FROM THE EDGE

BOOKS 1-3

BY EVIE RILEY

From The Edge
Books 1-3

Copyright © 2022
Evie Riley
Second Edition
ISBN: 978-1-77357-698-5
Published by Naughty Nights Press LLC
Cover Art By Willsin Rowe

FROM THE EDGE
BOOKS 1-3

Shattered

Can two young gay men find love?
Jimmy Ashford knows he is one of the lucky ones when it comes to support and love. He's gay, out, and proud. Being an artist is all he's ever dreamed about, and he can't wait to go off to Art School. Well, except now there's the new sexy-as-sin Zane Hamilton. Life is suddenly a lot more interesting, but can Jimmy tolerate being Zane's dirty little secret?

Runaway

Can love be enough to embrace that dangerous thing called hope?
Daryl Hamilton is finally free and looking

forward to his new life. Coming out of the closet is the best thing he's ever done. He has his art, his brother, a safe place to live, and that's really all he needs to be happy. A new flame in his life is just the icing on the cake.

Will Daryl's unconditional love be enough?

Jaded

Friends to lovers...

Detective Roland Wright lives a lonely and solitary life, filling his waking hours with work and volunteering. When a young man shows up at the soup kitchen where he volunteers, Roland tries to convince himself the attraction he feels is purely platonic. At least the handsome stranger is older than he looks, but can Roland risk getting close when his new friend isn't even gay?

SHATTERED

BY EVIE RILEY

FROM THE EDGE SERIES

BOOK ONE

SHATTERED

Can two young gay men survive the hate and find love?

Jimmy Ashford's senior year is looking good. His part-time job hours are lining up perfectly with studying and his future goals. With his parents behind him all the way, he knows he is one of the lucky ones when it comes to support and love. He's gay, out, and proud.

He can't wait to graduate and go off to Art School. Being an artist is all he's ever dreamed about. Well, except now there's the new sexy-as-sin Zane Hamilton. Life is suddenly a lot more interesting, but can Jimmy tolerate being Zane's dirty little secret?

Zane Hamilton only has a few more years before he will be free of his controlling parents and is finally able to start his dream for the future. If only he can make it that long. His father is determined he work in the family business and marry a woman he has zero interest in. If he doesn't comply, his whole future is at risk.

As manager of the quaint little diner in town, he has no business staring at one of the staff, but Jimmy is so free and confident, gorgeous too. Everything he wants. Everything he needs. Keeping his eyes, and hands, off Jimmy is torture, and he hates keeping Jimmy in the background like a dirty little secret, but if his parents find out he's gay all hell will break loose.

Is Zane willing to stand up for Jimmy, for their love?

CHAPTER ONE

Jimmy

THE SOUND OF the final bell going off had never sounded sweeter to me than right this moment. I had a love for school, but that last class in the day, political science, could really drag on for centuries. Some days, like today, it took all of my strength just to physically keep my eyes open.

I quickly got the hell out of there and made my way toward my locker. Being eighteen and a senior in high school came with a good batch of mixed feelings. Sadness, because the school you had spent the past four years in, growing up in, was no longer going to be in your life. All of the teachers and friends you had made along the way weren't going to be sitting next to you at lunch or making you laugh in the library just to upset the world's crankiest librarian. It was a piece of your life that was finished and it was bittersweet because your future was waiting for you right around the corner. For me, my future was waiting for me six blocks from here, at my part-time job.

I hastily said goodbye to the people I knew in the hallway as I made my way out of the building. I had to get to my work so I wouldn't be late. I had made a habit of never being late for work and I was not about to start now.

Working at the diner wasn't fascinating, and it didn't help me with my art, but it paid me every two weeks and that money went toward art supplies and my savings for when I went off to college in the fall.

Plus, working at the diner was not that bad. There were certainly worse part-time jobs I could be doing. In a city like Gaithersburg, Maryland you still had that small town feel, even though there was a decent size population, just under sixty thousand. Most would find that small, but when you think about how some cities only have a couple thousand people, I would say Gaithersburg was a decent size.

With that small town feel, though, you still had people with small town beliefs, like religion, politics, and sexual orientation. Two out of the three you could easily hide, but the sexual orientation part was a bit harder. Eventually, someone would notice you holding the hand of someone that was the same gender as you. Don't get me wrong, there were a lot of forward thinking people. A lot of accepting people who didn't care who you loved as long as you were happy. It was those people that got someone like me, a gay teenager, through the harder days.

My parents are some of those people.

They are truly amazing. I'd been such a nervous wreck when I'd decided to come out to them when I was fourteen. I'd been terrified with how they would react. They'd always been supportive of me where my art was concerned, but I also knew it was one thing to accept that your son was never going to be a football player and another that he was gay. They had taken it like a dream.

I was all prepared for a big showdown. I'd practiced what I was going to say to them and I was prepared for any argument they were going to throw my way. All of my hard work was wasted when my mom just simply said they knew and asked what I wanted for dinner. I had gone in fully prepared that my parents were going to be shocked. Only for the tables to be turned, leaving me the one that was stunned stupid in the living room.

All of my stress and worrying had been for nothing, absolutely nothing. I was so shocked and ecstatic that I went to school the very next day and told my friend Danny all about it. He had wanted to tell his parents about being gay, but he was really worried with how religious they were. He finally told them earlier this year. Only it didn't go over so well.

He'd called me that night crying his eyes out because his parents had kicked him out. All he had left was his backpack and a single duffle bag with his clothes and personal belongings. They completely threw him out without even a second thought about where he would go. I had immediately told him to come to my house and my parents both agreed that he could stay with us if he couldn't stay with his older brother who had his own apartment in town.

Thankfully, Danny's brother was not a jerk and had been pissed at his parents for kicking out his kid brother. Danny moved in with him and never had to hide who he was again. Neither of them have spoken to their parents since that night and I doubted they ever would.

That night, though, gave me a whole new level of respect for Danny. He had shown some true courage to tell his parents and then when they forced him to leave, he didn't try and put the genie back into the bottle. He held his head up high and became a proud gay kid. It was only proof to how strong he was and I couldn't have been more proud of him.

The aroma of the diner welcomed me as I stepped through the door for my shift. Most would find it gross, I suppose, but to me it smelled like the fifties. I can't explain it, but the odor from the grill with the eggs, the sweet sugar smell of waffles, the rich scent of brewed coffee, it always reminded me of poodle skirts and really bad hairstyles.

It didn't look like the fifties, but the Main Street Diner had been here since then. The one wall to the left of the diner was covered in photos from the past eight decades. They weren't organized at all, either, just thrown up where there was a spot. The owner, Anthony Blackstone, had taken over the diner from his father. It had been in their generation since the very first day. They were a pillar in the community and everyone still came here, even with some of the National chain restaurants just down the street. You just couldn't beat the food here, especially for breakfast.

"Hey, Sal, how are you?" I called to one of my regulars.

He was a very sweet seventy-year-old man who used to come here with his wife. They had been married for forty years before he lost her to cancer two years ago. They used to come here every Thursday night to have date night. They had their first date right here in the diner almost fifty years ago. Every Thursday, they would come in and sit in the same booth every single time. We would make sure no one sat in it before they had the chance to get here.

Sal had been coming here after her death, still. He would sit in the same spot and place her framed photograph across from him. It sounded really sad, I know, but to him it was his way of still having their date night together.

He once told me that there were many days where he missed her so much it hurt, but when he came to the diner for their date night, he felt connected to her. The pain didn't hurt so much and he truly believed that she was sitting in that booth seat right across from him. It was the sweetest thing I had ever heard, still to this day.

I didn't know if I believed in spirits or not, but what I did know is that I hoped it was true. I hoped that Martha was sitting right there in that booth with Sal, spending time together until they could be reunited again.

"I'm still moving, Jim," Sal said, flashing a toothless grin.

"I'm happy to hear that. This place wouldn't be the same without you, Sal."

I made my way toward the back room so I could drop my coat and bag off. I was hoping it might be a little dead tonight so I could get a jump-start on my homework. Dead was never good for tips, but it did allow me to get my homework done before getting home, allowing me the time to relax and watch a couple episodes of my favorite show before I would have to go to sleep.

After clocking in, I made my way behind the counter and gave Stella a big smile. "Hey good looking, how's it been?" I asked.

In her thirties now, Stella had been working here for ten years. She'd dropped out of high school at sixteen when she got pregnant. Her boyfriend at the time was a high school senior and he took off right after graduation before their daughter was even born. She came from a single mother, who kicked her out once she discovered that she was pregnant. Stella didn't let it get to her, though. She persevered and she created a life for her daughter. She had been working odd jobs for the first four years before she was given the opportunity to work here full-time. Mr. Blackstone was really good with her and even gave her health benefits for her daughter after she had worked here for six months. Stella had been eternally grateful to Mr. Blackstone and as a result, she always came into work and even worked extra shifts if they had no one to cover. She was a hard and loyal worker and I loved her from the first day we met.

"Not too bad, Jimmy. You know how Thursdays are. How was school?"

"It was uneventful, which is exactly how I like it. I have some homework, but if it's dead in here later I can always work on it."

"You must be getting excited with graduation creeping up," Stella said, flashing a warm smile.

"I guess I am. I don't know, it doesn't feel real yet. Maybe it would be different if I was going to travel the world or move to a completely different State. But to me, it just feels like I'm going to school in the fall. Only this one will be like a boarding school that I get to come home for on weekends," I said with a shrug.

"Don't worry about that too much. It will feel more real once you are living in the dorms. Then, in your second year, you'll be getting your own place. It'll sink in once you're there and taking classes."

That sounded about right. I wasn't the type of person who got excited to begin with, really. Of course, I was looking forward to it, but I wasn't jumping up and down with excitement.

Before anymore could be said, the little bell above the door chimed and we both looked up, expecting to be greeting a customer. Instead, we saw our new manager walking in.

We had been told a few days ago that we would be getting a new night manager. Stella had been offered the job, but she liked being a server. She liked the lack of responsibility more than anything. She said she had enough going on with raising a teenager; she didn't need more of a headache. She was open to the idea at a later time, though, when her daughter was off to College herself.

I had been prepared for the new manager to be someone like the old manager, Mr. Wilson, older and not really attractive. This man, though, he was nothing like I was expecting.

He had short brown hair; much like myself only mine was blond. He had a clear five o'clock shadow that he had no interest in trying to get rid of, which was fine by me. I liked a man that looked a bit rough. He was well built, like he spent some time working out at the gym in his day, but he wasn't so muscular that it was the only thing he did in the day. He walked with his head held up high and his back straight.

He didn't appear to be nervous at all for someone starting a new job. He glanced over at us and I felt a quick, warm shot of arousal at seeing his emerald green eyes. It was only for a moment before he was heading into the back, but I could have sworn he had mesmerized me with them. I couldn't take my eyes off of him, even after he had disappeared into the kitchen area. My gaze lingered on the door, hoping he would come back out.

"Earth to Jimmy, come back, you're drooling," Stella teased.

"I don't drool," I said, feeling my cheeks warm as I forced myself to look back over to her.

That granted me a chuckle. "Man, if I knew the new manager was going to look like that, I would have worn tighter pants." Stella winked.

"I think I should have worn looser ones," I joked back. But in all honesty, getting a hard-on at work was not a good idea. Thankfully, I had a server's apron on that would hide any issues should something get out of control. And by something, I mean my imagination. Hey, I was an artist; I had a remarkable imagination.

One that had gotten me through many lonely nights.

"You're so bad. What do you think, straight or gay?"

"You know, most people worry if their new boss is going to be a dick or not. Not what team they play for," I said with a playful smirk as I leaned my left side against the counter. I was not going to admit out loud that I was wondering the exact same thing.

And praying it was the latter.

"I doubt he's a dick. He doesn't look old enough to be a dick. He's like twenty, maybe twenty-one. And I'm allowed to wonder all I want. I'm just not allowed to ask. I'm going with straight, though. He's got that straight boy look."

"Can't argue with that. He's very pretty, though."

He was most likely straight. Odds were in his favor for being straight, but that didn't mean I couldn't window shop to my heart's content.

I didn't have much time to ponder my new boss, because a table of four teenagers walked through the door. I went back to focusing on my work. Whatever was going to happen with our new manager would happen regardless of what I wanted. For now, I would wait until I would get to be introduced.

***

It was a good two hours later when I had a moment to catch my breath. The dinner rush had come through and it was always busy for a few hours before everyone started to head out for home. Then only a few stragglers would come in for a late dessert or a coffee before they got back on the road. While I was in the middle of filling the napkin dispensers once again, Mr. Wilson made his way out of the kitchen with the new manager.

"Jimmy, meet our new night manager, Zane Hamilton," Mr. Wilson said.

Zane.

The name suited him. Strong, masculine, but unique. It wasn't a name you heard every day in your life. Seeing Zane up close like this only allowed me to realize that he looked even more sexy up close and personal than he did from a distance.

His eyes were to die for. I had never seen eyes this green before. He had a strong jaw and chiseled facial features that gave him a model like look. He was truly breath-stealing to look at up close. This man was a heartbreaker and I had no doubt that he would have a trail of hopeful lovers behind him.

I sighed inwardly, knowing working for this sexy-as-sin man would be a challenge of the worst kind on my active imagination.

"Hi, it's nice to meet you, Sir," I said, trying to remember that this was my boss and I needed to be polite and friendly. I was leaving for College come the fall, but I needed this job to make sure I could have enough saved up until I found a job up there.

"Call me Zane, please." His voice held a slight gravelly tone to it, but it wasn't from something like smoking. It was completely natural and it sent a shiver right down my spine.

"Well, it's nice to meet you, Zane. I'm sure you will love working here, the customers are great and the other employees are really friendly. If you have any questions, don't be afraid to ask."

God, yes, please ask me anything you want.

I would love to talk with him for my whole shift. Anything that would allow me to get close to him. I bet he smelled amazing.

"Thank you, I appreciate that. I'm sure I

will love working here."

I knew *I* was going to love him working here. This job just got so much better. I couldn't stand around and talk, though, because I had a new table come in and the last thing I wanted to do was leave a bad impression on my new boss.

I sighed, made my excuses, and quickly went back to work, waving goodbye to Mr. Wilson as he headed out. I did my best to focus on my work, but I could feel eyes on me. Zane's eyes. I knew it without even having to look at him.

I didn't have a problem being watched. I mean, it's common when you get a new boss. A good manager would always look around, check out how you work and what habits you had, or even what routine there already was in place. So Zane watching me throughout my shift wasn't that out of the norm.

The thing was, though, he wasn't looking at me like he was evaluating my skills. He was just following me around with his eyes. It was a little awkward and it left me feeling a bit weirded out by it. That was, until I saw just the slightest glimmer of what could only be described as lust in his eyes when I bent over the table to wipe the far end of it. I looked up just in time for him to snap his eyes away and look over at another customer.

Oh my god!

Is he checking me out?

That couldn't be right, right?

There was no way that he would be checking me out. Even if he was interested in guys, why would he be interested in someone like me? I couldn't be his type. As badly as I wished I was his type. Guys like him wouldn't go for the artistic type like me. I had enough experience in my dating life to know that.

Still, though, the thought of him checking me out didn't leave me feeling awkward or creeped out. It left me feeling a tingle of excitement. I knew nothing could come from it and I was perfectly okay with that.

One thing I did know, work was going to

be so much more enjoyable.

CHAPTER TWO

Zane

WALKING INTO A new job on that first day was always daunting, but this time around it was a little bit different. Today, I wouldn't be working some low level position; I was going to be in management. Yes, it was only managing a diner, but I was still responsible for the staff and ensuring that everything went according to plan on my shift. It was not a responsibility I would be taking lightly.

Today was so much more than just another job, though. Today was the first day that I would be getting true hands on experience in the industry I wanted to build a career in. It wasn't a diner I wanted to own, but a resort. Not just any resort, though, the best on the East Coast.

A place where people came from all over the world to visit.

Something that would prove to my father that I was worthy of my name and his respect.

Most people have their parents' respect by just being themselves and doing their best, but not me. My father liked to say that we come from old money and with that came a responsibility and prestige that we needed to upkeep. Anything less than perfection and we were not only letting ourselves down, but every family member that came before us. It was a lot of pressure to be perfect. To get perfect grades all throughout school. If I came home with anything but A's, I would be grounded and forced to take summer school to better my grade. I could have understood it if it was to ensure I got into an Ivy League school, but my father made it very clear that I was to not go to University. That it wasn't needed and would be a waste of money. I would be working for the family business, learning everything I could so I could take over it one day. Most people would find that comforting. To know that you would always have a job, but to me it was just one more way my father could control my life.

My whole life had been the same. He didn't care that I wanted to play baseball. He put me in golfing instead. Said it would help me to meet the right type of people that I could network and build connections with for future business deals. I was eight at the time.

My life had been planned out without any say or input from me. When I was younger I should have spoken up more, should have rebelled and done what I wanted, what would have made me happy. At the time, though, I just wanted my parents' love, my father's love. What all little boys wanted.

Now, at twenty-one, I was terrified of my father discovering the truth. That I didn't want to manage a pharmaceutical company. I wanted to build a resort that would go down in history. That would allow me to build an empire that could sustain the test of time. Something that could be passed down to my children, assuming they wanted it.

What I wanted to scream at my father most, though, was that I didn't want to marry whatever woman he picked for me. I wanted to marry the *man* that I would pick for me. I was gay, very much gay, and it was a secret that I would never be able to tell them. You would think with it being the twenty-first century that people wouldn't have to hide their own sexuality. Well, the twenty-first century has yet to meet my parents, specifically my father. If he were to discover that I preferred the company of men over women, he would go absolutely nuclear. I would be shipped off to some conversion camp for the rest of my life if that is what it took to make me see things his way, get over *those* perversions. He would never allow for his son to be gay, for any of his children. Thankfully, my kid brother was straight and he would never have to deal with the pain of having to hide something like this.

Having to hide this part of myself, this huge part, has not been easy. There have been guys I have dated since I discovered that I was gay. I was sixteen at the time and all it took was one look from Shawn Roman, the school's baseball shortstop, and I knew I was different. I wasn't interested in girls, even the ones that obviously flirted with me. But when Shawn walked into Math class, oh yes, I noticed. And he noticed me.

Being with Shawn was easy, he was in the closet just like me and he had zero interest in breaking out of it. He had his eye on a sports scholarship so he could work his way up to the major league. It was perfect for a long time, well, seven months, but back then it felt like years.

Shawn had come to school one day with

Daisy on his arm, his new girlfriend that he had no problem making out with in the hallways for everyone to see, myself included. That is when we broke up, a difference of opinions.

To Shawn, it wasn't cheating because she was a girl and he was gay. She didn't turn him on. She was just what he needed so people wouldn't suspect he was gay. She was his beard.

To me, kissing was kissing and it didn't matter if it was a guy or a girl. They were still making out and fooling around. I wasn't going to be sharing him and ultimately he picked her over me. Or I guess I could say, he picked his closet over me.

The thing is, I couldn't really be pissed at him for it, because when I was nineteen I was the one having to pretend that I was straight while seeing Chris. Chris who was out and proud and the most flamboyant gay person I have ever met. He didn't want to be a dirty little secret, not that I could blame him, but I couldn't leave my closet. That was the end of that relationship, and truly the last time I have tried to date anyone.

I've had one-night stands with guys that I've hooked up with at one of the gay clubs within the nearby towns. Nothing ever serious, though, since Chris. It wouldn't be fair to date someone that would have to live a lie, be a secret, until the day came when I could finally come out to my family. That day wouldn't be until I was twenty-five and able to secure my trust fund. With my trust fund in my own name and my father no longer having control over it, I could open my resort and come out to them. It would mean I could finally just be me and not someone they wanted me to be, someone *he* wanted me to be. It was a day I was counting down to, literally. One thousand, two hundred, and seventy-five days until I was free. As if I was counting down a prison sentence, and in a lot of ways I was in prison. I had been serving a twenty-five year sentence for a crime I didn't commit. My freedom would come though and it was going to be remarkable. At least, I hoped it would be.

"All right, you are all set," Mr. Wilson said with a warm smile.

Today was my first shift, but he seemed pretty confident that I wouldn't screw anything up. Though, with the checklist that I had to follow before I could leave, it would be pretty hard to make a mistake.

"Thank you for all of your help, Mr. Wilson."

"You are doing me a huge favor. Now that you will be working at night, I no longer have to. I get to go back to my nice day shifts and be home at a decent hour. Come on, I'll introduce you to the staff that is here."

Mr. Wilson stood and slowly walked out of the office. The man was old, too old to still be working, in my opinion, but it was a sad fact that retirement was not an easy concept to achieve anymore.

It was one of the things that I wanted to make sure I offered my employees once my resort was successful and profitable. I would make sure they had medical insurance and a pension. If you worked your whole life, you shouldn't have to be penalized because you couldn't work for a company that offered you a pension so you could retire.

We made our way through the small diner and Mr. Wilson introduced me to the night cook, Matt, then he took me to the front where I met two of the servers. First, Stella. She was a bit older than me, but she seemed very friendly and didn't seem to have a problem with having to listen to someone younger than her. Then Mr. Wilson introduced me to quite possibly the most beautiful man I have ever met. Jimmy.

"Jimmy, meet our new night manager, Zane Hamilton."

"Hi, it's nice to meet you, Sir," Jimmy said, and flashed the most beautiful white smile I had ever seen.

"Call me Zane, please," I managed to get out without looking like a complete fool—I hoped.

I couldn't get over how beautiful he was, and his voice... God, it was smooth and rich, like high-end milk chocolate. I could listen to him talk all day and never get tired of it. Hell, he could read the phonebook and he would captivate me. It shouldn't be possible for a man to be this beautiful. His skin was a smooth porcelain color. It wasn't white in the sense that he never went outside, it was his natural skin tone and he clearly took care of himself. He was cleanly shaven, not even a hint of a five o'clock shadow on his face like I had. His eyes were as blue as the ocean and I could easily get lost within their depth. His hair was a sun kissed, light brown that was kept a bit longer. It wasn't long, but it wasn't short, that nice middle ground like I had.

This was not good. I was supposed to be his manager; someone working for me could not be this attractive. There was no way I was going to be able to keep my eyes off of him. I was already looking forward to him walking away so I could see his ass. I was in so much trouble.

"Well, it's nice to meet you, Zane. I'm sure you will love working here, the customers are great and the other employees are really friendly. If you have any questions, don't be afraid to ask," Jimmy said, a warm smile turning up the corners of his mouth.

There was only one question that mattered to me right now. Well, two.

The first, was he gay?

And the second, if yes, how much trouble would I be in if I pushed him down onto a table and had my way with him?

"Thank you, I appreciate that. I am sure I will love working here."

Jimmy gave me one last smile before he turned to head over to a new table. Sure enough, his ass looked amazing in the black skinny jeans he wore. It took every ounce of strength I had to keep the moan in my head.

I gave Mr. Wilson a warm smile goodbye as he said he was heading out now, leaving me in charge of the diner. When I started, my biggest concern was making sure it was still standing come the end of the night. Now, my biggest concern was making sure I didn't get a sexual harassment lawsuit by the end of the night.

The vibrating of my phone had me moving into the back office. A quick look at it had my heart plummeting into my stomach.

My father.

Most kids call their parents Mom and Dad, but not me. I'd always been raised to refer to them as Mother and Father. It was to show a higher level of respect for their sacrifice and position within the family. That was exactly how my father explained it to me when I was just four years old. At the time, I had no idea how screwed up it was, I figured everyone must call their parents that. It wasn't until I started getting older that I came to discover it was screwed up.

There was always that doubt within me that my parents, especially my father, actually did love me. Love me and my kid brother. They weren't affectionate; they weren't the type of parents that tucked you in at night when you were younger. Even if we were sick, we were pretty much on our own. It's why I've always made a point of being there for Daryl. I didn't want him to have to grow up being stuck in bed sick and miserable knowing that no one was going to be there to help him. I wanted him to know, on some level, at least, what love was supposed to feel like. What it felt like to be hugged and taken care of. I couldn't change my own childhood, but I could have some say and control over the outcome of his. It was one of the reasons why I had been trying so hard to keep my father's attention on me. If he continued looking at me and my future, then Daryl was free to fly under the radar and discover who he was.

Letting out a sigh, I closed the office door and answered my phone. Letting it go to voicemail was never a good idea where my father was concerned.

"Hello, Father."

"Zane, I just received confirmation for dinner tomorrow. Make sure you are here by six o'clock sharp, and look presentable. This dinner with the Millers is very important for the future."

How could I possibly forget about dinner

tomorrow night?

Henry Miller owned a head corporation that boasted fifty hospitals within the country. All of them were privately owned and made millions every year in profits. My father had made friends with him five years ago in an effort to push his pharmaceutical company to the next level. It had worked, but ever since that day the Millers had been a serious pain in my ass. It wasn't Henry, per say, but rather the fact that he had a daughter, Kayla, who was my age. Both of our fathers thought we would make the perfect power couple. A way to merge both of our families together, and potentially, one day, the two companies. Kayla was all for it, which didn't help the situation. Obviously, I was not all for it.

"I know, Father. I will make sure I'm home and ready for when they arrive." I just needed to humor my father and bide my time. Soon enough, I would be in the clear.

"This dinner is very important, Zane. If all goes according to plan, it will cement the future of my company. I want you respectful and paying a great deal of attention to Kayla. Make her feel special and let her know you have a genuine interest in her. Henry has told me she is already interested in you. You just need to seal the deal now."

Leave it to my father to refer to a relationship as a deal. Though, I suppose in his eyes that is exactly what he saw this as. To him, it didn't matter if I wanted to be with her or not. Hell, he didn't even ask if I thought she was attractive or even had an interest in dating her. He did what he always did. He ordered and controlled without a single thought about how anyone else would feel.

"I will be very respectful, Father. I have to go, though, I'm at work and I need to make sure everything is in order. I want to make a good first impression on my boss."

"You better be making a *great* first impression. The Hamilton name is not one that can be squandered. Even if you are slumming it working in a diner," he said, not even bothering to hide his disdain for my new job.

"I am, Father. I really must be going, though."

In all honesty, I didn't have anything I needed to do. All I could do was wait for closing time and make sure nothing blew up. I just had no desire to keep talking with him. I would much rather stand in the corner and watch Jimmy work all night. It was pathetic, I was aware, but at this point all I could do was window shop when it came to men. If I was going to be stuck window shopping for the next three years, I might as well do it with a man as breathtakingly beautiful as Jimmy.

"Do not be late tomorrow."

That was all my father had to say before he ended the call. What was odd, was how he kept repeating for me to not be late. I still lived at the house, not by my doing but his, so it wasn't like I wouldn't be home at some point within the next twenty-four hours.

Pocketing my phone, I headed back out to the restaurant section of the diner. It was surprisingly busy considering it wasn't quite dinner hour yet. I had never been here before I applied, but I could see that there was a steady flow of regulars. And from what I had seen so far, the food looked and smelled delicious. I couldn't help but wonder what Jimmy smelled like.

Would he have his own scent, or would the scent of the diner be on him?

I was a firm believer that you could tell what type of a man someone was by their scent. Guys who had a woodsy smell to them, tended to be very outdoorsy and good with their hands. Guys who smelled like aftershave and overpowering cologne, tended to be jerks and had no life skills. I would take an outdoor man over a boardroom stiff any day of the week.

Leaning against the entrance between the kitchen and the dinning room allowed me to have the perfect view of Jimmy, without it looking like I was watching him. He moved with grace from one table to the next. The easy smile on his face as he talked with the customers told me he was friendly and kind, but also confident in himself.

He was thinner, so he clearly didn't workout all day or play sports. He wasn't a stick either, though, so he did do some form of working out. My guess was a runner if his thighs were anything to go by. It wasn't just his appearance that had caught my attention. It was how easy he smiled. He seemed so carefree and not weighed down by life and expectations. His parents probably not only loved him, but liked him. He probably had a girlfriend he was madly in love with. He was free. Free to be himself and live his life how he saw it. I wanted that freedom. I wanted to be able to smile with ease just like him.

Four years. Four more long years.

***

Ten minutes, that's how long I had left before the circus would start. Ten minutes left of being able to be myself before I would need to play straight and interested for an entire dinner. I was really not looking forward to this at all, but I also knew I had no choice in the matter. I would just need to get through this and then I could focus on my work and my life.

I headed outside for a quiet moment alone before all the fanfare began but the sight of my kid brother crying quickly interrupted that plan. Daryl was always a tough kid. He didn't cry. He didn't get emotional. He was athletic, but he was also artistic. I knew he hid that side of himself quite often because of our father. Our Father wasn't one for creative outlets. He believed men to be a certain way and a painter was not one of them. Daryl had always done his best to live up to our father's expectations. I knew it was hard on him, though, because he didn't fit into one category. He was a jock that could paint a mural that would leave you speechless. All of the emotions that he had seemed to come out on the canvas. He was different compared to me, in that sense. I kept everything inside. I put up a front and just pushed through the day with a mental clock ticking down the days in my head.

I quickly made my way over to the bench by the pond where he sat. I made a point of not sitting next to him, wanting to give him some space. We were close, but we weren't that close, either. We used to be really close when we were younger, but then I became a teenager and started to hang out with my friends. I didn't want my kid brother hanging around. He started to get busy with being in different sports, plus when he had free time he was always drawing or painting. He was seventeen now and months away from turning eighteen. He was set to graduate this year and I had no idea what he was going to do after high school. I was really going to have to get better with him, do better. I was supposed to be his older brother and I didn't even know what his dreams were. What his plans were for his life.

"What's wrong, Squirt?"

The snort that came from him only caused me to smile. It was a nickname I had for him since he was born. He used to love it, but once he became a teenager he hated it. Still, it was his nickname and I would always call him Squirt.

"Nothing," Daryl said as he wiped at his eyes to try and stop the tears from flowing.

"I can count on one hand how many times you've cried since you were twelve. You don't care for nothing. Hell, you didn't cry when you broke your arm. Something is going on, what is it?"

"Like you care."

That cut deep, but he had a valid point. I had been a pretty shitty brother in the past few years. "I know I haven't been around much. Me not being here, though, that much isn't because of you. It's just Father, I don't want to be around him. So it's easier for me to be working or out all night so I don't have to deal with him. That doesn't mean I don't love you or care about you. Something is going on with you. Tell me. I might be able to help."

I was really hoping he would open up to me. Clearly something was bothering him and he shouldn't have to feel like he had to face this world alone. Daryl sniffed a few times before he cleared his throat and spoke.

"I was dating someone for the past year now almost. I just found out they had been cheating on me for half of that time. Then I was the one dumped so they could be with someone else."

Okay, not what I expected. I had no idea he was even dating someone.

How could I have missed something this important in his life?

For a year he had been dating a girl and I never even met her. At seventeen, a year was pretty serious.

"I know it hurts, but if she is dumb enough to cheat on you, then she's a loser and you deserve someone so much better. I know it hurts and it will for a little bit, but you will find another girl and she will make you forget all about your ex. She doesn't deserve your tears."

"He," Daryl said softly.

"He who?"

"I wasn't dating a girl. I was dating Brad. I'm gay, Z," Daryl admitted as he looked at me out of the corner of his eye.

He was waiting to see how I would react. He knew just as much as I did how our parents felt about homosexuality. It would be logical that he would be worried about what I thought about it. I was shocked, though. I had no idea he was gay.

We are both gay.

It was this moment, though, that I realized something about my brother that I had never realized before. He was braver than I was, because he actually said it out loud. While I had been trying to nail the closet door shut so it would hold for another four years, he was trying to pry the nails out with his bare fingers just so he could be free.

My entire future relationship with Daryl was hanging in the balance on this single moment. How I reacted would change everything between us, and I was not about to screw it up.

"Then he's a loser," I said, and flashed him a warm smile.

"You're not bothered by it?" Daryl asked

with both surprise and uncertainty. I could understand both of those.

"I love you and I want what I would want for you if you were straight. For you to be happy, healthy and loved. That's all that matters to me. Whether I stand next to you at the end of the aisle as you marry a woman or a man, it's all the same to me. All I care about is being there and seeing that smile on your face."

"That's all I want for you, too. Even if it's with someone as annoying as Kayla," Daryl said with a smirk.

I couldn't stop the groan from escaping. "Yeah, I don't know what to do about that. I know she's into me, but I just can't imagine spending the rest of my life with her. I gotta figure out how to let her down gently or make it seem like it was her idea and she dumps me before we even date."

"Good luck with that. Both of our fathers seem pretty hell bent on it. Maybe you should take her on a date to help feed the homeless or something. She doesn't really come across as the giving back kind of a girl."

"She is a princess."

I had to agree with him on that one. Kayla was the type that showed up dressed for a gala every time you saw her. High-end clothes, hair and makeup professionally done. It didn't matter if she was just running to the grocery store—not that I believed she actually did her own grocery shopping—she still always dressed to impress. I knew there were guys who liked that kind of woman. A trophy wife. The problem is, even if I was into girls, Kayla wouldn't be it. I was going to have to figure out how to squash this before it went too far. I just wasn't sure how to make that happen yet.

I bumped my shoulder against Daryl's as I spoke. "Come on, let's get in there before we get in trouble for being late to our own dinner party. Tomorrow we can brainstorm some ideas on how to make Brad pay."

"Deal," Daryl said with a genuine smile.

It would hurt for a little while, but I knew he would bounce back soon enough.

The first time your heart gets broken, it's always hard, but then you get tougher and learn how to protect yourself better. He was going to be okay, because I was going to make sure of it.

CHAPTER THREE

Jimmy

NEVER, EVER AGAIN. And I do mean never again. When I agreed to go on this blind date, it was completely due to peer pressure. I love my friends, but they seriously suck at finding men for me. Ali and Kristy had good intentions, I know they love me, but this has to stop. They kept going on and on about how I needed to find me a man to date. Like being eighteen meant I was destined to be alone for the rest of my life if I was single come graduation. Don't get me wrong, I get that we're high school seniors and on the cusp of starting our adult lives. I completely understand how we should be having fun, dating, going to parties, thinking about prom, and I do all of that. But, I also have zero desire to be a drunken idiot when I go away to College. Yes, a boyfriend would be amazing, but that wasn't a top priority in my life. I needed to focus on my grades to ensure my scholarship and my acceptance into Maryland Institute College of Art was bulletproof. Yes, I had already received the scholarship and acceptance, but that could be taken away if my grades fall, something I wasn't going to allow. So, tonight marks the very last night that I am going to be entertaining any of my friends with dating. There will be absolutely zero future blind dates.

I headed into my house and saw that my parents were waiting up for me. My parents had always been amazing, but tonight they deserved an award for saving me like they did. One simple text message asking for 9-1-1 help and they were calling up saying I needed to get home, that my dog was very sick.

God I love them.

Whiskers instantly came running over to me with his tail wagging. My parents had surprised me with him when I was thirteen and Whiskers had been my best friend ever since. He was a mutt that they rescued from the shelter when he was only eight weeks old. I didn't care that he was all mixed up. To me, he was perfect. He was a good, medium size dog that loved to spend the hot summer months in the kiddie pool in our backyard. He was my dog and I was going to miss him when I would be off staying at the dorms.

"He's made a miraculous recovery," my mom said with a big smile.

"God, you have no idea how amazing you are," I said as I collapsed into the chair.

"It couldn't have been that bad," my Dad said.

"I would have rather spent the night

scrubbing the bathrooms at the diner with my own toothbrush."

"That's bad. Was he a jerk?" my Mom asked, the concern in her voice evident.

"More like a pompous air head. Honestly, I have no idea how he managed to get his head into his shirt. He spent the night talking about himself and how great he is. And then, when I did get to talk, the conversation was remedial at best. He's an idiot, and I say that in the nicest way possible."

"That's too bad. I'm sorry you had such a bad time tonight. Maybe next time hold your ground with your friends," my Dad advised. And he was absolutely right.

"Oh, believe me, they will be getting an earful from me come Monday morning. I need to get this night out of me, so I am going to go and paint for a bit," I said as I stood.

"Okay, sweetie. We're going to head to bed, so don't stay up too late," my Mom said as they both stood as well.

"I won't. I love you guys."

"We love you, too," my Dad said, a warm smile turning up the corners of his mouth.

We all headed upstairs and into our respective rooms. After I quickly changed into some old jeans and a t-shirt, I made my way back down the stairs and into the garage.

The garage was another reason why I loved my parents so much. Not only had they accepted me as being gay, but they also accepted my passion for art. My dad had converted the garage into my own art studio. I couldn't believe it when I came home from school three years ago to see it. My dad had always kept his car in the garage so he could work on it. He constantly called it his man cave, and he had given that up so I could have a place to pursue my passion, my future career. I couldn't have loved him more.

I grabbed a new canvas and started the process of grabbing different paints. I needed to paint away this night to cleanse my heart and soul. Dylan needed to go away.

As I moved the brush over the canvas, I allowed myself to think back to last night and meeting Zane at the diner. I still couldn't get his face out of my mind. The way his eyes seemed to track me as I moved from table to table.

I knew being a new manager it would be natural for him to keep an eye on his employees. To see how they were working, see how they interacted with customers. It made sense and Zane wasn't the first new manager that I'd had at the diner.

Still, I couldn't stop thinking about him. I couldn't stop wondering if maybe his eyes were on me for another reason. I wasn't sure, but I could have sworn there was lust in his eyes when he saw me bending over to wipe the tables. It was gone, though, before I could really confirm it one way or the other.

It should have been creepy and disturbing and I'm sure it would have if he wasn't so sexy. If he was a forty year old man, it would have given me the creeps. But Zane wasn't forty, he was twenty-one, from what we were able to gather out of him. We couldn't get much more out of him. We had no idea if he was dating someone, if he was straight, gay, in College, literally nothing. The man was like Fort Knox in the sharing department. It should have told me to back off, but I couldn't help but think about how sexy he was, the mystery about him was not helping either. I was in so much trouble, because he was my manager, which made him my boss and I could not oogle my boss all night long.

What I did in my fantasies, though, was well within my freedom. I wish I knew if he was straight or gay. That would really help me to be able to figure him out. If he was straight, then he was just another manager. But if he was gay, then he was attracted to me. Didn't mean anything could happen, because, again, he's my manager, but it was a fun thought.

Maybe Ali and Kristy were right, maybe I needed someone to have some fun with. Dylan was not it, but maybe I should be trying to get out. I could certainly use the sex, I'd always been able to paint more freely if I wasn't stressed or tense and sex was the best stress reliever in the world. Maybe it was time I lived a little, and tonight I would be doing just that with Zane.

In my dreams anyway.

***

There was nothing better than spending my Saturday in the art supply store. I could seriously live here and never get tired of it. There was a peacefulness to being in an art store.

Most just see paint, brushes, pencils and blank canvases. But to me, I see what they could become. I see the sunset with a bend of yellows, reds, and oranges that rests upon the water. I see the tranquility it brings, the warmth it brings within a household. How the owner picks it because it matches their lives or simply because they need it in their lives.

It's so much more than just liquid color in a bottle. It's what it makes a person feel when the masterpiece has been created. It's those feelings that make it all worth it for an artist, knowing that we brought that level of emotion out in someone. It's the biggest compliment that any artist could have.

Just as I turned the corner, I instantly hit a wall. Only this wall was not made of wood and paint, but hard and warm flesh. Looking up to apologize immediately, I was shocked to see it was none other than Zane.

"Hey, sorry," I said, as I tried to get my mind to work. My boss was standing here in an art supply store and he was looking as sexy as ever. He was wearing dark blue jeans with a black t-shirt and a black leather jacket. I couldn't help but wonder if maybe he had a motorcycle. The image immediately popped up in my mind of him sitting on a motorcycle and it had my mouth watering.

God, I gotta get a grip.

"Don't worry about it, I wasn't paying attention. Are you okay?" Zane asked, flashing me an easy smile.

"Oh yeah, I'm fine." Aside from the heart attack. "I didn't know you were into art."

"Oh, I'm not. I can barely draw stick figures. My kid brother, Daryl, is the artist in the family. He just got dumped so I figured I would get him a couple of things to help cheer him up."

That made more sense. I didn't get artist vibes from Zane, but it was sweet he was grabbing stuff for his brother. He was compassionate, a very good quality in a man.

"That sucks that he was dumped. Painting it out, though, can really help."

"I'm assuming that means you paint."

"Since I can remember. My mom says I was born with a paint brush in my hand. They have been really great about it. My dad even turned the garage into an art studio for me a few years ago," I said proudly.

God I love my parents.

"That's awesome. Are you gonna go to art school when you graduate?"

"I've already received an acceptance to

MICA, Maryland Institute College of Art. It's in Baltimore. I'm so excited for it, it's going to be amazing," I said with a smile so big I must have looked like a psychotic person, but I didn't care. The excitement at getting to go to MICA was exploding inside of me. I doubted it would ever get old.

"That's awesome, Jimmy. Why so close, though? Don't you want to be as far away from this town as possible?"

He wasn't the first person to ask me this. When people think of art, their minds go to New York or California. They don't go to Baltimore, all of thirty minutes up the road from here. I know it was close and, yes, I could have applied for other schools in New York or Los Angeles, but I didn't want to. I didn't want to be thousands of miles away.

"I like this town, for starters, but more importantly, I wanted to be close to home. I don't have any siblings or relatives. It's just me and my folks. I wanted to be close to them, still. To be able to drive home for family dinners or holidays. I didn't want to have to book a plane ticket just to come home for the weekend. And MICA is an amazing art school with unbelievable resources. I get to have a wonderful education while still being able to be close to home."

"Sounds like the best of both worlds for you. Think you can lend me some expertise on figuring out what to get my brother?" Zane said with wink and a grin.

Oh damn.

"I would love to." Any extra time outside of work that I could get to spend with him, I was going to be taking it.

"You are a lifesaver. Maybe if you have time afterward, we could grab some lunch," Zane offered.

"Sure." I couldn't stop the smile this time. I would not only get to be helping him in a place I considered heaven on earth, but I would get to sit with him for lunch, too. This day was turning out way better than I could have ever imagined. And trust me, I can imagine a hell of a lot.

***

We ended up at just a little cafe not too far from the art supply store. They had amazing pastries and some of the best coffee I'd ever had. Despite really wanting to just order sugar confections, I forced myself to order a ham and swiss sandwich along with my pastry.

Spring was fully in the air and I was relieved for the warmth it brought. We sat outside with how balmy it was. I couldn't help but notice how the sunlight played with the different shades of brown within Zane's hair. It was all natural, but it looked like he paid a few hundred dollars for highlights in it. The brown in his hair only made his emerald green eyes shimmer even more and I knew I could easily get lost in them.

"So, do you like working at the diner?" I wasn't really sure how to get the conversation going. If I was sitting with my friends we would have already been talking up a storm. Zane was different, though, he was new in my life, my manager, older, and I still had no idea if he was gay or straight.

Not that the last one truly mattered, but it would have been nice to know.

"So far, yes. It's only temporary, but it's decent work."

"Why only temporary?"

"I wanted some hands-on experience working with hospitality in a management position. It also allows me to pay for my tuition to the online hospitality management course I'm taking."

"That's cool. Why didn't you go to a physical College compared to online?" Most people jump at the opportunity to get out of town. For someone his age, it would only make sense that he would leave home and get some life experience with being in College and living on his own. I guess he could be living on his own in town, not everyone lives with their parents here. He might have had to stay so he could help his parents and be there for his kid brother.

"My father didn't see it as being necessary. He preferred for me to work for his company, but I wanted real life experience first, before working for his pharmaceutical company."

"That makes sense. It must be hard to have parents who own a corporation. Most would assume you would want to be in that company, to pass it on to you. You obviously want to be within the hospitality industry. What's your dream?"

I was very lucky in the sense that my parents worked medium income jobs. They didn't own a business. My mother was a grade school teacher and my father was an accountant at the only firm in town. There was no pressure for me to join the family business or have to take over one day. I was completely free to be myself and chase after my own dreams without any guilt. It seemed like Zane didn't have that, and that was truly sad.

"I would like to open a resort, similar to one you would find in Las Vegas or other vacation destination locations. Something that would bring tourists into the town to help other local businesses. I want something that can withstand the test of time and be something I can be proud of and pass on to my children, should they wish it. Mostly, I just want something that is mine and not connected to generations of Hamiltons."

Oh, that's right, he's a Hamilton. They own a massive pharmaceutical empire. That explained a few things. I could tell even with how he was talking that he was expected to take over the family business. That there was pressure from his parents to take it over. Pressure like that could be crippling to someone, I would imagine. Still, though, he was pushing through it and chasing after his own dreams. It was admiral and impressive.

"I don't have a family business or generations of high expectations. I can't imagine how hard that must be for you to deal with. I'm lucky in that sense. My parents have always encouraged me to pursue my dreams and carve out my own life. I think it's impressive and very brave of you to chase after your dream and go against the wishes of your family. You shouldn't have to feel like you need to conform to what they want. They got to live their lives, it's your turn to live yours so you can be happy."

The warm smile that spread across his face had my stomach filling with butterflies. I'd seen him smile before at work plenty of times, but this was different. This wasn't some polite smile you gave to someone you just met or because you had to. This was a genuine and true smile. It lit up his face. And his eyes became even more green, if that was even possible.

"Your parents sound like really amazing people."

"They are the best. I won the lottery with them, seriously. They are completely supportive of me wanting to be an artist, where most parents would be trying to convince me to get a *real* job. And when I came out at fourteen, they just said, "we know", and asked what I wanted for dinner. They didn't bat an eye when I brought my first boyfriend home, or object if I ever need to talk to them about something. They've always been supportive and I know that makes me very lucky. I've heard and seen firsthand some horror stories with people coming out to their parents. My one friend got kicked out, but thankfully, he had an older brother who had his own apartment and was very accepting of him."

I couldn't take my eyes away from his face. I was used to telling people I was gay and there was always a reaction. People couldn't help it, the second they heard it there was either shock, disgust, confusion, or complete acceptance on their face and within their eyes.

To me, I am who I am, and I don't care to change. But depending on how you react would dictate how our interactions would be. If you didn't like that I was gay, well you and I were never going to be talking again. It was just that simple to me and there were people I hadn't spoken with again because of it.

I was relieved to see no form of disgust within his eyes. There was a calm understanding there. But what was also interesting, for a second I could have sworn there was lust. Once again, this man was giving me mixed feelings. One second, I am confident he was straight and then he would look at me a certain way and my confidence would go right out the window. I had to know if he was gay or not. I couldn't keep playing this guessing game any longer. It was going to drive me insane.

"So, are you dating anyone?" I asked with a lot more bravery then I was feeling.

"No, I'm single. You?" he said with a small smirk.

That so did not answer my question at all. It wasn't like I could just flat out ask him if he got turned on by guys or girls. That smirk told me that he was toying with me. I would almost say flirting slightly. That coy answer was designed to keep me wondering and it was going to drive me crazy. He had no idea how much it was going to bother me not knowing the answer officially. Hell, maybe he was bi-sexual. No matter the direction he swung, he seemed to be enjoying torturing me.

"Single, and if the blind date that I was

dragged into going on last night was anything to go by, I'll be single for a while," I answered as the waitress brought our food over.

"Why, was he that ugly?"

I gave a small laugh at that. Dylan would have been very attractive if he didn't talk. "No, that wasn't his problem."

I told him all about how pompous and self-centered the guy was. We both had fun laughing about it and talking about other people we'd known who had been downright terrible.

The conversation between us flowed so seamlessly and smooth. It was as if we had been friends for years compared to only knowing each other less than forty-eight hours. He was smart and funny. He was not boring at all and he could listen, too. He had no problem sitting there listening to my stories and adding his own input to them. It felt amazing.

We had talked for so long that by the time we left, it was almost dinner time. We had been talking for four hours, but it only felt like minutes. We had exchanged numbers and were going to meet tomorrow to go bowling. I wasn't really a bowler, but I was willing to do anything if it meant I could see Zane again.

We were building a friendship and I knew that even if he was straight, a friendship with Zane was a hell of a lot better than nothing at all. He was a good man and he was someone I wanted in my life. Now, I just had to make sure my attraction to him didn't turn into a full-blown crush.

At least, not until I discovered if he was gay or not.

CHAPTER FOUR

Zane

THE LAST FEW weeks had been a mixture of emotions for me. The pressure coming from my father was getting intense, more so than it had been previously. He was constantly asking me about Kayla and talking about the company. He was not pleased with me working at the diner and he would often ask me when I was going to quit and come work for a *real* company. Thankfully, he was still completely in the dark about my online courses. I could only imagine the explosion that would come out of him if he discovered my secret.

It was ridiculous when I thought about it. I shouldn't have to hide my education from my own parents. I shouldn't have to keep this as a secret from him. Going to school, wanting to better my education, shouldn't be something that I had to treat as a secret. I shouldn't have to hide it like I'm selling drugs on the street corner. The fact that I couldn't let my parents know about my courses only solidified that I could never tell them about being gay, not until I was twenty-five. They would kick me out and disown me, not that it would bother me all that much, but I wasn't going to lose my inheritance. I had earned that money and it was set for my future. I couldn't risk losing it.

Aside from my inheritance, I couldn't risk Daryl and his safety. I wasn't worried about his physical health, but his mental and emotional health I was worried about. He was gay, and apparently more open about it than me, if our conversation was anything to go by. He wasn't going to make it until he was twenty-five in that house. He was seventeen, soon to be eighteen in three months, so if my parents discovered he was gay they would be free to kick him out. He would have nothing. He'd be a senior in high school living on the street. I had to be there for him. I had to make it four more years so he would have a safety net. So he could come out in four years and not have to fear being homeless. He would have a place to stay with me, where he would be free to be himself and to chance his own dreams. We would have to fight so he could keep his inheritance, but that was a fight we could face together.

The highlight of the past few weeks had been my time with Jimmy. He was the light in the very dark tunnel that I was trapped in. We had been able to spend most days together, even if it was just grabbing a meal together or working together. Seeing Jimmy made all of the sneaking around and frustrations worth it. Seeing him was like getting fresh air. He was breathing life back into a dying man and, fuck, I needed the breaths.

There was one hiccup, though. The more time I spent with him, the more I was haunted by him. His face would invade my dreams, my fantasies. I would wake up as hard as a rock and no amount of cold showers would make it go back down. The only way I could get rid of my erection was to jerk off. The dirty little things we would do in my fantasies...

Fuck, I couldn't think about that now or I would be hard at work.

The one thing I truly admired about him was how easy it was for him to just be himself. He was so open and accepting of who he was. He was gay and he was very proud of it. He didn't have to hide. He was free to be out and proud. His parents loved him and supported him in not only his sexual orientation, but his dreams.

God, my father would shit a brick if I went to him and asked if we could turn the garage into a paint studio. He hated that

Daryl loved to paint and draw. To him that was feminine and completely unacceptable for a man.

Jimmy had the kind of parents that everyone dreamed of having. The kind *I* always dreamed of having. I was happy for him, don't get me wrong, but it only confirmed how screwed up my family truly was.

Letting out a sigh as the last customer of the night left, I made my way over and locked the door before turning off the open light. It was only me and Jimmy left tonight to get everything closed up.

Normally, I would be very happy with that outcome, but tonight had been rough. Everything going on with my father, plus my growing desire for Jimmy, didn't make me very good company tonight. Something needed to give. I knew my father wasn't going to, which meant my attraction to Jimmy needed to. The problem was, you couldn't just turn it on and off. There wasn't some light switch in my head that I could flip to end an attraction. If there was,

I could be straight and have one less thing to worry about in my life.

"Are you okay? You've been quiet and a bit broody all shift," Jimmy asked from behind the counter, concern shining in his eyes.

Oh my God, this guy is so amazing.

I guess broody was the right word for it. Normally, at work me and him would talk and joke around. I'm more free to be myself there, but tonight I couldn't shake off the frustrations from life. I had been more quiet and kept to myself. Focused on some work in the back office and basically avoided people. It wasn't how I liked to run my shift.

"Sorry," I said, as I got the blinds all closed off.

"Don't be, but you can talk to me you know."

I made my way over behind the counter as Jimmy removed his server's pouch and started to get everything put away. We only had one customer in the diner for the past hour, so most of the closing jobs had already been done.

It had been a slow night tonight, something I was also grateful for. I knew I could talk with him, but I also knew he was still trying to figure out if I was straight or gay. I suspected he knew I was gay. He had caught me looking at his lips way too many times. I couldn't help it, though. They looked so kissable. We hadn't talked about dating, really, outside of that one conversation a few weeks ago. That was focused on Jimmy's horrible blind date and it had nothing to do with my love life, or lack thereof.

I had other friends, but those were the friends picked by my father as being *suitable* for our family. They were all the same, stuck up rich guys that talked way too much about which girl they were banging. They weren't people that I could talk to about Kayla and how I felt about her. They would not only *not* be interested in any of my feelings, but they also wouldn't understand. To them, a girl like Kayla was perfect. She would look good on your arm, she would put out as much as you wanted and wouldn't care if you cheated on her as long as she got to spend money. I couldn't talk to anyone, but maybe I could talk to Jimmy about it. Maybe, I could finally unload my thoughts and feelings on the situation I was being forced into.

"I had to go out on a first date with this girl, Kayla," I started. I wanted to see how he reacted to the news that I was "straight". If he seemed a bit confused, then that would tell me he suspected I was gay, so discovering that I was gay wouldn't be a shock. It was putting off the inevitable, I was aware of that, but it would help for me to know that I was making the right decision in telling him.

"Oh, did it not go well?" he asked, and flashed a sort of half-smile.

The tone in his voice and that look of 'trying to appear happy but not really feeling it' told me everything I needed to know. He wasn't fully shocked, but he was disappointed. He might not have known if I was gay one hundred percent, but he'd been hoping I was. It seemed like I wasn't the only one with an attraction between us.

"It was terrible. *She* is terrible, and I know that sounds bad, but she is really terrible. A complete airhead and self-centered. The whole dinner I had to keep reminding myself that I couldn't stab her with the salad fork."

"Wow, a salad fork, eh? Very fancy for a first date," Jimmy teased.

"Not my idea. She comes from old money so she expects a certain level of luxury. Which does not help her case at all."

"If you didn't like her, then why ask her out?"

It was a very simple question, one that should have had a simple answer, but this one really didn't.

"You know how my father runs a pharmaceutical company, but what I didn't tell you was that it's Hamilton Pharmaceuticals. It's been in my family for generations so I come from old money. My father has been trying to make a deal with another company that owns fifty hospitals all across the country. It would be serious revenue and profit for the company if they can secure the deal. Kayla Miller is the daughter of the current owner, Henry Miller."

"Ah, so he wants you and her to get together to help solidify the deal. If his daughter is dating you, and if you are making her happy, then that will help persuade him into signing a contract," Jimmy said with complete understanding.

"Exactly. He wants me to date her and eventually marry her. He doesn't care what I want. He doesn't care if I'm attracted to her or if we're even a good fit. All my father cares about is expanding the company. To him, my being with Kayla is a sacrifice I should be honored to make."

And that was the thing, my father should have asked what I thought of her. Even if I was straight, he shouldn't have assumed I would be attracted to her. He should have pulled me aside and talked to me like a normal father would have and asked what I thought about her. Asked me if I could see myself being with her for the rest of my life. He didn't, though, because to him it was just another line in a contract. I was something he could use to better a deal. He didn't care, not one bit about me, and that really hurt.

"Well, what do you want, then?" Jimmy asked gently.

It was a simple and innocent question, but it was one I hadn't really heard all that often. Everyone told me what I was expected to do. No one tended to ask me what I wanted. This might be a mistake, but I think the bigger mistake would be to let this moment pass me by. If I was going to regret this night, I want it to because I took action instead of doing nothing.

Before I could change my mind or chicken out, I was moving. As I moved closer to him, Jimmy moved back. I kept going until his back hit the counter. Placing my hands on either side of him on the counter, I spoke.

"I want you." Without giving him a chance to say anything, I pressed my lips against his. The second our lips made contact there was an explosion of fire that spread through my entire body. It was like nothing I had ever felt before. Something as simple as a kiss should not leave me feeling like this. The gentle press of his lips back against mine had me instantly hard. The kiss was simple and he was uncertain, I could feel that in his hesitation against my own lips. But he wasn't pulling back. I wanted more of him. I needed more of him, but before I could deepen the kiss, he was pulling back.

CHAPTER FIVE

Jimmy

HE KISSED ME.

Zane kissed me.

Holy shit.

I needed to think. I needed time to consider what all of this could mean. But, I couldn't think, because all I could get my mind to focus on was how amazing it felt to have his lips against mine. The same lips that were millimeters apart from my very own right now.

Screw thinking, it's overrated.

Grabbing the front of his shirt, I pulled him back to me, crushing our lips back together. This time, though, the kiss was anything but light and gentle. The gloves were off and we were both allowing our attraction to the other to explode.

Zane easily dominated the kiss and I was more than happy to allow him. Once I felt his tongue against my lips, seeking permission, I easily granted him it. I parted my lips so his tongue could dance with mine.

The second his tongue reached mine I couldn't help the moan that crept from my throat. Kissing was one of my favorite parts. There was just something about it that told me everything I needed to know about the man I was with. If it sent a shiver down my spine, I knew the attraction, the chemistry, was going to be off the wall. If he was gentle and hesitant, then I knew he was going to be uncertain about every step that came after.

Zane's kiss, though, not only did it send

shockwave after shockwave of electricity all over my body, but his kiss was confident and strong. He knew exactly what he wanted and he was not holding back or afraid to go after it.

The need to feel his skin against mine became too great. I needed to touch him. Pressing my hands to his chest, I casually trailed my fingers over his warm pecs, down to his rippled stomach, and then up underneath his shirt.

Zane apparently felt the same because before I even knew it, he had my shirt open and off, leaving me in just my jeans. This was stupid, I knew messing around with my new boss could end things for me at the diner, but I didn't care. I couldn't think of anything else but feeling Zane against me.

I quickly removed his shirt, pushing it off his shoulders as Zane broke the kiss and peppered his way up my neck to the sensitive spot below my ear, causing me to moan once more. I tilted my head back to grant him better access to my neck as shivers flared up and down my spine.

His hands went to my ass and he pulled me closer, tighter against his hips. The second our hard cocks rubbed against each other, even through our jeans, it was pure bliss. Both of us moaned deeply and I started at the electrified sensation that shot through my belly to my balls.

"I need you," Zane said in a breathy voice that vibrated against my lips. In this moment that was the only thing I needed to hear.

"Fuck, yes," I breathed back.

It was like a switch had been flipped at my simple confirmation. Zane's hands were everywhere, all over my body. The need we both felt was explosive. The desperation to feel the other's skin against our own bodies took over all logic and reason.

My hands were instantly going to his pants, quickly undoing them so I could free his hard cock. It felt huge trapped within his jeans and the need to see it, to feel it with my own hand, was all I could think about. I was rewarded with not only a large and solid cock within my hand, but Zane let loose a deep, throaty moan at the contact.

He made quick work of divesting me of my pants. I kicked off my shoes, allowing him to pull the jeans off each foot and toss them to the floor. Once I was completely naked, I was expecting to feel Zane's hand on my cock. Only, I was pleasantly surprised when he dropped to his knees, licked his lips, and then gave my engorged tip a lick, slurping up the white pearl of pre-cum that had gathered at the slit.

I couldn't stop my eyes from fluttering shut as intense pleasure scorched through me. I couldn't stop the cry that slipped from my lips as his hot mouth took my cock all the way down to the base. Clearly, he was very good at this.

Zane moved my left leg up so it was sitting on one of the shelves behind the counter to give him better access. I opened my eyes and looked down as he worked my cock with his full lips. The sight of it was almost enough to make me come.

Zane pulled back off me with an audible *pop.* Licking his lips, he reached into his pants pocket and pulled out his wallet. He dug around for a brief moment, and then tugged out a condom and a small packet of lube.

I wasn't going to allow myself to think about why he would have those in his wallet. Zane wasn't going to even give me the chance to think about it, because he was once again taking me all the way down to my base, his moans reverberating through my shaft and into my balls, driving me dangerously close to the edge already. The vibrations had me whimpering from the pleasure. My eyes closed again and I surrendered myself to Zane's magical tongue.

When I felt his finger tracing cool lube over my puckered hole, excitement shot through me. I couldn't wait until I could feel him inside of me. Until I could feel his cock buried balls deep within me. I was a very happy bottom. I knew some guys who liked to switch back and forth, but for me, I was a definite bottom. I had zero desire to be a top and I loved to bottom far too much to give it up.

Zane worked his two and then three fingers quickly inside of me, stretching me enough so that he would fit. His mouth was moving slower on my cock, and I knew he was trying to hold me off. I wanted to come so badly, but I wanted him to be buried inside of me when I did.

"Zane, please, fuck me." A deep moan escaped me as his fingers hit my sweet spot and stars danced across my eyes.

I don't know if it was the moan or what I said, but Zane didn't need any more incentive to move things along. He slowly pulled his fingers out and the next second I was laying flat against the counter and Zane was in between my legs.

"It's gonna be hard and fast," Zane warned and I knew he was teetering on the edge along with me.

"Fuck yes," I easily agreed. That was the only way I wanted this to go. Don't get me wrong, I've got no problem with slow and sweet, but tonight I wanted it hard and fast. I was a volcano waiting to blow and I needed to explode.

Zane quickly rolled on the condom and then I finally felt his tip against my ass. He pushed in slowly. Even though I was stretched, he was so big there was still a slight sting to it. I didn't care, though, because the second his tip breached my opening the world shattered all around me. Inch by inch, he pushed inside of me, going deeper and deeper than any guy had ever gone before. His cock was large and long and it felt glorious inside of me. By the time he was all the way down to his base, we were both breathing heavy.

"You okay?" Zane asked.

"I'll be better once you move."

Zane flashed me a sexy smirk and he kept his eyes on mine as he slowly pulled out almost all of the way before he snapped his hips forward, burying himself deep inside of me again. The sensation and pleasure had me arching my back and moaning, only fueling him on. Zane kept true to his word and fucked me hard, fast, and deep. When the tip of his cock hit my sweet spot all control went right out the window.

"Zane," I moaned as I wrapped my legs around his hips.

Zane continued to hit my sweet spot dead on with each thrust. The contact and friction was bringing me closer and closer to my release. I was a moaning mess on the counter, but I wasn't the only one. Zane's moans bounced off the walls of the diner as his own need for release was fast approaching.

"Come for me, baby," Zane said, as the walls of my ass started to tighten around him.

I was so close, so fucking close, and with one final direct hit on my prostate, I was all but screaming Zane's name as I came hard, spurting hot, white ropes of cum over my belly.

The tightening of my walls around Zane's cock pushed him over the edge and I was blissfully rewarded with feeling him pulsing inside of me. My whole body was tingling. I was still coming, something that was remarkable all in itself. It was rare when I was able to come from sex without my dick being touched. Zane had a serious talent and I had a feeling it was one I would never grow tired of.

The only sound in the diner was the sound of our heavy breathing. I knew I should be moving, but I wasn't fully confident that my legs would be able to hold my weight right now. That was easily the best sex of my life. I could still feel Zane pulsing inside of me and it was complete bliss.

Zane gave me a very sweet and slow kiss before he pulled back and slowly pulled out of me with a groan. He moved back and quickly removed the condom and tossed it into the garbage before he turned his attention to me. I slowly sat up, the room spinning for a second. I wasn't worried about it, though. I knew it was from breathing so heavy. I just needed to get my breathing back to normal.

"Are you okay? I didn't hurt you?" Zane asked, slightly concerned with how fast he had gone.

"Fuck no. That was amazing. I don't think I can walk right now," I said with a goofy smile.

I knew this was all going to click in soon, but right now I was just going to enjoy the after bliss I was in right now. The sexy smirk Zane shot my way sent a shiver down my spine. This man was sex on a stick.

Zane got his clothes back on and went to take the garbage out to the dumpster. By the time he got back, I had managed to get dressed and to stand. We were basically done with closing and now we were starting to reach the slightly awkward part of sleeping with someone for the first time. I mean, was this a one-night stand type of deal? He said he wanted me and the way he could suck cock and fuck told me it was not his first time being with a man. Yet, he was dating a girl, or supposed to be, so what did it all mean?

"Why don't you grab your bag and I'll give you a ride home," Zane suggested.

All I could do was nod to that and head

off into the back to grab my backpack. It took everything in me to not comment that he already gave me one hell of a ride.

I quickly grabbed my bag and headed out with him. We got into his car, and after telling him my address, we were off.

Awkward didn't seem to cut it for the first five minutes of the drive. I wanted to say something, but I wasn't sure what to say. I wanted to know what this all meant, but at the same time I was afraid of the answer. If he said it was only a one-time thing, I would have to accept that and go back to working around him. It would suck, though.

"I don't want this to be a one-night stand. If that is what you want, then I'll respect it, but I'm hoping that isn't what you want." Zane's voice snapped me out of my thoughts and for a moment I had to make sure he actually said the words and it wasn't my imagination.

"I'm not a one-night stand type of guy. I like you. I just don't know what you want. I mean, you said you were dating that Kayla girl.”

And technically, he just cheated on her with me. Not good. I was the dirty mistress in this situation, not something I ever thought I would be.

"We aren't officially dating, I've never even kissed her or held her hand, and I have no plans of doing either with her. I like you, Jimmy. I'm gay, but I'm in the closet only because of my parents. If they discovered I was gay they would not only kick me out, which I wouldn't care all that much, but they would also remove my inheritance. I need that money for my dream. Once I turn twenty-five, it automatically goes to me and there is nothing they can do or say to change that. I just need to go another four years without them finding out I'm gay. Afterward, I don't have to hide anymore. And I know it's a lot to ask someone who is out and proud to be kept in the shadows, and if you can't handle that or don't want to, I completely understand. I would never hold it against you. But if you are okay with that, if you want to pursue something with me, then I'd really like to take you out on a date."

A date?

Could I really go out with him on a date knowing I would have to be a secret he keeps for the next four years?

Yes, four years was a long way away and anything could happen between now and then. Hell, in three months we might not even still be together.

What could one date really hurt, right?

"I'd like that."

The big smile that Zane sent my way told me everything I needed to know. He really did have feelings for me. Maybe this would turn out to be a terrible idea, but for right now it didn't seem like such a bad idea. Sex at work on the other hand, though, not the best idea I've had.

"Great, I'll text you in a couple of days and we can figure something out with our work schedule."

I just gave a nod and then enjoyed the silence between us. It was no longer awkward, but now a comfortable silence, something I was very pleased about. I didn't live that far from the diner, so it only took another ten minutes before we were pulling up front of my house.

"Thanks for the ride," I said as I removed my seatbelt.

"No problem. I'll text you tomorrow."

"Goodnight, Zane."

I wanted to kiss him, but he seemed to be unsure about it. I could see his eyes darting around the area to see if anyone was watching us. I was starting to get a picture of what it might be like if I did date him.

"Night, Jimmy," he said with a warm, rich smile. It was a nice smile, don't get me wrong, but I would have preferred a goodnight kiss.

Accepting that it wasn't going to happen, I got out of his car and quickly made my way inside, relieved that my parents were already in bed. Once I was safely in my room, I couldn't help but slowly sink down to the floor with my back pressed against the door. Shock. I could safely say I was in shock. It was a good shock, don't get me wrong, but shock nonetheless. Never have I ever had sex in a public place before, much less my work. Thankfully, there were no cameras at the diner so we weren't going to be fired. I could only imagine the rumors about that going around town. In a town this size, the rumor mill was always turning. There was always someone that was sleeping with some married person. Always some scandal that was going around, and with Zane being in the closet, the last thing he needed was for the whole town to hear about him having sex on the counter in the diner.

I can't believe I did that. I had never done anything like that before. Anytime I've had sex it was always behind closed doors. A closed *bedroom* door. I've never done anything out in public. Well, I've kissed, but never anything more. I don't know what happened. One second we're talking, then the next his lips were on mine and it was like my mind completely shut off. All logic and reason went right out the window.

I needed him.

I had never needed someone that badly before. I had never had a desire for another person that strong before. It was like my whole body was on fire and his hands were the only thing that could put it out. I could still feel his hands lingering all over my body. His scent was covering my skin and it was intoxicating. My body was craving him, craving his touch all over again. If I wasn't careful I could become addicted to his touch and that wasn't something I could afford.

I swore I would never be with someone that was in the closet again. That I wouldn't put myself in the position of where I would have to hide who I am with. I couldn't hide who I was, most people knew I was gay, but I wasn't the type that enjoyed having to be some dirty secret. I wanted to be shown off. I wanted to see the proud smile on my boyfriend's face when he introduced me. I wanted kisses and hand holding. I wanted it all, and being with someone in the closet took it all away. Save those kisses and moments for when we were alone. Having to hide in the closet with someone was not something I was looking to do. And yet, here I was actually thinking about it. Actually agreeing to going out on a date with him. It was absurd and chances were this was only going to end in tears. My tears. Even though I know all of that, I was still going to go through with the date. I wanted him, I had wanted him from the very first second he walked into the diner. I never thought he would be gay, much less interested in me, but he was. Maybe this would turn out to be a mistake, but it was my mistake to make and I had to take the risk.

I would be protecting my heart, though. I was taking a huge risk by going out with him. I understand why he has to hide, why he can't come out, I truly do, but I also needed to keep myself safe. I had to protect my heart, because chances were, this relationship was going to go down in flames and when the smoke cleared it would be me left heartbroken in the soot.

CHAPTER SIX

Zane

THIS WAS INSANE. I couldn't be this nervous about something as simple as a first date. I had been on plenty of first dates. Well, not plenty, but enough to make me anything but a novice. Still, here I was standing in front of my mirror after changing my outfit eight times. It was ridiculous, and yet here I was in my ninth outfit trying to convince myself that I looked good.

All of this was crazy. We had already had sex. At work, on the counter, admittedly not the best idea, but if it was a mistake it was the best mistake I had ever made. This wasn't my first time having a one-night stand, but generally those guys were the ones I picked up in the bar. They weren't someone that I wanted to date. Someone that I wanted to have conversations with and to curl up on the couch with.

Jimmy, he could be that person. He's different, he's smart and funny and very creative. He is so free to be himself and he embraces every aspect of himself. He shares who he is to this world and I wanted that. I couldn't wait until I could have that.

Letting out a deep breath and giving myself one last look in the mirror, I headed out of my room and made my way down the stairs. I moved quickly in order to avoid running into my father. The last thing I needed tonight was to see him. I was in a good mood and he would only ruin it.

"Zane."

Of course.

I was almost at the door.

I was so close.

Another ten feet and I would have been free from him. I quickly turned around, hoping to get this over and done with so I could leave. The last thing I wanted to be was late for tonight. It wasn't anything special, just going to the movies, but still. It was our time together and I didn't want to miss a single second of it.

"Father."

"I have just finished speaking with Henry. Kayla has been enjoying your time together, though she wishes it was more often."

Great.

There was a lecture coming. I could see it all over his face and hear it in his tone. He wasn't happy that Kayla wasn't getting enough of me. That she wasn't getting more of my time. The problem wasn't just because I had zero interest in her. I was also working while taking courses online. I didn't have much free time and any free time that I did have, I wanted to spend it with someone I was actually interested in. Not some girl that her only goal in life is to marry someone rich. Even if I was straight, Kayla would not be the woman that I would pick for myself. She was the exact opposite of who I would pick.

"We both have busy lives and our free time doesn't always line up. We still text and speak with each other every day, though."

The conversations were kept very short. I'm not a rude person at all, but Kayla, she was dumb. There really wasn't a nice way to put it.

She was stupid.

An airhead.

Literally nothing inside.

The only thing she wanted to talk about was gossip about her other idiot friends. Something I did not care about. Or she was trying to sext with me, again something I did not care for. Jimmy sending me naked photos, now that I could get into.

Kayla was your typical shallow, self-centered rich girl. She had no problems, she had no responsibilities, and she had no desire to make something of herself. She couldn't understand why my working was important to me. To her, I should have quit and just worked for my father. To land a cushy upper management position and just coast. She considered my working in a diner as a low-life position and it was something she needed to be ashamed of. Point of fact, her friends all think I work for my father already, because God forbid she told them the truth.

"That is not enough. A woman needs more than words on a screen or a phone call. You need to prioritize your future. Kayla is part of that. You need to get your mind focused. You are working at the diner, something that was only supposed to bring you experience, and yet you are treating it like it is your career. The work you do there is pitiful compared to the work you will be doing for the company. It is a waste of time, one I am humoring you on for now, though I will not be doing it for very long. Whatever little rebellion you have going on, I strongly advise you to get it out of your system and do it quickly. I will not allow you to jeopardize my company's future. A company that has been in this family for generations. A company you are set to take over within the next few years."

I had heard this lecture all before, not exactly this version, but the bottom line was all the same. I wasn't living up to his expectations or to the family name. That I needed to get my head out of the clouds and focus on the company and how to make it better for the future. That future included me being forced to marry a woman just so there could be a merger with her family. To my father, it wasn't just my duty to the family but my way of bringing honor to us. It was beyond old fashioned, and this was a lecture I quickly became annoyed with and often tuned him out.

"Plan the proposal."

That had me snapping back into attention. I had clearly missed something, something very important that he had added on this time around.

"Proposal?" I asked, trying to make it seem like I hadn't tuned him out. That wouldn't have gone over well.

"How you propose to a woman matters, Zane. They want to remember it for the rest of their lives. You can't just place a ring box down on a table. A woman of her caliber needs a big gesture for it. Just like the ring matters. You should take your mother this weekend to look at rings."

Okay, now I know my father is certifiable. There was no way in hell he was actually talking about me proposing to Kayla, a woman I had only been dating, and I use that term very lightly, for a few weeks. This was turning out to be a shotgun wedding, only this time around the shotgun would be pointing at me and not the bride. He couldn't seriously believe that after only a few weeks of dating I would propose to her.

"There's no need for that just yet, Father. We have only been seeing each other for a few weeks, now. I understand that this is important, but it is also important that we develop a relationship to ensure a marriage works. If she is not happy, it would not look good to have her filing for divorce."

I needed to get my father to see logic. If it was his idea for us to wait, then he wouldn't keep bringing it up. He wouldn't start to pressure me into a proposal.

"A woman like her will not wait that long to see a true commitment. You cannot drag your feet for very long or she will grow tired of waiting and find someone else that will give her what she needs. You need to start thinking about the future and how you are going to propose to her."

He wasn't going to let this go, which meant I would have no choice but to appease him. I would have to figure out how to get out of this later.

"Yes, Father. I need to go and pick her up now, though. I don't want to be late."

A simple nod from my father had me instantly moving to the door. It was easier for him to believe I was seeing Kayla. I didn't need to deal with any further questions about where I was going and who

I was seeing. Not to mention why I wasn't going to see Kayla. I just wanted to see Jimmy. Seeing him would make this night better.

I quickly got into my car and headed off for the downtown movie theatre. We would be meeting there. As much as I would have loved to pick Jimmy up at his house, I was still nervous with people knowing I was gay. You never know who was going to accidentally let something slip to someone else. I had to be vigilant, especially in the beginning. Once people got used to seeing us around and seeing us as being just two guys who were friends, I could pick him up at his house. I could hang out with him there and no one would think twice about it. The movies would allow us to be close while in the dark. I've taken a few dates to the movies before and it always worked out well. I couldn't wait until I could get Jimmy alone in the dark.

Once I parked, I made my way to the front of the building. Downtown tonight wasn't very busy with it being a Wednesday.

With mine and Jimmy's work schedule a Friday or Saturday night date wouldn't work. We would be working while everyone else was enjoying their weekend. It being not that busy would help in our favor in the movies, too. It would give us more privacy, and with more privacy, more fun could be had.

Jimmy was already here, standing out front looking sexy as hell. He wore a black t-shirt with a black denim jacket. His jeans were dark blue and I could see paint splatter on them. His black converse shoes also had paint splatter. Most would find it unattractive, but to me, no one had ever looked sexier.

I can't even begin to explain how badly I want to watch him work. I wanted to watch as his creative juices poured out of him and onto the canvas. And once he was finished, I wanted to strip him of his clothes and lay him down on the tarp. I wanted to create our own masterpiece together.

The rich warm smile he sent my way caused a chain reaction within my body.

Electricity ran down my spine that was quickly followed by this heat that exploded in my chest and traveled all the way down to my crotch. This man could make me hard with something as simple as a smile.

"Hey, you made it," I said, and flashed him a warm smile. I wished I could have reached out and kissed him.

"I had to set an alarm so I wouldn't get lost in my art. I always paint when I get home from school," Jimmy said with a small shy smile.

"I would love to watch you paint," I said softly as we made our way toward the cashier. I could see the blush creep over his cheeks out of the corner of my eye and it only made him look sexier. Tonight was going to be so much fun.

Once we had our tickets, we headed inside and grabbed some drinks and popcorn to split. I guided us into the theatre and made sure we sat in the back in one of the darker corners. Most people wouldn't want to sit back here and that was what I was counting on. It would allow us to have some privacy that we would need.

"Interesting seats," Jimmy whispered.

"Trust me, these are perfect," I said with a playful smirk. Jimmy had no idea just what I had in store for him.

"It's not very busy." The slight nervous tone to his voice told me that he was feeling anxious. I was as well, but I always was when I was out in public with another guy. My mind was constantly going over the chances of someone discovering that we were on a date.

"It's Wednesday. I would have been shocked if it was. How was school?" I was hoping the topic of school would be enough to help put his nerves at ease.

"It was good. I was able to get most of my projects done ahead so I don't have to stress too much over them. Danny was pretty upset today."

"Danny?"

"He's my friend that I was telling you about that was kicked out. His older brother, Thad, had to have this big meeting with their parents. Apparently, it did not go well."

"What happened, if you don't mind my asking."

"His parents wanted Thad to place Danny into a conversion camp. Technically, Thad doesn't have custody of Danny so his parents can still make all the decisions. Thad is trying his best to protect him. It's looking like it's going to get ugly. Danny was talking about Thad having to get a family lawyer and sue for custody," Jimmy said with pain in his voice for his friend.

"Shit, I'm sorry. That really sucks and shouldn't have to be like that. How old are Danny and Thad?"

"Danny is sixteen. He's a year behind me in school. And Thad is nineteen. He works as a mechanic. I don't know where they would get the money for a lawyer, but Danny has two years to go before he's legally an adult. From what I gathered, they don't want to roll the dice with that much time left."

"No, I wouldn't want to wait either. That's insane. Why the push for the conversion camp? Or do they just believe they work?"

Conversion camps weren't unheard of, especially in a small town like this one. Still, most parents didn't jump to it.

"They are very religious. They were always strict with him and Thad growing up. They had to only wear certain clothes, they only ever ate healthy food, they went to church four times a week. They weren't allowed to be alone with a girl, no dating. I mean, insane, controlling, strict. Being gay is completely against their religion and means he would be going to hell. Danny said they had apparently been hoping the phase would be washed out of him by now," Jimmy said as he rolled his eyes.

"And now they want to put him through conversion therapy. What are they going to do?"

Conversion therapy wasn't a route that my parents would take. Only because they wouldn't want to have it out in the open that one of their sons was gay. That didn't change the fact that I was worried about

Daryl. He only had a year left, but he would still be expected to live at home until he was twenty-five. My parents had their own beliefs and ways. Keeping us home until we get married to the woman they picked and we received our inheritance was their way of controlling us. If we left, our inheritance would be changed and we would lose everything. I was going to make it, but I had serious doubts about Daryl.

"I don't know. Danny didn't know. I think he is hoping that Thad can convince them to wait it out. I doubt he would be able to afford a lawyer. He works all the time now to pay the bills and to put some money away for Danny's college fund. All they can really do right now is wait and see."

It was clear that Jimmy was worried about his friend. I couldn't blame him. It was a terrible situation for them to be in. Hopefully, it would work out and they would able to avoid having to go through the court system. That could be a lengthy and expensive experience. Mechanics didn't make minimum wage, but they didn't make a huge amount of money, either. With having a two bedroom to pay for, plus trying to save money, there wouldn't be much room for unexpected expenses.

"Hopefully, Thad can come to some sort of an agreement with his parents to put a stop to all of this. I'm sure it'll be okay," I said. I reached over and took his hand in mine as the room got darker for the trailers to begin.

"I hope so," Jimmy easily agreed, flashing me a warm smile.

We turned our attention to the movie. While Jimmy was watching it, I was waiting for the perfect moment to make my move. That moment came roughly twenty minutes later when everyone was invested in the movie.

I moved my left hand over to Jimmy's crotch and started to rub it through his jeans. The second my hand made contact, Jimmy jumped slightly in his seat and I couldn't help the small, soft chuckle that escaped my lips. I looked over at him and I could see the shock and confusion on his face, but I could also see the excitement in his eyes.

"You didn't think we'd just watch the movie did you?" I whispered into his ear, causing him to shiver.

"Someone could see," he countered as I started to unzip his pants.

"They are all watching the movie. The only reason they would look at us is if you make a noise."

I freed Jimmy's cock from his pants and he was already hard. I brushed my lips over his neck, nipping and licking at the sensitive spot below his ear as I started to slowly jerk him off.

Jimmy must have decided that holding the popcorn bucket was too much effort right now, and he placed it down on the seat beside us. What he did next, though, did surprise me. He reached over and started to unzip my own jeans to free my already hard cock.

A quick scan of the room only confirmed what I already knew, everyone was looking at the giant screen. I let out a huff at the contact of Jimmy's warm hand along my hard shaft. He felt amazing. I wished we could have had sex right now, but people would notice that for sure. Handjobs, not so much. Still, what I wouldn't give to be buried deep inside of him again.

It wasn't long before we were both breathing heavy and having to keep our moans and groans internal and not out loud. If we didn't have to worry about the thirty some odd people in the theatre hearing us, these walls would be echoing with our pleasure-filled sounds.

"Zane," Jimmy whispered, and I felt his cock getting harder within my hand.

He was reaching his peak and I was closely following behind him. Normally, I could last a lot longer, but there was something about Jimmy that made me go crazy. Every single touch of his felt amplified by a hundred times.

Jimmy moved and buried his face into my neck as he gave a groan and came hard, his cum quickly spilling down my hand with each pulse. Feeling his cock pulse in my hand, feeling his warm cum spreading over my skin, pushed me over the edge and I had to bite down on my lip to keep what would have been a very loud groan from escaping.

We both fought to catch our breaths as we pulsed in the other's hand. And just like that, all of the nerves and anxiety about tonight were gone.

He was amazing.

We were amazing together.

Jimmy turned his head toward the screen and after a moment he spoke.

"Who's that guy?"

I couldn't help the small chuckle. "I have no idea."

Jimmy laughed as he pulled his hand away from my still hard cock and grabbed us some napkins. We were both a mess, but it was a good mess.

After quickly getting cleaned up and settled back into our pants, we sat back and tried to catch up on the movie. I had no idea what was going with it, but so far it was my new favorite movie.

CHAPTER SEVEN

Jimmy

IT HAS BEEN a month now since Zane and I started dating. Everything had been going amazingly. I had forgotten what it was like to date someone. To have someone in my life that I could talk with and share different personal aspects of my life. I know I can tell my parents anything, just like I could tell my friends anything, but it's different with a boyfriend. Having someone know you on a physical and intimate level brought a stronger connection and it was that connection I'd missed.

I missed the little moments, the kisses goodbye, the quick kiss on the cheek, holding hands, being curled up in his arms while we watched television or lying together in bed. Being with Zane brought a certain feeling to my chest. A warmth I didn't think I needed, but he had proved me wrong. There was something real brewing between us and I wanted to experience more of it.

My parents were in absolute love with him, not that I could blame them. They weren't happy that he was in the closet, but they had to respect it. Their worries were put at ease when they discovered that it would only be short-term. I think to them, though, they were looking at the big picture.

Statistics weren't exactly on our side. Chances were we wouldn't still be together in five years time. I would be going off to College and he was staying here. I understood that the odds were not in our favor, and that was before you factored in our ages.

Still, I wasn't going to let that get to me. I was going to live my life to the fullest and if Zane was standing by my side, then I would be eternally happy. I could hope, though, that it worked out. I could hope we could make it work and last long enough for Zane to be able to come out to his parents.

At the same time, though, I was keeping a piece of my heart safely tucked away behind a cement wall three feet thick. I had learned enough from my past relationships to know that a man in the closet brought pain with him. Brought feelings like you weren't good enough, annoyance, frustration, and impatience.

He had to stay in the closet, and I understood fully, but he was also going to have to understand that I was going to have to keep some level of emotional distance with him. At least, until we'd been dating long enough for me to see how exactly this was going to work.

Sitting down outside at the cafe once again for lunch, I could tell that something seemed to be bothering Zane. He tended to furrow his eyebrows when he was stressing about something. When he had something on his mind he would look down and not really notice anything that was going on around him.

This is where we differed greatly. Me, I'm an open book. If something is bothering me you will be hearing all about it. I never keep things bottled up inside of me. It was bad for my art. Now, yes, there are plenty of times when I paint my emotions and my pain away, but that is to cleanse my mind and soul from it. I have to talk in order to be able to properly paint, to properly draw and release my creative juices.

Zane, though, kept everything under lock and key. It made sense, considering he had to hide the biggest part of himself from the world. Having to keep a secret that personal and enormous took a toll on you. Plus, based on what little he had spoken about his parents, they weren't the 'hug you and make it all better' type. They didn't come across as people who wanted you to spill all of your secrets and emotions out to them. Zane's mom would not be sitting curled up in bed with him with a pint of mint chocolate chip to listen to his boy problems. He was used to going through life keeping things bottled up and going through it all alone.

It was clear even with past boyfriends he didn't open up to them. I wanted Zane to know, to understand, that he could tell me things. That if something was bothering him, I was there for him. That I would be on his side and it wasn't just because we were dating. It was because he clearly needed someone to just be on his side. Right or wrong, he needed a person standing in his corner ready to face the world with him.

"What's on your mind, Z?" I asked, using the nickname for him while we were outside. I was the type of guy that loved pet names. I loved calling my boyfriend 'baby' or 'honey', but we couldn't do that right now. So I call him Z while we are outside around people so he knows that he's special to me.

"Nothing, J," Zane said with a teasing

smirk.

A quick roll of my eyes told him I was not impressed with his new nickname. He was still trying to find something that would work for me while we were out in public. That one was a serious no go.

"Never, ever, again."

The rich chuckle that escaped him only warmed my heart. It would have brought flutters to fill my chest if his smile had actually reached his eyes. Something was seriously bothering him and we were not going to enjoy our day together until we cleared it up.

"I'll keep trying, but you're the creative one between us."

"Yes, I am, but I refuse to give myself a nickname. Now, what is bothering you?"

"I said nothing."

"Yeah, tell that to the troubled look on your face or the distant look in your eyes. Something is bothering you. Tell me what it is so we can work it out," I said calmly. I knew this was going to take a wee bit of teeth pulling, but it would be worth the work.

"It's fine, I can work it out myself," Zane said, looking to dismiss the conversation all together.

"I know you are used to handling things on your own. Just like I know it will take you some time to get used to having someone in your life that you can talk to. I am respecting your pace, but every now and then I need to give you a little tiny push up the hill. This is me pushing nicely," I said and flashed him a warm smile.

Zane took a deep breath in and slowly let it out. I had discovered that meant he was debating internally and needed a moment to get his thoughts in order. Needed that minute or two to list the pros and cons before he would make his decision. Hopefully, the pros would be in my favor this time around. The waitress brought our drinks over and we quickly placed our food order. Once we were alone again, Zane spoke.

"My father has been asking me when I am going to propose to Kayla."

That was not what I was expecting to hear. I figured it might have been something to do with his school work or his parents. I didn't expect for it to be about Kayla. I didn't even know they were still seeing each other. I know they had gone on a date before Zane and I kissed. Before we started to see each other, but I figured he was finished with her.

Was he still seeing her while seeing me?

Was I the dirty mistress?

"I didn't know you were still seeing her," I said in a hushed voice, doing my best to keep the pain from my voice. I didn't want him to know that it bothered me that he might be seeing her along with me. It was one thing to be in the closet, but another for me to be just someone else that he was sleeping with. Even if the other person was a woman.

"You are the only person I am with. You are the only person I am seeing. The only person I am spending time with. You are the only person I *want* to spend time with," Zane reassured with a deep strength to his voice that instantly had me feeling better.

"You are the only person I want to spend time with, Z."

It made me feel good to hear him say that. To hear that he was only sleeping with me, only dating me. Still, it brought up more questions about Kayla.

Why would his father be asking when he is going to propose if he wasn't seeing her?

"My father thinks I'm still seeing her. We keep texting, but I keep blowing off her requests for a date. I just tell her I'm working or have to do something for my father. My father, as you know, has basically promised me to her and her to me. I didn't get a say in it, it's all business to him. The sooner we get married, the better it will be for the family company."

The bitter tone to his voice was subtle, but I could easily pick it up. Not that I could blame him. He was basically being forced into an arranged marriage and it wasn't because of his religion, but so his father could make more money and have more prestige. It was despicable in my opinion and no way for a father to be treating his child.

"Have you thought about how you are going to do this long-term? I mean, Z, you're almost four years away. You can't just keep leading her on, that's not fair to her."

I had never met her and Zane didn't say much. I just knew from what Zane had told me that she was more interested in being a trophy wife than actually working and making something of herself. I couldn't hold that against her, lots of women can be like that if they grow up in a highly wealthy family. How she was brought up or her personality didn't mean she deserved to be lead on. To be thinking that she was going to get married and eventually fall in love with someone only for the other person to hold zero interest in her. That wasn't fair to her at all and she didn't deserve to have that level of pain placed on her.

"I know, I know," Zane said, as he rubbed both hands over his face before he continued. "I'm hoping that maybe she'll be the one to quit. To get tired of me blowing her off. She spends all day long with other rich guys, she's bound to find someone that will give her the attention she needs. I've just been trying to avoid her and hope for the best at this point."

"And I hope for both of your sakes that it works that way. That she finds someone else and her father just wants her to be happy and doesn't care about the merger. But, Z, what if they do care? What if they don't care if she falls in love with someone else?"

I know what I was asking him was a lot and I know it wasn't an easy answer. The reality was, he didn't have the answers to any of these questions and he was never going to. It was something we would have to wait and see on, that was our only option. The problem was, I hated that we would have to wait. I hated that there wasn't a clear move we could make to put an end to Kayla and their impending engagement.

"I know this puts you in a shitty position, and I can't tell you how sorry I am that I've put you in this position. I wish I had answers for you. I wish I had answers for me, but I just don't right now. It's something I'll have to figure out down the road when a problem presents itself. I would completely understand, though, if you can't do this, if you don't want to do this."

The calm and understanding tone to his voice told me that he wouldn't hold any of this against me. That we could just go right back to being friends and co-workers. The problem was, I didn't want that. I didn't want to go backward. I wanted to move forward. And in moving forward, I would have to accept a higher level of uncertainty, of the unknown, than I would in a traditional relationship. It was a bigger risk that I was placing myself in, but it was my decision to be here and I wasn't about to change that now.

"I appreciate the out, but I'm not going anywhere. I know this is hard for you, more so than me because you have to deal with it all everyday. You don't get to escape it. I'm not looking for an out. I'm not looking to go back to just being friends. It's early days, I know, but I also know we have something. Being with you feels differently than my previous boyfriends and I know you feel it, too. I believe it's something worth pursuing, so we will face the problems as they come up together. We'll work through them and see what happens."

I wasn't the type of person who needed a plan for everything. I could roll with the punches and just see where the chips would fall. This was a very different situation compared to anything I'd ever been in before, but Zane was worth it. Whatever was going to happen in the future could all be worked out. I was just going to enjoy the ride and enjoy the time I got to spend with him. Hopefully Kayla would just be a blip in the very far distance soon enough.

"Being with you feels special. You feel special and I don't want to lose that. I'm going to do my best to do right by you while navigating my father's demands. Because what we have *is* different and I want to explore it to the fullest with you. But if there is ever a time, if you reach a point where you can't do this anymore, then I need you to promise me that you'll tell me. I won't be mad. I won't try and convince you to stay. I'll let you go, because I just want you to be happy and I know what I'm asking of you won't be easy and the last thing I want is for you to be miserable."

"I promise."

It was the least I could do for him. This wasn't going to be easy and I was confident there were going to be plenty of times where I was going to be frustrated and wanted to scream at the world. At the same time, though, I also knew there were going to be moments that I would cherish forever. Moments where I felt unbelievable and cared for.

It was those moments I would need to hold on to. Those moments that I would need to remember when times got hard. Those moments would get me and him through this until we reached that finish line. And I wanted to reach that finish line more than anything else. It wasn't just so we could be free to express our feelings in public. It was so Zane would finally be able to be himself. To walk hand in hand without feeling like he had to hide something. For him to just be free to openly show affection toward the man he cared for. He deserved it and I was really hoping I would be around to see it. To watch as he bloomed into his own true self. He was going to be remarkable and, hopefully, together we would be remarkable.

CHAPTER EIGHT

Zane

FIVE MONTHS, IT was crazy to think that we had been together for five months, now. Time had flown by and I am fairly certain there are a lot of people that would think something is wrong with me that I would expect for five months to be a long time, but to me it was.

I hadn't dated someone this long since my very first boyfriend back in high school. Most of the time it was only a friends with benefits situation or a one-night stand at the club. There were no dates, no cuddling, no hand holding, it was just sex and then a see you next time. It was beyond casual and simple. So to me, five months was a huge accomplishment.

Tonight we had gone to the movies, it was our new favorite spot because we could hide in the back and be alone. We tended to now go and watch movies that we didn't care about so we could enjoy the other's body while it was playing.

The past five months, Jimmy had been my salvation. Spending time with him in and outside of work was the only thing that kept me from going insane. I was still dealing with Kayla and all of the drama that came with it. She was upset that we weren't going on dates and that I wouldn't sext with her. There were only so many times I could tell her I was a proper gentleman and preferred to take things slow with her to build a better relationship. She was getting annoyed and both of our families knew it. That was putting more pressure on me from my father, who was all but demanding that I go and buy her an engagement ring. Things were getting intense, to say the least, so any time I got to spend with Jimmy was my saving grace.

Being around him made me feel light, as weird as that sounds, but when I was around him I didn't have to be weighed down by all of the pressure and stress from my daily life. I didn't need to have all of the walls up to protect myself. I could just be me and Jimmy made me feel like being myself was enough.

We had been getting closer over the past five months, spending a lot of time together will do that. I was falling for him. If I was honest with myself, I had already fallen for him. It was so fast, too fast, but it had happened. I hadn't told him yet. I couldn't tell him. It was too soon and I didn't want to scare him away. If there was one thing I couldn't lose, it was him. I had never been in love before; it was all new to me and I wasn't exactly sure how I felt about it.

When I wasn't around him, I was

constantly thinking about him, dreaming about him. Sometimes I would get so caught up in my mind that I wouldn't even notice that my parents were speaking with me. I had easily covered it up by lying, saying I was thinking about Kayla or work. When we were together, though, it took all of my strength not to touch him. I wanted to hold his hand, to kiss him, hug him. I wanted to scream from the rooftop that he was my boyfriend. I couldn't do that, though. Not yet.

It was different for me, because before I never cared about any of that. I was perfectly content to play friends and not get personal with them. Jimmy was different. He made me feel things I never expected to ever feel in my life. He made the logical part of my brain shut off when were alone.

"This place is so pretty at night," Jimmy said, snapping me out of my thoughts.

We were currently walking through a park that wasn't too far away from the downtown strip. It was dimly lit with a few light posts scattered around. It wasn't too dark that we couldn't see, but it was dark enough that I could hold his hand without anyone seeing us.

"It's not the only thing that is pretty at night," I said back to him.

It wasn't a line; he was breathtaking in the moonlight. The way the muted light played across his face, and his eyes actually sparkling in the moonlight, he was beautiful, absolutely beautiful.

I stopped and pulled him into my arms. I just couldn't help myself. I knew I shouldn't be doing this, but the need to feel his lips against mine was far too great. I pulled Jimmy in for a kiss and I could feel the shock through his lips, but it only lasted a split second before he was responding and kissing me back.

The world around us completely disappeared. All that was left was Jimmy and his lips, his sweet tasting lips. I had never been a huge fan of kissing, I much preferred to skip that step and go straight to fooling around, but with Jimmy, I could spend all day long kissing him and never get tired of it.

"Well, look at what we have here, boys. We got ourselves some faggots."

The foreign voice instantly had us pulling apart. I quickly looked over Jimmy's shoulder to see eight twenty-something year olds not too far from us. I was so lost in the kiss and what I was feeling that I didn't even hear them coming. I moved so Jimmy was behind me as I spoke.

"We're not looking for trouble. We're just heading home."

I wasn't sure what would happen with them. I hadn't come across something like this before, but I could guess it would only go one of three ways. They left, they stayed and said horrible shit to us, but allowed us to leave, or they attacked us. I was really hoping it wouldn't be option number three. I could fight, but I knew Jimmy couldn't and even if he could, we were still widely outnumbered.

"You should have thought of that before you decided to kiss in public. Ain't nobody wants to see that disgusting shit," the man said, as the other seven started to move around us. It looked like they were going to go with the third option. All I could do now was try and protect Jimmy as best as I could. Maybe if they saw me as the bigger threat they would leave Jimmy alone.

"Then walk away. We're not bothering you," I countered.

I could feel Jimmy shaking slightly behind me. He had yet to say anything and that was a good thing right now. I wanted their attention on me.

"You're bothering us by existing," another man said from behind us.

They were closing in, so I did the only thing I could think of. I moved back toward the one large tree just off to the left of us. I made sure Jimmy was directly behind me so he would have his back to the tree, putting me right in their sights. It wouldn't protect me, but it would protect Jimmy.

"I want you to run toward the street. Go as fast as you can and don't look back," I softly whispered.

"I can't leave you," Jimmy countered.

"Yes, you can. You have to so you can get help. I mean it, run."

I knew what I was asking him would be hard and that he wouldn't want to do it, but he had to. The only way we were both going to get out of this alive would be if he could get away.

Before any more could be said, the guys were moving on us. I swung out at the first one I could and my fist connected with his jaw, knocking him down. I was hoping if I could hold their attention for a minute or two, then that would give Jimmy enough time to run. I didn't have time to check and see if Jimmy was running or not. I had fists flying at me in all directions. I was trying to keep up, but there were just too many of them. I was being grabbed and thrown around.

By the time I ended up on the ground, I was a good twelve feet away from Jimmy. Jimmy, who hadn't gotten very far from the tree where we started, had five guys on him. He was on the ground trying to protect himself. I could see through the punches and kicks that connected with my body, that they were kicking him repeatedly to his leg.

His eyes were closed and I was praying that he was unconscious and they would leave him alone. A sharp kick to my head sent blackness circling my vision. I couldn't really see, but I could vaguely hear them talking. I could hear their voices and the words, but I couldn't really tell how many were talking or where they were coming from.

"Come on, we don't have to do this. Let's just leave."

"These faggots need to learn a lesson."

"Not like this. We've already given them a beat down, let's get the hell out of here before we get caught."

"Relax, no one is going to come looking for these faggots. Get his pants off."

Hearing those words had me forcing my eyes to focus.

What the hell were they talking about?

Whose pants were they taking off?

I looked around, blinking hard as I felt

my body giving in to unconsciousness. I forced myself to stay awake. I had to know what was going on, what was going to happen. To my horror they were removing Jimmy's pants and the ringleader had a small branch in his hand.

Jimmy was completely unconscious; he had no idea what was going on. I was praying that someone would stop them, that someone would see us and save Jimmy from what was about to be done to him. I could just vaguely make out the evil smirk on the ringleader's face as he got down in between Jimmy's legs. I couldn't hold on any longer, though, as the ringleader moved the branch closer to Jimmy, everything went black.

***

Pain, that was the only word for it. Everything hurt, my entire body was screaming out in pain. I had no idea where I was, but the thought of having to open my eyes was unappealing. It hurt to think, I couldn't imagine actually seeing.

I settled for lying there, trying to use my other senses to tell me where I was or what was going on. There was something soft underneath me, a bed it felt like.

Maybe me and Jimmy had made it back to his place, but why would I be in pain?

Why would my head feel like I had a hundred jackhammers going to town inside?

If I was hung over, this was the worst hangover of my life. I couldn't have gotten drunk last night, though, that wouldn't make sense. I was with Jimmy and he's not old enough to drink.

What the hell happened last night?

Okay, focus.

Last night...

What did we do last night?

I got ready to meet up with Jimmy. We were going to the movies and then something, it's that something that I needed to figure out. That something led to whatever this is.

If I could just get my head to stop pounding, I might actually be able to think, to remember. I needed to open my eyes, that would at least tell me whose bed I was in. Maybe Jimmy knew what happened.

Slowly, I forced my eyes to open, I had to know where I was and what happened. I couldn't keep lying here all day or all night. I realized I didn't even know what time it was. I had to blink a few times to get rid of the blurriness that greeted me. Only, when I could see, it didn't ease my confusion at all.

I was in an all white room and the distinct smell of disinfectant told me it was a hospital room. A quick scan told me I was alone, so my parents either hadn't been called or they had and were just not here.

The dim light that made its way through the window told me it was morning. It also told me I had a concussion, if the extreme shot of pain from looking at it was any indication. I'd never had a concussion before, but I had a couple of friends that did from playing sports. They all said the same thing, it was like having a hangover times a hundred. Even your eyeballs hurt and you couldn't always walk a straight line in the early days. I was not looking forward to that. The concussion would also explain the haziness over last night.

Did I crash my car?

Cautiously, I moved the blanket down and saw a hospital gown. I couldn't help but groan at seeing it. I moved slowly, but I could see that my arms were both covered in bruises and my hands were banged up and sore, like I had been in a fight.

Oh shit.

I had been in a fight.

It was as if a switch had been flipped in my mind. Suddenly, the images of last night came pouring back in. We'd been in the park and I couldn't help myself, I had to kiss him. All logic went out the window and the need to feel his skin against mine became all consuming. Those few moments of kissing, though, brought us both a world of pain.

Eight guys jumped us.

Jimmy, I had to get to Jimmy. I had to know if he was okay. What they did to him... *Oh fuck,* what they did to him. I have to see him. I need to talk to him.

Pushing through the pain, I forced my body to sit up. I couldn't suppress the groan that escaped from the pain shooting all across my ribs, stealing my breath. I had no idea if any were broken, but they sure as shit felt like they were.

None of it mattered, though.

I had to get to Jimmy.

I could see a small black duffle bag on the one chair, so someone had been by since last night and was kind enough to bring me a change of clothes. Whoever it was, I loved them immensely right now.

Bit by bit, I managed to stand up. I had to hold onto the bed as the entire room spun on me. Still, I managed to get to the chair and pull out some sweatpants, a long sleeved shirt, and some socks. My shoes were on the floor underneath the chair and I was not looking forward to trying to get them on. I would do it, though. Any pain I felt would be nothing compared to the pain Jimmy was in.

If anyone asked how long it took me to

get dressed, I would be embarrassed to answer. I would also deny the fact that getting my shirt on almost made me curl up into a ball and cry, but I was dressed.

Making sure I held onto the walls, I made my way out of the room and slowly made my way down the hallway. I had no idea where Jimmy was, but if I could find a nurses' desk or something, I could ask where he was and find his room.

After finding a nurses' desk and going through the annoying conversation about how I was supposed to be in bed, she finally told me what floor and room Jimmy was in. He was two floors up from me in the ICU wing, something that had my heart plummeting into my stomach. She couldn't tell me anything about his condition because I wasn't family, but I was hoping his parents would be up there. They were good people. They wouldn't leave his side like my parents apparently had. I would have to face that tidal wave of emotions later.

Right now, the only thing that mattered

was Jimmy.

After taking the elevator up and heading down the hallway, I was finally standing out front of Jimmy's room. Just like I thought, his parents were there, sitting beside his bed, ready for whenever he woke up or needed something.

My gaze only lingered on them for a moment, before they focused on the only person in that room that mattered to me. Seeing Jimmy did nothing to ease my fears. I had no idea what any of the machines did, but he wasn't intubated so he was breathing on his own. I wasn't certain, but the heart monitor looked okay, the beats looked good, but what the hell did I know? I barely passed biology. I knew nothing about any of this stuff.

The injuries on Jimmy that I could see only made me feel worse. His right eye was swollen shut and he was covered in bruises; I could see them even from where I was standing. He also had a black leg brace on his right leg from his thigh down to his knee. It must have been broken or sprained. Based on the bruises and the swollen eye, he must have had a concussion as well.

What worried me and confused me would be why he was up here and I wasn't. I knew that Jimmy would have an additional injury from the assault, but why would he need to be in the ICU? Something else had to be wrong, something that I wasn't seeing.

I should be going in there. I should be sitting next to his bed and holding his hand, but I couldn't bring myself to open the door.

This was my fault.

I should have prevented this.

I should have protected him.

I should never have lost control and kissed him. If I hadn't, then they wouldn't have known that we were gay and none of this would have happened.

I knew logically it wasn't my fault. That they were homophobes and I wasn't responsible for their actions, but I didn't feel that way right now. There was no logic running through my mind at the moment, only deep guilt that brought tears to my eyes.

It was that moment that his parents turned to look at the door. Maybe they sensed my presence. They were both getting to their feet and coming out. I was prepared for them to tell me to leave, to get the hell away from their son. It would destroy me to do it, but I would out of respect for them. I just needed to know how bad it was and to let them know how sorry I was.

"Zane. Sweetie, you should be in bed. You have a serious concussion," Jimmy's mother said in a soothing voice that only made the tears start to flow.

"I'm sorry. I'm so sorry. I tried to get them away from him. There were too many."

Jimmy's mother instantly pulled me into her arms as she spoke. "No. Oh, Sweetie, no. You did nothing wrong. This is not your fault. None of this is your fault. They were in the wrong. He's going to be okay. You both are going to be okay."

Hearing that Jimmy would recover from

his injuries made the dam break inside of me. I held on to his mother for dear life as the sobs shook my entire body. I felt a firm hand on my shoulder from his father, providing me with what comfort he could. I wasn't sure how long we all stood there as I let the pain out before I was pulling back. I quickly wiped away the tears from my cheeks as I cleared my throat so I could speak.

"How bad are his injuries?"

"He has a concussion, bruising all over his torso and arms, his eye is still swollen, but it was only just last night the attack happened. The doctor said it would go back to normal in a week or so. He needed to have surgery on his right thigh, there was blunt force trauma and damage done to the nerves. He needed to have a graft made in order to save the function of his leg. It was successful, but he will need to go through physical therapy to relearn how to walk with that leg. He'll be on crutches for a few months, at the least. He needed stitches from the assault, but the doctor assured us that he would make a full recovery and there won't be any permanent damage. With his concussion, there's a good chance he won't remember any of the attack, which will be a blessing. You, though, you have a concussion and two very bruised ribs and should be in bed resting still."

"I'm fine. I should have done more. I should have done something. I love him. I love him and I couldn't protect him from this." Tears welled up in my eyes all over again and I fought to hold them back from spilling over.

"What did you just say?"

The sound of my father's voice had me snapping my head to the right. The room spun for a moment at the sudden movement and I had to close my eyes for a second to prevent myself from falling over. When I opened them, I saw my father standing there with a very pissed off look on his face. With him, though, was my mother, looking indifferent as always, and Daryl.

The shocked look on Daryl's face told me that they had heard everything I just said.

He wasn't expecting me to say that I was in love with another man. The shock was justified. I had never confided in him that I was gay, not even after he admitted it to me. It was just further proof that my kid brother was braver than me.

"Father, what are you doing up here?" I needed to buy some time. I needed to figure out what I wanted. I really only had two options, deny my love and explain it away as something else. Or I could admit to being gay. I wasn't sure which road I was going to take yet.

"We went to your room and a nurse said you were up here looking to see the other boy. Now, what the hell game are you playing at here, Boy? You are not in love with that faggot. Tell me I did not just hear you say you were."

There was a sharp edge to my father's tone and for the first time in my life, I wondered if he would actually snap and attack me. He had always kept himself composed. Yes, there were times he teetered on the edge, but he never went over. Today, though, he might actually tumble off that edge.

This was the moment where my life could either change, or I would continue to be stuck in limbo, waiting out my prison sentence before finally having my freedom. The problem was, I don't know if I wanted to wait. I was standing here at a parole hearing and the judge was telling me to just admit it and I could go free right this very second.

Was staying in prison really worth my inheritance?

Was the money truly worth having to continue on lying and denying a huge part of who I am?

I couldn't help but look over at Daryl and see what his reaction to all of this was. His eyes told me everything I needed to know, they always did. He was completely expecting me to deny it, to lie and keep on pretending. Underneath that, though, there was hope. Hope that I would stand up to our father, not just for myself, but for the both of us.

It was at this moment that I knew I couldn't lie. I couldn't do that to myself, but more importantly, I couldn't do that to Daryl.

"I don't know what you heard, Father, so allow me to clarify. I am madly in love with Jimmy. I have been with him for months, now. Just like I have been with other guys since I was a teenager. I'm gay, whether you like it or not, and I am done denying who I am just to make you feel more comfortable."

Previously, I would have cringed at the very idea of ever telling my parents I was gay. I thought it would leave me feeling empty and nervous, ashamed even. But it didn't.

There was this joy that flooded my chest. There was no shame, no guilt, nothing but pure joy and the sweet breath of freedom. This feeling, it was worth it all. It was worth every bruise on my body. Every dollar that he would steal from me. It was all worth it just to finally be free from him.

"You are a disgrace to this family. You have brought disgrace to my name. If you want to be a fag, fine, but you are not welcome in my home. You are not welcome in this family. You're dead to us," Father said with a deadly calm that I knew did nothing to showcase how furious he truly was. If we were at home, things would have been broken, but he wasn't about to put on a show here in the public.

Him and my mother quickly turned and started to head off. I was expecting for Daryl to follow them, but instead he ran toward me and wrapped his arms around me. I held in the groan of pain; I didn't want him to feel bad for hurting me. He clearly needed the comfort and I was happy to give it. I wrapped my arms tightly around him as I whispered into his ear.

"It'll be okay. I'll be okay, I promise. You just stay quiet and out of his way for a little bit. Don't tell him. We can do that together when you're eighteen and free to make your own decisions. I'll figure something out for you, I promise, Squirt."

He just gave a nod against my chest before he spoke. "I love you, Z."

"I love you, too. Now go on, before he comes back looking for you."

I didn't want to send him away, especially with our father, but I couldn't do anything just yet. We had to wait until Daryl was legally an adult before we could get him away.

Daryl pulled back and quickly took off down the hallway to catch up.

Once they were gone, the adrenaline began to wear off and I was feeling it in my body as weakness set in hard and fast. I moved back and used the wall to help support my weight.

Jimmy's father placed a strong hold on my arm to help steady me.

"I'm okay. Sorry you had to experience that." This would have been the first time Jimmy's parents met mine and that didn't exactly go the traditional route.

"You don't have to apologize for them. They are the ones that are ass backward here. I'm very proud of you, though. What you did was very brave and you should be proud of yourself for finally standing up to them. For accepting who you are and knowing that there is nothing wrong with you," Jimmy's father said with a deep truth to his voice.

His words instantly soothed my fears and I could see, now, how Jimmy was so comfortable and confident with himself. He had two amazing parents that got him there.

"Thank you."

Though the simple words didn't seem like enough, it was all I had. I didn't know what else to say other than that. Maybe if I hadn't been concussed and flooded with all sorts of different emotions right now, I would be able to find the words. Thankfully, they both seemed to understand how deeply I meant them.

"Come on, you need to be in bed. I know you want to see him, but he just came out of surgery not even two hours ago. The doctor said he's going to be out for at least eight hours. He's stable, but he's sleeping right now. There isn't anything we can do for him right now but sit in very uncomfortable plastic chairs. Something your body does not need to experience, especially in your current state. Let's get you back into bed. I am sure now that you are awake deputies will be coming to speak with you about the attack. We can work everything else out tomorrow," Jimmy's mother said warmly, as she placed her hand on my arm and started to guide me back toward the elevator.

I didn't want to leave. I wanted to sit next to Jimmy, even if that was in an uncomfortable plastic hospital chair. I wanted to be able to see him and be there for when he opened his eyes. The problem was, Jimmy's mother was right. There wasn't anything I could do right now and my body was already screaming for sleep.

I was so tired and dizzy that if she wasn't holding my arm, I was sure I would be on the floor. I didn't even think about deputies or the sheriff coming down to speak with me. This whole situation could turn into a nightmare if the men were never caught or if anyone within the Sheriff's department were homophobes. With the likelihood of only myself being able to remember, it would fall onto my shoulders to testify and do whatever I needed to do to ensure Jimmy got justice.

And I would do it.

I couldn't help him right now, but I could by being ready to make my statement. I owed it to the man that I loved and I was not about to let him down. Not again.

CHAPTER NINE

Jimmy

WAKING UP IN the hospital for a second time was a lot smoother than the first.

When I first woke up, it was to discover my body in a world of pain and I had no idea why my natural instinct was to cry. Thankfully, my parents were both with me and they quickly soothed and calmed me down.

I was still in a lot of pain, but at least this time I knew why and where I was. It was a surreal experience to know that I was attacked, assaulted, but to have zero memories of it all.

It didn't feel real, like it was someone else's story and I was just playing a role. There should have been emotions attached to it. I should have felt violated and upset, and to a degree I did, but without the physical memories it was as if there was this disconnect within me. It left me feeling weird, like I was supposed to be a certain way. What I was, though, was grateful.

I didn't want those memories. I didn't want to wake up and remember everything with perfect clarity. I wanted to stay in my blissfully ignorant bubble and never leave and I didn't think people would blame me.

After all, who would want those memories by choice?

Forcing my eyes to finally open, I was surprised not to see my parents right next to my bed. I was very surprised and happy to see Zane's head next to me. He slept in a hospital chair and bent over onto the bed. It did not look comfortable at all. I didn't want to wake him just yet, though. I used this time to look him over for myself.

The last time I woke up, I wanted to see him, but when my mom had gone to get him he was asleep. She said he desperately needed the rest and she would go back and check on him later to see if he was awake. They had told me he was injured from the attack, had a concussion like me, but he also had two badly bruised ribs and was covered in bruises. Looking at him now, I could see all of the bruises that were all over his arms and his face. He should still be in bed.

The one thing my parents did tell me, Zane wasn't as lucky as me in the forgetting department. He remembered it all and it broke my heart for him. I was the lucky one, in my opinion. I was more physically injured, yes, but I would heal.

Zane would have to heal with all of the memories from that night. He would always remember it. He would have to do a different type of healing, one that didn't have a set number of days that you could count down from.

I reached over and ran my fingers through his hair. It only took a moment before Zane took a deep breath in and his eyes fluttered open. It only took him a moment before his mind clicked in and then he was sitting up as he spoke.

"Hey, you're awake. How are you feeling? Do you need me to get the nurse?"

His concern and worry for me was sweet, but I didn't want him to worry over me. My body would heal and, eventually, I would put all of this behind me. I wasn't looking forward to the recovery time or with having to learn how to walk again with my right leg. I was also worried about school. I couldn't lose this semester, everything was riding on me graduating. Zane had his own healing he needed to do, and he wouldn't be doing it if he was too busy being focused on me.

"I'm okay. I have pain meds, so that helps with the bulk of the pain. How are you? You should be in bed still, Baby."

Zane grabbed my hand with his while

his other moved over to run his fingers through my hair. "There isn't anywhere else I would rather be right now. I'll be fine. I just have to take it easy. I'm so sorry."

"Don't. I don't remember what happened, but I know without a doubt it is not your fault. The guys that attacked us are assholes. Have the police come by?"

I wouldn't really be able to give them much, but I knew they were hoping to speak with me in a few days. The doctor said if my memory came back, it would be within the next week. If I didn't get it back by then, I was never going to. I was torn between hoping it didn't and hoping it did. I didn't want it back. I wanted to save myself from that level of pain. At the same time, it wasn't fair that only Zane remembered. If the guys were arrested, it would rest solely on his shoulders to get us justice and that was a lot of weight for one person to carry. At least if I remembered, we could both carry that weight.

"Real early this morning. I already spoke to them and gave them my statement. They were going to look into it and see if they could find them. The doctor said you could leave in a week and then you'll start physical therapy a month from now. Your parents went to get something to eat and shower. They've been here for the past two days."

"Good, that's good. They need to take care of themselves. They get so worried about me that they forget to eat and sleep. I don't want them to get sick. What about your parents? Have they come by to see you?"

I wasn't really sure how it would work for Zane. He wasn't eighteen like I was, he was twenty-one, so it would make sense for his parents to not sit by his bedside all day and night long. Though, my parents still would no matter how old I was. Zane's parents, though, they were cut from a different cloth to mine. The hurt that spread throughout his eyes told me that something happened.

"What is it? What happened?" I asked gently. I knew you couldn't push with Zane or he would shut down, but we had made a lot of progress within the past five months. Zane was opening up to me easier now and I was hoping that would continue.

"They came by yesterday not long after I woke up. They found me up here talking with your parents and they overheard me saying that we were together. My Father was pissed and started to demand that I say it was a lie. I know I could have lied, but I just didn't want to anymore. I thought I could make it until I was twenty-five, but there is a difference in not admitting it and lying about it. I could go the next five years not admitting it, hiding it, but I couldn't lie about it. He was furious. He disowned me and kicked me out before they stormed off."

Unbelievable.

I could understand that some parents, especially fathers, may have an issue with their son being gay. I mean, I didn't understand it, but I could wrap my head around the concept. But to disown him after he had been attacked, after he could have been killed? It was disgusting. There was no excuse for it. Even if you don't agree with your son's sexuality, he's still your son.

How could they stand there in a hospital and see him injured and then kick him out?

"I'm so sorry. He had no right to do that to you. What happens now?"

"Daryl, he was able to pack up some of my stuff for me before my father got to my room. He's got it in his room right now, until I'm ready to grab it. Your parents have offered for me to stay with you guys until I can get an apartment. If you would be okay with that."

The uncertainty in his voice cut me deep. He shouldn't feel uncertain about our relationship and I could tell he was feeling a bit off with everything that had happened. It was natural, given the events in the past forty-eight hours.

"I would love for you to stay with us."

Zane being with us was exactly what he needed. To be able to just be himself and be around people who accepted him. I thought it would really help him start to accept and embrace this new path he was on. He didn't have to hide anymore, he could just be himself and proud of who he was.

"It's just temporary. I've already called the diner so I can get more hours next week. I'll work and save up so I can get my own place. Find a two bedroom so Daryl can stay with me once he's eighteen, if he wants. I'll be there, though, so I can help you with your PT and healing."

It was going to be nice having Zane around the house. Being able to sleep in his arms, getting to wake up next to him. It was going to be exactly what I needed to heal from this attack. Even if it was just temporary, I think it would be really good for us. Give us the chance to just be ourselves in and out of the house, allow our connection to grow. We could heal and recover together and hopefully come out of this stronger than ever.

"Come here. You're too sore to be sitting in that chair all day. I got plenty of room for two," I said with a warm smile as I wiggled over further.

"You sure? I don't want to hurt you."

"You won't. Come on, you need sleep and to rest your ribs."

Zane gave in very easily. I had a feeling he would. He made his way onto the bed with me and lay down with a bit of a groan. He was in a lot more pain than he was letting on with me. I was annoyed, but I couldn't hold it against him. He was used to having to always be the strong one. It was going to take him some time to get used to being vulnerable with me. We would get there, though.

Together, we would get through this and, no matter what, I would be there for Zane.

CHAPTER TEN

Zane

THIRTY DAYS HAD never felt so long and gone by so fast at the same time before. The past month had been filled with pain and drama. The pain part was on both me and Jimmy, though he was in a lot more of it then I was.

My concussion and ribs had improved quite a bit before Jimmy was even able to leave the hospital. Still, for the first week that we were at the house, I was pretty useless.

Jimmy was in a lot of pain, mostly from his leg. The doctor had given him some prescription pain pills, but he didn't like taking them. I couldn't blame him, I was the same way.

For Jimmy, they made his mind cloudy and he wasn't able to be as creative as he was used to being. It blocked him from being able to express himself properly on paper. He spent most of his time in bed resting with a sketchbook in his lap and charcoal over his hands. Watching him sketch had actually been some of the best moments within the past month for me. There was a deep peace that took a hold of his entire body when he was drawing. He was gorgeous and I couldn't wait until I could sit back and watch him paint.

Unfortunately, the drama within the past thirty days was all on me. Jimmy and his parents were really good about it all. They had opened their home up to me and even allowed me to sleep in the same bed as their son. They helped me when I was too dizzy or in pain to do much. They were remarkable human beings and proof that nurture really did outweigh nature.

Three weeks ago, before Jimmy was cleared to leave the hospital his father had driven me to my parents' house. I wasn't cleared to drive yet and I needed to get my things that Daryl had managed to save. I thought we were in the clear, but we were only there for two minutes when the sheriff's department had shown up. My father had called them and reported trespassers on his property.

Thankfully, Jimmy's father had been calm enough to explain that I had been kicked out and was just looking to gather my property. The deputy had been very kind and escorted me inside so I could collect whatever was left in my room. There wasn't really anything left that wasn't destroyed. My father's rage had clearly exploded within the room.

After gathering my bags and saying goodbye to Daryl, we were out of there. It was only a week later when the letter came for me in the mail from a lawyer. I still have no idea how my father discovered where I was staying, but he did. I was expecting the letter from the lawyer, but it still hurt to receive it. My inheritance had been revoked and was being allocated to Daryl. I was happy for him, but I also seriously doubted that he would ever see any of his inheritance, either. I couldn't imagine he would be able to hold off until he was twenty-five with them.

My boss had been really great, he was able to give me extra shifts in the week and he had me on the call list if someone had to cancel their shift. It wasn't amazing money, but I was making a bit more than minimum wage. It was enough that it allowed me to keep doing my online program and to save up.

I had offered to pay rent to Jimmy's parents, but they completely refused it. Told me to save it so I can get my own apartment for me and Daryl. I was looking at two bedrooms, but so far I hadn't found one. I was hoping soon one would pop up and I would be able to secure it. It was just a matter of time, now. I didn't have to hide my schooling anymore, so I was spending most of my free time completing my courses so I could start working toward a better job. I was still going to work on the resort, but it would be a bit of a larger process now. That was okay. I wasn't about to let my dream go, not for anyone.

I hadn't spoken to my parents in the past month, but Daryl and me had been texting each other and even calling. I'd made it a habit of texting him everyday so he knew that I was okay and that he wasn't alone. I didn't want him to feel like he had to face the hurricane that was our father without help. Things at the house were getting intense and I hated that Daryl had to be there on his own with all of this. He would be eighteen in less than a year and then he would be free to move out and live the life that he wanted. I was going to be ready for him.

"Do you think it's going to hurt a lot?"

Jimmy's voice snapped me back into the

present. We were currently heading back to the hospital so he could attend his first physical therapy session. His parents had to work today and they weren't too happy that they wouldn't be there for it. I was, however, able to take the day off so I could be there for Jimmy. There was no way in hell I was letting him go through this alone.

"I don't know, Babe. Everything I've read said it can be pretty painful the first few times as your nerves get used to working again. This is only your first session, so you might not be doing too much that would cause any pain. No matter what, though, we'll get through it together," I promised with a warm smile as we pulled into the parking lot.

It was natural for him to be worried. Hell, I was worried and I wasn't the one injured. I had done extensive research into physical therapy and it all depended on the type of injury you had. Learning to walk was a process. At first, you learned how to stand up without having to hold onto the bars, then you worked on taking steps, and eventually, walking without support.

Jimmy would be able to switch the crutches for a cane once he was able to hold his weight and walk. Recovery time varied from a couple of months to a year or more.

"I just want to be able to walk for graduation."

I knew that was very important to him. I couldn't blame him. He was so close to graduating high school, it was only natural that he wanted to be able to walk across that stage like everyone else. I was determined to help him achieve that goal.

"You will. You can do anything. This is going to be a breeze for you and that determination of yours," I offered flashing him a warm smile.

It had the reaction I was hoping for. Gone was the doubt and in its place was my Jimmy, confident and ready for a fight.

We got out and we made our way through the hospital to the physical therapy wing. I walked slow, allowing Jimmy to set the pace. He was still a bit awkward with the crutches, but he was getting a lot better at it. I was surprised to see that there were no other patients there, but it was also nice that we could just be ourselves and Jimmy could focus on what he needed to do without feeling like others were watching.

"You must be Jimmy. I'm Sarah and I'll be your physical therapist," Sarah greeted us both with a warm smile, her eyes crinkling at the corners.

"Hi, this is my friend Zane."

"I'm his boyfriend, actually," I instantly corrected.

I had never truly said it out loud to someone like this before and I had to admit, it felt amazing. Jimmy gave me a big, proud smile, and I could tell he was very happy to hear me say that I was his boyfriend. I was enjoying it, too, and I knew that I would be saying it many, many times.

"It's great that you can be here, the first session can be hard on the patient," Sarah said with understanding.

"How does it work?" Jimmy asked.

"Well, today we are going to get you up

on the bars and you are going to work on putting weight onto your leg. The first step to walking is standing. Much like when you were an infant, you had to learn how to stand up before your first step. All we are doing is strengthening your muscles and getting your nerves used to working again," Sarah easily explained.

"You ready, Babe?" I asked, knowing that Jimmy had to be the one to make the decision to get started. It was his body and he would be the one going through the pain.

"As I'll ever be," Jimmy said, shrugging and making it clear he was completely unsure about this. He was nervous again now that we were actually here, but he would be okay. I was going to make sure of that.

"So, we are going to be over here," Sarah said as she led us over to the parallel bars. "You are going to grab each bar and stand with your left leg holding your weight. Then you are going to slowly put some weight onto your right leg. Now, this is going to hurt, I'm not going to lie or sugarcoat it.

The first time you do it, it's going to hurt, but it will get better as your body gets used to the movement again. Before you know it, standing won't hurt. Then, when we move on to walking, the process will start all over again. I need two things from you."

"Don't cry?" Jimmy said, trying to joke to ease the mood.

Sarah gave us both a friendly smile. "You can cry all you want. Believe me you will not be the first. I've had patients that have cried, screamed, and even swore. You name it, they've done it. The two things I need from you are honesty and faith. I need you to be honest with me when the pain gets too bad so we can take a break. There is pain and pushing through it, and then there is pain that could cause damage and push your recovery back. As determined to get better as you are, you can't let that determination add months onto your recovery. And faith. Faith that the system that I am going to do with you is going to work. If you give me those two things, we can get you walking within four months, assuming you do your exercises at home and give your leg proper rest. We got a deal?"

"If you can get me walking that fast, I'll do whatever you want me to do," Jimmy easily agreed.

I was surprised that Jimmy's leg could be better within four months. That was a huge deal to both of us. It also gave Jimmy something to fight for. The possibility that he could be walking across the stage at graduation was all he needed to hear to put a fire inside of him.

"Perfect. Grab onto the bars and Zane, if you could stand behind him just in case his leg gives out that would be great," Sarah said as she took Jimmy's crutches.

We both moved into place and I put my hands on his hips, ready to hold him up should I have to. I gave him a quick kiss on the cheek before I spoke. "You got this, Babe."

We both turned our attention to Sarah as, together, we started to get Jimmy on the road to walking.

***

I helped to get Jimmy up the stairs to his bedroom. He was pretty sore still from his first session, but I knew from the research I did that his leg would be pretty sore after his physical therapy for a little while yet. The nerves had to get used to working again and that could send a pretty strong pain wave throughout his leg.

His parents were still at work, so we had the afternoon to ourselves.

Jimmy placed his crutches down by the door. He was able to hop around a bit so he wouldn't have to use the crutches all day long. The second I closed the door, he was on me, though. My back hit the door and Jimmy's lips were on mine. I easily kissed him back, but once I felt his hands going to my pants, I placed my hands on his arms gently and pulled him back, breaking the kiss.

"What the hell is wrong? Do you not want me anymore?" Jimmy asked, pissed off, but I could also hear the hurt tone to his voice.

"That's not it at all, Babe." I knew this conversation was going to happen eventually, but I was hoping it would have been a bit longer. I wasn't fully prepared for this discussion.

"Then what is it? In the past month you have barely even kissed me. So if you still want me, then what is it?"

I knew he had been feeling frustrated and annoyed with me. He wanted to be close, to be intimate with me, but I kept pulling back. It wasn't because of him, it was me probably over thinking things, but I couldn't help it. I didn't realize what it could be doing to him, though, what he could be taking it as.

"I don't want to hurt you," I softly admitted.

He didn't remember and I was happy about that, but he was still assaulted and the very last thing I wanted was to hurt him. Or god forbid, he did remember while we were in the middle of it. I couldn't hurt him like that.

"The doctor cleared me. He said I was completely healed from the assault. I'm not in pain or anything. Nothing you do to me will hurt me. What hurts me is being pushed away every time I try to touch you. When I try to be intimate with you. It makes me feel like you're not attracted to me after the attack. That you don't want me anymore. That hurts me."

"I do want you. And you will always be the most beautiful man I have ever seen. I always want you, it's why I've been pushing you away. Because if we get started, I won't be able to stop and I don't want to hurt you in any way."

Jimmy moved and he placed his hands on my hips as he spoke. "And I appreciate that, but I want you. I want to feel your hands on my body again. I want you to make me yours." Jimmy moved closer until our lips were just a breath away from the others. "Make me yours, Zane."

I couldn't deny him. Everything in my body wanted him, wanted to feel his skin underneath mine. I closed the distance between us and devoured his mouth. I would never get tired of kissing him. The sweet taste that flooded my mouth when our tongues danced only fueled the fire within me. I was making him mine again today, but this time we would do it differently. I pulled back when the need for air became too much and spoke.

"We'll take it slow this time. I plan on savoring every single second of it."

The arousal and excitement in his eyes told me exactly how badly he wanted this. Today we were taking back the last piece of us that had been taken from us and it was going to be magical.

CHAPTER ELEVEN

Jimmy

FINALLY, WE WERE finally going to have sex again. I knew it'd only been a month since the last time we had sex, but it felt like years to me. It was insane, because before Zane, I could go years without the need for sex. I could easily focus my attention on school or my art. Sex wasn't that high on my priority list.

Yet, with Zane, it felt like I couldn't breathe if he wasn't touching me. The need for his body was overwhelming and to have gone the past month without it, it hurt worse than any of my bruises. I didn't remember the attack. I had been told about it from the doctor, but I didn't have those memories. The doctor's words felt as if he was telling me a story about someone else, there wasn't this deep personal connection that I had.

Still, I knew Zane had that connection. He saw it. He didn't get to have the relief of not being conscious like I had. He didn't get the lucky break of not remembering that night like I do. Even though I had to heal physically from the assault, Zane had to heal emotionally and mentally from it.

I was trying to respect his pace, respect his need to go slow, but it had been hard. It was hard seeing him pull away from me. It was hard to feel him kiss me on the cheek and not my lips. It was hard to know that there was a possibility that Zane didn't want me like that anymore. That he saw me as this broken and damaged man, now. After a month of healing, of distance, I couldn't do it anymore. If we were never going to be able to move past what happened to me, then I needed to know. I couldn't keep giving my heart to him. If this was the end, then I needed to know.

It was a huge weight off my shoulders to hear that Zane still wanted me. That he was still attracted to me and was just afraid to hurt me. It was sweet, but I didn't want him to be sweet right now. I wanted to feel his hands on my body again. I wanted to feel him inside of me, claiming me as his own.

Zane moved his hand over to my cheek and to the back of my neck as he spoke, "Tell me if you need me to stop."

"Don't ever stop," I easily said back.

Zane gave me a small smirk before he pulled me to him, closing the gap between us. The second his lips touched mine, it was fire all over again. The way this man could kiss always stole my breath. It made my knees go weak and everything inside of me was screaming for more.

My hands were instantly going to his shirt as he went to mine. We pulled apart for a second so we could remove the pesky material blocking us from the other's skin.

The second our shirts were removed, tossed recklessly to the floor, our lips were back on the other as we began to explore the other's body. I was never going to get tired of the feel of his muscles underneath my fingertips.

Zane moved his hands down to my ass and he lifted me up. I instantly had my legs wrapped around his hips as he moved us over to the bed. He gently placed me down on it before he covered me with his body. With a firm grip on my ass we rubbed our cocks together, moaning at the pleasure the friction brought us.

It wasn't enough, though. I needed more.

I quickly moved my hands down to the front of his jeans, fumbling with the button and zipper in my haste. Zane clearly felt my urgency as he quickly pushed down my sweats. I kicked them off as Zane stood for a second to remove his jeans and boxers the rest of the way.

I sat up and instantly ran my tongue

along the tip of his hard dick. I was rewarded by a surprised hiss of pleasure from him. If there was one thing that I had truly missed within the past month, it was the feel of Zane's dick along my tongue, inside of me. He tasted so sweet and I could never get enough.

I ran my tongue along his long shaft before I worked his dick into my mouth, taking him all the way down to the base. The feel of Zane's hand in my hair caused me to moan, sending vibrations down his dick.

"Oh fuck, Babe," Zane moaned breathly.

It had only been a month since we had done anything, but I knew Zane was just as pent up as I was. When you go from nothing, to having sex almost every day, and then back to nothing, it was hard to get used to it. You had all of this energy and need just bottled up inside of you and I knew we were both going to explode soon. The first time was going to be fast, but we had the whole afternoon alone to enjoy the other's body. Zane proved my point when he pulled my head back after a moment.

"I'm too close. I want to be buried inside of you when I come."

I wanted that, too, but I also had this uncontrollable desire for something more, as well. I wanted to feel him pulsing inside of me, but I also wanted to feel it without a barrier up between us.

I had no idea how Zane felt about it, but it couldn't hurt to ask, right?

"I don't know if you've ever done it or want to, but I'm clean."

"I've never done it before, but I'm clean, too." I was relieved that Zane understood what I was talking about. "Are you sure?"

"I want to feel you, I want you to claim me as yours. But if you don't want to—"

"I want to more than anything," Zane said, cutting me off.

Zane's body was once again covering mine as we moved back further on the bed. He reached over and grabbed the lube from my bedside dresser before he started to kiss his way down my body.

I knew what was coming so I easily laid

back and allowed him to worship me. The second I felt the heat of his mouth around my dick, I let loose a deep, throaty moan. I simply couldn't help it and it slipped from my lips. In the past month, I hadn't even touched myself. I was wound up tight and Zane knew how to loosen every single knot within me. He worked my dick like a pro as he started to stretch my ass. He took it slow, making sure he didn't cause any pain. I knew there wouldn't be, but it warmed my heart to know that he was still being careful, even with his own need increasing.

"Baby," I whispered. I was right on the edge; he was keeping me there with his talented mouth and fingers. The need to come was so strong, but I couldn't fall off the cliff yet. I needed just a bit more friction, but he was purposely missing my sweet spot.

I whined when he pulled his mouth and his fingers back. The warm chuckle he gave me did nothing for my annoyance.

"I want to be buried inside of you when you come," Zane said as he kissed my neck, my shoulders, nibbled on my earlobe.

He moved my right leg carefully, spreading my legs so I would be wider for him. He then grabbed the lube and slicked himself up. I couldn't help the butterflies that filled my stomach, only they weren't from nerves, but excitement.

I had always wondered what it would feel like to have sex bareback, but I never actually thought I would do it. That I would find someone that I trusted to this level. It warmed my heart to know that Zane trusted me with this as well. It would be a first for the both of us and it was romantic that we could share it together.

Zane leaned down and gave me a slow and sensual kiss. I was so lost in the feeling of his lips against my own that I almost missed the feel of his tip breaching my hole. There was a slight sting, but that was always expected and I knew soon enough he was going to have my eyes rolling into the back of my head from the pleasure he could bring me.

We continued to battle each other with

our tongues as Zane pushed deeper and deeper inside of me. I didn't really think there would be much difference in the feel of it, but I was wrong. It felt amazing to be feeling Zane's actual skin inside of me. There was a warmth to it that a condom never brought.

I could tell that Zane was feeling it, too. Every time he moved forward he moaned into my mouth. When he was finally down to his base, he pulled back from the kiss, breathing heavy.

"Fuck, you feel so good, so warm." Zane groaned, his cock pulsing inside of me as he fought to get control of his need to move.

"You feel amazing, Baby. I'm okay. Move. Oh God, please move."

I wanted him to move more than anything in this world right now. It seemed like Zane was on the same page as me, because he was instantly slowly pulling out before he pushed back in. He kept his pace slow and smooth. It should have driven me insane, but surprisingly enough it didn't. We hadn't had sex like this before, slow and sensual, it brought a whole new level of pleasure to me. Zane reached over and grabbed a pillow before he lifted my hips and slid it under them. The new position of my hips caused Zane to hit my sweet spot dead on each time.

"Zane!" I called out as pleasure shot straight up my spine, my balls pulling up tight to my body.

"That's it, Babe, let it out. I want the world to know that you are mine," Zane said as he kissed all along my neck before he sucked on it, giving me a hickey.

After our attack, I thought Zane would try and hide that fact that he was gay and in a relationship with me. But the opposite happened. He was all too happy to hold my hand and introduce himself as my boyfriend. It was like this wall had been blown up and Zane was now free to just be himself, and he loved it.

I loved it, too.

I was a sucker for a hickey. To have a mark that told people I belonged to someone.

Zane continued to hit my sweet spot and each time it made me see stars. I was so close. I just needed a little more. I moved my hand down to start touching myself, but it was quickly snatched up by Zane's hand. He moved my hands above my head and he took them into his own, keeping them there.

"Zane, please, faster. I'm so close."

"Not this time. Just close your eyes and feel it. Let it build and then when you explode it's going to feel so fucking good." Zane's breath against my ear caused me to shiver and I slid my eyes closed, marveling at the pleasure just his words brought to me.

I had rarely come before without my cock being touched, but Zane seemed determined to make that happen and I was more than happy to lay here and be pleasured.

Zane's lips were back on mine, but his grip remained firm on my hands. I don't know what it was, perhaps a combination of everything, but my body was tingling from this position. I wasn't able to move my hands and touch him, but being held down, even just gently like this, sent an extra wave of pleasure throughout my body. It was something we would need to play around with later.

I could feel Zane getting closer. His dick was getting harder, swelling inside of me and I was right there with him. I was so close. That moment finally came when Zane hit my sweet spot once more with a hard thrust and I exploded.

"Zane!" I screamed out as my back arched and I felt my dick pulsing hard and long. I couldn't stop moaning as my cock throbbed and the cum continued to pulse out of me, covering my belly and chest with slippery white ropes. I had never come this hard or long before, it was like it was never going to stop. My whole body was trembling from the pure pleasure that this single orgasm had brought to me.

The tightening of my walls was enough to push Zane over the edge. He screamed my name as his hot cum shot inside of me. The heat from it and the sensation of feeling him pulse only caused me to come more. I had no idea it would feel like this. The heat alone was enough to drive me mad, but to feel it in combination with his dick throbbing within me, I was in heaven.

Condoms between us definitely needed to stop.

I could never go back to using them after this.

I opened my eyes and saw Zane staring back at me. The arousal was clear in his eyes, but so was something else. A deep passion, a connection that we now shared with the other. It was sacred and something that would always remain special between us.

He leaned forward and began a session of slow and sweet kisses. He removed his hands from mine, allowing me to run them through his hair as our bodies started to come down from the intense high we just felt.

When the need for air became too much for the both of us, Zane pulled back, but only slightly. He cupped my cheek with his hand before he said the words I had been longing to hear.

"I love you."

My heart actually fluttered.

I thought that was just something they wrote in books or in the movies, but it actually happened. Hearing those three simple words coming out of Zane was a dream come true. I knew I had fallen in love with him a few months ago, but I never wanted to say it. Too afraid that it would scare him off and I would be left alone and heartbroken. He was taking a huge risk by telling me, but it was going to be a risk that paid off very well.

"I love you, too," I said with as much love in my voice as I could muster.

The warmth and joy that filled his eyes told me everything I ever needed to know. His love was true and deep within him and to know that I loved him back was all he needed to hear.

I pulled Zane in for a kiss, one that quickly went from slow and sweet to hard and heated. I could feel Zane's dick getting hard once again inside of me and I knew that our afternoon was just starting.

***

Lying here in Zane's arms made everything feel perfect. Since the attack, things between us had been different. He was different. I couldn't hold it against him, though. After all, he was the one that remembered. I didn't have those memories, something I still felt blessed about. I didn't want those memories. I didn't need those memories to haunt me for the rest of my life.

What hurt me was knowing that Zane did have the memories. He remembered everything from that night and I hated that for him. I knew it would take time for him to recover from the mental scars the attack had left him with. I completely understood that, but that didn't mean it wasn't hard.

When he had been pulling away from me, afraid to touch me for the past month, something felt like it cut very deep inside of me. I wanted to be intimate with the man I loved. I wanted to be held and kissed by him and, damn it, I wanted to have sex with him. I wanted to know that he still wanted me that way. That he was here with me because he wanted me and not out of some obligation built on false guilt from what happened that night in the park. The attack aside, he'd acted like he was avoiding me, and that cut deep after all we'd meant to each other. It scared me.

So, to feel his hands on me again, to see that desire in his eyes, it completely obliterated my worst fears. Zane did in fact still want me, he still found me attractive. Our relationship was still intact and that eased all of my worries and fears. I felt the most immense relief once all that uncertainty had been laid to rest.

The sound of Zane's phone dinging made him pull away. I knew he had been texting with his little brother a lot in the past month and Zane was making a real habit of being there for him. Whenever Daryl texted, Zane always made sure he responded. He would call him to check in and see how school was going at least once a week, too.

I knew he was worried about him and I couldn't blame him. Zane had said his parents were different, that his father was strict and had very traditional beliefs. Part of me, though, foolishly believed that his parents would be okay with him being gay, as long as he was happy. It was a stupid idea considering how Danny's parents had reacted to him coming out. I mean, I'd seen it before so I should have known it could easily be the case with Zane's parents. Maybe it was me just being hopeful for Zane that things with his parents wouldn't be as bad. Boy, was I wrong.

Still, though, Zane admitted it in a hospital after getting attacked. He was injured and in pain.

How could any parent just walk away from their child when they were like that?

I knew it was bothering him, even if he didn't want to show it or say it. Him getting that letter from their family lawyer telling him he was no longer getting his inheritance, it cut him deep. It wasn't just about his dream of opening a resort, it was the act of his parents trying to erase him from their lives.

To begin with, that money was money he earned. Money that was left to him by previously deceased family members, it wasn't like his parents put the money into the account. It was from generations as it was passed down through the family. That was his rightful money and they had no right to try and take that from him.

I told him I felt he should fight it, that he shouldn't let his parents away with it, but he was so worried about what that could mean for Daryl. He didn't want to rock the boat and potentially put his brother in a worse position. I could understand that, respect it, but it was still hard seeing him struggle with this.

I reached over and opened the bedside table drawer and pulled out my sketchbook and pencils. After moving my pillows up, I sat back and started to sketch the man that I loved lying in my bed. He always looked so sexy after sex. The way his hair was slightly messy from my fingers, this peaceful look on his face, as if all of the pieces that make him up were perfectly in place. There was no outside stress, no pressure or expectations from his family or so-called friends. He was just Zane and he was breathtaking.

"How is Daryl?" I asked, after he placed his phone down. He didn't move, though, knowing that I was sketching him. I had told him in the early days of our relationship that I wanted to sketch him, that he was the perfect model. Today, after six months, I was finally getting my wish.

"I think he's lying to me," Zane said, clearly feeling completely troubled.

"About what?"

"About how bad it's getting."

"What makes you think that? I thought he'd been open and honest with you about what has been going on this past month."

I knew things were a bit rocky at the house for Daryl. It was natural that after his parents discovered that Zane was gay it would change the dynamic at the house. All of that disappointment and anger had to go somewhere and with Zane not there, it was logical for Daryl to be the target of those emotions. It wasn't fair, but with Zane not there, it would naturally progress down to Daryl.

"He was in the beginning. He was telling me everything that was going on. Now, though, his answers are getting shorter, he's taking longer to answer my texts, and he's avoiding my calls. It seems like he's trying to hide things from me," Zane said with a great deal of worry to his voice.

"Maybe he's been busy. He's seventeen and in high school. School is over in three months so he might have a lot of projects going on right now," I said, trying to find a more positive reason as to why Daryl's texts were getting shorter and further apart.

"After the attack, he said Father was constantly yelling and throwing things. Trying to figure out who to blame for my *disease*. Going on and on about faggots and how he was worried about Daryl catching it. He destroyed my room, everything that

Daryl wasn't able to pack up for me. He was ranting and raving about how he was going to have to cover it all up now, try to explain why me and Kayla weren't going to work. How me being a disgusting fag was going to destroy this big deal."

I could hear the hurt within his voice. He was trying to hide it, trying to put up a front that his own father's words didn't bother him, but they did. I hated that he felt like he needed to be strong right now. That he needed to always be strong.

He had been working a lot of hours at the diner to try and make enough money to get a two bedroom apartment for him and Daryl. Daryl couldn't move until he was eighteen, eight months from now, but Zane wanted to be ready for when he was able to legally move.

What I wasn't sure about was why he was so worried about Daryl. I knew he liked to draw and was creative, but Zane seemed very worried about how Daryl would be at the house. He didn't like that he was there alone, but I couldn't help but wonder if there was more to it.

"There isn't anything wrong with you. You don't have a *disease*. We were born this way. Just like he was born straight. You can't take his words personally, Baby. Is there something going on with Daryl? Something that you haven't told me?" I asked gently. I didn't want to make it sound like an accusation or that I thought there was something wrong with Daryl. That wasn't it at all. I didn't really know Daryl, I had yet to meet him. All I knew about him was what Zane had shared, which wasn't much really.

"I forgot I never told you. Daryl, he's gay," Zane stated.

Holy shit.

That explained a lot.

It explained everything that Zane was going through. Why he was so worried about him, why he was working all of these hours to save up enough for a two bedroom apartment. He didn't want Daryl to have to go through what he did. To feel like he had to hide a huge part of who he was. It wasn't an easy life for someone to go through and not one anyone would wish upon another, especially someone you love.

"I'm sorry. I'm not sorry that he's gay," I quickly clarified. "I'm sorry he's having to go through the explosion of negativity and nastiness that is your father. I hope he knows that whatever garbage your father says, it's not a reflection of him. Neither of you have a *disease*. There isn't anything wrong with you or him. Unfortunately, some people don't understand and their mind is too closed off to see what is right in front of them."

"I don't know how he feels about what is being said. He doesn't talk about it. He'll tell me about it, but he doesn't tell me what he's feeling. I'm worried he's bottling it all up, pushing it down. He used to paint, but now Father has gone through the entire house and taken everything away that he could use for a creative outlet. He said only fags draw and paint. He's pushing Daryl into more *manly* activities. Before this, Daryl seemed to be pretty comfortable with who he is. He seemed to be in a better place with his sexuality than I was at his age. But anything could change if you hear enough poison being yelled all day long." Zane sighed.

"It can be, but you also have to remember he has you. He sees you and your life and he knows that you aren't some horrible person. It sounds like he's more at peace with who he is than you were at that age. That's a really good sign. He just needs to make it eight more months and then he can leave and live with you."

"If I can get him through these next eight months," Zane said.

The first stage of doubt was starting to creep in and I could tell he was seriously starting to worry if he could get his brother through these next eight months.

"We will get him through this. Together," I said with as much strength to my voice that I could. Zane needed to know that I was in his corner and I was also in Daryl's corner. They didn't have to go through this alone. I would be there to support them in any way that I could.

Zane gave me a warm smile as he reached up and pulled me in for a kiss. Even after all this time, the feeling of his lips against mine still sent shivers down my spine. The connection I felt with Zane was the most intense connection I had ever had. I couldn't imagine what my life would be like without him in it. I didn't want to. He pulled back after a moment when the need for air became too much for the both of us.

"I love you."

Butterflies filled my stomach at hearing those sweet words again from his lips. I was never going to get tired of hearing them.

"I love you, too," I easily said back. "Now, stay still. I'm trying to create my best masterpiece yet."

Zane's rich laugh filled my chest with a deep warmth. It was good to hear him laugh. I hadn't heard it since before the attack. It was music to my ears.

"Should I remove the blanket?" Zane said with a playful wink.

"Hell no. The only one that gets to know

what your dick looks like is me. That massive friend of yours is only for my eyes and pleasure." And oh was there ever pleasure with this man.

"The only body my friend wants is your body. You never have to worry about that, Babe."

"I know. Have you had any luck with finding an apartment?"

The real estate world in town wasn't that great. It wasn't often people were moving, so it could be a bit of work finding an apartment, especially a two bedroom. Thankfully, my parents were amazing people and had no problem with Zane staying here.

"Not yet. I'm just working as much as I can and saving up so I will be ready when one comes available. I'm not real picky about where it is or what it looks like."

"What are you going to do about the resort? I know you don't have your inheritance anymore, but you shouldn't let that stop you from pursuing your dreams."

I didn't want Zane feeling like he needed

to settle, now. He had a dream. Something I believed could really work for the town. It was something he was passionate about. He shouldn't be giving that up. Yes, not having his inheritance was a roadblock but it was one he could get around. I truly believed that.

"I'm not giving up. I'm focusing on completing my business course right now. Then I'll get a business plan put together and start looking for investors. I'm not letting anyone stop me from building it. My Father doesn't get to win," Zane said with a deep determination to his voice.

It made me very proud and happy to hear that Zane was still going to pursue his dreams of opening a resort. I had no idea how it would all work, I wasn't a business person at all, but I was willing to help him with whatever he needed and I would always be a sounding board to him. No matter what was going to happen in the future, we would face it together.

EPILOGUE

Zane

I COULDN'T BELIEVE it had been eight months since I first kissed Jimmy. These past eight months had been a roller coaster ride, to say the least, but it was a roller coaster I never wanted to get off. If you had told me that working as a manager in a diner would lead me to finding my soul mate, I would have thought you were insane.

Yet, that is exactly what happened.

The best decision I had ever made in my life was applying for that job. It led me to Jimmy and I wouldn't trade him for anything in the world. Even though I had lost my parents, I had gained so much more. I had Jimmy and his amazing parents on my side.

His parents were truly wonderful human beings and I am a better person, a better man, for having them in my life. The loss of my parents was hard. Even though we didn't get along, we didn't see the world the same way, they were still my parents. I still wanted to have their approval, their love. Having to accept that it wasn't something that was going to happen was hard, maybe harder than it should have been. It wasn't like I didn't know it would happen, eventually. I guess I just had myself believing that in five years they might have felt differently.

I was coming to peace with it, having Jimmy and his family in my life had definitely helped me come to peace with it all. Now that I was out and proud, I was finding that, internally, I wasn't so torn up. I felt complete, like the weight that had been on my shoulders was finally removed. I had no idea that something like coming out would make me feel this good. Finally, I was able to be myself completely without having to hide pieces of myself or live a double life. I could focus on the future.

My future with Jimmy.

Today was a very big day for him. Today he was finally graduating high school and what made it sweeter, was that he would be able to walk across the stage without crutches or a cane.

The past two months had been hard on him with his physical therapy, but Jimmy never gave up. He pushed through all of the pain and did every single exercise that he was told to do. He worked his ass off just for this single moment. Just so he could walk across the stage for his diploma without needing any help. It was the one main driving force pushing Jimmy through all of the pain and endless hours exercising. He wanted to be able to graduate high school as he had always envisioned he would. He wanted to graduate and put the attack completely behind him and have his future clear in front of him. All of his hard work was paying off and I couldn't have been more proud of him.

"I'm so nervous for him," Jimmy's mother said beside me.

We were all sitting in the third row, the closest we could get as the first two rows were reserved for the graduating class. We had gotten here an hour early just so we could get a good seat in the front. Both of his parents had been balls of nervous and excited energy. We all had our phones ready and they were constantly checking the battery life on theirs, even though they had charged them all night and before we left the house.

I could understand why they were excited. It wasn't just the fact that their only child was graduating high school with honors, but he was going to be walking without his cane.

Jimmy had been able to complete his

last physical therapy session a week ago and he had been walking without his cane for the past three days. His leg was doing a lot better, but it was still healing so he had to be careful for the next few weeks to not aggravate his injury.

"He's going to do great," I said, flashing his mother an encouraging smile.

Jimmy had worked hard on not just his physical therapy, but with his schooling. He had been out of school with his leg injuries and physical therapy for a good six weeks before he could go back. He had been working from home on his schoolwork so he wouldn't get behind and potentially lose the semester, making him unable to graduate.

Not graduating was not an option for Jimmy. For any of us. He had a full ride scholarship waiting for him, there was no way in hell any of us were going to allow what those assholes did to him to cost him his future. He was going to school in the fall and he would be doing it without a limp or any lingering pain.

"How is your apartment?" Jimmy's father

asked.

I had stayed with them for two months, something I would always be grateful for, before a two bedroom finally became available. I jumped on it right away. Especially because it was in a good location. It wasn't far from work, so I could walk and save money on gas without having to drive. It also wasn't too far from Jimmy's house, which made it easier for us to see each other more.

Now, I was just working on saving up some money so I could afford to buy a bed for Daryl and some things for his bedroom so he would be all set to move in when he turned eighteen in six months. Having my own place for the first time in my life, though, felt amazing. I could just be myself and not have to worry about always having to be on guard. At Jimmy's, I could relax as well, but there is something different about living on your own. I have every intention of enjoying it while I can before Daryl moves in.

"It's great. I have everything set up and

now I'm just getting used to being on my own and making sure I actually have food that I'm cooking." I chuckled.

Cooking was an interesting experience for me. Most people at my age have cooked or have the knowledge and skills to make simple things. However, we had always had someone else cooking for us, even breakfast. My father refused to cook and my mother held zero interest in it, so a cook was what we grew up with. Now, I had to figure it all out for myself.

Thankfully, YouTube was a huge asset that I had right at my fingertips. There had been plenty of days where I'd cooked along with whoever was on my screen. I was getting somewhere and, it turns out I actually enjoyed cooking. It made the food taste better somehow to know I'd actually created it myself. And then there was that sense of accomplishment, too.

"Well, you just remember that if you ever need a cooking lesson, I am available. I love to cook and bake," Jimmy's mother said with that warm smile of hers.

"I would love to learn how to bake, but I think I'm going to stick with cooking for now. Maybe once I have more dishes under my belt, I'll start to figure out baking." I flashed her a grin.

The idea of baking did appeal to me, but I needed to make sure I didn't burn down my new apartment before I attempted to bake anything. Not burning the eggs was a new accomplishment recently. It was a slow growth, but I was getting there.

Music started to play and we all sat up in our seats as the ceremony started. I could see and feel the energy in the auditorium. Everyone was excited for the graduating class, including the class themselves. Most of them could barely sit still.

I easily remembered when I graduated high school. Most of the people in my graduating class were all excited to be getting the summer off to relax and travel before they went off to their colleges. I just remember feeling like I was stuck in quicksand, unable to move, otherwise I would sink to the bottom and die. I didn't get to go and travel for two months. I didn't get to apply for any colleges. My future had been dictated to me and there was nothing I could do about it.

This time, though, I could enjoy the energy and atmosphere within the auditorium. The excitement and anticipation of their whole lives laid out before them, it was something that I could relate to this time around. This time, I could share in their excitement. Because now, my whole life was mine to control and dictate. I was free and it was intoxicating.

"Jimmy Ashford," the presenter announced once they started giving out the diplomas.

We were instantly on our feet cheering and clapping. He looked amazing in his black cap and gown as he walked up the four steps and across the stage. You couldn't even tell that he had a leg injury. He walked strong and confident, with his head held up high. He was breathtaking and I couldn't wait until tonight when we could sneak away to my apartment.

Jimmy turned and gave us a brilliant smile and wave as he received his diploma, and then he had to make his way off stage and back to his seat. It took everything in me not to run over there and hug him, but I would have to wait until the ceremony was over. Then he would be mine.

I would need to remind myself that we were in public, so all I could do was hug and give him a simple kiss. Tonight, though, I would be showing him exactly how proud of him I am.

***

The backyard was packed back at Jimmy's house. He had his parents, his grandparents, and his friends here, including Danny and his older brother, Thad. I could see that Thad was exhausted. He clearly had been working a lot of hours and was feeling stressed.

I felt bad for him. They were going through a lot and there was no telling just how bad the fight could be with their parents. I hoped they got some sense knocked into them soon and left Danny and Thad alone.

I couldn't help but look down at my phone again for the hundredth time. I had invited Daryl to the barbeque, but so far he hadn't shown. He said he would, but that was a week ago and I hadn't heard from him since. Our conversations were getting shorter and with more time in between. Even when I texted him, he would send me a response, normally one word, a week later. Something was going on at home and I was worried about what it could be.

"Hey, Baby, you okay?" Jimmy asked, flashing me a big smile, but there was a hint of worry in his tone.

I put my phone away and forced my mind to focus on what was going on around me. I would simply have to keep reaching out to Daryl and make sure he knew that I was at least there for him for whenever he was ready.

"Yes, I'm good. Have I told you how sexy you are today?"

Jimmy currently wore dark blue skinny jeans that were one of three pairs of pants that didn't have paint on them. He'd paired them with his paint splattered converse shoes and a red t-shirt. He looked very sexy tonight.

"You may have mentioned it a few times. I have been told we can't sneak away until after the cake."

"Oh, you've been told? Did we get found out?" I asked, flashing him a grin.

"My mom figured it out. She even gave me a wink to go with it," Jimmy said with a small chuckle. His parents were amazing, they seriously were.

The smile on my face instantly disappeared when I saw my brother walking into the backyard. Him being here wasn't what took my smile away. It was the very clear black eye on his face.

My anger mounted and I could feel the heat infuse my face. Jimmy glanced over his shoulder to see what I was looking at and when he saw Daryl, his face paled.

"I'm just going to go over here," Jimmy

said, putting a reassuring hand on my shoulder and acknowledging that he knew I would need a minute alone with my brother. Just another reason why I loved that man.

Daryl made his way toward me and I could see he was feeling defensive already without me even saying anything. I had no idea what happened to him, though I had a few guesses. I was going to find out.

"I'm fine," Daryl instantly said before I could even open my mouth.

"Who did it?" I demanded with an edge to my voice. I swear to god, if our father laid a hand on him, I was going to kill him. Jail or no jail.

"Just some guy, it's not a big deal. I'm fine," Daryl said, but he couldn't make eye contact with me. He sucked at lying to me. He could lie to anyone, but he couldn't do it with me for some reason. He had been like that since he was a little boy.

"Bullshit. Did Father do that to you?"

"No, I'm fine, okay? You don't have to worry about me. I'll be eighteen in six months and then, legally, I'll be an adult and can do whatever I want."

He put up a brave front, for sure. I could see through it, though. He was worried, he was uncertain, and he was scared.

Six months might not sound all that long, but it was forever when you were in a place that wasn't safe. A place that could hurt you physically, but also emotionally and mentally.

I hated knowing I had to leave him there. If my parents weren't rich, it would have been easy to have Daryl just stay with me. They wouldn't have an image they needed to upkeep. But they did have an image, and my father would kill to protect it. Me trying to take Daryl from them, it would only make his home situation worse. That didn't mean I couldn't still be there for him, though. And I would, no matter what.

I reached into my pocket and pulled out my spare key that I was going to give Jimmy tonight. I handed it to Daryl as I spoke.

"This is your key to my apartment. If you need to get away, just say you are staying at a friend's place. I have a two bedroom and I'm working on getting a bed for you, but one of us can always crash on the couch. I want you safe, that's all that matters."

Daryl looked at the key for a moment before he finally took it and pocketed it. "Thanks, but I'm fine. Really, Z."

No, he wasn't, but he clearly needed the break from the drama and stress today. I would have to talk to him more about what was going on at home later, but giving him some peace now, that was something I could do for him.

"There's still some food, why don't you grab something to eat and relax," I suggested, giving him a warm smile.

The relief was evident on his face as he gave me a nod and headed off.

I watched as he made his way over to the food table. I was hoping he would mingle with some of Jimmy's friends and maybe make some that wouldn't care he was gay.

The second I was alone, Jimmy instantly came back over to me.

"He okay?" he asked, his voice laced with

a deep concern for my brother.

"He's lying about where it came from. I think our father did it, but he won't admit to it. Just keeps saying he's fine. I gave him the key that I actually made for you to my apartment," I said with a shy smile. That was technically his graduation gift.

"He needs it a lot more than I do, Baby. We can always make another one. They are easy to replace. But it gives him something irreplaceable, a safe place he knows he can go to if he needs it," Jimmy said with a deep understanding.

"I'll have to talk to him more about it, but I don't want to push him tonight. He looks like he could use the break from our family. He needs a few hours to just be a seventeen year old kid."

"He's not the only one that needs to relax and have some fun," Jimmy said as he put his arm through mine. "Come on, let's mingle and have some fun."

I couldn't deny him that. This was his day and I wanted to make sure he had a great time. He was so special and we both had our whole lives ahead of us. I had no idea what the future would hold for either of us. But what I did know, with the utmost certainty, was that my future would involve this amazing, kind, creative and brave young man.

Both of our futures looked bright, now, and I couldn't wait to see what life had in store for us.

Thank you for reading!

Turn the page for Runaway, From The Edge, Book Two.

RUNAWAY

BY EVIE RILEY

FROM THE EDGE SERIES

BOOK TWO

RUNAWAY

Can love be enough to convince a gay homeless man to embrace that dangerous thing called hope?

Daryl Hamilton is finally free and looking forward to his new life. Coming out of the closet is the best thing he's ever done. Nothing and no one will take that freedom away from him ever again, even if it means his father is out of his life forever.

He has his art, his brother, a safe place to live, and that's really all he needs to be happy. His goals are set and he's on his way to becoming the man he's always wanted to be. A new flame in his life is just the icing on the cake.

Devon St. James left home at seventeen and has lived on the streets ever since. He longs for the stability of a home and permanent job but doubts his crap luck will ever change. The catch twenty-two of his situation simply makes it seem impossible.

Suddenly, Devon is offered a chance at everything he desires. As usual, it's too good to last. It physically hurts to leave his new family behind but Daryl deserves a better man than him and he's determined to leave town before he hurts the only man he's ever loved.

Will Daryl's unconditional love be enough to convince Devon to stay?
Can he brave his fear and embrace the chance for a family?

CHAPTER ONE

Daryl

THE WARM SUN against my skin felt better than it ever had before. It sounds crazy, but feeling the sun against your skin after finally becoming free, there's just something exciting in it. Exhilarating, even.

Free.

It sounds like I was in prison or locked away in some dark and damp cellar by a serial killer. The truth is, I was just outside yesterday and every day before that. I've never been in prison. I've never been trapped in a small room and told what I could do, what I could eat. There was no serial killer causing me harm. I had every freedom that a normal human being has, and yet, I felt as if I *was* trapped. Not physically, but mentally and emotionally.

It had been almost a year since my older brother, Zane, came out to our parents. It wasn't planned. More of a heat of the moment type of deal when he was in the hospital after him and his boyfriend, Jimmy, were assaulted. They still hadn't found who had committed the brutal assault, and chances were they were never going to. They had both made peace with it, something I don't think I could have done. They were happy, though.

Zane had found a two bedroom apartment and Jimmy went off to University in Baltimore. He stays with Zane on weekends and on breaks. Currently, Jimmy was back for his four month summer vacation and, from what I have been told, they are inseparable when they aren't working.

I was proud of Zane. He was my big brother and I looked up to him a lot growing up. We have almost four years between us and when we were younger it was great. He was always teaching me something.

That four year difference, though, started to matter once he was thirteen and he didn't want to have his nine year old kid brother hanging around. We drifted apart for a while. A long while, really. It wasn't until he started working at the diner did we start to reconnect. I hadn't realized how much I had missed him until that day in our backyard.

When he came out, a flood of emotions hit me. I was slightly annoyed, because I had come out to him just months prior and he never said he was gay, too. That would have been the perfect opportunity for him to share something very personal with me.

Especially the fact that he was gay.

I was also very proud, though, because I knew what he gave up. I had made peace with the fact that I would lose my family, lose my inheritance. I was prepared for it and, to me, it wasn't worth more stress and having to deny who I was at my core.

Zane, though, he had plans. He had big plans for that money and he wasn't willing to go against our father if that meant he would lose his inheritance. When he threw it all away for love, I couldn't have been more proud of him. He made a huge sacrifice, one I knew I would be making soon enough. That sacrifice, though, became a lot less terrifying knowing I would have him in my corner.

The past ten months hadn't been easy. The exact opposite. My mother had always been indifferent with us, but now she was completely checked out. Most days, she didn't even say a word to me. It was like a zombie had taken over her body and she was just going through the motions. As for my father, well, he got worse.

Before the *incident*, as we'll call it, he was tolerable. He wasn't loving and he had never been the type of father that checked under your bed for monsters. There were no hugs, no I love yous. He was just there and you knew not to cross him. He cared about the image of his company above all else and we all knew that we had to live up to his expectations.

When you are young and innocent that is very easy to do. However, when you start to grow up and hit the teenage years, it's natural that you would want to rebel and come into your own.

We didn't do that.

The fear had already been instilled into us, even though he never raised a hand to us. My father had this unique ability to destroy you with just a few words and we knew by a single look just how much trouble we were potentially walking into.

I was twelve when I discovered that I had zero interest in girls. Changing for gym class was always hard for me. I had to make sure I kept my eyes down and didn't look at anyone for fear that my body would react. It turned out, I wasn't the only one who had that issue. Billy Swanson was fighting his own feelings of confusion and attraction.

I was thirteen when we had discovered that the other was gay as well. We had decided to create a pact with each other. A safe zone, if you will. We would get to explore our sexuality, but with each other. We shared our first kiss, first handjob, and even first blowjob, before Billy started to date a guy from another school and I was left without my safe zone.

That was, until I was sixteen and discovered Brad, my recent ex. He was deep in the closet like I was, so it seemed perfect. We had hit it off right away and within a week we were having sex.

I guess I'd always moved fast when it came to boyfriends. I don't really see the point in waiting for the right time or some special time to make a move. If I'm attracted to someone and they feel the same, then why wait? Life was short and I had zero interest in wasting any of my time on this Earth.

Brad and me didn't work out. He went and cheated on me. With a girl, no less. Since then, I'd kept to myself, trying to hide out from the hurricane that was my father. With the bomb that his oldest son, the one that was supposed to take over the company and bring it to a whole new level with marrying Kayla, was gay, he got worse.

I had no idea my father could yell so loudly and that much. He was constantly breaking things, throwing things, ranting and raving about how Zane had this *disease* and we couldn't let it infect me.

I knew I had to get out of there. I just needed to bide my time until I could graduate high school and be on my own.

Zane already had a place for me. He knew one day I would be living with him. All I needed to do was say the word.

I'd been working my ass off these past ten months to graduate early. I was now eighteen and, as of yesterday, a high school graduate. I had four months off before I would be heading for University in Baltimore.

The past ten months hadn't been easy.

Zane and me were texting and calling each other, but it'd been getting further and further apart. That wasn't on him. It was completely on me.

I'd been distancing myself from him to save him from the stress and drama of the house. He had enough on his plate, he didn't need to worry about me to go with it.

My father's words hurt, but I knew I couldn't take them personally. It was hard, because he was my father and I thought that he would love me regardless, but that just wasn't the case.

Zane had suspected it, but I'd never confirmed that our father had been hitting me. I'd stopped counting how many bruises he had put on my body.

There wasn't one thing over another that would trigger my father to lash out at me. Sometimes, I would wear something that he felt was gay clothing. Sometimes, it was just talking about a male friend. Sometimes, it was when I was painting.

Straight men aren't artistic in my father's eyes.

It was always when he could justify my appearance or actions as that of someone *infected.* Apparently, his cure was beating it out of me. It's why I worked my ass off to graduate early. The sooner I could get out of that house, the better.

Today was that day.

I was free.

I had no home, barely any money, and no job, but I did have my car and I had Zane. Most importantly, I had my freedom. Everything else could be worked out.

I walked into the diner where I knew my brother would currently be working. I wasn't sure if Jimmy was on shift or not, but I didn't see him in the dining room. There were a few customers, but they didn't pay me any attention.

I headed behind the counter, past the kitchen, and into the back office. I knew technically I wasn't supposed to be back here, but it wasn't the first time.

I easily found Zane in the office filling out paperwork. He looked up at the sound of the door closing and I could instantly see the surprise, and then the anger, that flashed across his face.

I expected both.

The bruising from my most recent beating and the resulting black eye was still visible. It wasn't as dark as it had been a few days ago, but it was still noticeable.

"For fuck's sake, I'm going to kill him," Zane said with a deadly edge to his voice.

"Don't bother, he's not worth it." It was the first time I had admitted that the bruises had come from our father. I didn't feel one way or the other about it. It just kind of became a small piece of my history and I was determined to not let it affect me. I wasn't going to let him have power over me. "I graduated yesterday."

"What? No, your graduation is in June," Zane said, furrowing his brows, clearly confused by what I was talking about.

"The ceremony is, but I took extra courses so I could graduate early. Officially, I'm a high school graduate as of yesterday. I packed my bag this morning, went down to have breakfast, where I told Father that I love sucking dick, and then I left. I heard the table flip over as I was shutting the door."

It was a risk telling my father that I was gay, but even if I had it to do over, it was one I would always take. I wanted him to know the reason why I was leaving. I wanted him to know that not one, but both of his sons were gay and there was nothing he could do about it. That I wasn't going to hide. I was going to make sure this whole town knew I was gay. He wasn't going to disown me and pretend that I was dead. He was going to have to deal with my face around town.

"Good for you. I'm so proud of you," Zane said, flashing me a big warm smile as he got up and pulled me in for a hug.

I easily hugged him back. I had missed how his hugs felt. He had a way of making me always feel loved and safe. After a moment, he pulled back and I spoke.

"I hope I still have that room at your place."

"It's our place and always. I have two rules, though, but they are simple and easy to follow."

"Okay," I said, slightly unsure. I wasn't really certain what type of rules Zane would have for me. Truth be told, I was hoping to live rule free.

"You go to University and get yourself a degree so you are not working in a dead end job for the rest of your life. And you need to get a part-time job to help cover your expenses. I can cover the rent, but you need to pitch in for food and to cover your car expenses."

"So, be an adult. That I can do," I said with a warm smile. I'd already planned to look for a job to help out with bills and cover my own needs. I wasn't expecting him to do that.

"Perfect. Jimmy is at his parents for dinner so he will be home late. I'll text him and let him know you'll be there. You have a key already and your room is all set up. Let me know if you need any help with University applications or figuring out a program to take."

"I've already been accepted to the University of Baltimore for the computer programming degree. I'm going to learn how to build video games. I even got a scholarship from my gaming app that I designed." I flashed him a brilliant smile, the first true smile I'd been able to let out in a very long time. I was proud of all I had accomplished, despite my father and his abuse.

I had a love of painting and drawing, but what people didn't realize was what I was doing with it. I would draw characters for video game ideas that I had floating around in my head. The work was peaceful and it allowed me to see what the characters were supposed to look like.

"I had no idea you designed a video game app. Why didn't you tell me?" Zane looked surprised, his eyebrows arched.

"I didn't think you would really care. We didn't really have the best relationship for a few years there. I just kept it to myself," I said, and shrugged.

I wasn't too sure how people would react to discovering that I was really into video games and developing them. Most teenage boys like playing video games, but to me it wasn't a hobby or a pastime. I was in love with them. I would always try to find glitches in their programming, constantly look for hidden programming in the game. They were my passion and I wanted to grow my skills and spend the rest of my life creating pieces of art.

"I know I was distant with you and I'm sorry for that. I want to know *you*, though. I want to know these things. I think it's amazing that you love playing video games and have found a way to take that love and passion and turn it into a career. That's really great, Squirt," Zane said with a warm and proud smile that reached his eyes.

I hated that nickname, but apparently it wasn't going to go away. Oh well, could be worse. Right now, I was simply happy that Zane appeared to be proud of me. That *someone* was, finally.

"I'll start looking for a job tomorrow and then I'll probably stay on campus during the week and be home on weekends."

"Yeah, that's what Jimmy does. It's not

much of a drive, but it is if you are doing it twice a day. He's looking to rent a room in someone's house next year. You guys might be able to find something together."

"Yeah, I wouldn't mind that. He doing okay?"

"He's doing great," Zane said proudly, and puffed out his chest. His love for the younger man shone in his eyes whenever he talked about him, and it was very clear Zane was proud of Jimmy, too.

Jimmy had gone through a lot from the attack, including physical therapy. He never got his memories back, but I think they were taking that as a blessing.

It had taken time, but Zane seemed to have recovered from it. They had gone through something horrific together and they came out stronger than ever in the end. I couldn't have been more proud of either of them.

"That's good. All right, I'll get out of your hair. I have to unpack and start looking for work. I'll see you tonight."

"Yes, you will. At home," Zane said, and

flashed me a wink and a grin.

I couldn't help the chuckle that slipped from my lips. It sounded so weird that I was going to be living with my brother, in our own apartment. I never expected for this to ever happen, but I was looking forward to spending more time with him.

We weren't kids anymore.

We could have a real relationship. Not only between brothers, but friends, too. I really looked forward to that.

Zane and Jimmy were the only family I had left, now. We were a small family, but that never mattered to me. We all had each other and Jimmy's parents, who are amazing people.

Together, we would grow our own family and there was nothing that could stop us.

***

I arrived at the apartment and a flood of emotions hit me the moment I walked through the door.

The first, was disappointment.

Frustration in myself because I hadn't

been here before.

Zane had been the one to put some distance between us growing up, but it was me that placed that wall there this time around. I had been focusing all of my energy on making it through each day, so much so that I couldn't allow myself to get close to Zane. I couldn't afford the disappointment if something were to go wrong. It was just easier to not come by whenever I was invited. Seeing the apartment for the first time shouldn't have been now and that was all on me.

I was also hit with excitement.

Anticipation of what was to come.

I had my whole future now free to do whatever I wanted with it. I was very happy about it.

The last emotion was a shockwave of anxiety that took over my body from my toes all the way up to my head. It was gone within moments, but the fact that it was there to begin with told me I hadn't exactly walked away from my father's abuse as cleanly as I thought I did.

The anxiety of him finding out where I lived, of trying to get me back, was something I would need to deal with. I had no idea if he would let me go as easily as he had Zane. I was his youngest, but also his last child that could take over the family empire.

He cared about his image and that meant if he couldn't leave his family empire to one of his sons, an empire that had been in the family for many generations, it would leave a black stain on his image. The only way to prevent that would be for him to leave it to one of his *gay* sons.

My father would never be able to leave it to a gay man, which meant he would have to try and convince one of us to go back into the closet. Considering Zane and Jimmy were not shy about kissing in public, the only one that could go back into the closet was me. I wasn't about to let that happen, but it meant I would be hearing from my father eventually and my gut was telling me it would likely be sooner rather than later.

Pushing that thought aside, I made my way through the apartment to check it all out. My room was a decent size and there was a bathroom separating mine and Zane's bedrooms. I had a feeling I was going to appreciate the added sound barrier between us.

I tossed my bag on the bed and sucked in a deep breath. I let it out slowly. This was the start of my future and I wasn't going to let anyone ruin it. Least of all, my father.

CHAPTER TWO

Devon

ST. MARKS SOUP Kitchen was one of my favorite places to be. It was not only a warm and inviting place, but the people who volunteer there were very nice. Some of the other soup kitchens and homeless shelters had some pretty judgmental volunteers.

Places like these had to take who they could get to help out, without being paid, so they got a lot of the high school kids looking to get their community service hours in so they could graduate. Or people who were court ordered to do community service. Not the most open-minded and friendly crowd. Which was something most didn't want to deal with if they were already homeless.

I wish I could say I was here to volunteer, but I fell into the latter category. I was homeless, had been since I was seventeen and had left home. That was three years ago, now, and unfortunately, my situation hadn't improved. It wasn't for lack of trying, but when every job application asked for your address, things got a bit tricky. I'd had the odd jobs here and there, things like mowing someone's grass for twenty bucks. Sometimes, if I was lucky, I could get a laborer job for a day or two, but nothing ever stuck. It was a catch twenty-two, because I needed a place to live in order to get a proper job, but I couldn't get a place to live without a proper job. This was why the homeless community never grew smaller. We couldn't get out because we were trapped in this vicious cycle.

I made my way up to the serving area

and was greeted by Roland. He was older than me. My best guess was by at least ten years. He had kind brown eyes, though, that had a way of putting you at ease, despite his rather muscular size. He was a detective for the decent size police force we had in town.

We weren't a huge town, but crime did happen and it needed to be investigated, occasionally. I had no idea what he did when he didn't have a case. In my mind, he spent his free time like some prisoner, just lifting weights all day long. The man was *huge*. I could appreciate a man that took the time to work out.

I may have been homeless, but I still enjoyed using what I had around me to stay in shape. Sometimes working out was the only thing I had to pass the time. Plus, it was free. It didn't cost anything to run through the forest or lift fallen branches. My older brother always said, keep the body strong to keep your mind sharp.

Fuck, I miss him.

"Hey, Devon, how are you doing today?"

Roland asked, his New York accent poking through.

"Same as always. You?" I asked, in my terrible fake New York accent. It drove him crazy when I did it.

I had no idea what brought this man from New York over to a relatively small town in Maryland. I had never asked, afraid it was too personal. He was a detective so I had to imagine it would have been better for his career to be in a big city where there were always a hundred cases sitting on your desk.

"I'm good. You know, with the amount of times you use that terrible accent, you would think you would get better at it," Roland teased.

"I guess I'll never be an actor," I said, and let out a dramatic sigh.

Roland let out a chuckle. "You're looking better. Last time I saw you, you looked like death warmed over."

I'd felt like death had taken a hold of my body last time I was here. I had caught a really bad cold after being caught in one of

Maryland's spring storms. I was soaked for a couple of days and that resulted in me getting very sick. For a bit, I was worried that I would have pneumonia. But I lucked out.

There wasn't always room at shelters. You had to get there early enough to secure a spot, and they kicked you out every morning at nine, whether you had a place to go or not. There had been plenty of times where I wasn't able to get a bed and slept rough. After three years, though, I was used to it.

"Just a bad cold. All better now."

"Anything I should know about? Any injuries I need to look over?" Roland asked, still not giving me the plate of food in his hand.

It wasn't the first time he'd had to look me over. Injuries happen when you live on the streets, but in my case especially. I was never one to look the other way like a lot of the other people do.

We had a crime rate, it wasn't astronomical, but it was there and people knew about it. The gangs were laughable, at best, but they still dealt drugs and committed violent crimes.

If someone was in trouble, I wasn't going to look the other way and pretend like I was blind and deaf. That wasn't who I was. It wasn't the type of man I was, the type of man I wanted to be. My brother would roll over in his grave if he ever saw me walk away from someone in trouble. I was not about to spit on his grave, on everything he sacrificed for me.

The end result, though, was a lot of scars from knife wounds and even a gunshot wound. Whenever I came in banged up or moving slowly, Roland always checked me over. We had an agreement between us, if I needed help I would go to him, no questions asked. If he said I needed a hospital, then we went. That was the deal and, to this day, we have both honored it.

"Nah, I'm good. With the amount of times you try and get my clothes off, people are going to think you have a thing for me," I said playfully.

I knew Roland was gay. He knew a bit about me and why I left home. We had gotten to talking one night when I had a concussion. He wouldn't let me leave for a good six hours to make sure my brain wasn't going to leak out of my ears.

It was about six months after getting to know him through St. Marks when I told him about my old man beating the hell out of me. Maybe it was the concussion that had me opening up to a virtual stranger, but that night had changed things slightly between us. We weren't really friends, but there was a shared understanding between us.

He had told me about being gay himself and how hard it was for him when he was younger. Which I had to imagine was pretty rough, considering he had ten years easily on me. Times had changed, but people wouldn't have been anywhere near as accepting of a gay man back when he was a teenager as some were now. He was a good man and had become one of my closest confidants.

"Well, as sexy as you are, you're not my type. I prefer someone smaller than you. Not to mention you're a tad hairy. I like my men clean shaven and smooth." He winked.

We were both pretty buff, and definitely had more scruff on our faces than type I went for would, and that made it perfectly clear that we would never work out. I had zero interest in a man with a hairy chest, either, and I knew Roland had that in spades.

"That is true. Looks like we have one more thing in common. We're both a sucker for a twink," I said with a smirk.

Roland laughed at that as he handed me the plate. "Be safe out there, and make sure you are checking in with me."

"Always."

We both knew that wasn't exactly true, but if something was seriously wrong I would go to him.

I took the plate and turned to face the semi large room. A quick scan had me heading over to a table closer to the back of the room where a new friend of mine was sitting.

Tyler.

We had met just a month or so ago and something had clicked instantly between us. Maybe we were kindred spirits.

Tyler and I had quite a bit in common. He had been homeless since he was eighteen, four years now. He worked odd jobs to try and earn some form of an income.

The main difference between us, though, he was straight. Even though he knew I was gay, he never cared. I think the fact that he didn't care, that he had no problem sleeping next to me, cemented our friendship.

"Hey, how are you, man?" I asked as I sat down.

Tyler gave a small shrug in response. Sometimes he got pretty quiet. I had a feeling it had to be with how he grew up. We'd never talked about it. He wasn't very chatty about his past. I had a feeling it was a rough one and I wasn't about to push or pry. I had my own rough past and I had no interest in having someone pry information out of me.

One of the larger men walked behind Tyler on his way up to the front, and Tyler instantly tensed up until the man walked by completely. Tyler had always been wary of larger men, something else I suspected was connected to his childhood.

"Have you found any work?" I asked, looking to hopefully distract Tyler and get him talking.

I wasn't sure what got him like this at times, but I knew if I asked simple questions it could get him to open up and talk. Once he was talking, he was very friendly and easy to get along with. Some days were just harder than others, which I completely understood.

"I did a painting job a week ago. You?"

"Not for a few weeks, now. I go out everyday hoping to get something. This is not how I thought my life would turn out."

And wasn't that the truth.

I know no one expects to become homeless, I sure as hell didn't. When I left at seventeen, I was only six months away from being eighteen, a legal adult. I figured it would be a short-term solution. Staying at home wasn't an option anymore. Not if I wanted to live, at least.

I figured I would bounce around on the street while still going to school. I just needed to graduate high school and then I could apply to be in the army. I wanted to be a Ranger just like my big brother, Jay. He had always been my hero. He was technically my half-brother but that changed nothing about how I felt about him.

I was only seven when he left at eighteen for the army. He made sure to call every night, though, so we could talk. He came home every chance he got leave and on holidays. There had been a few times when he came home injured, but he always said he was fine, for me to not worry about it.

He was the first person I told that I was gay when I was twelve. I was so scared of how he would react. I couldn't lose him. But, as always, he was amazing. He just told me to be careful and to always welcome love. That heartbreak would always be painful, but love was the best feeling in the world and it made the potential hurt worth the risk.

My whole world came crashing down when I was thirteen when there was a knock on the door. On the other side of it were two men in uniforms coming to deliver us a devastating blow. Jay had been killed in action while on tour.

I was devastated. I had lost my hero that day. My protector.

Things at home went downhill pretty fast after that. They were already rocky and Jay knew it.

When we were cleaning out his apartment, I found custody papers. He was going to sue our father for custody of me. Apparently, he was putting things in place so he would become an instructor and no longer in the field until I was older and could be left alone while he was on operations.

My father went from being hard to be around, to impossible. Before, he would yell, throw things, but he'd never laid a hand on me. He drank a lot, and the more he drank the more violent he got.

Jay was barely in the ground when he hit me for the first time. I got good at lying to the people at school about where the bruises came from. We lived in a rougher area of town, so it made sense that I was having problems with gangs. I dealt with it. I pushed through, knowing that one day I would be able to leave and never have to see him again.

The very day after I graduated high school, I went down to the army recruitment office and signed up. I passed the aptitude test with flying colors. I aced the physical and everything looked like I was going to be heading out to boot camp within weeks.

I was so excited.

But it all went up in smoke when they saw my full medical file, which included the fact that I had no spleen. That instantly disqualified me for the military. Without a spleen, I was at risk of bleeding out from a non-fatal wound.

I was born with a spleen, but one night when I was fourteen my father walked in on my current boyfriend and me making out.

He lost it.

Absolutely lost it.

My boyfriend, Stan, ran out of there faster than I could blink, and he didn't look back. I broke up with him after that, I didn't need a coward in my life.

My father, though, he was uncontrollable. He beat me so badly with his fists and anything else he could get his hands on. He caused so much damage that my spleen ruptured. I almost died and the only way the doctors could save my life was by removing it.

I have to take a pill every day, now, just so I don't bleed out. Thankfully, it was covered by government insurance when I was younger. Now, I have to get it from a free clinic, but I get a month's supply. It doesn't make you high so they have no problem giving me a month's worth at a time.

Even though I couldn't be in the military, I still figured I could get a job somewhere. I was so naive. I didn't even realize how difficult it would be to get a job without an address. The second someone discovered I was homeless there were judgments about why. They assumed I was mentally ill, or a junky. They never even bothered to ask me why.

It'd been three years, now, and I was still drowning. I needed to figure out how to swim, soon, or I would be just another statistic.

"I've been thinking about moving to a bigger city, but I'm not sure my car will be able to handle it," Tyler said.

I had been thinking the same thing. At least in a bigger city you had more opportunities to work under the table. There were more places that were willing to look the other way if it meant they could pay you a lower wage and didn't have to pay taxes for you. The trick was, I didn't have any money to afford a bus ticket. I thought about walking, but that idea really wasn't too appealing.

"I keep bouncing around with that idea, too. Larger homeless community, yes, but more opportunities for illegal workers. If I can get some money saved up, I might make the move."

"If I could just find stable work, then I wouldn't need to move. Rent in town would be cheaper here than in Baltimore. I just need to find something," Tyler said, sounding completely frustrated.

I couldn't blame him. He had been doing this a year longer than me and I was frustrated.

I noticed that Roland kept looking over at us, but his gaze was focused on Tyler and not me. I could tell that Roland wasn't checking him out, but he still kept looking his way.

"Hey, did something happen between you and Roland?" I asked.

"Who?" Tyler asked, slightly confused.

That wasn't surprising. Tyler didn't really have a habit of talking to strangers. He kept to himself and small talk wasn't one of his strong suits.

"The big guy behind the counter in the black t-shirt, leather jacket. His name is Roland. He's a detective. He keeps looking over here at you, I didn't know if he said something to you."

"Didn't know he was a cop. And no, nothing has happened."

"He's a good guy. If you're ever in trouble and I'm not around, you can go to him. He'll help. He's gay, too, so he knows how it feels to be different and judged. He won't hit on you or anything. You don't have to worry about that. I'm just saying, he knows what it feels like to be different."

There were plenty of cops that were judgmental assholes. They saw homeless people as some sort of scum and they had zero interest in helping them or treating them like a person. Roland wasn't like that at all. He saw you as a human being who just happened to be homeless. It wasn't the first thing he saw about people, and that difference is what made me start to trust him.

"Sure," Tyler said, and I could tell he was just placating me, but I was taking it for now. "It's supposed to storm real bad tonight, do you want to crash in my car?"

This wasn't the first time Tyler had offered me a place in his car. It wasn't very comfortable, he had a small car, but we always made it work. I had noticed that the only times he offered was when it was supposed to thunderstorm. I got the feeling he was scared of storms and having me around with him helped him to feel safe. I got the impression that feeling safe wasn't something Tyler was used to. I had Jay for a while, but it seemed like Tyler didn't have anyone growing up.

"Yeah, sure, that would be great. I don't think I'll get a spot in a shelter and I don't really fancy getting soaked and sick all over again," I said, flashing him a warm smile.

I might have been able to get into a shelter for the night, but there was never a guarantee. Even if I did have a bed, I would still have agreed to Tyler's request. If me sleeping in the seat next to him helped to get him through the night, I was more than happy to do that for him. We would get through the storm together and maybe one day, we both would be able to get off the streets and make a real life for ourselves.

CHAPTER THREE

Daryl

THE PAST WEEK had been amazing. It was the first time in my life that I felt completely at ease. I didn't have to wake up to yelling. I didn't have to wake up worried about what the day was going to bring. There was no floating anxiety throughout the day. I could just be myself and be carefree.

Living with Zane was awesome. We were getting to know each other as adults and becoming more than just brothers. We were becoming friends.

He had been teaching me how to cook. We weren't very good at it, but it was fun trying out different meals and recipes. Jimmy's mother had been a wealth of knowledge that we could rely on when we got stuck. Even something like cooking dinner was fun.

We were never even allowed in the kitchen half the time growing up. So to be able to make food that we liked, instead of having to eat all this fancy shit that didn't even taste good, it was freeing. I'm sure some people would find that outrageous and weird, but whatever. Until they had lived my life, they would never truly understand how simple things are downright wonderful to me.

Another change I had enjoyed was living only ten minutes away from a park with a basketball court. I loved playing basketball. It was really the only sport I did like.

Maybe because it wasn't one my father wanted me to learn. He was always going on and on about professional quality sports that every growing businessman needed to learn. Sports like golf and fencing. Somehow they had class and things like basketball didn't. Apparently, poor degenerate people played basketball, but golf was for the upper class, those with money who could afford to be in a country club.

I never saw it that way, but because my father did it meant I couldn't be on the basketball team. That didn't stop me from playing at school and whenever I could sneak away for a few hours.

I had been going by the court every day for the past week, just shooting some hoops with the local kids that were there. I had made a few friends in the area and it felt nice to meet new people again.

Over the past week, I had noticed that there was one man in the area who would just wander through the park. He never spoke to anyone. He never joined in any of the basketball games or soccer games going on. He kept to himself, but his eyes always seemed to be scanning the park. He would watch, leaning against a tree sometimes, before he would move on.

At first, I wasn't too sure about him. I mean, it was a man alone in a park just watching. It had a creepy factor to it. However, after getting a closer look one day, I noticed that his clothes looked old. He seemed to always be wearing roughly the same thing. Normally, a pair of old blue jeans and an older jacket. Sometimes the jacket was done up and sometimes I could see the old worn out t-shirt underneath. I knew he had more than one pair of jeans and one shirt because I had seen him wear old black jeans and a different t-shirt.

He always carried around a small black duffle bag that looked like it was about to fall apart. He had some scruff to his face, so he didn't shave every day, and some days he looked unkempt, like he hadn't showered in a few days. It was then that I figured out he wasn't watching people in a creepy way, but in an envious way. He wanted to be involved, he wanted to join in, but his obvious state of homeless was keeping him at arm's length.

It wasn't any of my business, but I couldn't help but wonder why he was homeless.

What happened to him that made him this way?

Was he on drugs?

Did he drink?

Did he lose his job and was just never able to recover?

I knew most people would automatically go with the thought of him being on drugs or a drunk, it was their natural assumption of a homeless person. I knew, though, that life was far more complicated than that. Sometimes what you see isn't always how it is.

Take my family for a perfect example.

If you saw a photo of us or saw us at one of my father's company parties, you would assume we had it all. That our lives were perfect and there was nothing that could ever stand in our way. When, in reality, that photo was fake as hell and the only time we were all smiling and together was when the photographer made us.

Everyone had a story and it was not always the story you'd expect to get out of them. Whoever he was, he had to have a story and for some reason I couldn't stop thinking about him.

I *really* couldn't stop thinking about him.

Even when I was home, I wondered where he was. On the nights when it rained, I wondered if he was somewhere warm and dry.

Was he safe?

I mean, I knew this wasn't New York City or anything, far from it, but I knew we had crimes. We had gangs that sold drugs and attacked people. Being homeless made you an easy target.

It might seem silly for me to be so worried about a complete stranger, but I had never been the type of person who walked away from someone that needed help. There was also just something about him. I don't know what, but something that made me not want to forget him.

After seven days of seeing him walking

the park, I decided it was time for me to finally open my mouth.

"Hey guys, do you know who that man is?" I asked the three guys I was playing basketball with.

"Who, Shadow?" Lucas asked with a slight nod toward the man.

"Is that his name?" I asked. That couldn't have been his real name, but I would take what I could get right now.

"Nah, we just call him that because he's always hanging around in the shadows. He never talks, never approaches anyone, just hangs around for a few hours and then leaves," Lucas said with a shrug.

"So, no one knows anything about him?" I pressed.

"We know he's been hanging around in the park for a good year, at least. Other than that, nah, man," Dave answered.

That made sense, I guess. They wouldn't have a reason to go up to him and ask him questions. I wasn't wired that way. I wanted to know and when I had a question, I didn't stop until I got the answer. Today, I was getting some answers. At least, I hoped I would. It would really all depend on if Shadow wanted to talk to me.

After playing ball for another hour, we all started to pay up and head out. Shadow was still over by the trees, so I made my way toward him. I was pleasantly surprised when he didn't immediately start walking away. I had literally no idea if he was friendly or if he had a mental illness that would make him skeptical toward me. The last thing I wanted to do was get into a fight with someone.

"Hey, I'm new to the area. I'm Daryl," I said, flashing him a warm smile as I held out my hand to him.

He looked at it for a moment, slightly uncertain, as if I would pull him in to attack him or something. After a moment, he reached out and shook my hand. I was surprised to find that he had a strong grip. I don't know why I was expecting he would have a weak and shy handshake.

The second his hand touched mine, though, I noticed two things.

The first, his hands were rough, indicating he must have worked the odd job as a laborer or something equally physically demanding.

The second, and the most shocking, was when I felt a jolt of electricity go down my spine and land right in my groin. My dick pulsed for a second at the feel of his skin against mine, which was ridiculous because all he did was shake my hand. A hand I was still holding onto and really needed to let go.

"Devon," he said, as I pulled my hand back and slid it into my pocket.

His voice was a rich, deep sound that slid smoothly across my nerve endings, and it was doing nothing to calm my arousal. I couldn't help but think this man could read me the phonebook and the just the stimulating tone of his voice would have me begging for more.

"It's nice to meet you. I've seen you around for the past week as I played basketball." I nodded in the direction of the court. "I didn't know if you wanted to grab a cup of coffee or something."

It sounded like I was asking him out, but I wasn't, and I really hoped he understood that. He was attractive, though. He had dark, chocolate brown hair, and his eyes were a light caramel brown with these gold flecks in them. They were breathtaking and something I would never tire of looking at.

I could see and feel the hesitation radiating off of his body. It was almost like no one had ever asked if he wanted to grab some coffee before. That brought up more questions. Him being homeless and not getting offers for coffee made sense. But he didn't look that old, surely he couldn't have been homeless that long, so how was it he had never been asked to grab a coffee? Even with friends, it didn't have to be a girlfriend, just someone that he could hang out with.

"I'm not a prostitute," he said after a moment, clearly figuring that was something I was after.

"Perfect, I'm not either. I would make a terrible prostitute. Not the gay part, I got that covered, but the moment they go to hand me money I would feel really awkward and probably tell them not to worry about it," I said, and flashed a grin.

I wasn't sure how he would feel about me saying I was gay, people could go either way with it. It warmed my heart, though, to see a friendly smile on his face.

"You would be a terrible prostitute," Devon easily agreed. "Coffee sounds good."

"Perfect, there's a shop just down the street."

We made our way out of the park and we walked in silence, a comfortable quiet, which was surprising considering we had just met. I wanted to ask more questions, I had a bunch, but I also wanted to give him some time to get his own thoughts and emotions in order. I had no idea what he had been through, but I had to imagine it had been hard on him.

Once we arrived at the coffee shop, we both ordered a coffee and I ordered us each a pastry. With our order in our hands, we made our way back outside to sit on the patio to enjoy some more of the warm sun.

"Thank you for this," Devon said once we sat down.

"It's no problem. Thanks for keeping me company," I said and flashed him a warm smile.

"You didn't have anyone else to go for coffee with?" Devon challenged with a light tone.

"Honestly, no. I just moved into the area a week ago to live with my older brother and his boyfriend, who comes by on weekends. He's in Baltimore for school. I don't really know anyone in the area except for the few guys I've met playing basketball. All of my old friends from high school, I left them in my rearview."

"Why give up friends?" Devon asked, and I could tell he genuinely wanted to know.

"A week ago, I was seventeen and just about to graduate high school. I had a bunch of friends who I had basically grown up with. They all came from wealthy families like mine. They had their future mapped out for them. They were stuck up, entitled rich kids who were homophobes.

So, I worked my ass off to graduate early and the day after I got my diploma, at the breakfast table, I told my homophobe parents that I was gay and moving out. I left everyone behind that would never love and accept who the real me is."

"Good for you. So many people compromise who they are just to make other people happy or to make them feel better about themselves. No one should ever have to be less than who they are just to make people more comfortable. It's better to have a handful of true friends than a hundred fake friends that you can't even be honest with. Not a lot of people understand that at your age," Devon said with a proud smile.

The fact that this complete stranger's words were making me feel all warm inside told me that there just might be more to our meeting then I thought.

A lot of people didn't believe in soulmates or fate. I don't know about soulmates, I go back and forth on the concept, but I do believe the universe has a plan for us all. That sometimes, the universe puts people in our path, people that we are supposed to meet and have in our lives for one reason or another. It would appear that Devon was one of those people that I was supposed to have in my life.

"Life is short, I have no interest in wasting any of the time. What about you? How old are you?" I wasn't sure what he was comfortable talking about so I figured it would be better to let him decide and set the pace.

"I'm twenty. No family and I have a couple of people I could call friends," Devon answered, and then paused for a moment to look at me before he continued. "You can ask, you know. I'm not going to be mad."

Ah, the elephant in the coffee shop. Well, if he was good with it, then I had no reason to make it awkward and uncomfortable.

"How long have you been homeless?" I asked gently.

"Three years, now. I left when I was seventeen. Needed to get away from my abusive father. It was either stay and potentially not see my eighteenth birthday, or leave and take my chances on the street." He shrugged.

I was shocked at how much alike we were in that sense. I wasn't worried that my father would kill me, but the abuse was all the same.

Devon's childhood sounded like it was a pretty hard one, for at least part of it. I couldn't imagine being homeless, much less at seventeen.

I was lucky that I had Zane in my life, someone I could lean on and could count on to be there for me when times got hard.

It sounded like Devon didn't have anyone in his corner. That made for a very lonely life. A very hard and lonely life. No one should have to live that way. Life shouldn't always be a struggle. I knew everyone struggled, life wasn't perfect, people weren't perfect, but it wasn't supposed to always be a fight to see the next morning.

"Not much of a choice to make. I'm sorry you were put into that position. I was lucky in that sense. I knew I had a place to live when I left home. My older brother, Zane, he would never turn me away. When our father kicked him out for being gay, he worked as many hours as he could at a diner just so he could have a two bedroom apartment. I told him I was gay before he came out, and when he finally did, he wanted to make sure I would have a safe place to go once I was legally an adult. I don't want to think about where I might be right now if I didn't have him. I would probably be living on the streets, too."

And that was the thing, if I didn't have Zane, I wouldn't have a place to live. I know that I wouldn't have been able to live in the closet forever. I wouldn't have made it to twenty-one like Zane did. There was a very real chance I would have ended up on the street just so I wouldn't have to hide who I was.

"You're lucky to have him and it sounds like he's lucky to have you. My father discovered that I was gay when I was fourteen. He walked in on me and another kid making out. Everything pretty much went downhill after that."

I would be lying if I said there wasn't a little version of me inside doing a very happy dance. He was gay.

Holy shit, he was gay.

Maybe the universe did have a plan for me, after all, and this was fate telling me this man very well could be the one who made me believe wholeheartedly in soulmates.

"I'm sorry. My father was nothing like yours, I'm sure, but in the past ten months there had been times where his punch landed on me. I couldn't imagine having to deal with it for years like you had to."

It had to have been terrifying for him to go through all on his own. At least, it sounded like he was all on his own.

"I'm sorry you had to go through what you did," Devon said, his eyes reflecting his understanding and the pain I'm sure his own life had cost him.

We spent the next hour just sitting there talking about little things. We kept the conversation lighter, though. I wanted to know more about him, but I didn't want it to feel like I was prying, either. We had just met and even though the conversation was easy, extremely easy, and the connection was there, we were strangers. Still, though, I didn't want the conversation to end. Mustering up some courage, I asked a question that I really hoped he answered in the affirmative.

"It's getting close to dinner time. I don't live that far from here. Do you, maybe, want to come back to my place? We can keep talking and have something to eat."

I did my best not to hold my breath as I waited for his answer. I had no idea if he would even want to keep going with our conversation or if he was looking for a polite way to leave. I really hoped it wasn't the latter option, and that he felt this connection between us as deeply as I did. I was pleasantly surprised when he didn't even take a minute to think about it.

"I would like that," Devon said, a warm smile perking the corners of his lips and reflecting in his eyes.

"Awesome," I said, with a ridiculously big smile bursting out on my face.

After tossing our garbage out, we made our way down the street toward my apartment.

"Are you sure your brother will be okay with me being there?" Devon asked, and I picked up the slight uncertainty to his voice.

"He's out with his boyfriend, Jimmy, at Jimmy's parents' place. They won't be there. But even if they were, neither of them would care," I easily said, knowing it to be true.

That was one of the best things about both Zane and Jimmy. They didn't make rash judgments on people. They were both always open-minded and understanding. Especially Jimmy. That man was a saint in another life. He also made my brother really happy and that was the only thing I cared about. I had no idea what was going to come from having Devon over for dinner, if anything, but I hoped it would at least be the start of a new friendship.

CHAPTER FOUR

Devon

WHAT THE HELL am I doing?

I don't ever grab coffee with someone I don't even know. Hell, I don't get coffee with people I *do* know, though that could be because everyone I know is homeless. When Daryl approached me, I should have turned away, I should have ignored the outstretched hand and kind eyes. Yet, no matter how much and how hard I told myself to do just that, my body reacted on its own.

The soft skin of his hand, god, I never wanted to let it go. He was a sexy man and he had no business talking to someone like me. He was eighteen and had a lot to offer the world and someone else. I was not worth his time.

Still, he wanted to have coffee with me. He wanted to talk and know who I was. Surprisingly, he was really easy to talk with. The way the conversation flowed between us was so fluid and natural, like we were old friends just catching up. It was crazy, almost as insane as me actually going to his apartment for dinner. It's like I stepped into the twilight zone, only I never wanted to leave.

I had long since given up hope that anything good would happen to me. I knew I could never expect for someone to stand by me and help me out. If I wanted to change my life, I would have to put in the work to make it happen. I *had* been putting the work in, in fact, but it was a lot harder than I ever expected it to be.

I can't even remember the last time I had a home cooked meal. The meals at the soup kitchens were often not even hot by the time I got my plate and the taste left something to be desired, but it was food and I couldn't afford to be picky.

Growing up, a home cooked meal was whatever I could put into the microwave, and that didn't always work. One frozen dinner should not have to be microwaved for twenty minutes. Even once it was hot enough to not be frozen, it still tasted terrible. I couldn't help but wonder if Daryl could cook or not. Even if he couldn't, I was willing to bet he could make burnt toast taste good.

This could be reckless and stupid on my part. Going to a complete stranger's house was not something I did, or something I ever thought I would do. I should have told him no. I should have passed on the coffee and just walked away. That would have been the smart and safe choice to make.

Yet, here I was, walking the short distance to his apartment that he shared with two other men that could be there. Despite him saying they were at Jimmy's parents, I had no way of knowing for certain that he wasn't lying about that. All logic dictated that I run, that I turn away right now and never look back. That would be perfectly solid logic. But here I was, still putting one foot in front of the other all the way to his apartment. I couldn't get my mind to tell my legs to turn and run. So even though it went against all reason, I followed him up the stairs, down the hallway, and into his apartment.

The apartment itself looked pretty close to what I expected for the area. It was an open concept with the exception of the island that divided the kitchen and the dining room. The walls were the stereotypical off-white color that every landlord seemed to be a fan of. There was an old wooden dining table with four chairs that were all wood, but different styles. As if they were picked up at various garage sales or second hand stores. There was an older coffee table and two end tables, a dark brown chair and sofa, and that was it for furniture. The walls, though, they caught my eye, because they all had different sized canvases on them. They were hand painted and beautiful. The artwork spoke for the room and that was clearly what made it a home.

"It's not much, but it's home," Daryl said hesitantly, mimicking my thoughts, and I could tell he was a bit self-conscious of the space. I had no idea why, especially because I lived on the streets. Anything was better than a cardboard box.

"It's great. I love the paintings," I said as I moved over to the closest one to look at it better.

"Yeah, they're great. Jimmy, he did most of them. He's going to University for art," he said proudly.

Jimmy had real talent. They were beautiful. "They're stunning. You said most of them, who did the others?"

"I did, actually," he said, his eyes downcast, cheeks pink, and a shy smile crossing his mouth.

He could paint.

I don't know why, I didn't know him well enough to know for sure, but that seemed to suit him. Looking around at all of the artwork, my gaze kept going back to the same one. It was in the living room and held some darker colors to it. It was a storm with just the slightest bit of sunlight poking through in the top right hand corner. It was my favorite out of all of them and I knew, without even having to ask, that Daryl painted it. I spoke as I moved over to it.

"This one is breathtaking. It's my favorite out of all of these pieces. You poured your heart into it."

"How did you know I painted it?" Daryl asked with the slightest bit of shock crossing his features, his eyes going wide, brows raised.

I turned to give him my full attention. Looking directly in his eyes, I spoke from the heart about the emotions running through me as a result of his painting. "I don't really know anything when it comes to art. I don't know about reading brush strokes to understand the painter's emotions at the time, or anything like that, but I do know darkness and pain. It's pretty clear in this piece that the painter was going through hard times, but was still trying to see the light through the clouds."

It spoke to the strength that he had inside of him. He had been going through a lot, that much was clear in his words at the cafe and in this painting, however, he still tried to see the light in the world and that was inspiring.

"I painted it a month before my graduation. My parents were gone for the weekend so I broke the rules and bought painting supplies. I used to paint all the time, but after Zane came out to my parents, my father made any art forbidden in the house. He thought it was something only gay men did."

"That's bullshit. You have a real talent, Daryl, never give it up for anything," I said with a deep strength to my voice as I turned to look at him. I could see he was warmed by my words. It seemed like he wasn't used to strangers complimenting his work. I had no idea why, though. He was talented, even I could see that. People should be telling him how amazing he was, how talented he was.

He headed for the kitchen as he changed the conversation. "Are you allergic to anything?"

I could tell he felt a bit self-conscious at my words, which only stirred some anger within me.

"No, I'm easy when it comes to food. What can I do to help?"

"You can sit down and keep me company," he said, flashing a warm smile.

"I can help you cook." I wasn't going to just sit there and let him do all of the work. That wasn't fair.

"You're my guest, I'm not making you cook. Seriously, sit down and relax. If you want to do something, you can talk to me. Tell me something about yourself."

I could see he wasn't going to back down on this, so I had no choice but to cave. I went and sat down on one of the stools at the island countertop.

"What would you like to know?" I was pretty much an open book. I didn't have anything to hide and I always tried to be honest with people. Didn't really see much point in lying when eventually the truth would come out.

"If you could do one job, what would it be?"

That was a loaded question. It was a simple question, something you would ask a person on a first date to get to know them. For me, though, it was not that simple. But I would answer it all the same.

"I wanted to be in the Rangers, like my older brother, Jay." That seemed to surprise him, though I wasn't sure which part.

He turned to look at me slightly as he spoke, "You have a brother?"

"I had one. He died overseas when I was thirteen." The pain from losing him was still raw and my chest hurt at just the mention of him. I forced myself to remember it wasn't a real pain and to stop myself from rubbing my chest. I wasn't really sure I would ever get over losing him. Especially like that.

"I'm so sorry, Dev. That had to be really hard. I couldn't even imagine," he said with a deep level of sympathy in his voice that told me he truly felt my pain.

"It was hard. Still is at times. He was my hero. I wanted to be just like him. So when I was twelve, I decided that I would become a Ranger and we would serve together. When I left home at seventeen, I had convinced myself that I could live on the streets until I turned eighteen and then I could enlist. I just had to make it until my eighteenth birthday. At the time, it seemed so easy to do."

Naïve.

So naive.

"What happened? I can't imagine they would turn you away if you didn't have an address. As long as you passed all of their tests, why would it matter where you were living?" he asked as he turned to work on the island counter, flattening the hamburger meat into patties.

Fuck, I love burgers.

"They were good with me being homeless, I didn't hide it from them. I passed all of their written tests with flying colors and the eye exam. I passed the physical test like it was nothing. The instructors were all impressed, said it was like I was born to be a soldier. But then the medical test came back and they discovered I had no spleen. My father had walked in on me and my secret boyfriend making out when I was fourteen. He beat me so bad, it ruptured my spleen and the only way to save my life was to remove it. I was automatically disqualified, and just like that, everything was gone."

A deeply pained look crossed his face, as if he could feel every ounce of hurt I felt at the loss of my career, my dream, my way of honoring my brother's memory. He didn't know me, I was a stranger to him, and yet, he felt empathy and concern for me. It was something I had never experienced before and I wasn't too sure how to handle it.

"I'm so sorry. The doctors never asked

you what happened? Your father got away with it?"

"He did. He lied and said I had been attacked by a gang, and at the time they believed it. They had no reason to think otherwise, I guess. It wasn't like I was a frequent flyer. There were no past suspicions of abuse. I just never went to a hospital and my father was smart enough to ensure he didn't break any bones."

"Asshole. You were never able to get back on your feet?"

"Not yet. It's hard to get a job when you don't have a set address. People assume because I'm homeless I must be a drunk or a junkie. I work out, still, use whatever I can that is lying around. That way, when I get picked up for manual labor jobs I can handle the work. I keep hoping that if I work hard enough at one of the sites they will hire me on full time, even under the table. No luck yet, though. I've been thinking about leaving town, going to a bigger one. Somewhere where there's more of a homeless population, but where they are also more open to paying someone under the table and not caring about a permanent address. I've been thinking of saving up and making the move. What about you? What's your dream?"

I was much more interested in him than talking about myself. My life was depressing enough as it was, I didn't need to drag him down with me.

"I got accepted to a University in Baltimore for video game design. I get to build my own video games. The dream would be to have my own video game company," he answered as he slid the burgers into the oven.

I couldn't stop the groan that escaped me. "God, I miss video games."

He spun around with shock and excitement plastered all over his face. "You're a gamer?"

"A very sad excuse for one. I love playing them, but I tend to be terrible at them. Unless they are the fighting or racing ones. I don't know if you'll remember this, but I used to go to the arcade that was down on

Main Street."

"Crazy Ricky's Arcade, right above the pizza shop, yeah, of course I remember it. I wasted so much money on those games," he said, with a big nostalgic smile crossing his features and a chuckle slipping from his lips.

God, that laugh sounded so good.

"I know, me too. My brother, Jay, he would always take me when he was on leave. He would only play Deer Hunt, though. He held the highest score for years."

"Wait, your brother was G.I Jay? Seriously? Do you have any idea how much money and time I wasted playing on that thing just to try and beat it? I literally spent one entire summer going down there and playing it for hours every single day. All of us did. We all thought Ricky put it there just so people would keep paying to play it," he said. His tone implied he was completely amazed by the information.

"Nope. Oh, man, it was all him. There's a reason he was a sniper. He could hit anything. He taught me how to shoot playing that damn game." I subconsciously rubbed my hand across my chest again as another pang of loss and pain shot through me. I pushed off the negative thought, intent on not letting the memories get to me and ruin what was already turning out to be a great evening. It'd been so long since I'd enjoyed myself like this, with conversation and food, and, hopefully, a new friend.

"That's unreal. I actually have that game. A few years ago, they made a Nintendo game system, a new version but with all of the old arcade games built into it. I even have the guns for it. We can play later, if you want."

"Hell, yeah," I instantly said, flashing him a big smile. I hadn't played a video game since I was fifteen when the arcade closed down, taking the last of my childhood with it. I would probably be terrible, but getting to play it again sounded like the best thing in the world. I was one lucky man tonight. I was getting a burger and to play a video game. This night might not be so bad, after all.

***

"Oh come on, how are you this good at this game?" Daryl said as he tossed his hands up in the air.

I couldn't stop laughing. For the past couple of hours, we had been playing Deer Hunt and he was terrible at it. I wasn't my brother, but I was no where near as bad as Daryl was.

"How are you this terrible at it when you own it? No wonder you could never beat Jay's score," I teased.

"I don't play it much. Why do they have to make the deer look so cute and harmless? I feel like I'm shooting Bambi."

That only made me laugh more. He was too cute for words, he really was.

"Laugh it up. I'm gonna shoot you, see how you like it." Daryl pushed me playfully on my shoulder as he spoke.

I could hear the fake clicking of the gun and I easily grabbed at it and pulled. The movement caused us both to laugh as we pretended to fight with the gun. He tossed his weight my way and it was enough for me to end up falling over and lying down on the couch with him on top of me. Suddenly, the toy gun became irrelevant with the feel of Daryl's body pressed against my own.

My desire to have him only increased and he must have felt it, too. I should have been the one to pull back, but when he closed the small gap between us, I was completely powerless. The second his lips touched mine, all sense of logic left my body.

The smoothness of his lips, the taste of him, his scent, the whole thing was intoxicating.

I wrapped my hand around the back of his neck and pulled him closer to me. I opened my legs ever so slightly, just enough for him to slip his between them, causing our rigid dicks to rub against each other. The second his rock hard erection touched mine, the only thing between us the barrier of clothing, a delicious moan escaped his lips, shattering my resolve completely.

His tongue flitted against my lips, seeking permission, and I easily gave it to him. He tasted like sweet honey and I wanted more. I could feel him, stiff against me, his throbbing heat making its way through the cloth covering him, and I knew I was just as hard, my own pulsing cock straining against my jeans to be set free.

Things between us were quickly becoming heated, our hips pressed together firmly, both of us bucking and grinding against one another, and I knew if one of us didn't stop now, we would be having sex right here on his couch. As tempting as that was, I was also fully aware of the fact that I hadn't showered in a few days. This couldn't go any further, not with me like this. After a moment, I broke the kiss, panting, and pulled back.

"Mind if I borrow your shower real quick?" I looked into his glittering, lust-filled eyes and could see his mind trying to function as he tried to catch up, change course from the scorching path we'd just been on, and he did after a brief moment.

"Yeah, second door down the hallway, right hand side."

I wanted to kiss him again, but I knew if I did, I wouldn't be able to stop. I gave a nod and started to roll, forcing him to move as well and back off of me.

I grabbed my bag and headed down the hallway and into the bathroom. After locking the door, I quickly removed my shirt and I couldn't help but look in the mirror. At one point, my skin had been unmarked, smooth and clean. Today, though, the man looking back at me was a man that had been through war. Only, it wasn't actual war. Maybe if it was, the scars that littered my body would have caused a different reaction within me. They would have represented a warrior, someone who fought bravely for this country.

Instead, mine were from abuse and years on the street. It didn't matter, in my mind, that I had gotten most of them from protecting people. I had put myself in this position when I made the decision to leave home. Had I stayed, I would have been able to get a job and I could be in my own apartment right now. It was irrational and the logical part of my brain was screaming at me that it wouldn't have mattered. I would be dead if I'd stayed. It didn't make it any easier to see the scars, though. I felt disgusted as I looked at them.

This was a mistake.

Someone like Daryl would never want someone like me. The second he saw my multitude of scars, my unflattering body, he would be horrified and disgusted, too. I shouldn't have kissed him. This was all a mistake. I knew better than this. I needed to shower and then head out. The shelters would be getting fuller by the minute and if I left it any longer I would be back on the street tonight. It was time for me to get back to reality and stop living in this fantasy world that I had been in today. We lived two different lives, in entirely different worlds, and they would never mesh together. It was time to get back to the real world.

But first, I was ready to get started with

a hot shower. At least I could do that before I had to face the life I'd made for myself again. It was something.

CHAPTER FIVE

Daryl

OH MY GOD, I can't believe that just happened. I kissed him. I actually kissed him. Not only that, he kissed me back.

I knew Devon said he was gay, I had no reason to doubt him, but I just never thought he would go for a nerdy artistic guy like me. I could tell through his shirt that he worked out. I was surprised, at first, but him doing what he could outside to stay in shape for labor jobs made perfect sense to me. If employers were looking for cheap labor, they were going to go with the guy that had some muscles to him over the skinny dude.

Still, though, to feel the ripples underneath my hands, to feel his very sizeable dick rubbing against mine, it felt like a dream come true.

This hadn't been my intention when I first approached him. Not even when I invited him over for dinner. He was interesting and so easy to talk to. I didn't want the conversation to end, so it made complete sense to bring him back here to chat. I was glad I did, even before the make out session started.

He seemed like a genuinely good man who'd had a hard life. I was crushed when he spoke about losing his older brother and then losing his dream to honor him by joining the Rangers. I couldn't even imagine losing an organ because my own father had beaten me that severely. Had hated me to that level. It was soul crushing. Yet, Devon still found the strength to keep going, to carry on, and still fight for his dream. He was inspiring.

It bothered me when he spoke about leaving town. I didn't want that to happen. He had no obligation or loyalty to me, but it felt like he was leaving me behind, which was insane because we had only just met today. I shouldn't feel this close to him, this strongly connected, and yet, I did. I hoped he was feeling it, too, that it wasn't just all in my head or one-sided, because that would really suck.

The sound of the locks being turned instantly had my heart plummeting to my stomach and my hard on going soft. Great, Zane and Jimmy were back already. There went the potentially amazing sex with the gorgeous man in my shower.

"Hey, you guys are back earlier than I thought you would be," I said, but in all honesty I didn't really have an idea as to what time it actually was. A quick glance at the clock told me it was almost eight.

Shit, time flies.

"It was just dinner. Did you eat?" Zane

asked.

"Yeah, I made a couple of burgers. Um… Listen, I have to tell you guys something." I wasn't too sure how they would react to this. I was positive that Jimmy would react better than Zane.

Jimmy was the easy going one in their relationship. Don't get me wrong, I love my brother, but he needed to relax every now and then. I knew it was hard on him, though, he worked a lot of hours to pay the majority of the rent plus his car. On top of that, he was also working on a business plan for his resort and having to meet with investors. There was a lot on his plate.

"Is everything all right? Did dad contact you?" The worry was evident in Zane's voice and I hated that I had put it there. I didn't mean to.

"No, this isn't about Dad," I quickly reassured my brother. "I brought someone over. He's a really nice guy. His name is Devon."

"Oh, do you have a boyfriend?" Jimmy asked with a big teasing smile as he flopped down on the reclining chair.

"He's not my boyfriend, no. I just met him today. Officially, anyway. I'd seen him around the park for the past week and today I finally introduced myself to him."

"So you brought a stranger over?" Zane asked, his eyebrow arched and his tone telling me he was not too impressed with me right now.

I could understand why he might not be too happy. I'd had every intention of making sure Devon was gone before they got home, but we were having so much fun, I completely lost track of time. Now, I was going to have to explain this away very quickly and pray that Devon came out of the bathroom with clothes on.

"You can't exactly expect him to never bring someone over. It's his home, too, baby," Jimmy said lovingly, making it clear he was in my corner, for which I felt extremely grateful right at that moment.

"We went for coffee and we had such a good time talking that I invited him over for dinner. We were playing video games and we just lost track of time. He's taking a quick shower right now."

"Why would he be in the shower if you were just playing video games?" Zane asked, confusion showing on his face. He sounded skeptical and I knew I had to be honest and get it out there before things turned odd. The last thing I needed was Zane thinking anything dishonest or underhanded had been happening.

"Because he's homeless right now," I answered slightly awkwardly.

"You brought home a stray?" Zane instantly snapped.

"Zane Hamilton! You change your attitude right now," Jimmy said with a deadly edge to his voice.

I had never heard Jimmy get angry before, and based on the look on Zane's face, he knew he'd screwed up. I didn't take it personally. I knew Zane wasn't the judgmental type. I knew he was tired and stressed. I wasn't going to hold this against him.

"I'm sorry, I'm just... It's been a long

couple of weeks," Zane admitted, his voice softening.

From what I had gathered, he was having a hard time at the diner. They were not only down a dishwasher but also a cook. Zane had been working extra shifts and double shifts just to cover everything.

Finding people willing to work in a diner was easy in a larger city, but in a small town like this, it was hard to find anyone that wasn't already working. Part-time was fine for servers, but the cook was the day cook so they couldn't be in school. He had tried to get the night cook to move to days, but he could only work at night because his wife worked during the day and they had a toddler at home. The end result, my brother was ready to explode at any moment.

"I'm sorry for dropping this on you. That wasn't my intention. I didn't expect to bring him back here, but he's a good man and we were having the best conversation, so I invited him. He's twenty and has only been homeless for three years. He's worked the odd job, but he can't get anything to stick because he doesn't have an address. He left home when he was seventeen because the physical abuse by his dad was so extreme he didn't think he would make it until he was eighteen. His dad beat him so badly when he was fourteen because he found him making out with his boyfriend, he had to get his spleen removed." I knew I had rushed out all that information in a single breath, and I hoped Devon didn't get annoyed with me telling my brother about his past, but I just felt it was important for Zane to know a bit about the stranger before he met him. He needed to know.

It was hard for me to even talk about it, truth be told. The brutality of it, the fact that his father had done something like that to him and hid it from everyone, it was heartbreaking. No child should ever have to go through that, especially by his own father's hand.

I could see the information instantly affected both Zane and Jimmy. Their attack not long after they got together was still a fresh wound with them. Especially Zane.

Jimmy still doesn't remember what happened to this day, but I knew it still haunted Zane. They had never found their attackers, something I suspected would leave the mental wound open until they got justice.

"Where does he stay at night?" Zane said, after a moment.

"On the street or in a shelter, if he can get in," I answered as the bathroom door opened.

My heart went into my throat and didn't go back down until I saw Devon fully dressed. He was clearly shocked to discover that we were no longer alone.

"This is my brother, Zane, and his boyfriend, Jimmy," I supplied at the slight confusion on his face.

"Devon. It's nice to meet you both," he said with a nod, before he turned to look my way. "I really appreciate today, but I have to get going if I don't want to lose a bed."

Before I could even speak up, Zane surprised me by speaking first.

"Why don't you just spend the night

here. It's getting pretty late for the shelters. I know they tend to get all booked up not long past seven. I know it's not a cot, but the couch is pretty comfy to sleep on."

Instant shock went across his face and I wasn't sure if it was because I had told them he was homeless or that Zane had offered him a place to sleep tonight. I suspected it was more of a sixty-forty split in favor of the offer. Not that I could blame him. I was shocked, too.

"That's very kind of you to offer," Devon started, but Zane cut him off.

"No thanks necessary. Besides, I kinda have an ulterior motive. If you crash here tonight, that gives me more time to try and convince you to work at the diner as a dishwasher."

"What?" Devon asked, completely shocked.

"Yeah, well, the job sucks. I'm not just saying that, either. I've been told by the last five dishwashers that I've hired within the past three months. One even told me he would rather pick up roadkill instead. It's not just washing the dishes by hand, because we can't afford a fancy machine, nor would we have anywhere to put it. But the dishwasher also has to help unload the delivery truck every week so you have to be able to lift fifty-pound bags over and over again. If you crash here tonight, that gives me some time to try and convince you why it would be a fun job to have," Zane said with a grin.

He wasn't lying, I knew that. The job as a dishwasher at the diner was brutal on your body. It was easy work in the sense that you didn't have to think too much while doing it, but it was long hours and heavy lifting. The way Zane was going about it, though, allowed Devon to not see it as a handout, but rather doing something to help Zane.

My respect for my brother and the way he just handled this situation rose dramatically in the space of a few seconds. This idea was perfect. It'd help Devon, and Zane.

"I'm not afraid of hard work. If you are

offering me a job, I would be happy to take it," Devon easily said, still looking slightly surprised but easing into a more comfortable stance.

I would imagine even if it was picking up roadkill, he would be happy to take it just to have a job. From what I had seen in him, he didn't appear to be a man that was happy to do nothing all day. He wanted to work and I got the sense that he enjoyed working, feeling like he accomplished something in the day.

"You're hired. You can start tomorrow at nine. You don't have to worry about a uniform or anything, because you will be in the back. Tomorrow morning, we can go over the paperwork and get you official."

"Thank you, I really appreciate it," Devon said as he held his hand out, a grin turning up the corners of his lips.

My brother easily grasped Devon's hand and the two shook briefly before pulling back and stepping away with almost matching looks of relief in their eyes.

I could tell Devon seemed a bit

overwhelmed with it all, not that I could blame him. He went from expecting to sleep in a shelter or on the street tonight with no job, to sleeping on our couch and getting a full-time job offer. It would be a lot to process for anyone.

I was happy that Devon would be able to spend the night here tonight. It just sucked that he would be on the couch and not in my bed. But maybe now that he would be working, he might consider staying here in town, getting his own place.

I knew Zane wouldn't fire him as long as he was doing his job. He could build a life here and maybe that would mean we would get to spend more time together. Maybe the connection we felt would have a true chance to grow into something more.

At least I hoped it would.

***

It was just after seven the following morning when I crawled from my bed. It had been hard to fall asleep last night knowing that Devon was right in the living room on the couch. I couldn't stop thinking about sneaking out there and continuing our intimate time on the couch together. Or him sneaking into my room and we could have one hell of a time in my bed. Neither happened, unfortunately, but I would get to see him this morning. After a quick stop in the bathroom, I walked into the living room and my heart sank. Devon wasn't there.

"He left thirty minutes ago. Said he needed to check in on someone before he would meet me at the diner," Zane supplied from the kitchen where he was cooking at the stove.

I knew I didn't have any right to be disappointed, but I was. I really wanted to see him this morning. To wish him a good first day at work and maybe sneak a kiss in when Zane and Jimmy weren't looking.

"I appreciate you giving him a job. He's been through a lot, but I'm pretty sure he can get back on his feet if given the chance."

"He needed a job and I needed someone that would appreciate the work even though it sucks. It made good business sense. You need to be careful around him," Zane warned.

"He's not dangerous, Z," I instantly said in Devon's defense. Just because he was homeless didn't mean he would be a danger to me and I wasn't going to tolerate anyone telling me otherwise.

"I'm not saying to be careful because I believe he's dangerous. If he wanted to physically hurt you, he could have easily done it while you were alone. I'm saying you need to be careful with your heart. I know how you are. You get attached to people very quickly. You've always been like that with friends and past boyfriends. The end result is always you getting your heart broken. Devon, he could stick around, he might get an apartment and be happy to stay in town. But he is also a transient and they tend to move around, especially if they don't have any family or friends keeping them here. Devon is on his own, there's nothing here that would make him want to put down roots. I just don't want you to get hurt if he disappears, that's all, Squirt."

He was right.

I knew he was right.

I did have to be careful with my heart this time around. I felt a connection with Devon, but we were also strangers. I wouldn't be enough for him to stay in town if he wanted to leave. It wasn't like we were in love or had been dating a long time. And with no family, he didn't have any obligation to stay here. I hoped with him working at the diner he would want to stay, put down roots, but I couldn't allow myself to be naive in thinking that he definitely wouldn't leave.

Zane was right. I needed to be cautious and protect my heart, because if Devon did leave, I would be the one left with a broken heart. And I truly wasn't sure how many more broken hearts I could handle in my life.

CHAPTER SIX

Devon

OF COURSE, IT'S raining.

Why wouldn't it be raining?

It seemed like the rainy season was never going to end this time around. It had been raining on and off for the past week, but I had lucked out and was able to be inside for it.

Tonight, not so lucky.

I had been working at the diner for the past week and, surprisingly, I loved it.

Being a dishwasher wasn't hard work, but it allowed me to do something with my hands. It felt good to get up every day and go to work, almost as if I was a normal person. A functioning member of society, once again, and it felt really good.

Daryl had come by the diner a few times to see me and we'd chatted during my break. Every day, I looked forward to when I would get to see him. I often found myself looking up whenever I heard the front door open, hope in my heart. Just setting my eyes on him caused my heart to flutter and a warmth to spread throughout my body.

I couldn't get the feeling of his lips out of my mind. How it felt to have his lithe body against mine. It drove me insane, haunted my dreams every time I closed my eyes. Still, I would rather have Daryl appear in my dreams than any other memory within my mind.

I shook my head to try and get some of the water out of my hair. It was pouring out tonight and because of the time I got off from work, there weren't any spots available at one of the shelters. I also hadn't been able to find Tyler, so I couldn't sleep in his car tonight. All of that left me stuck outside during this storm.

I had managed to find an overhang on one of the shop doorways that was empty. It was large enough to cover my body and shelter me from the heavy rain overhead, but when the wind blew in the wrong direction, I got the mist blown my way. Hopefully, this wouldn't make me sick. The last thing I wanted to do is not show up for work because I was too sick.

I only made minimum wage at the diner, but considering I wasn't making anything before, I was more than happy to get ten dollars an hour for cleaning dishes. I only needed to work there for a month or two and then I would have enough money saved up to be able to afford a bus ticket, and maybe rent a room from someone in a bigger city. I could find a job working in a diner or restaurant as a busboy or dishwasher. I just needed some money saved up to do it and this job might be the answer to my prayers.

"Devon."

The unexpected sound of my name had me snapping my head up. I knew that voice. I would never forget that voice. Daryl was walking toward me with an umbrella over his head. It was nearing eleven at night. He shouldn't be out in this weather, at this time of night, especially in this area. That wasn't smart and I knew the only reason he hadn't come across a problem on his way here was because of the rain.

"Daryl, what are you doing out here? It's not safe in this area, especially at night," I chastised once he was close enough.

He bent down so we were on the same level and a small piece of my heart went out to him. Most would have just stood there and looked down at me. He actually made the effort to bend down so we were on the same level.

"I'm looking for you. It's really bad out tonight and it's supposed to get worse. You shouldn't be out in this, either. It's not safe and you'll end up sick. Come back to my place with me."

It was sweet of him to offer, but I doubted his brother would be too pleased by that. No, he didn't give me any grief about being there last time, but that wasn't late at night. He'd offered me a job and the last thing I wanted to do was disrespect him or give him cause to fire me.

"Your brother—" I started, but Daryl cut me off.

"Him and Jimmy are already asleep. He won't care, but we can always sneak you in and then out again in the morning. Come on, Dev, it's not safe out here for you. Not with the weather like this."

I didn't have the heart to tell him that I had been out in worse, that being in the rain or other elements was second nature to me. If it had been anyone else, I don't think I would have agreed, but the worry was thick in his voice and I knew if I said no, there was a very real chance he would just stay right here with me. I couldn't allow that to happen.

"Okay."

The biggest smile spread across his face and it damn near killed me. No man should have a smile that beautiful.

It was deadly.

We both stood up and started down the street. He made sure the umbrella covered us both and with his body close to mine, warmth began to flood through me once more.

"How has work been?" he asked after a few moments.

"Good. Your brother has been really nice and the other workers there all seem great."

"Yeah, they are a good group of people. Jimmy used to work there before he went to school. I know from Zane that they have missed him. They're a good group. Is the work okay?"

"Yeah, it's fine. I like working. I like doing things with my hands. It's nice having a steady job right now. It's been a long time since I've been able to have steady work. I really appreciate your bother giving me the job."

"He's good like that. And he said you've

been doing well."

That made me feel good. I took pride in my work, regardless of what it was. I always believed that if you were going to do something, you do it right and to the best of your ability, no matter what it was. It felt good to know that Zane was pleased with my work.

"How has work been for you?"

Daryl had been working at the community center teaching art class to kids. He had landed the job roughly a week ago and he had been really enjoying it. He loved to paint and draw so being able to make money doing it was a blessing.

"It's been amazing. The kids aren't too bad at it. Some of the younger ones are pretty terrible, but they are four or five so I can't expect much. They all really love it, though, and they are willing to give anything a try. I love how creative they all are. The things these kids think of are incredible."

"I always believed we were all born creative and then life takes that creativity away. We're all taught that it's wrong to have invisible friends: Santa Claus, the Easter Bunny, Tooth Fairy. They all become made up stories that we can't believe in anymore. Society and parents take that creativity away and kids conform to what society dictates they have to be. It's sad to think about what the world could be like if we allowed children to be as creative as they wanted."

"I completely agree. It's why I tell all of my students, regardless of their age, that they should never stop being creative and dreaming. Especially kids. They should be allowed to believe in magic and have invisible friends. Let them explore all aspects of their mind and what they are capable of."

It was nice that we could agree on that. Some people felt that kids shouldn't have their head in the clouds. But if you couldn't believe in magic and unicorns when you were younger, then when could you? It was a major part of growing up and it should be embraced.

As the wind picked up, we hastened our pace and made the rest of the journey to his apartment in a comfortable silence. Once we were inside, we made sure to be very quiet to avoid waking up Zane or Jimmy.

"You should take a shower and get warmed up. I'll meet you in my room," Daryl whispered.

I simply nodded and made my way down the hallway as quietly as possible. Once in the bathroom, I allowed myself a moment with my racing heart. I didn't think we would be sleeping in his room. I expected that I would be on the couch like last time.

My body already tingled with the prospect of being able to feel his skin against mine. He might not want anything sexual from me, though, so I would have to be careful and make sure I didn't overstep. I prayed that he did want to make out again, at least. I can't lie, I was really hoping for something more, though. I desperately wanted to feel him wrapped around me. To be inside him. My cock was already hard and throbbing just thinking about it.

I let out a slow breath to try and calm myself down. I pushed away from the door and got the shower running. I couldn't take too long in here, otherwise I risked waking up Zane or Jimmy.

Ten minutes later, my body was both clean and warmed up. I quickly dressed in some dry clothes and made my way quietly back down the hallway to Daryl's room. I slipped inside and closed the door behind me.

Standing in Daryl's room was both nerve wracking and surreal. I couldn't stop thinking about the feel of his lithe body on top of mine when we were on his couch.

It had been a good year since I had been with someone in a sexual sense. I'd touched myself when the need became too much, but it wasn't often I found someone that I could be with. The last person I'd slept with was Jaz, a twenty-four year old prostitute that was just looking for someone to make him feel good. We'd both needed a bit of positive physical contact at the time, and when you were homeless or a prostitute, your choices were limited. That had been a year ago, though, and the itch was quickly becoming a burning sensation that was flooding my body.

Daryl was standing there, leaning against his dresser, in just a pair of black boxers and that was it. I hadn't been able to see his body fully last time, though I felt his muscles against mine. Seeing him now made my mouth water. He was even more beautiful than in my dreams.

He had well-formed muscles, but it was clear he wasn't a heavy weight lifter. He obviously worked out enough to stay in shape, but not to bulk up. His whole torso was smooth and held no hair. His skin was smooth and I couldn't see a single mark on him.

He was the complete opposite to me in that sense. His skin was unmarked and mine was covered in various scars from my father and years on the street. Despite the fact that he was standing there practically naked and I was fully clothed, he didn't seem to feel the slightest bit of shyness. He appeared fully confident in his body and his looks.

He made his way over to me and fingered the bottom of my shirt as he spoke. "You're wearing too many clothes."

I couldn't agree more, but I also knew scars were a topic where people either were bothered by them or they weren't, and I was terrified to find out if he was disgusted by them. I moved my hands down to cover his, stopping him from lifting my shirt.

"Do you not want to?" he asked gently.

I knew if I said no, then it wouldn't be an issue. We would just go to sleep. The problem wasn't that I didn't want to, I wanted it badly. I just didn't want to see disgust on his face.

"I want to, very much so. I've had a hard life, between my father and being on the streets. I'm not unmarked like you are," I admitted softly, my eyes downcast.

I hated that I felt insecure at this moment, but I couldn't help it. He had no marks on him. His skin was perfect.

"I don't care about scars. Your body is

perfect to me, exactly the way you are. You don't have to hide from me, Dev."

I let out a shaky breath as he continued, raising my eyes to his and licking my lips.

"Can I take your shirt off?"

I was trying to find words to tell him that he could. But my emotions were stuck in my throat after his words to me. All I could do was nod, but thankfully that was all he needed.

Daryl grasped the bottom of my shirt and lifted the material up.

I raised my arms, letting him pull it over my head. I kept my eyes locked on his face to see what emotions would play across his features as my marked skin was revealed. I was surprised that I didn't see shock or disgust, but rather there was heat in his eyes. He somehow still found me attractive, even though my body was a roadmap of hell.

When he placed his lips against the scar on my collarbone, I couldn't help the shiver that snaked down my spine. He kissed and licked along each scar on my chest before he moved down to my stomach. His hands went to my belt. With expert fingers, he got my pants open and pushed them down as he kissed his way down my stomach.

He mesmerized me. I couldn't tear my eyes away from his face, in fear that he would either disappear or I would miss something important. He moaned at the sight of my hard dick and I knew he was very pleased by what he saw. I was not on the small side, I knew that. I had been told many times I was above average. He was clearly pleased by it and the thought sent a rush through me, my cock hardening even more.

Daryl licked his lips and then gave it a long lick from the base all the way up to my tip, groaning his appreciation.

I moaned the second the warmth of his tongue made contact with my skin.

He took my tip in his mouth and sucked, moaning at the taste of my precum on his tongue. He was so sexy like this.

I couldn't take my eyes off of him as he worked his way all the way down to my base, not an easy task. I couldn't remember the last time a man could take me all the way in his mouth. I threaded my hand through his hair, and he hummed his appreciation.

"You like that?" I asked in a husky whisper so there was no chance that anyone would hear us. I gave his hair a slight tug and Daryl moaned as a response, the vibration sending shockwaves of pleasure straight down my dick.

I could only allow him to continue for a few more minutes before I pulled his hair, forcing his mouth off me and pulling him up to me. I crushed my lips on his and instantly slipped my tongue into his mouth. As we kissed, I toed off my pants and boxers that had pooled around my ankles, then went for his, slipping the boxers down his hips to fall on the floor.

My hands tangled in his hair once more, mouth ravaging his, I moved us over to the bed. Once the back of his knees hit the edge of the mattress, I followed him down and we wiggled ourselves up the bed until his head was on the pillows, never once taking our mouths from the other.

Daryl opened his legs for me, hinting, but I knew if we started to grind against each other, I was going to come and that was not how I wanted this to go. I needed to be inside him.

Pulling back from the kiss, I spoke, "Where's your stuff?"

He reached over to the bedside table and pulled out a condom and some lube.

I wasted no time in grabbing the lube and putting some on my fingers. I kissed my way down his body until I reached his gloriously hard dick. I instantly took him all the way in my mouth, sliding down to his base. He let loose a very loud moan and I knew he was going to be a vocal partner in bed.

I loved it when my man was vocal. Moan and scream all you wanted. I loved it. The only time it wasn't a good thing was when you needed to be quiet.

Before I slipped my first finger inside of him, I moved my left hand up to his mouth and covered it. I wasn't sure if it would muffle everything, but it was better than nothing. He proved me right when I pressed my finger to his puckered hole and breached him, and he gave a deep moan at the intrusion. I was going to need to gag him at this rate.

I worked my mouth over his dick fast. I quickly added a second finger and then a third as he relaxed and pressed back against my hand. I focused on seeking out his sweet spot and I knew I hit it when he arched his back off the bed, a muffled cry escaping his lips behind my hand.

After a few more moments, I pulled my fingers out and moved my mouth off his dick with an audible *pop*. I didn't want him to come just yet. I wanted to be in him when he did. He was getting way too close.

He gave me a delectable whine at the sudden loss of contact, but I knew he would be happy soon enough. I looked around and found exactly what I needed on the floor, a tie.

"Sit up."

"We getting freaky? I'm not saying no," he said with a sexy smirk.

I would be logging that information away for another time.

"You are loud and I love it, but your brother probably won't. We need to keep you quiet, Sweetheart," I spoke as I wrapped the tie around his mouth.

With the tie in place, I coaxed him to lie back down before I grabbed the condom and slipped it on over my throbbing erection.

He looked so sexy with that tie in his mouth. We were both rocking on the edge and I knew this was going to be fast, but I also knew we could go around again before we got too tired.

I lined the head of my cock up with his hole and slowly pushed into his heat. I couldn't contain the moan as my mushroomed tip breached his muscles.

He pushed back against me, trying to get more of me inside of him. Taking the clue from him, I knew he was enjoying this moment just as much as I was, and I continued to push into him until I was all the way down to my base.

"Fuck, you feel so good, Sweetheart," I whispered as I rocked my hips gently, causing him to whimper.

I pulled out slowly before gently pushing back in, giving him time to adjust to my size. Once I felt him loosen up enough, I picked up my pace. I pulled out almost all the way before slamming back in, causing us both groan deeply.

I angled my hips, seeking out his sweet spot, and I knew I hit it when he all but screamed. I quickly placed my hand over his mouth once more to try and muffle his sounds. All the while, I continued to snap my hips forward and back, slamming into his tight heat, hitting his sweet spot dead on. We were both close, there was no stopping that.

I snaked my hand between us, curling my fingers around his throbbing dick, and started to jerk him off in time with my thrusts. I wanted to feel him come first. He was close and it only took a few more thrusts before he was coming hard and long. The tightening of his ass muscles and feeling his hot seed pour over my hand, pushed me over the edge. With a small growl, I came hard, pumping jet after jet of cum into the condom buried deep inside of him.

I removed my hand from his mouth, but left the tie there. Both of us panted hard as we fought to catch our breath.

Once I stopped pulsing, I gently pulled out and took the condom off, tossing it into the garbage can. Daryl went to remove the tie, but I stopped him. We weren't done yet.

"I didn't say I was done with you," I said as I bent forward and ran my tongue along his stomach, licking up his sweet juices.

"You taste so sweet, baby."

I kissed and licked my way back up to his neck as I reached over to his bedside nightstand. I moved away as I pulled out a condom and gave him a sexy smirk.

"I am nowhere near done with you, Sweetheart." I shot him a cocky grin.

A visible shiver of anticipation rippled

through his body and he was already growing hard again. This night was nowhere near finished and neither of us wanted it to be.

***

Waking up with Daryl in my arms, his head against my chest, was one of the best feelings in the world. It felt remarkable that he was here with me, that we were together like this. I never expected anything like this to happen to me, especially with someone like Daryl. He was good, pure hearted, and saw the light within this world.

I used to be able to see the light, but over the years it only became dimmer and dimmer. My years being alone with my father and living on the streets had made me jaded, in a sense. Now, I generally expected for people to be bad. I didn't see the good in everyone anymore and quite often I was waiting for when they attacked me.

Daryl was the complete opposite of me. He had every reason to not approach me that day at the park a week ago. I was clearly homeless and that normally sent other people running in the opposite direction. Not Daryl, though. He walked right up to me and shook my hand, as if we were new friends meeting up. There was no hesitation, no fear inside him like there probably should have been with meeting someone like me.

Last night had been like a dream. Even if it could only happen that one time, it would be a memory and experience I would cherish forever.

A quick glance at the clock told me I had to get up and get moving. It was just before seven and I needed to get out of here before Zane or Jimmy saw me. I was torn between waking Daryl up and not. I didn't want to disturb his sleep, but I also didn't want to just sneak out on him. That wouldn't be fair to him, for him to think that last night meant nothing to me. I began to rub my hand up his back as I spoke.

"Babe."

Daryl sucked in a deep breath before he

let out a soft groan. I knew he was waking up, though, so I continued to rub my hand along his back. I never wanted this moment to end, but I knew it would have to. I had to go back to reality, but at least I would always have this memory with me.

I hoped I would be able to see Daryl again and be with him, but I was also not holding my breath. Too much disappointment in my life to allow myself to truly hope. I had learned a long time ago it was better to expect the worst and never be disappointed. Sometimes, I was even surprised in a good way.

"It's too early," Daryl said, his voice groggy.

It was too early, especially considering how late it was when we finally did go to sleep. But I needed to sneak out before we got caught. I had no idea how his older brother felt about me. Yes, he gave me a job, but that didn't mean he wanted his kid brother dating some homeless guy. I really didn't want to lose my job because I had slept with Daryl.

"I know, but I gotta get going or we risk getting caught." A physical pain shot through my chest at the thought and I winced but he didn't see it, thankfully.

He sucked in another deep breath and I knew he was trying to wake up now. He slowly moved off my chest and rolled to the edge of the bed as he spoke. "Yeah, okay."

We both went through the process of getting dressed and then slipped out of his room. I didn't hear anyone moving around so I felt a twinge of hope that we were going to make it, to get me out of the apartment before anyone even knew I'd been there.

I should have known better than to hope, though. Hope never worked out for me.

As we came to the end of the hallway, there sat Zane and Jimmy, drinking coffee in the kitchen. I hadn't even heard them get up. Apparently, I must have been more exhausted than I realized.

"Good morning," Zane said with an ever so slight edge to his voice.

I couldn't tell if he was upset with my

being there or if it was because we were trying to sneak around behind his back. I had to give it to Daryl, though, he acted as if nothing was out of the norm.

"Morning. How did you guys sleep?"

"We slept good, until someone started to make a lot of muffled noises very late last night," Zane said.

I cringed internally, heat filling my cheeks. I had gagged Daryl, but he was so very vocal when it came to sex. It drove me crazy, but in a good way. It only made him more sexy, but I had wondered if we would wake someone up.

"I told him it would be Daryl, but he didn't seem to believe me," Jimmy said, flashing a big smile at Zane. There seemed to be something they weren't telling us and my money was on some sexy bet that Zane had just lost.

"I'm paying rent, I get to bring someone home if I want," Daryl said, and I picked up a slight defensive tone to his voice.

"That's not my issue at all. My issue is getting woken up by it. The last thing I want to hear is my kid brother having sex. The decent and responsible thing to do is wait until you are alone, like we do. I also don't appreciate you sneaking someone in. If you are going to do it, then don't hide it. It's not fair to the one you are trying to hide," Zane explained.

"I'm sorry we woke you. I didn't know how you would react to me bringing him home with me, and I really didn't want to make a big deal of it all. It was really nasty out last night and I just wanted to make sure Devon was okay," Daryl explained.

I stayed quiet as the conversation continued. This was between the brothers and I had no place butting in. I could understand Zane's point of view as well as Daryl's. I didn't take any of this personally, either. If I was Zane, I wouldn't be too happy that my kid brother wanted to sleep with a homeless man. It wasn't like I had a lot to offer him. I still couldn't figure out what Daryl wanted with me.

Why did he hold any interest in me?

I wasn't anything special. In fact, I was

the exact opposite of special.

"It sounded like he was a lot more than okay," Jimmy quipped, a playful smirk on his mouth.

Zane closed his eyes for a moment and I could tell he was trying to mentally bleach his mind. I felt bad for him. I wouldn't want to listen to my brother having sex, either, but there was nothing I could do about it now.

"I know over the past week you have been worried about Devon, especially with it being the rainy season. I don't want you wandering around at night outside in bad areas alone and looking for him, though. We are willing to allow Devon to stay here, at least until he gets his first paycheck. Afterward, we can re-evaluate and see if there's another option for him to go where he would be safe," Zane finally said.

"Really?" Daryl asked. A huge smile turned up the corners of his mouth and made his eyes glitter in the morning light filtering in from the big glass window of the balcony door.

I gasped and shot a questioning look at Daryl, but he wasn't paying attention and didn't seem to notice. I felt shocked at what I had just heard. They were going to allow me to stay here until I got paid. This was unbelievable. No one had ever offered me a place to live. Tyler had allowed me to sleep in his car, but that was not the same thing. It wasn't for my own safety and welfare, but rather for the fact that he didn't like being alone. Zane and Jimmy were willing to open their home to me, allow me to have a place where I could sleep, in a bed, and get food. It all felt overwhelming and surreal.

"Yes. We don't want anything to happen to him, either. But there are ground rules," Zane warned.

"Very understanding ground rules," Jimmy added so we didn't think there would be any unfair expectations on either of us.

Jimmy seemed like the more fun loving type of guy compared to Zane who appeared to be more serious. At least, from what I had discovered about him at work.

He did a great job at work and everyone who worked there all seemed to like him. He was easy to work for. As long as you did your job, he was happy with you. I had yet to hear him yell or demand anything from an employee. He was a good boss, one of the easiest ones that I'd worked for.

"He helps out like the rest of us with cooking and cleaning. And any sexual activities happen when you are alone," Zane stated. "I really don't want to wake up to those sounds at two in the morning again.

All of which were very reasonable rules and something I already planned to do.

"That's more than fair. I truly appreciate you allowing me to stay here temporarily," I said.

I didn't want to overstay my welcome, but I was relieved that I wouldn't have to be out on the street for the next week. I wasn't sure where I would be going once I did get paid, but I would at least have some money that I could use to figure it out. Maybe there was a cheap motel room I could rent out on a weekly basis.

"Thank you, Z," Daryl said with a warm smile on his delectable mouth.

"You're welcome, Squirt," Zane said, and flashed him a grin and a playful wink before he continued. "I need to shower. I have to go into work early today. Inventory."

"I'll cook breakfast," Daryl offered, heading toward the fridge.

"I'll help you," I offered.

I wasn't much of a cook, but I could handle breakfast pretty easily. Besides, it was the least I could do after them allowing me to stay here. I had no idea what was going to happen in a week, but I was going to enjoy the time I would get to spend with Daryl while I could.

Odds were, Daryl was only interested in me because I was something forbidden. Soon enough, he would lose interest in me, but that was fine. I would at least get this time with him and it would be something that I cherished forever.

If Daryl wanted to use me for sex, I was perfectly fine with that. He had already given me more than anyone else in my life had. Because of him, I now had a real job that I could make a steady paycheck from. It was more than I'd had since I'd been living on the streets. Maybe, just maybe, I would allow myself to hope a tiny amount.

CHAPTER SEVEN

Daryl

THIS WAS PROBABLY the worst idea I'd ever had and chances were I was going to regret it. My father had been calling me every day since I left. Sometimes, I would let it go to voicemail, only to torture myself later by listening to the messages, and then sometimes I hit the decline button right away.

After almost three weeks, I thought he would have given up. I knew when Zane left home after the explosion of discovering he was gay came out, our father wanted nothing to do with him. All of Zane's photos were gone, his room was completely cleared out, and our father even went as far as hiring a cleaning company to sanitize the whole room.

He had never once tried to reach out to Zane. If he could have, our father likely would have denied even having two sons. The only thing stopping him was that it was public knowledge that my father had two sons that were active within the community.

All of the voicemails were essentially the same. He was asking me to call him back, that we needed to talk about this. I hadn't told Zane about any of it. I wasn't really sure how he would react. Our father was not a man who gave up easily and if he cast you aside, that was where you would always be.

Logically and rationally, I knew what he was doing. He wanted to try and convince me to go back into the closet or that this was simply a phase. It would be easier for him to try and convince me to not come out publicly about being gay, than to try and put the genie back in the bottle with Zane.

If my father wanted to leave the family business to one of his sons, that son would need a wife and children one day. To him, it was better for the company to force me to live a life of unhappiness just so he didn't have to leave his company in the hands of someone outside of the family. Or to leave it with one of his sons who were gay.

The irrational part of my mind, though, that emotional side, foolishly allowed me to hope that maybe, just maybe, my father wanted to meet with me so he could apologize. To express regret for all of the yelling, the bruises, the abuse that he threw my way out of his anger toward my brother. That he would see the error of his ways and want his family back, exactly the way we are.

It was foolish of me to allow myself to hope for a different outcome. It wasn't going to happen, and I knew that. Still, there was this part of me that wanted my father in my life. The part that remembered those rare moments when he was home and not working. Those exceptional moments when he would actually act like I felt a father should.

Not the times when I was so sick and he would allow me to place my head on his lap, because that never happened. And not the times he'd tucked me into bed and check for monsters under the bed, because that simply wasn't him either. But rather how, once in a while, he would give me a genuine smile when I got an A on a test or an assignment, some accomplishment that said his intelligent son lived up to the expected standards he had and he was proud of me.

My most precious memory, though, and it was one that I had never shared with anyone, not even Zane, was the one I hung onto the most and complicated the need to separate myself from my father entirely with the desire to believe even he might really care about me enough to accept me.

One day, when I was eight, father came to the school and pulled me out. At first, I thought I was in trouble, but he just smiled at me and took me to his car. He wouldn't tell me where we were going, just kept saying it was a surprise and that I would love it.

I was a ball of nerves and energy, because nothing like that had ever happened before. From as young as I could remember, I had always been told that school was important, that it was my job. I was to go to school every day and learn as much as I could, to always do my best to make my parents proud. So for my father, of all people, to take me out of school completely randomly, it was a huge deal.

I didn't know what to expect, but I didn't anticipate for my father to take me to an art museum, of all places. I had always loved drawing and painting. Zane used to tell me that I came out of our mother with a paintbrush in hand. Up until that moment, my parents had never really spoken on that matter. I always believed that to them I was just a kid being a kid.

After all, what kid doesn't draw and paint all day?

Walking into that museum only fueled my love for art. The paintings were all unbelievable and suddenly I had doubted myself.

How could I ever paint something that looked as breathtaking as the ones hanging on the walls?

How could I ever paint something that invoked all of these emotions with just a single look?

I was young, but even I understood the talent and emotions that went into every piece in that museum. There was a reason those artists had earned their place on those walls.

Father had picked up on my conflict and what he did next would never happen again. He grasped my shoulder, looked me right in the eyes, and told me to never doubt myself. That if I wanted something badly enough, I would make it happen. All I had to do was work hard and never stop believing in myself. He told me that he brought me there to show me where my art could end up one day and that he couldn't wait until he would be able to purchase a ticket to my own art viewing. It was the first and only time he had shown me any indication that he believed in me, in my art.

When I was a kid, my dream was to be an artist, but that started to change when my love of video games entered the picture. It started out as a doodle, just an idea for what a character could look like if I combined different aspects of other games. It was only a doodle, done so out of boredom sitting in my chemistry class, but that single drawing changed everything for me. It was when I discovered I could combine the two things I loved the most.

My drawings started to turn into virtual worlds filled with different possibilities. From paper, I moved to learning how to draw using a computer. There was a serious learning curve, but I had figured it out and now I planned to design video games for a living.

It was a dream come true.

As for today, I was meeting my father for coffee. He wanted to meet for lunch or dinner, but that would require me to be fully committed to the meeting. At a restaurant to share a meal, you couldn't just up and leave. If things went south, I would still be stuck there, required to share a meal with him. Coffee allowed me the freedom to get up and walk away at any point. It was a freedom that I desperately needed, because I had no idea what he was going to say to me. I wasn't doing this for him, I was doing it for me. To give me the closure that I needed. I owed it to myself to hear him out and know for one hundred percent certainty that this relationship was not repairable.

As I headed into the cafe, I easily spotted my father sitting at one of the tables in the back. I couldn't help but wonder if he chose a table in the back so we wouldn't be seen. After placing my order and grabbing my coffee, I made my way toward him.

Something that should have been

normal, should have felt common, had my stomach all in knots. There was no telling why he wanted to meet so badly, why he felt the need to talk. There was no telling what he wanted to say or how it would all make me feel. I could hope for the best, but I also knew there was a higher chance I would leave here today feeling upset and hurt.

I slid into the seat across from him and took a moment to look at my father. He was dressed in a typical suit, it wasn't often I would see him out of one. He looked just how I remembered him, a blank look on his face.

The perfect poker face.

We never could tell what he was thinking or feeling, something that added to the nerve-wracking experience.

"Father." I acknowledged him with a nod.

We used to be able to call him dad when we were younger, but things started to change with him. From the age of ten it went from dad to father.

"Daryl, thank you for taking the time to meet with me today, he said, his face stoic and impassive." His professional tone got on my nerves. I was his kid, not some client.

"This isn't a business meeting, Father. I'm supposed to be your kid. You used to be able to talk to me like a parent, like a dad. If you can't do that right now, then I'm leaving. I'm not going to be treated like some client of yours."

Ground rules. We needed ground rules and they would be set by me. If he couldn't play by my rules, then we weren't doing this.

The slight tick in his jaw told me that he wasn't happy about what I had said, but he didn't get up and he didn't immediately argue against it. He was annoyed, but I expected him to be. He liked to be in charge, in control of every conversation, and I had just all but demanded that he refrain. He sucked in a slow, deep breath before he spoke.

"How have you been, Son?"

"I'm good. Zane is good, too. He's been working a lot at the diner and putting together a business plan for his concept.

I've been working at the community center teaching beginners art to a lot of great people."

This was about me and him, but I wasn't about to let him forget that he also had another son. He helped to make us. He didn't get to disown us when we don't fit in the perfect box that he designed for us.

"Teaching art to children, is that really what you want to do?"

The way he said it had me on edge.

First, it wasn't just children that I taught and even if it was, so what?

Why not let a child explore their creativity?

Why not teach them something that they could use later on in life either within their career or as a stress reliever?

Teaching wasn't something to be looked down upon.

"I enjoy teaching them. All of them are different ages, from five year olds to sixty year olds. It allows me to use my passion to earn a living. To share it with people who enjoy it just as much as I do. As for my career, I got accepted into a Baltimore University for video game design. I even secured a scholarship from a video game that I designed. I'll be using my love for art and video games to create works of art that can not only be enjoyed, but also to be utilized as an escape. To give people from all walks of life and age a break from reality when they need it."

"I didn't know you knew how to do that. When did you learn how to make a video game?"

He sounded genuinely surprised and confused. To him, I was always up in my room playing a video game or drawing. He never expected for me to do something with it. Mostly because, in his opinion, I would go into the family business, regardless of if I wanted to be or not.

"I taught myself, mostly. I used some of my allowance and money that I saved up to take an online coding class. From there, I used YouTube to help me learn the rest. I started drawing on my computer to create the worlds that I wanted to explore myself, with characters that I wished existed. Now, I get to learn more about it and learn new tricks and skills to start making more games. I'd like to have my own video game company. You told me once to never doubt myself, that you couldn't wait to purchase a ticket to my own art viewing. It's not a painting that can be hung on a wall, but it is a work of art that can be enjoyed and bring out emotions within someone."

"When I was fourteen, we didn't have much in the way of video games. However, we did have a few arcade games. Whenever I needed a break from reality, a break from home life and stress, I would go down to the corner arcade and I would play for hours the different games and the pinball machines. I can understand the joy and the escape that video games bring people. I stopped playing them when I was sixteen, when my Father started grooming me to take over the company." He looked thoughtful as he reminisced about his own past.

"Did you always want to take over?"

I had often wondered if this was what my father wanted for his life. To work for the family company and have all of the stress on his shoulders for it. I knew it was a stressful load he carried. That was why I never held it against him when he came home in a bad mood. Or if he had to work late and missed a birthday or holiday.

"No, it wasn't. I was a lot like you, actually. I was constantly drawing. I had sketchbooks all over the house full of drawings. Only, I drew buildings. I wanted to be an architect, but that wasn't what my father wanted for me."

That shocked me. I had never seen him draw. Even growing up, all of the times he would come into my room or when I was at the dining room table drawing or painting, he never said anything. He never sat down and joined me. He never taught me anything he knew. It would have been the perfect opportunity for him to spend time with me.

"Why didn't you ever say anything, ever join me?"

"I gave it up a long time ago. Your grandfather was a man built on old traditional values. The business and public appearance came first. Anything outside of that didn't matter and was not allowed. Being the only child, the only son, I had to take over the business and drawing wasn't acceptable to him for a man to do. Even picking whom I would marry. I only met your mother once before we got married. That was how he was and there was no changing his mind."

"You do realize that you just described yourself, right? You tried to force Zane into a marriage so he could take over the company. A company he doesn't want to run. You disowned him, rid him of his inheritance, all because he fell in love with a man. You talk about how Grandfather was traditional and controlling, but you are doing the same thing to your sons that he did to you. Do you not see that?"

I needed him to see that. I didn't want to not have my parents in my life. I wanted to be able to go home for dinner or to just hang out with my parents, with my father. I wanted to be able to share my good news, or to talk through a problem. I wanted to bring the man that I loved over for dinner and not have to worry about knives being thrown.

Don't get me wrong, I was still pissed and hurt at his behavior toward Zane and me for the past ten or so months. Trust would have to be earned. Our relationship would have to be built from the ground up. He was in no way, shape, or form, off the hook for what he did, and if he wanted something to do with me, he would have to repair the damage he did with Zane. We were a package deal and that was something he would need to accept.

"I did not grow up in a society like you did. Being a homosexual was not openly talked about. It was something that was treated as a disease, something that needed to be kept hidden. That's not how society works for the most part now, I understand that, but I didn't expect for it to hit so close to home. I didn't handle it well when your brother came out. I was raised to be a certain way and it's ingrained deeply within me."

"Why are we here, then? I don't get it. When Zane left, you cut him off completely, erased him from the house, even had his room professionally cleaned. Yet, I leave and you won't stop calling me."

He gave a slow nod as he sucked in a breath. I knew he was trying to get his thoughts in order and for the first time, I could tell this was hard for him. He wasn't one to talk about feelings. He tended to avoid those conversations like the plague. He was going out of his comfort zone for me and I appreciated that.

"How I handled everything with Zane was wrong. My behavior in the past few months has been wrong and I apologize for that. Parents aren't supposed to have favorites, but it does happen. You have always been my favorite. I've always felt more connected to you. Perhaps it's from our love of drawing. You remind me so much of who I used to be when I was younger. I wanted you to be free to pursue your own dreams. It's why I pushed harder on Zane to take over the company. It would relieve you of that burden and you would be free to be yourself. I'm not okay with either of you being gay. I don't understand it and I don't like it. However, I don't like not seeing you more. I don't want to lose you and I know my behavior was unacceptable. I never wanted to be my father and that is exactly what happened."

"I'm not going to hide who I am, not for anyone. You don't like that I'm gay, but that isn't about to change. It's a piece of who I am and I'm not going to hide it away like I have something to be ashamed of."

I was never going to hide it again. I was out, I was proud, and the very last thing I was going to be doing was going back into that closet to be miserable.

"I'm not asking you to. I'm simply asking for you to give me a chance. It's going to take me time to accept that you are a homosexual. It's not easy for me to acknowledge it, but if I have to in order to have you in my life, then I will."

"You can't have me in your life and keep Zane dead. He's your son, too, and he doesn't deserve to be cast aside because he fell in love with a man. If you want to make things right with me, you also have to make things right with him."

I wasn't going to budge on that, either. If my father couldn't start making an effort to make it right with Zane, then he wasn't getting me. I refused to be accepted only to have my brother not be. That wasn't okay and it never would be with me.

"I know, and I will. Things between your brother and I are more complicated, but I will do my best to try and repair that relationship. I want to be in your life. I want you to be in my life and I'm sorry for everything, Son."

He sounded sincere, but I was also apprehensive about the sudden change. He had always been adamant about not accepting homosexuals. It went against everything in him, and now he was willing to try and accept it? It seemed a little too good to be true. I wanted to believe him, but I also had to be rational and safe. I couldn't put myself in the position to be hurt either physically, emotionally, or mentally. There was no trust and it would take a very long time before I could even begin to remotely trust him.

"It's going to take time. I can't trust you right now, and that trust needs to be rebuilt. I'm willing to try, but I'm apprehensive toward the sudden change. I hope you truly do mean what you say."

"I do mean it, Son. I know it will take time, and I am more than willing to put in the time and effort to repair the damage that I've caused. All I'm asking for is a chance to make it right. With you and your brother."

"I'll give you that chance, but like I said, you have to make it right with Zane, too."

"I will. Thank you. I know it's a big ask from me."

"Time will tell if I live to regret it. Please, don't make me regret it."

This could turn out to be one of the

biggest regrets that I had in my life. But it could also turn out to be the best decision I'd ever made, too. It was a toss up and the coin really could go either way on me.

Businessmen would tell you some of the best investments are the ones with the highest risks. They can cripple you, but they also have the power to give you more than you could ever hope for. My hope was that this wouldn't cripple me, but only time would tell what way the coin would land.

CHAPTER EIGHT

Devon

LETTING OUT A grunt, I lifted the heavy box of oil from the back of the delivery truck. The driver, a very overweight middle-aged man, kindly left me alone with the entire truck to unload.

Zane had told me that the job sucked and he went through quite a few dishwashers. At first, I thought he was just putting up a front so I would be able to feel like I was doing him a solid instead of me feeling like I was being given a hand out. As it turned out, I was wrong. This job really did suck.

It wasn't just washing dishes like it would be in a larger restaurant. It was on me to help unload the delivery truck and to jump in to help the cooks with whatever they needed when a rush hit and I didn't have any dishes backed up.

The thing was, I liked this job. I had done a lot of random jobs over the past few years since being homeless. Washing dishes and unloading heavy boxes didn't even come close to the worst job I'd done. I didn't work in the rain or cold weather.

I did miss the cash at the end of the day, though. It was nice to be able to have some cash in my pocket so I could get something that I needed. Right now, I was stuck having to wait for a paycheck and it was hard. I wanted to be able to contribute to the house I was currently staying in. I had been cooking and cleaning and earning my keep, but it would have been nice to help out with the bills.

The past couple of weeks had been surprisingly really good. It was the longest I had been able to stay in one place for since I left home at seventeen. I hadn't really been sure how well it would go over, at first.

Daryl and me were the very definition of new. I wasn't really sure what we were. It wasn't like what it used to be when I was younger and first started dating. People didn't ask someone to be their boyfriend once you reached my age. You had to just figure it out based on actions and the situation you were in. We were sleeping together, that was beyond amazing, but I also knew we weren't sleeping with other people.

Normally, that was a good sign, but I also knew it would be hard for either one of us to be sleeping with someone else when we were basically living together. We were trying to get to know each other on both a surface and deeper level. I was being honest with him and I could tell he was being honest with me.

As for a label for what we were, I had no

idea. I would have liked to be dating him, but at the same time I would have preferred to have a more stable life before I dated someone.

I would like to have my own place, even if it was a bachelor apartment. It would give me the privacy to be with someone. More than that, though, it would be my own place. It would be a place that would be *all* mine. It would be a safe place. The first safe place I had ever truly had. It was a huge step and it was one I desperately wanted to take.

That desire was why I was more than willing to work overtime whenever Zane needed someone. The more hours I worked, the more money I would make when I finally did get my paycheck.

The sound of the front door opening drew my eyes away from the work in front of me. I knew it was locked. I was the only one here, so anyone that entered had to have a key. I couldn't stop the smile that instantly spread across my face at the sight of Daryl walking in. He locked the door behind him and headed straight for me.

"Hey, what are you doing here?" I asked.

Daryl often came by when I was working, to share my lunch or dinner breaks with him. It was one of the best parts about working here, getting to see him every day. He had been working himself and I knew he often preferred to chill when he got home. I did as well.

We had spent many nights hanging out on the couch playing different video games or watching some television. I liked that he didn't always want to go out. He wasn't old enough to drink, but even still, most guys his age were always looking for a party to sneak into. Not Daryl. He was perfectly content to stay at home and relax.

Even if I wasn't homeless and broke, I still wouldn't go out to parties. I was more introverted in that sense. I could be polite and social, but only with the right crowd. I wasn't one for large parties, bars, or clubs. A group of friends over for dinner and a few beers, though, that sounded like a good time.

"Jimmy is back in town, so you know what they are doing," Daryl said with a smirk as he went and sat down on the counter where, typically, the dirty dishes would go.

I couldn't help but shake my head a little at that. Whenever Jimmy got home for the weekend, those two were constantly going at it. Thankfully, I worked most of the weekend so I never got to hear any of it. Daryl, though, he hadn't always been so lucky. There had been a couple of times when he came running in here because he'd walked in on them having sex very loudly.

"Well, it could be worse, they could *not* be having sex. At least the passion is still alive," I offered as I moved the last box.

"True, but a little warning couldn't hurt, either. Aren't people in the dorms supposed to leave a sock on the door or something?"

"A tie I think, actually. You could always mention it to him."

"He probably won't remember."

That was probably true. From what little I knew about Zane, he was forgetful at times. When he was at work, he always remembered everything and kept the place very organized. At the house, it was the same thing with his work for his own company. Anything that didn't fall within the two categories, though, he had a habit of forgetting.

I couldn't blame the guy. His mind was clearly busy with work and his pending company. It was natural for little things to slip and none of us held it against him. Even I could tell how hard he worked, pushed himself.

With the last box put away, I washed my hands to get rid of the dirt from the boxes before I went over to Daryl. I ran my hands up his thighs and he easily opened his legs for me to fit in between them.

"I could probably think of something fun we could do to pass the time," I said as I moved closer.

Daryl wrapped his arms around my neck and pulled me in, closing the gap between us as his lips crashed down on mine.

Being with him never got old. I had been

with a few friends with benefits over the years and they tended to get boring very quickly. With Daryl, the sex was not only unbelievable, but it was also exciting no matter how many times we'd done it.

Our need rose quickly and the kiss turned heated very fast. Both of our hands were moving at a rapid pace to rid the other of their clothing. Even though we had just had sex last night, it felt like it had been months since we had seen each other.

Before my pants were removed, I grabbed my wallet and pulled out the small packet of lube and the condom that I kept there. I grabbed the edges of Daryl's jeans and he lifted his hips enough for me to be able to pull them off, along with his boxers. I grabbed him by his hips and pulled him down closer to the edge of the counter so I would have proper access to his hole to stretch him.

"I need you." Daryl moaned the second my first finger breached him.

"I know, baby. I need you, too. But I don't want to hurt you. I'll be quick," I promised.

We were both in desperate need to feel connected to the other. It was almost as if there was a string that connected us to each other and if we let that string get too tight, we would break. I didn't believe in soulmates, not even for a second, but there was just something about Daryl that made me question that belief. I couldn't help but wonder if he felt it, too, but I was too much of a coward to voice my question.

Once Daryl felt stretched enough I pulled my fingers out of his ass and rolled on the condom. Lining my tip up with his hole, I slowly pushed myself inside of his ass.

We both moaned at the invasion. No matter how many times we'd had sex, he was still so tight, as if we were made for each other. Bit by bit, I pushed my dick inside of him until I was finally balls deep.

I held still for a moment to allow Daryl to adjust to my large size. He was already breathing heavily and I knew he wouldn't last too long. I also knew he could handle more than one round back to back, though.

I had always had a high sex drive and I could stay hard for four or five rounds before I needed a break. Most guys thought it was amazing and perfect, until they started to go for multiple rounds. I was fairly certain they thought I was bluffing or exaggerating. Most could only handle three rounds before they were the ones in need of a break.

I placed my hand in the middle of his chest and slowly pushed him down onto the counter so his back was flat against it. The counter wasn't very wide so his ass hung off, causing him to wrap his legs around my hips, which wasn't exactly what I wanted tonight. Placing my hands on his inner thighs, I pushed his legs open as wide as I could so I could watch as my dick moved in and out of his sweet hole. Pulling out almost all of the way before I pushed my dick right back inside of him, slowly, all the way down to my base. I kept my pace slow, a mixture of not wanting to hurt him and to drive him crazy. His soft moans echoed off the bare kitchen walls and I knew he was getting impatient as he tried to wiggle his hips for more friction.

"Stop teasing," he whined at me.

I couldn't help the smirk that played across my lips. "I guess we should hurry. We wouldn't want our new boss to catch us."

His deep moan told me he was more than happy to role play. "I can't lose this job. You better fuck me hard and deep."

"As you wish."

I pulled out all the way before I slammed right back in, hitting his sweet spot dead on. I was pleasantly rewarded with a deep moan. I couldn't contain my own as I watched my dick move quickly in and out of him. He was completely at my mercy, but he didn't seem the least bit bothered by it.

I continued to snap my hips hard and fast, getting as deep as humanly possible inside his tight heat. We were both a moaning mess as our need for release continued to build. I was getting close, but I wanted to feel him come first. I wanted to feel his walls close around my dick.

"Touch yourself for me, baby. I want to watch as you come."

Daryl gave me the most delicious whimper in response to my words. He moved his hand to clasp around his erection and started to jerk himself off. I knew he wouldn't last long. I could already feel his walls tightening around my dick. His dick was hard as a rock and pulsing with need, the vein on the underside visibly swollen and throbbing. It was only minutes later when he was coming hard.

"Dev!"

I watched as line after line of cum shot out of him and landed on his stomach. The added tightness of his ass pushed me over the edge with him.

"Dar," I moaned as I came hard deep inside of him.

I placed my forehead against his as we both continued to pulse, our breathing heavy. I don't know what it was about him, but our sex was always earth shattering. It was insane, but also so unbelievable I never wanted it to stop. Maybe I was living in a fantasy world right now, but it was a world I was happy to continue to live in. At least until the bubble popped.

CHAPTER NINE

Daryl

THE DAY HAD gone by so fast I almost couldn't believe it. One second I was at work and the next thing I know, I'm looking up from my canvas and it was time to go.

The group of students that I worked with today had been amazing. The energy in the room was very positive and it really brought out the creativity in everyone. It was a great group and I was already looking forward to working with them again next week.

Devon was working tonight, so I made my way toward the diner. Over the past three weeks, since Devon had been living with me, we would often meet at the diner on his dinner break. It was a way that we could continue to get to know each other and spend more time together.

I found myself growing more and more attached to him. I knew I needed to be careful with my heart, but my heart was never a very good listener. It often fell for the wrong guys, the ones who would inevitably hurt me in the end. No matter what I did, though, my heart always seemed to go all in and it was something that was happening all over again. I had been doing my best, trying my best, to not let it happen.

There was still so much up in the air where Devon was concerned. He hadn't brought up leaving for a bigger city again, but the threat of that happening was constantly playing out in my mind. I didn't want him to leave, but I had no right to ask him to stay. He had been working for the past three weeks and he was set to get his first paycheck in a couple of days. It was also going to be a decent size one with how the pay periods went. He would be getting three weeks worth of hours on it, close to a hundred and twenty hours. It was going to be more than enough for him to go to Baltimore and potentially find a room to rent for a month. That would give him the chance to find more work and he would have an address he could use for a proper job.

He didn't have family here. There truly was nothing keeping him in our small town. It only made sense for him to spread his wings and move to a larger city. It would grant him more opportunities. I hated that I had no say in this. I hated that what we had could all come to an end and I would be the one left behind with a broken heart all over again. I knew I was doing this to myself, but that didn't take the pain away any less. I wished I could have been more like Zane. He was harder to get to know. He kept a wall up around his heart, always had. Maybe it had something to do with his relationship with our father. Or maybe he was more like our father than he thought or wanted to admit. For me, maybe it was the artist in me that made me feel things differently, more deeply than the average person.

Heading into the diner, I easily made my way around the counter and headed into the back. It wasn't unusual for me to be coming in and heading straight back. Everyone who worked here was used to it. They knew I was Zane's brother and people suspected that Devon and me were dating. Neither one of us had said we were dating. We didn't call each other boyfriends, but Devon did tend to call me pet names.

I was doing my best to not get my hopes up that those pet names meant he cared about me. I knew some guys used them just as a way of not saying the person's name. It wasn't always a term of endearment. Still, whenever he called me Babe or Sweetheart, my heart fluttered a bit.

I found him just finishing up the dishes

from dinner rush. He was wearing a black t-shirt and I couldn't help but admire the view of his arms. He was the most muscular man I had ever been with and I was finding myself enjoying it.

I didn't date really skinny guys, but the guys I did tend to date weren't that muscular. They "worked out" once a week at a gym. Only, their definition of working out was using the treadmill or rowing machine. If they did lift weights they were ten pounds.

I didn't care. I was the artistic gamer guy. I had muscles, but just enough to feel confident when I took my shirt off. Devon, he had the kind of muscles that could pick me up and toss me around. I was really enjoying that level of strength.

"Hey, Babe," Devon said, flashing a warm smile in my direction.

"Hey, I brought dinner for us. Nothing fancy, just some spaghetti."

"I love spaghetti. It's my favorite."

"Worked out nicely, then," I said and flashed back a warm smile.

We had been opening up to each other for the past few weeks. Nothing too crazy and emotional, but we were learning new things about the other. There were a lot of those first date type of questions, at first. They felt awkward, though, because we had talked more in depth about our lives and growing up. It seemed weird to be asking him things like his favorite color when I knew his father had beaten him so horribly it caused him to lose his dream. Still, we were doing it so we could know each other on a surface level.

It did help to ease my nerves and fears about him leaving, just slightly, but some.

After all, who wants to get to know a person better if they were only going to leave in a month?

If he was taking the time to get to know me, he must feel something toward me and hopefully maybe he'd want to stay.

Once he finished with the dishes, we strolled out into the dinning room to sit for dinner. We were the only people out here with the dinner rush being over. The couple of servers were busy trying to get things cleaned up so they would have less to do tonight for closing.

"How was work?" Devon asked.

"It was amazing. The class that I had at the end, the energy in the room was just phenomenal. I can't wait to see 'em again next week."

"That's good. Do you paint while they are?"

"Sometimes I do, yeah. I'll paint whatever subject they are working on. It just depends on their skill level and if I need to be watching over them throughout the whole class."

"Have you been working on anything special? I know you said you were thinking up a new game to develop."

I had been mentally designing a new game that would be different to anything else out there. For starters, I was going to have it where you could choose what your character's sexuality was. For the most part, any role playing games currently out there didn't have romance involved, really, and if it did, it was always a straight guy and girl. It would appeal to the masses.

I wanted to create a game where you could choose if your character was straight, gay, bisexual, or transgender. Then the algorithm would change the game based on your choice.

So if there was a love interest and you picked gay, your love interest would switch from a woman to a man. The coding would be more intense and you would need to have serious skill to be able to keep the different scenarios functioning, but I thought it would be nice for people who are gamers, but don't fall within the traditional heterosexual category.

The other aspect of the game I wanted to create was to combine gamer favorites into one. My thought process was to have it start off in a normal, everyday realm and as the game progresses you get pulled into different portals that take you to different realms that you have to fight your way through. Like a Lord of The Rings realm, a World Of Warcraft realm, a Call of Duty realm. All of these different realms that you would have to adapt to and survive, in order to complete the quests. It would be a massive undertaking in terms of coding just to keep the different realms functioning, but the goal was it wouldn't be like anything out there.

"I've been drawing up different sketches of what I would like the characters to look like. I also have a document going of what the quests could be and how it can all connect. It's going to be a big project and most likely will take me a few years to develop."

"Well worth it, though, if it ends up being something you are proud of. From what little you have told me, it sounds like something the gaming world would love. I would be happy to be your beta tester," he said with a grin.

Hearing that warmed my heart, because maybe it meant he might be planning to stick around. He could use his paycheck to find a room to rent for the month in someone's house here. Then he could save up enough money for his own apartment. He already had a job and Zane was very pleased with him. He worked hard and he was always willing to put in the extra time and effort to get the job done right. He was a great worker and employee. Maybe he would stick around and we could have something real together.

My phone beeped and a quick glance told me that my father had sent me a text. Ever since our meeting, he had been reaching out to me almost every day to check in. He had switched from phone calls to text messages. Maybe he figured I was more likely to talk with him if I could just text him back. Either way, it did work. I had been messaging him back, but I also kept my guard up. I didn't send him one back right away, at first. Normally, I waited an hour or two before I would actually reply. Maybe it was me being petty, but I wanted for him to feel like I was in control of our relationship and not him. Waiting even an hour made me feel like I had the power and not him.

Some type of emotion must have flitted across my face because when Devon spoke concern laced his tone.

"Everything okay, Sweetheart?"

I hadn't told anyone about my father reaching out to me or about our meeting. Honestly, I wasn't sure how anyone would react, especially Zane and Devon. After everything that Devon went through with his own father, I didn't know what he would think of me trying to repair the relationship with mine.

As for Zane, he was protective of me and I knew he would be worried that our father would hurt me again. It was wrong to keep this a secret from Zane and I knew, eventually, it would come out. Our father would be reaching out to him soon to try and repair their relationship, too. I honestly doubted Zane was going to be willing to give our father a second chance. It was his choice and he had every right to want to keep that door closed, but I hoped that speaking with our father, even just once, would bring him closure.

"My father has been reaching out to me. He used to call every day since I left and now he texts me," I finally admitted.

It had been weighing on me keeping this secret. It shouldn't have to be a secret, but it felt like I was doing something wrong. He was my father and it should be my choice if I had a relationship with him and what type of relationship it was.

"Is he harassing you?" Devon asked, worry evident in his voice now.

"No, no. At first, he would call and I would let it go to voicemail. He just wanted to meet and talk with me about what happened. I actually met with him at a cafe for coffee about a week ago."

"You met with him? Why didn't you say anything?"

Devon was clearly worried and slightly upset. I could hear it in his voice and he had every right to be a bit upset with me. I knew what he would say. He just wanted to make sure I was safe. That even in a public place my father could have tried to hurt me. It was a valid argument and one I didn't think of at the time.

"To be honest, I wasn't sure I was even going to go, and then I figured I deserved the closure."

"I can understand that. And now he's texting you? Does that mean you are talking with him now?"

"I was expecting a lecture when I met with him. I thought he would try and convince me to go back into the closet or that I was going through a phase. He didn't. It actually went pretty well. A lot better than I ever expected it to go, honestly. He said he loved me, that he didn't understand homosexuality and it would take him time. But he did say he didn't want me to be condemned to a life of misery. He seems to be trying and he apologized for everything that happened between us. He seemed really genuine."

"That's good. Hopefully, he was being authentic. Just be careful, though. Abusers, they become nice when they think they are going to lose the person they are abusing. They tell them what they want to hear to get them back close to them, only to turn around and hurt them once more when they feel like it's safe enough to."

That had been something I had thought about as well. I believed people could change. I believed that there were people out there that would change for someone they loved. I also knew that abusers liked to be in control and have all of the power. If they felt like their partner was slipping away from them, they would change temporarily to give the other person a false hope of a better life. Only to go right back to their abusive ways when they felt like their partner was under their spell again.

I hoped my father wasn't doing that with me. That he wasn't playing the long game and looking to get me back into the house to abuse and control me. I was being extremely cautious with him and it would stay that way until I saw real change in him. It was the best I could do, and I knew I had to give it a chance or I would regret not trying.

"I know. I'm being safe. I'm not letting

myself get my hopes up or making up this big false reality of a perfect family. I haven't met him since and if I do again it will be in public. I also told him he had to make things right with Zane. I don't know what Zane will do, but that will be up to him and at least he will have the option this time around."

"Being safe is all you can do. Only time will tell how it all plays out. I hope for your sake it ends how you'd like for it to. Some relationships are repairable, I know that."

"Have you heard from your father at all since you left home?"

It was a sensitive topic and I wasn't really sure what about it was off limits or not. So far, Devon had been good with talking about it. I did make a point in letting him know if there was ever a time I asked him something that he wasn't ready to answer, or comfortable with answering, to just say so. I would understand and I would never pressure him to open up when he wasn't ready.

"No. It wasn't like what it was between

you and your father. He was violent before he discovered I was gay, and with what happened afterward, there's no going back from that."

"I can understand that. I wouldn't be able to forgive him, either. I don't know if I can even forgive my father for what he did. I do understand, though, that a lot of parents handle it the wrong way when they discover their child is gay. Especially fathers and sons. I know my father was raised in a community that didn't believe in it and it was not allowed. I actually learned that he used to draw growing up. He wanted to be an architect, but his father said he had to take over the family business as the only son. He had only met my mother once before they were married. His father set it all up. I think he was forced into being someone he's not, into living a life that he wouldn't have picked for himself. Losing his last child, I think that made him reflect back on his actions and decisions. At least, I hope that's what inspired his desire to change all of a sudden. I hope it's real and not just a manipulation tactic that he's trying."

"I hope it's real, too, Babe. There are a lot of parents that react horribly at first, but at the reality of losing their child, they see that they have to change. It'll take time for him to come around, to fully accept that you are gay. There might always be a part of him that hates it, but he won't cause you harm because of it. Give it time and take it slow. If he truly wants this to work, he will put in the effort and jump through as many hoops as you want."

I hoped he was right. That my father really did want this to work and he would be willing to follow my rules and respect my boundaries. The problem was, though, only time could truly tell. All I could do was wait and see how it would all play out.

Tonight, though, I wasn't going to worry about anymore to do with my father. I was going to enjoy my time with Devon, for however long I would get with him.

***

I was pulled out of my drawing bubble when my phone went off. It was Zane's ringer, so I reached over and hit the answer button, putting it on speaker so I could keep drawing. Zane was at work, so I wasn't expecting any earth-shattering news.

"What's going on?" I asked, looking to cut to the chase so I could keep working on my new video game characters in peace.

"Is Devon there?"

That had me instantly stopping my hand and giving my brother my full attention. Devon was set to work the evening shift at the diner. He had gotten paid yesterday and seemed to be in good spirits. It had only been two days since we had dinner at the diner. Even though I hadn't asked him about his plans, he gave no indication that he was still intending to leave.

"No, he left for work an hour ago. He didn't show?" I asked, worried now that something could have happened to him.

"I wouldn't be calling if he did, Squirt. I know you said he had talked about leaving three weeks ago. Did he mention anything to you recently?"

"No, nothing. The way he was talking, it sounded like he was looking to stay. I never flat out asked him, though, and he never said anything. What if something happened to him?"

I was quickly reaching panic mode. Devon could have left, but he also could have gotten into trouble. He had been on the streets for years and from what little stories he had told me, he had often protected people out there. I suddenly couldn't stop thinking about all of the possibilities. All of the "what if" situations.

"I'll call Roland and have him look into it. He might know of places where Devon would go. He might not be hurt or anything, Squirt. He could have easily got caught up in something. He could have been arrested on an old warrant or something. We have no idea. Don't jump to any conclusions, okay? And stay in the apartment, in case he comes back."

"Yeah, okay. I'll wait here."

"We'll find him. I'll call Roland. I love

you."

"I love you, too."

Zane hung up before I could even get my body to listen to my mind to move. Zane had told me to stay here and I knew that made sense. Still, it didn't change the fact that all I wanted to do was get out there and find him. To go and search the streets for where he might be. I hated that all I could do was sit here and wait.

There wasn't even anyone I could call who might know where he was. He had no family and he didn't seem to have any friends. All I could do was wait, once again. I was really getting tired of having to sit and wait. When Devon was found, I wasn't going to wait any longer. I was going to let him know exactly how I felt about him. Life was too short to sit around and wait.

CHAPTER TEN

Devon

STANDING IN THE bus depot was a bit surreal and heart breaking. I didn't come to this decision lightly. It had been something I had been tormenting myself with for the past week or so.

It wasn't that I didn't appreciate all of the help that Daryl and his brother Zane had given me. They had given me a job, a safe place to sleep at night, but most importantly, they had given me the freedom of no judgments. They didn't judge me. They didn't make assumptions as to who I am or what I would be like just because I was homeless. It was as if I had always been there.

It was refreshing, but terrifying, all at the same time. I hadn't really been cared for since Jay died. I'd gotten so used to being on my own and only relying on myself. Having three people, now, in my life that seemed to care about my welfare, well, it was kind of overwhelming.

I never thought I had any self-esteem issues. I knew I was homeless and that generally meant I didn't have much to offer someone, but I was confident in myself. Yes, my scars were hard, but that was on the outside. Internally, I was confident in my skills and the type of person I was. Recently, though, I felt that wavering.

I'd found myself feeling a bit self-conscious because I didn't have anything to bring to the table. I only had a job because Zane took pity on me and offered it. I only had a safe place to sleep at night because

Daryl had decided we needed to be friends. They were supporting the household and I was just another freeloader. I felt like a burden and I hated that feeling.

I hated feeling like I wasn't contributing to a relationship. I hated feeling like someone needed to take care of me. I was my own man and I had always been the type in the relationship to be the strong one, to take care of my partner, and I couldn't do that with Daryl right now.

There was a huge part of me that wanted to stay here. A part that wanted me to try and find my own place and keep working at the diner until I figured out what I wanted to do for a career.

An enormous part of me wanted to be with Daryl and show him what type of man I truly was. My feelings for him were strong, stronger than any man I had ever been with. That, in and of itself, was terrifying because I wasn't used to feeling so strongly toward someone. It was almost overwhelming, even though it should be a good thing. It *was* a good thing, but it was also a new experience and with that came uncertainty.

I didn't want to hurt Daryl, but I also believed he deserved someone so much better than me. I didn't have anything to offer him. He deserved to have a man that had a good job and his own place. Someone that could make him feel secure. I might never be able to offer him that security. I might never be able to offer him the world, and he deserved to have the world.

Leaving town, leaving a place where I had a full-time job, might not seem like the smartest idea and I could agree with that. However, it wasn't just a job. It was the closeness to Daryl and his brother. I couldn't end things with Daryl and still live here, still work in the diner. I wanted to be with him, but I had to let him go. I had to let him find someone that would treat him better and give him everything he deserved.

This was breaking my heart.

I could admit to myself that I was no longer *falling* in love with him. I had fallen. That's how I knew I had to leave. I wasn't going to risk Daryl falling for me, too.

That's how I ended up at the bus depot with a one way ticket to Baltimore. It would be a big city with lots of opportunities for me. I could get a job as a dishwasher in any restaurant. Some might even pay me cash. I had enough for a ticket and to rent a room in a cheap motel for the month. I could use that as my address and hopefully find something quickly so I could continue to afford to stay at the motel. Then I'd just have to save up until I could afford first and last month's rent for a one bedroom apartment. This was the right move to make.

"Well, look who we have here, boys."

I couldn't help the internal cringe at hearing Luis' voice. I'd come outside to wait for my bus, which was set to arrive within the hour. I was on my way out of town and of course Luis had found me. Turning, I saw he wasn't alone. He had five friends with him. Of course. This was the last thing I needed.

"What do you want, Luis?" I asked,

making sure my shoulders were squared and my chest puffed out. There was no way I was going to let any of them know that fear had started to edge in. One on one, I could take him. Hell, I could take three of them. But six against one were not good odds.

"Payback for Juan. You should have gotten out of town months ago, bitch."

This had been coming. I'd known it was. We only had three gangs in town and the Draggos were one of the more violent gangs. The other two were happy to hang around on the streets and try and shake business owners down for money. The Draggos had complete control of the drugs coming and going in town and if there was a violent crime committed, you could guarantee it was one of their members. There was no reasoning with them.

I tossed my bag down as they started to circle around me. I knew this wasn't going to end well, but I would be damned if I was going to go down without one hell of a fight. One thing was for certain, come morning I was going to be very sore.

***

Beep, beep, beep, beep…

What the hell is beeping?

It needed to stop. My head was killing me. My whole body was killing me.

What the hell happened?

Beep, beep, beep, beep…

What is that?

There was only one way I was going to find out, but opening my eyes seemed like a terrible idea. It was going to hurt, I knew that much. I had no idea what happened or why I was in so much pain, but I did know that opening my eyes was going to be a decision I lived to regret. Still, I forced my eyes open. My need for answers was stronger than my need to escape the pain.

The first thing I saw was a white ceiling, followed by white walls.

A hospital.

How did I end up here?

The beeping sound was coming from my right and a quick glance down at my chest told me I had leads on it from a heart monitor. There was also that pulse or oxygen monitor thing on my right index finger. Looking down hurt my head more, but I ignored the pain for a few moments longer as I took in my appearance.

There were bruises all over my arms and my right hand was swollen and bruised. I must have been in a fight. It's the only way for it to get like that. I wore a god awful hospital gown so I couldn't see any damage done to my torso. It felt like I had a broken rib or two, though, if the pain from breathing was any indication.

Everything just hurt.

It wasn't unbearable, so I knew there was some form of pain medication going through my system. I did know, though, if it hurt this much with pain medication, I didn't want to know what it would feel like once the medication ended.

A knock at the door sent a blinding pain shooting through my skull. I had to squeeze my eyes shut just to try and stave off the increased pounding. I knew this feeling all too well. A concussion. A bad one, if the pain was any indication. Thankfully, I wasn't the type of person who threw up with a concussion. I was the type of person who needed to be left alone in a dark and quiet place until it started to heal. Not something that was easy to have living on the streets.

"Sorry," I heard Roland's soft voice say next to me.

Forcing my eyes open once again, I took in his appearance. He wore his typical black, straight cut jeans, his black t-shirt, and black leather jacket. For a detective, he always dressed on the casual side. But I suppose in a town like this, he wouldn't need to wear suits everyday.

"What happened?" My voice was hoarse, but it didn't hurt to talk so I hadn't been strangled, at least. I counted that as a win.

"You were at the bus depot, apparently looking to leave town, I believe. Six of the Draggos found you there and they apparently wanted get revenge for you attacking Juan a couple months back when he was going to rape that girl. You fought back, but they won. You got a concussion, three broken ribs, a bruised kidney, and your right eye is heavily bruised. It was swollen, but now it's gone down. When I got there they started to take off. I was able to grab one of the guys and we've been able to pick up the other five. They are in lockup for a few days until their bail hearing."

I was lucky I wasn't dead. When I had come across Juan in that alley with that girl, I knew what he was going to do with her. The police had been looking to take Juan off the streets for years for multiple counts of sexual assault, but none of his victims would report it or testify. He seemed to think he was untouchable and I wanted to make sure he knew he wasn't. I wanted to save that girl from a violent and traumatizing experience like that. Juan hadn't walked away unscathed. I made sure of that. I broke multiple bones, including his jaw. I knew the Draggos would be looking for retaliation, but I figured it would be after Juan healed. Apparently, I was wrong.

"I knew it was coming, I guess. I just thought I had more time. I don't remember anything after my shift at work last night."

It wasn't uncommon for people to lose their memory after sustaining a concussion. What was surprising, though, was that I had been at the bus depot. I had been toying with the idea of leaving for weeks now, but I was still on the fence. Apparently, I had jumped off that fence and had decided on leaving.

"You know that is not uncommon. You got lucky that I arrived in time. Any longer and you could have been dead."

"I guess I was lucky someone there called 911."

"No one called from there. I was already on my way to the depot to see if you were there. Zane called me when you didn't show up for your shift. You've managed to scare the living shit out of him and Daryl."

There was a lecture coming my way. It didn't matter that I was literally in a hospital bed. Roland was not going to hold any punches and I knew it. He was upset with me for leaving. Maybe because he found out I was dating Daryl or maybe because I was leaving without telling him. I knew he liked to know who was in town and who wasn't.

He was one of the few cops who actually did care about the homeless community. He liked to know if we were still in town so if we went missing he would know it wasn't because we decided to move on. I should have called him. I don't know why I wouldn't have. I must have been in a hurry or too emotional and not thinking straight. Most likely the latter.

I don't remember last night, but I knew for the past week I had been agonizing over staying or leaving. If I hadn't been with Daryl the decision would have been easy. My feelings for him had muddied the waters. I had apparently made the decision to leave.

"Why would he call you?"

I wasn't sure how much time I had lost, but it couldn't have been anywhere near the twenty-four hour mark. If Zane called to report me missing after not showing up for my shift, they wouldn't have investigated. They probably wouldn't have investigated if it had been a whole day with me being homeless. Most cops tended to assume when a homeless person went missing they had just moved on to the next town. Hoards of people didn't come together to search the area.

"Almost a year ago, Zane and Jimmy were attacked in the park. I took the case. We've gotten close since then. They were worried and asked if I wouldn't mind looking for you. I headed to the bus depot first. I figured with your new paycheck you would be running away."

"I wasn't running away," I said with as much strength to my voice that my body could muster.

"Right. That's why you are leaving not only a stable job, and a roof over your head, but also the man that you are madly in love with," Roland challenged.

"I'm not in love with him," I instantly

denied. It was a lie and, based on Roland's face, we both knew it.

"Come on, Dev. who are you trying to kid here? Me or yourself? I've known you for a few years now, and the last thing you are is a coward. You don't run away. So why are you running away from a great man like Daryl?"

He was a great man. He was sweet, kind, gentle, generous, positive, smart, beautiful, and creative. He was far too good for me and he deserved so much better. I couldn't remember last night, but I was willing to bet every dollar I had that I was leaving for Daryl's own good. So he could find someone that would be able to give him everything his heart desired. I was just some homeless guy that he took pity on.

"He deserves better than me. It's better for him if I'm gone. He can find someone who will give him everything he wants and needs."

"He cares a lot about you, Dev. Whether you are here or not, it's still going to hurt him. He's already falling for you. That window of getting out clean without causing any pain has long since closed. You both fell hard and fast. It happens. That can be terrifying, but it can also be the best love you will ever experience in your life. That's not a love you let slip through your fingers. Especially over something like insecurities. You have a lot to offer someone, a lot to offer Daryl, but I can tell you right now, the only thing he wants from a partner is to be loved and respected. Now, that is something I know you would be able to give him."

I could hear a slight hurt undertone to his voice and I couldn't help but wonder if maybe he had lost a love like that himself. I knew better than to ask, though. Roland was more tight-lipped than a Royal Palace Guard.

"Life isn't that simple." It was a weak argument, but it was all I had right now. My head hurt too much to try and come back with something stronger and bulletproof.

"If it was, we would all be bored. I can call him, tell him you are here."

"No, don't. There wouldn't be a point.

Once I can leave, I'm getting on that bus and he'll be free from me. It's what's best for him."

Roland patted the bed beside my arm as he got up. "Your body needs rest. I'll come by later to check in on you and sneak you in some food, if you're allowed."

My stomach turned at just the mere mention of hospital food. Nurses and doctors were always on your case to eat enough food so you could leave, but they never gave you anything you wanted to actually swallow.

Roland made his way to the door, but before he walked out of it he turned back to me one last time.

"A big part of respect is allowing your partner to make decisions for themselves. It's not up to you to decide if Daryl deserves better than you. That's on him to decide, and if you love him, you'll let him make that decision." And with that, he strode out the door.

He was right. I knew he was right and I hated it. Daryl did deserve to make the decision for himself, but I also knew it was one he would make based on emotions. He would pick me and that would only cause him pain later on in life. I was trying to avoid that for him, and for me.

A sharp pain shooting through my eyes told me I needed rest. I needed to get out of here and that was never going to happen if I didn't get some sleep to recover. Once I was able to leave, I would be getting on that bus and putting this town and Daryl in my rearview mirror. It was better for the both of us. I just hoped that Daryl would be able to forgive me one day.

CHAPTER ELEVEN

Daryl

WALKING INTO THE hospital was a terrifying experience.

The last time I was here was because Zane had been jumped. It had been terrifying then, too. At the time, we hadn't really been speaking all that much for a few years, but Zane had started making the effort. So when I walked in here after his attack, I was terrified that I would lose him before I ever truly got him back. Relief didn't even come close to what I felt when the doctor told us he would be okay.

I wanted to stay with him, but my parents had said we didn't need to sit there all night while he slept. By the time we got back in the morning, he was gone and my heart sank, fearing the worst. Only to find him outside of Jimmy's room and proclaiming his love for him.

When our father wanted him to deny it, I thought for sure he would. I thought he would give some lame excuse as to what he meant just to appease our father, only he surprised me again by being honest and strong. It was in that moment, I truly saw my big brother again and I couldn't have been more proud of him.

Now, here I was back at the hospital, and once again, someone I loved had been attacked and all but left for dead. If it hadn't been for Roland, Devon very well could have died. Roland had said he was pretty beat up, worse than what Zane had been, but that he would be okay in time. There were no permanent injuries and he was only beaten and nothing sexual happened to him. It was a relief to hear, but I knew it would have still brought up painful memories to my brother and Jimmy. Unlike their attackers, Devon's had been caught and would most likely face serious jail time for this crime.

"Remember, he's going to be fine. He's got a lot of bruises on him and his head and ribs are likely killing him. But he's going to be okay, and the Doc has him on some pain medication to help take the bulk of the pain away. He just needs rest," Roland advised us again and I could have sworn he was nervous.

I wasn't sure why Roland would be nervous about seeing Devon. He had already been by earlier to check in with him and stay with him until he woke up. The doctor hadn't allowed visitors until Devon was awake, but with Roland being a detective he could stay with him. It was something I greatly appreciated. I didn't want Devon waking up all alone and scared in a hospital bed.

"And he doesn't remember what happened?" Jimmy asked for clarification.

"Last thing he remembers is his shift the night before. Doc said it was perfectly normal given the level of concussion he has. He may never remember the attack. Thankfully, we don't need him to. I was there at the end of it and the bus depot had cameras all along the outside. They got the whole thing. It's an open and shut case. Hopefully, with the bulk of the more dangerous members of the Draggos behind bars, other victims will come forward and finally press charges."

I could hear the slight hopefulness in his tone. He had been frustrated with victims not wanting to press charges because of the blowback that would be awaiting them. It was terrible, to be a victim but to be so afraid to press charges that they just lived with the injustice. They lived with knowing the one who hurt them was out there on the street, that they could easily see them walking by. For the sake of all those victims, and to prevent any future ones, I hoped they did come forward and band together to end the Draggos reign of terror, once and for all.

Roland led us down the hallway to Devon's hospital room. My heart pounded in my chest and I was fairly certain it was trying to escape. Either through my chest or up my throat. Despite knowing that Devon would be okay and nothing permanent was wrong with him.

I still found my hands trembling and my body flooded with fear. My mind was filled with endless "what if" possibilities. The most prominent, what if he took a turn for the worse and when we walked through those doors he wasn't there?

Could I handle losing someone that I loved?

I didn't even want to think about it, but my mind wouldn't stop going over the possibility that I could lose him before we had a chance at having something real. I wasn't kidding myself, either. I knew he was at the bus depot when he got attacked. He was leaving. Leaving me. But I refused to believe it was because he didn't care. The way he looked at me told me he cared. The sweet tender touches and moments that we shared told me he cared. Him leaving was not because he didn't care for me and I suspected it had a lot more to do with fear than the prospect of better work.

We had a lot we would need to talk about and, hopefully, I would be able to get him to see that he didn't need to leave. That he could stay here and have a life with me, with our family. He wasn't alone anymore, and I knew it was going to take him some time to get used to that concept.

He had been struggling on his own since his brother died. First, it was with his father, and then on the streets. He didn't have to be strong and brave all the time. He could let himself feel and be vulnerable without the fear of being hurt, being hit. He had a lot of trauma he had to work through, but I was more than willing to work through it with him. He wasn't alone anymore and he needed to realize that.

"This is it. You ready?" Roland asked,

keeping his gaze on me.

Letting out a slow, deep breath, I gave a nod.

Roland opened the door.

Walking into the room, my gaze immediately went to the bed, to Devon. He was awake, but he looked tired, as if he didn't get much sleep since Roland left. I could see the telltale signs of pain in his eyes and the crease on his forehead. Roland had warned us that he was covered in bruises, but hearing it and seeing it were two very different things. Seeing the state he was in, it instantly had tears building up in my eyes. The reality that I could have lost him last night was too fresh, too painful to even put into words.

"What are you doing here?" Devon's voice broke me out of my trance and I forced my body to move to the side of the bed.

"I'll give you guys some time," Roland said, before he purposefully strode out, closing the door behind him.

Zane and Jimmy moved around to the right side of Devon, but stayed back a bit, giving us some time.

"What are *we* doing here? You're in a hospital after getting attacked by six guys. Where else would we be?" I countered.

I wasn't expecting for him to be all open arms with us being here. He was in pain and I knew better than anyone when you weren't feeling great you just wanted to curl up and be alone. But the slight confusion and defensive tone to his voice had kind of pissed me off. It bothered me that he thought we wouldn't be here, that we wouldn't want to see him after what happened. Yes, we had only known each other less than a month, but that didn't change how I felt about him. It didn't change that we all lived together for three weeks. It didn't change that we were good people and would be worried about him, especially in his current state.

"Anywhere else. We've only known each other for three weeks, Daryl. It's not like I'm anyone important."

I could hear the sadness in his tone, even though he had tried to hide it. He wanted to be someone important to me. What he failed to realize was that he already was someone important. No, three weeks wasn't much time, especially in the grand scheme of things, but that didn't change how I felt.

It didn't change that I had been falling for him almost from the moment he took my hand in the park. I was in love with him and I wasn't going to over-analyze that. Most would. Most would think it was impossible to love someone after such a short amount of time, but I wasn't most people. My brain and heart were wired differently and I could feel a deep love for someone if we made a strong connection.

Devon and I had made a strong connection. We made it that night we met and spent time together. You want to talk about love at first sight, this was it for me and I was not about to lose him now.

"Time is only a number. It doesn't matter if it has been three days or three years. When you feel a true connection with someone, time holds no meaning. Yes, it's only been three weeks since you walked into my life, *our* lives, but it's been the best three weeks of my entire life."

"You're a part of the family now, Devon. I know you aren't used to having one, but you're just going to have to start getting used to it, because we aren't going anywhere," Jimmy added.

"It was hard at first for me, too. I was used to being on my own and not relying on anyone. But then Jimmy took a chance on me and it was the best thing to ever happen to me. I couldn't imagine ever going back to how I used to be. To being alone. You became a member of this family when Daryl brought you home that first night. Family, true family, doesn't give up on each other. No matter the struggles that one of us is going through. We're always there for each other, no matter what," Zane said with strength to his voice.

I couldn't have been more proud of Zane. He had worked hard to get used to opening up to people. To us. Jimmy had been his saving grace and I was so very thankful that he had been there for my brother when he needed him the most.

I snapped my gaze back over to Devon and I could see the emotions playing out in his eyes. This was all new to him and he wasn't handling it very well. He was clearly overwhelmed by the sheer emotions coming from all three of us. He obviously expected to remain alone in this world. He expected us to forget about him and move on with our lives. But I couldn't do that. None of us could. Whether he was here in town or not, we would all worry about where he was and if he was okay. He was so used to people hurting him, letting him down, not wanting him, that the concept of love and a family was completely foreign to him.

No more.

He deserved to know what love felt like.

He deserved to know what comfort and stability felt like.

I moved and sat down on the edge of the bed, being careful not to get too close and potentially cause him harm. "I know you went to that bus depot and I know you were planning on going to Baltimore. But I also know you care about me and I am willing to bet that scares you. That maybe you don't feel like you deserve to be with someone, or deserve to be cared for."

"You deserve better. You deserve better than me," he cut me off with a soft voice.

The fact that he thought he wasn't good enough for me was a load of crap. I didn't care that he'd been homeless. I didn't care if he was a dishwasher. I didn't care about any of it. All I cared about was how he made me feel. I cared about how he treated me and made me feel special and wanted. He was a kind, gentle, and sweet man.

Despite everything he had gone through, he still cared about people, still wanted to protect them and be a good man. He had every reason to throw in the towel and just give up, but he didn't. He continued to fight every day to keep people safe, to have a better life. He was a good man and I was lucky to have him in my life.

"That's bullshit. If you were going to leave because you didn't care about me, then I would have to accept that. But you don't get to decide what is best for me. You don't get to decide who is worthy and who isn't. I love you, and I don't care how crazy that sounds. I don't care that it's only been three weeks. I love you, Devon. It's my choice if I think you are worthy, and you are more than worthy of my love. You don't get to run away and take that choice from me. I know you care for me and I know you probably don't feel the same as I do, but—"

"Shut up," Devon snapped, and I could see the heat in his eyes, the fire. "You are a smart, beautiful, creative, kind, gentle, caring, and confident man. There isn't anything about you that I don't love. I love you, Daryl, and all I want is to be with you. If you'll still have me."

If I'll still have him?

Is he serious?

Of course I'd still have him. He's all I'd wanted. He's who I had been waiting for, and I couldn't imagine not having him in my life. Hearing that he loved me flooded my body with a warmth that I never wanted to get rid of.

I had dreamed of this moment. Of where we would finally say *I love you* to each other. I had pictured us out having a romantic dinner or watching the sunset at the park. I had never envisioned it would be in the hospital with Devon lying battered on the bed.

But it couldn't have been more perfect. The setting of which we said those three words didn't really matter. All that mattered was that we did finally say them to each other. We finally admitted it.

He loved me.

Just the thought brought a huge smile to my face.

"I love you, you idiot. Of course I want you."

Devon reached up with his left hand and wrapped it around the back of my neck and gently pulled me down. I was very careful to not put any weight against his chest as I gently pressed my lips to his. I made sure it stayed light, though, because he was injured and I didn't want to cause him any added pain. After a moment, we were forced to pull back when Jimmy's voice broke out into the quiet room.

"All right, you two. We don't need any alarms going off from lack of oxygen," he quipped.

I couldn't help the small chuckle at the images that brought forth. I could only picture how panicked the nurses would have been.

"We'll go grab some coffee and give you two a few minutes. Nothing crazy, though. We need him out of the hospital, not staying longer," Zane advised with a pointed look in my direction.

"What? I'll behave," I promised.

"Whatever you say, Squirt," Zane said with a playful wink before they both turned and left the room.

I shook my head and turned my attention back over to Devon, who was looking even more exhausted than when we came in.

"You sure you want more of them in your life?" I teased.

"I'm sure I want more of *you* in it," he responded with a smile that only caused my heart to flutter. "Come here, lay down with me."

"I don't want to hurt you," I said. I would have loved to lay down with him and provide him some comfort. But I also knew that broken ribs were no joke.

"You won't. My broken ribs are on my right side. Lay down with me."

I couldn't deny him that request, especially with knowing his ribs on his left were perfectly fine.

I kicked my shoes off before I got up and crawled under the covers. I made sure that none of my weight was on his chest, instead tucking myself into his left side.

Devon put his left arm around me and left his right on his stomach. I suspected it was the only comfortable position he could put his arm in. He placed a kiss on the top of my head as I spoke.

"You need sleep. I'll be here when you wake up, baby."

"I love you, Sweetheart."

"I love you, too."

I had no idea what the future would hold for the both of us after today. What I did know, though, was that I was really looking forward to experiencing it with the man that I loved.

CHAPTER TWELVE

Devon

Two Months Later

"YOU GOT EVERYTHING you need, Sweetheart?" I asked as I walked back into the bedroom I had been sharing with Daryl.

The past two months had been amazing and hard at the same time. Amazing, because I got to spend it with the man that I loved. Hard, because of my injuries that had just recently healed up. My ribs were still a bit tender if I turned the wrong way or if enough pressure was put on them. The doctor had said it was normal as they were just freshly healed. I still had some bruising on my ribs that was now an ugly yellow color.

Both Daryl and Zane had been terrific with me. Zane made sure I still able to work at the diner once I was healed up enough. Daryl had been overly cautious with me at first, terrified of hurting me further. It took a good week before I could finally get him to sleep in the bed with me again. It even took me until last week to convince him I was fine to have sex. Even then, he insisted on being on top, which was more than fine with me.

I never thought I would have this. A home with not only a man that I was madly in love with, but also brothers. Zane and Jimmy had taken me in when they didn't have to. They brought me into their family and welcomed me with open arms and no hesitation. I loved them both for that. I had finally found a family and I had zero interest in letting any of them go.

Hell, even Roland had become a member of my family, something I never would have expected. He was there every day I was in the hospital, always sneaking in food for me. It was the first time I had seen him outside of one of the soup kitchens and it turned out he was pretty amazing. He reminded me so much of Jay. Especially the fact that he had been in the Army for three years before he joined the police academy.

It was Roland who had shown me that my dream of helping people wasn't over. I couldn't be in the military without a spleen, but that didn't mean I couldn't help and protect the innocent people in this world. It was because of him that I applied to the Police Academy and had been accepted. I was set to start next month and I couldn't have been more excited. I was going to have a real future, a real career. I would be able to protect people, help those in town that were forgotten.

There was only one person I was missing. Tyler. I hadn't seen him since that night at the soup kitchen and I couldn't help but worry about him. I had been trying to find him so he could take over my job as a dishwasher. I knew he would be willing to do it, but I hadn't been able to find him. That didn't mean I would stop looking, though. I was going to find him again and I was going to make sure he was safe.

"I think so. If there's something I've forgotten then I can pick it up when I come back on the weekend," Daryl said, before he turned to me and I easily pulled him in for a hug. "This weekend only thing is going to suck."

"I know, but it's easier than you driving back and forth from Baltimore every day. That's too much strain on you, not to mention the gas money we'd need," I said flashing him a warm smile.

Daryl to let out a chuckle. "Might have to take out a loan with the gas prices right now. It's still going to suck and take a while to get used to."

"I know, Sweetheart, but we can video chat with each other every night and we'll see each other on weekends and holidays. A bit of space might not be so bad. Our relationship kind of went from zero to a hundred in no time flat."

Everything had gone very fast. I wasn't complaining, but I was worried that because we moved so fast and our emotions developed as quickly as they did, we would burn out. A flame could only burn so hot for so long and I didn't want us to lose what we had.

It was one of the reasons why I had agreed that it would be better for Daryl to stay on campus during the week. It would let us not only miss each other, but grow as individuals. Plus, I wanted him to have the fun experience of going to University. I wanted him to enjoy dorm parties and not having to worry about driving back home. This was an experience that I wanted him to have completely and not just part way.

It would be hard. There were going to be a lot of lonely nights and there would be arguments that happened in long-distance relationships, even if they were only

Monday to Friday. It would challenge us, but I knew we were up for it and it would make us stronger in the end.

"I know and I agree it's important for us to grow as individuals as well as a couple. It's just going to be hard for the first couple of weeks. But I will have Jimmy there with me so if I am feeling homesick I can always go over to his place," Daryl said, flashing me a grin before he leaned up and pressed his warm lips to mine.

The feel of his lips against mine was something I was going to miss. Not being able to kiss him or touch him whenever I wanted to was going to be a hard reality. I was fully prepared to go through withdrawals, like a heroin addict.

All too soon, Daryl pulled back and I knew he needed to head out. He was driving up with Jimmy and if they didn't leave soon they would hit the heavy traffic. The drive would be hard enough, they didn't need to be stuck in a traffic jam as well.

I picked up his last bag before we made our way out of the apartment and down to the awaiting car. Daryl went over to give Zane a hug as I put his bag into the trunk and closed it.

"I'll keep an eye on him," Jimmy said with a wink, and it had me opening my arms to the very sweet man.

Jimmy easily welcomed the hug and I knew he would keep Daryl safe and sane while he adjusted to being in Baltimore and in school. I wasn't worried, though. Daryl would make friends in minutes and he was so talented with creating video games. He was going to take that school by storm and he would become a famous video game designer one day. I couldn't have been more proud of him. Pulling back, we both made our way over to our respective man.

"This isn't goodbye, it's an I'll see you later. Remember that," I said as I wrapped my arms around Daryl's hips.

"I know. Still sucks, but I know. I left you a little surprise on your laptop for later on tonight. Just make sure you watch it alone and with headphones," Daryl said with a playful smirk. I couldn't help but groan at what could be awaiting me.

My need to feel his lips against my own one last time was too great. I needed to taste him once more before I had to go all week without him. Daryl melted at my touch and I had to remind myself that we were in the middle of the street with his big brother right there. If we had been in our room, he would already be naked and underneath me.

I forced every ounce of love that I had into the kiss. Focusing my mind on memorizing the smallest details of his lips and the way they felt against my own. It might only be a week, but to me it was going to feel like an eternity before I could kiss him again. If I had to wait that long, I was going to make sure it was a kiss that the both of us would not soon forget.

"I remember when you used to try and kiss my very soul out of me."

Jimmy's voice broke the spell between us. Both of us sent Zane and Jimmy a well deserved glare for their rude interruption. It only caused them both to laugh.

"Relax, it gets easier," Zane offered, but it was of little comfort to me at that moment.

"Come on, we need get on the road if we are going to stand a chance at eating dinner tonight," Jimmy said, giving Zane one last quick peck on the lips before heading for the car.

With a final squeeze, I had no choice but to allow Daryl to join Jimmy. Zane moved over to stand beside me and placed a comforting hand on my shoulder. It was nice, but it wasn't his touch I craved. Together, we stood there, smiling and waving goodbye as the men we loved drove off.

"It really does get easier and it will make the time that you do get to share together more special," Zane offered.

He was right. I knew he was, but that didn't make this hurt any less. Two months ago, I was fully prepared to leave all of this behind. Leave Daryl behind. I was dead set on putting it all in my rearview mirror. I never expected to be the one slowly disappearing in his rearview. At least I could be thankful that he was only going to school and we hadn't broken up.

Looking back now, I could completely say that getting on that bus would have been the worst decision of my life. In a way, I was glad that Luis and his thugs had jumped me. I would gladly go through all of that pain a million times over if it meant I would have not only Daryl in my life, but the lovely family that I have now as well. I had gone from the homeless man that had nobody, to the man who had not only a home and a family, but a bright future with the world's most amazing man.

For quite possibly the first time in my life, I could honestly say I was excited for what the future had in store for me. I just knew it was going to be a bright one with Daryl by my side.

Thank you for reading.

Turn the page for Jaded, From The Edge, Book Three.

JADED

BY EVIE RILEY

FROM THE EDGE SERIES

BOOK THREE

JADED
FROM THE EDGE
BOOK THREE

COPYRIGHT © 2022
EVIE RILEY
ISBN: 978-1-77357-382-3
978-1-77357-383-0
PUBLISHED BY NAUGHTY NIGHTS PRESS LLC
COVER ART BY WILLSIN ROWE

JADED

Friends to lovers...

Detective Roland Wright lives a lonely and solitary life, filling his waking hours with work and volunteering. It's been ten years since he lost the love of his life to a drunk driver, but he's still plagued by nightmares.

When a young man shows up at the soup kitchen where he volunteers, Roland tries to convince himself the attraction he feels is purely platonic. At least the handsome stranger is older than he looks, but can Roland risk getting close when his new friend isn't even gay?

Tyler Foster has lived on the streets since he aged out of the system. When a helpful police officer from the soup kitchen gets him a job, and a real place to live, Tyler feels like life is finally giving him the break he's prayed for.

Still a virgin, Tyler is confused when he feels an attraction to the larger man. Roland is unlike anyone he's ever met and he makes Tyler feel things he doesn't understand.

When he confides in Roland about his past, the truth hits closer to home than either man could have imagined. With Roland beside him, Tyler is willing to do anything to help build the case. Together, they are determined not to let any more children suffer the same fate.

Will Roland and Tyler escape the past and find a future together?

CHAPTER ONE

Roland

"YOU KNEW WHAT you signed up for!" The strength of my voice made the words echo off of our kitchen walls.

"I didn't sign up for this! I didn't sign up for a military life!"

"You knew I was in the military when we met, Shane. This isn't some new thing. I told you I wanted to be a Ranger and in order for that to happen I have to move to Georgia. Why can't you be supportive?"

"Supportive? Supportive of you going out on dangerous missions. Supportive of you getting injured or killed? How the hell am I supposed to be supportive of that? I've entertained you being in the military and humored you, because I thought it was a phase. I thought you would come to your senses and see that a life behind a desk was better for us. How the hell are we supposed to get married and have a real life together if you can't even admit that you're gay?"

"It's not that simple. You know that I can't just come out to the guys. If they have a problem with it, they might not have my back in the field. You said you didn't care. That it didn't bother you."

"And you actually thought I would be happy to live a life hidden in the shadows forever? That I would be happy to hear the man who supposedly loves me talking about whatever imaginary girl he banged just so the guys will feel more comfortable? You promised me marriage, you promised me kids, and now you have taken all of that

away. I won't be your dirty secret!"

"You're not, but you can't keep pressuring me like this. It's my life and I'll live it how I see fit!"

"Then it's a life you'll be living without me. I'm not going to be kept hidden away, and I'm not going to be left here while you are out there, never knowing if you're coming home to me." Shane grabbed his car keys and stormed toward the door.

"Fine, if that's how you feel I don't need you. You can get the hell out of my life!"

The house shook as the front door slammed shut.

My breath caught in my throat as I shot up in bed. My body was damp from the sweat that covered it and I could feel the tremble that threatened to overtake my whole body. This was not my first nightmare. Hell, this wasn't even the thousandth. They often plagued me and I was never lucky enough to wake up not remembering them. If it wasn't my time overseas from the war that I fought for three years, it was of my own personal hell. The night that changed everything in my life. The night I lost the most amazing man. A man that could very well have been my soulmate.

And it was all my fault.

My own stupidity that drove him away that night.

When you are twenty-one everything in life seems so simple. I was so stupid back then, so naive to believe that I could have a military life and be gay without it ever affecting my job or my home life. I thought the best solution was to hide it, like it was some disease that I needed to keep secret.

Stupid.

So unbelievably stupid.

A quick look at the clock showed me it was just after four in the morning and I knew I wouldn't be able to get back to sleep. Letting out a sigh, I forced my sore and tired body to move. After eleven years, I had become used to functioning off little to no sleep. Being in the army for three years had started the normalcy of little sleep between boot camp, training, and missions. Then my time as a New York cop solidified it. When you work as a homicide detective in a big city like New York, you get used to getting called out of bed at any hour of the evening and working two or three days straight with only bad station house coffee to keep you going.

Making my way into the bathroom, I did my best to avoid the mirror. I knew what would be looking back at me. A man with red, tired eyes that carried a haunted look in them. For the most part, I could cover up my pain, push through it and wear a mask during the day. People in this small town didn't know anything personal about me and that was how I wanted it to be.

I had only been there for four years, when the toll of being a homicide detective became too much. I was handling it just fine, but then the Michelle Wilson case came my way and I realized that I couldn't do it anymore.

Michelle Wilson was a beautiful four year old little girl who had been found dead in a dumpster four years ago. It wasn't just because of her age, it was because she had been raped and tortured thirty-six hours before her death.

She was never reported missing.

The investigation took me three weeks to solve. Three weeks of having to re-read the Coroner's report. Three weeks of having to see the photos of the brutal acts done to her. Three weeks of interviewing her parents who were completely devastated.

Three weeks for me to discover that her so-called devastated parents were actually her kidnappers.

Michelle Wilson's prints and DNA finally came back from the lab and they matched a missing two year old girl named Rebecca Watts. She had been kidnapped one night while the parents were away at dinner. She had been left with a babysitter who was killed trying to protect her. Rebecca Watts was one of thirty-six children that had been kidnapped for a child sex trafficking ring. Her death had broken the case wide open and with the help of the Feds, we were able to shut it down.

The case itself wasn't necessarily the part that broke me. It was afterward, when the whole precinct was celebrating the win. To them it was a win, but to me it was a great loss.

Because we had failed Rebbeca.

We had failed her parents and now they would forever be haunted by her death and what she had experienced in the last two years of her life. We had saved only ten out of the thirty-six that we knew to be out there. The other twenty-six were already sold and gone. We had lost them.

There was no win.

There was nothing to celebrate.

It was in that moment that I realized I couldn't do it anymore. So, when I saw the posting for a new detective here, I immediately applied, and given my experience in a large city, I was hired on the spot.

Now, three years later, I was trying to do what I could to keep this small town safe. There weren't really murders that happened here, but there were crimes, nonetheless.

There were three gangs that ran the criminal enterprises in town, two of which were small-time and nothing to worry about too much.

Drugs were in every town and we did our best to make sure we didn't have any labs cooking them. The Draggos were the ones that caused the most violence and harm in the town. We had been working on trying to get them shut down, but with no victims willing to come forward, it had put a serious delay in the process.

At least, until six of their top guys made the mistake in attacking Devon St. James at the bus depot two months back. The whole thing was caught on video surveillance and even if it hadn't been, I knew Devon would have testified against them.

He had been homeless since he was seventeen, but the man always made sure to help people and keep the streets safe. The whole reason the Draggos had targeted him was because he attacked their leader as he was trying to rape a young girl in an alley close to eight months ago. For the past two months, we had finally been able to start taking down the Draggos, and soon enough, we would have them all locked up.

After relieving myself, I headed back into my bedroom to change my sweat-soaked pants, something that was almost a daily task. I changed into some clean, dry sweat pants and a hoodie before I threw on my running shoes and hit the pavement.

Running had never been something I was interested in, until my boot camp days. I had discovered that it was a great way for me to get my spinning thoughts in order. Whenever I felt like I needed a moment to breathe, I would go for a run and it helped me to feel better. It helped to calm my racing mind and allow me to think clearly.

I wished I had just gone for a run that night with Shane.

Maybe everything would have turned out differently if I had.

Forcing that painful thought aside, I coaxed my mind to think about things that I could control.

Like Tyler.

He was relatively new to one of the soup kitchens that I volunteer at. That same soup kitchen was where I met Devon for the first time, and now he had become a member of my family.

Tyler was different compared to the other homeless people I'd interacted with. To begin with, he was young. If I had to guess, he was fifteen at most. He should have been in a home and not sleeping on the streets.

I had often tried to talk with him, but he was very shy. He never looked me in the eye and whenever I was around he seemed to shrink into himself.

I was used to that reaction, though, just because of my size. I did workout. I had always been a gym guy. Even when I was sixteen I would often work out whenever I got the chance. I still do it a few days a week to keep my body in good shape. The result, though, is that I was very buff and with that, intimidation always followed. Between being in the army and in the police force, my love for working out only deepened. It came in handy when I needed to intimidate a suspect, but it also meant it took victims a few minutes to get comfortable with me.

Living in a smaller town like this, I didn't have to worry too much about the victims. Everyone knew everyone, essentially, and people here all knew that despite my size I was like a teddy bear. If I could protect you, then I would. I would lay down my life for anyone in this town.

I was worried about Tyler, though, and I suspected there had been abuse in his life just by the way he reacted to me. He was afraid of me and I could tell. Anyone that saw us together could tell. I hated that he was afraid of me. I would never hurt him, but it was going to take time before he understood that. Before he truly one hundred percent believed that he was safe around me. It was going to take time, but I was never afraid of hard work.

My worry for Tyler had increased some over the past two months, though. I hadn't seen him at the soup kitchen and neither had Devon. I knew he had a car. How he was driving it without a license, I didn't know, but he could have easily driven off to another town.

I was hoping he hadn't left town. I would have loved to help him try and get back on his feet. Try and find a safe place for him to live. We didn't have many foster homes, but we did have some. It was why I reached out to my friend, Isaiah, in Child Protective Services. I need to know more of his story, but I also needed to know what foster home he was in hiding from so he could be put into a safe one.

What most people didn't understand about the homeless community here in town, was that they weren't all alcoholics or drug addicts. The majority of them had some type of mental illness that had been either undiagnosed, or untreated. Some were even runaways, like Devon, who had to escape an abusive situation and just could never get back on their feet.

Thankfully, Devon had managed to get back on his feet with the help of Daryl and his older brother, Zane. Devon was now going to be in the Police Academy, and I knew he was going to make one hell of a cop. I was looking forward to working with him and mentoring him.

Devon was safe and now it was time to make sure Tyler was. He was one of the few that I could help and I was not about to let him slip through my fingers.

CHAPTER TWO

Roland

"ALL RIGHT, I'VE gotten the bulk of the dishes cleaned up, Martha," I said as I dried my hands off.

It was just after seven and the mass of the dinner rush had finished. I had volunteered at St. Marks Soup Kitchen for close to three years now. I often volunteered my time for various charities in town. I wanted to make sure the community and the people in it knew that they could trust me.

That I was a friendly face whenever they needed it.

I knew that people in a small town didn't hate the police as much as they seemed to in a major city like New York, but I wasn't going to kid myself into believing that everyone loved the police in town, either. Small town or not, that didn't mean people weren't judgmental or corrupt.

In fact, I often found from my dealings with other local law enforcement agencies around New York City, that those small towns had all sorts of corruption within them. To some, it might not make much sense, but to me it did.

Who better to be corrupt than the mayor of a small town?

It wasn't like anyone would notice or suspect anything.

After all, what small town had corruption in it?

It was that novice assumption that made it possible for bad people to hurt a lot of innocent people, even if it was their pocketbook they were targeting.

"Thank you, Roland. You are so much help around here. I honestly don't know what I would do without you." Martha placed a kiss on my cheek and it warmed my heart.

Martha was the sweetest seventy-two year old you could ever meet. She was also the most fierce seventy-two year old I had ever met. She wasn't your typical grandmother. She ran ten miles three times a week, and she kept a bat next to her bed in case anyone was stupid enough to break into her house.

If you walked into her house, you would think you walked into a time warp. It was the perfect cookie cutter home from back in the fifties, right down to the ugly brown shag carpet. She kept it pristine and there was even plastic on the furniture.

She was one of a kind and she ran the show here. There were only two soup kitchens in town, there should have been more, but the officials believed two was more than enough, just like one shelter was more than enough. It wasn't enough, nowhere near it, but there was no money to be made helping the homeless. It was a sad fact, but it was a fact, nonetheless. The town was trying to grow.

I had been getting crap from my Captain about trying to get better control on the homeless community. Trying to get them pushed back into the shadows for when the developers come into town. Mayor Jenson was trying to win his reelection and apparently the way he was going about it was to make sure the town grew.

I wasn't against growth, but small towns survived off the mom and pop businesses that make up the town. They survived because of tourists wanting to come and see the quaint town. I wasn't sure how well it would go over to have large construction sites all over town, but it was something we would all have to deal with soon enough.

"Why don't you head home and I'll handle the closing tonight. I can see that your hip has been bothering you tonight."

"That's very sweet of you, but I can't

leave you here all alone to handle closing."

"It's not very busy tonight, there's only a few people hanging around. Go home, put your feet up, and watch your soap," I said, flashing her a warm smile.

She would cave.

I knew she would.

She loved her soap operas and she made sure to record them every day. I had even shown her how to use the DVR that she had gotten from her kids for Christmas. Once she knew how to use it, there was no stopping her. She was a recording queen with over two hundred hours of recordings to go through.

"Oh, all right. If you're sure."

"I am. Go on and get out of here," I said, flashing her a big smile.

She gave me a grin in return and then she headed off to grab her coat and purse.

I made my way back out to the front and started to put together the last few plates that I could store in the fridge for tomorrow. Normally around eight, the place got quiet and I would close up. The sole shelter in town tended to fill up quickly, so everyone who needed a place to stay the night would flock there in the hope of getting a bed.

It could be very busy here when there was a storm. Once the shelters filled up, anyone who didn't get a bed would seek sanctuary here for as long as they could. When I had been left to close up on those nights, I would try and hold off for as long as possible, especially if the weather was horrible. I hated knowing that I would have to kick people out who had nowhere to go, nowhere safe to be. I had been trying to fight with the town council about getting more shelters built so the homeless would have a safe place to be at night, but so far there was no budging them.

At the sound of footsteps, I turned to face whoever had approached the serving station. To my surprise, it was Tyler. I had been trying to find him for two months and when I finally saw him again, he had found me.

He also found me while he sported a nasty black eye. Seeing it sent a wave of anger throughout my body. He was just a kid. He didn't deserve to be hit.

"Who the fuck hit you?"

CHAPTER THREE

Tyler

MY HEAD WAS killing me. Over the twenty-two years of my life, I had lost count of how many times I had been punched. Of how many black eyes I'd had. My newest black eye was nothing new to me, but that didn't change the fact that it hurt like a bitch.

For the past two months, I had been working for cash at a construction site. I had been working as a laborer. The grunt, essentially. For the past two months, I had been doing back breaking work, lifting fifty to a hundred pound bags and wood loads and carrying them up multiple flights of stairs and across the job site. It was very painful and even after two months my entire body was still sore and ached from it.

I was confident in myself enough to admit that I was not a big guy. I was five foot eight and only a hundred and twenty pounds. It wasn't by choice. It was just hard to get enough food to eat. I worked as many odd jobs as I could so I could afford a meal a day, and some days, I would break down and get a second meal. When I didn't have a job and the money ran out, I would try and hold off as long as I could before I would go to the soup kitchen to grab something.

It wasn't that I thought a soup kitchen was beneath me. It was the harsh reality slap to the face that I was, indeed, homeless. It was easier for me to pretend that I wasn't as bad off as everyone else. I had a car that I could sleep in, after all, and up until the last five months, I could still drive it around and do deliveries. I had to stop, though, when it started to act up, and with no money to spend to fix it, it was better to baby it. Now, I just used it to sleep in and I'd only move it to get closer to where my current job was.

I grew up in the foster care system. I was a foster care baby. My parents were both foster siblings and my mother got pregnant when she was fourteen. They didn't want me, and their foster parents at the time didn't want them, or a baby, so all three of us got put into different homes.

I didn't know where they were, but I ended up bouncing from one home to the next for my entire childhood. Typically, infants and toddlers had a higher chance of being adopted, but no one wanted me. I was the kid who had "problems". Those problems were asthma and a learning disability. I just wasn't healthy enough for prospective adoptive parents to take a chance. The result of being born at thirty weeks, which probably accounted for a good part of my weight issue, too.

Eighteen years in the system and thirty foster homes. They were each different in their own way, mostly how many kids were there and the rules. But one thing they all did share in common was there were no birthdays, no holidays of any kind, no affection, no I love yous, and they never paid for anything that they didn't have to.

It was a harsh life, one that made me grow up to not rely on or trust anyone. When I wasn't being ignored, I was being beaten. I got very good at lying to my teachers whenever they asked about a new bruise.

I had learned from watching other kids what happens when you snitch. I had been abused my whole life, mentally, emotionally, and physically. I guess I could count myself lucky that I had never been violated like some of the other kids. Small miracle, in and of itself.

The worst home, though, was when I was twelve. I stayed there until I was fourteen. It was me and eight other kids, and we all slept in one room on old foam mattresses on the floor. Our foster parents were Dana and Jasper Monroe.

To the public, they were good people, valuable members of society. Jasper was a cop, now a detective, and everyone thought they were saviors. They had saved all these poor unwanted children. Behind closed doors, though, they starved us, beat us, and then used us to cook, weigh, and distribute the cocaine that they were making in the basement.

Every Sunday, we would all pile into a cargo minivan and travel to other smaller towns around ours and distribute the drugs to the town's dealers. Whenever one of us started to get too sick from inhaling the fumes we were surrounded by for almost twenty hours a day, they would just ship us off to the next home.

The worse part is, I still see Jasper wearing his badge, walking around town like he's this great person. People have no idea what he'd done and still does to the children he and Dana took in.

Yesterday's adventure was a shit show. I

got to work like normal and everything was fine. Then, at the end of the day, my boss, Armondo, came up to me with five other huge dudes and started screaming at me about stealing tools. Apparently, in the last few days there had been tools that had gone missing.

According to my boss—ex-boss—I was the only one it could be. I was the homeless guy, so I must have stolen them to get money for alcohol or drugs. It didn't matter that I was the one with the most to lose. I was only making fifty bucks a day, but that was two hundred and fifty a week, a lot more than I would normally be making doing other jobs. The job sucked, but at least the pay was decent, to me anyway. I would never jeopardize it by stealing tools.

Armondo hadn't agreed with me and proceeded to give me a black eye while his workers held me down and grabbed all of my cash in my wallet that I had saved up.

Now, I was back to being homeless and had moved my car to a parking lot where it wouldn't be towed or destroyed. I hadn't eaten in two days, so I walked my sad self to St. Marks soup kitchen for a hot meal. It was later at night, though, and I wasn't too sure if there would even be a plate left.

I had debated on going there or not. I didn't like being there. I didn't like the stereotyping and assumptions that were placed on people in there. But I was starving and I knew I needed to eat something. My painful, growling stomach and the lack of food shakes really made the decision for me, in the end.

Walking in, I immediately spied Roland behind the serving counter. This weird feeling flooded my body at the mere sight of him. I didn't know what it was about him, but it happened every time I saw him. What the feeling was, I had no idea, I couldn't put a name to it to identify what exactly it was that I felt, but it happened every time I went anywhere near him. It disturbed me, in a way, annoyed me, really, that anyone could make this rush of heat, fear, whatever it was, happen in such a way.

Roland was a very big man. He had

muscles for days. I knew he was a cop, a detective, and would often work out. That's all I really knew about him, outside of him being gay. I had overheard him and Devon talking about it one day a few months back.

Gay people didn't bother me. I liked Devon he was a good guy. Normally, muscular men bothered me, made me feel uncomfortable, but for some reason with Devon, it never did. He was the only man who didn't make me feel intimidated by his size. Whenever I didn't want to be alone at night, he would sleep in the car with me. Nothing ever happened between us, I wasn't gay, but it was as close to safe as I had ever felt and probably ever would feel.

I hadn't seen Devon since the last bad storm a few months back. I hadn't been by in two months, though. Too busy with working. Part of me felt torn between hoping to see him here and hoping I didn't. If he wasn't here, that meant he might have found work and didn't need to be here. That would be good for him. He was a good man and didn't deserve a life on the streets.

Not seeing anyone else volunteering there, I made my way over to the serving station where Roland was.

He was looking down as I approached and I was happy to have a few more moments to myself before I would have to talk with him. He was going to see my black eye. It wasn't like I could cover it up from people. With him being a detective, he tended to get nosy. He wanted to make sure everyone was okay, but I still couldn't figure out if it was an act or not.

After all, Jasper Monroe was his partner.

Devon seemed to think I could trust Roland, but I don't trust anyone, not even for a second. Once you trust someone, they have complete power over you, and in my experience, that kind of power was not something you ever wanted to give to someone.

"Who the fuck hit you?"

The deadly rage in his voice instantly set me on edge. For some reason, I didn't expect for him to ever sound like that, to ever get mad. He had always come across as an easygoing guy. To hear that level of fury, to know that it was in him, had the little boy in me curling up into a ball. I don't do yelling and I don't do conflict. Too many years of abuse programmed into my body.

I instantly looked down, shied away, and stumbled around to find the right words. Words I knew I would never be able to get right.

"Nothing... It's nothing. Just a... a door. Is there... ah, a plate left?"

I hated that I sounded like some young kid who got caught with their hand in the cookie jar, but I couldn't help it. Hopefully, he would just move on and let it go. I doubted it, but one could hope.

The deep sigh that escaped his lips told me exactly how unhappy with my answer he was. I knew it was a lame excuse, but I also knew I didn't owe him any explanation.

"Yeah, we got a plate."

He headed off to grab it and I didn't even bother trying to contain the sigh of relief that escaped my body. Thankfully, he was letting this go and wasn't in the mood to push. I couldn't understand why he would be so angry, though. I was just some homeless guy. I wasn't anyone special. Certainly not someone he needed to have that level of ire over. It made no sense, but I was far too tired and hungry to try and figure out why.

He walked back with a plate and handed it to me with a warm smile. I gave him a half-smile in return and mumbled my thanks before I headed off. I did not want to get caught in a conversation with him. I just wanted to eat and then head out.

Making my way over to a table that was empty, I sat down and started to eat. The food here wasn't too bad. I knew the one lady, Martha, cooked a great deal of it.

She was a very sweet old lady that was one hell of a cook. She would often chat about her life, her grandchildren, and some of the hoodlums that thought they could scam her. She was the definition of a badass grandmother and it was going to be a sad and dark day when she left this world.

My mouth watering and prompted by yet another growly pang from my belly, I immediately dug into the food. It was some type of meatloaf. I didn't really care what it was, though. It was warm and tasted good.

As I shoveled in the meatloaf, mashed potatoes, and peas, I could feel eyes on me. I could feel *his* eyes on me. I didn't know what it was about me, but he always watched me when I was there.

At first, I thought maybe he just found me attractive, but then there didn't seem to be any fire in his eyes when he looked at me. Nothing that would lead me to believe he found me attractive. If he wasn't attracted to me, I really didn't know what his fascination was.

The only thing I could think of was that he thought I was younger than twenty-two. I did look young. I knew that. I looked sixteen, at best. I had zero ability to grow facial hair and I had a baby face. If I drank, I would be getting carded well into my forties. It could very well be that he thought I was underage, but so far he hadn't ever asked me about it or given any indication that he truly believed that. In the very few conversations we'd had, he'd never pried for any personal information, something I was grateful for.

That gratefulness died the moment Roland came over and sat down next to me.

I had just finished eating and was debating on if I should stick around to see if Devon would come by. The second his considerable weight hit the bench, my whole body tensed. He wasn't close enough for our bodies to touch, but he didn't leave much room for a personal bubble.

"That eye looks pretty bad. Is the pain okay? I got some over the counter stuff you could take."

I wasn't against pain medication, but I tried not to take it unless I didn't have a choice. Medications just made me feel weird, even something as simple as an Advil. They had a way of making my head a bit foggy and loopy, not something I wanted to be when I lived on the streets. Yes, my head hurt, my eye hurt, but it wasn't something I couldn't handle.

"I'm fine."

I needed him to walk away. I didn't want to be sitting next to him. I didn't want to be in the same room as him. I seriously needed to start going to the other soup kitchen. The food tended to be terrible and some of the people who went there were rougher, but at least I wouldn't have to worry about running into Roland.

Normally, I could adjust to another man's size at a decent rate. It wasn't always easy like it had been with Devon. Most of the time, it took a few weeks of being around a person for me to start to feel even remotely comfortable. Yet with Roland, I could not for the life of me get this weird feeling to go away. I didn't know what it was, but I didn't like it and I was starting to get sick of it.

"I saw Devon the other day. He's doing really well. He fell in love with a good guy, Daryl, and they have been living together. Devon was injured, but he made a full recovery and now he's going into the police academy."

It was good to hear that Devon was doing okay, that he wasn't dead and hadn't left without taking me with him. I was happy for him. He was a good man and deserved to be in love and find proper work. It wasn't all that surprising, either, that he was going into the police academy. I knew he always wanted to be in the military but his lack of a spleen kept him out of it. I didn't even think of the police academy for him. I figured with him having no spleen it would be an issue there, too.

Apparently not.

I was happy for him.

"That's good. I'm glad he got out. He deserves it."

"He's not the only one that does. Isn't there someone I could call for you? A family that you have out there that could help you out?"

"I don't need help."

And I didn't. I had been taking care of myself for practically my whole life. There was no one that I could call. Some could argue that I could reach out to Devon, but he got himself free from this life and I was not about to drag him down into this world again. He didn't need me to worry about. I could take care of myself. I would figure it out, eventually. I would figure out a way to get off the streets and have a small apartment to myself.

"Everyone needs help from time to time, Ty. There's no shame in that. I can help you. I can help you find a safe place to be. You could go back to school. Life isn't supposed to be this hard."

He kept his voice calm, but it did nothing to calm the tightness in my body. He definitely thought I was a minor. Even if I was, there was no way I was going back to school. Me and school didn't get along. I didn't even graduate.

Teachers always told me I must have some learning disability, but what it was, specifically, they didn't know. I didn't have any foster parents that were willing to pay for the diagnosis. I didn't go to school to learn. I went because it meant I didn't have to be surrounded by abuse. Going to school was the only time I was safe from being hit.

I wasn't popular in school. The exact opposite. People thought I was stupid. They thought I was weird. They didn't like that I was a foster kid or poor. There was always something about me that someone didn't like. But they never put their hands on me so it was better to listen to their words than to be at home nursing another bruise.

"It's getting late. I need to get back," I said, and stood.

I wasn't going to sit here any longer. Devon wasn't going to show, and that was good, because he would demand to know who hit me and be looking for payback. He was getting his life on track. He didn't need to deal with any drama coming from me. I didn't want to be alone in my car just yet, but it was better than feeling uncomfortable under Roland's glances.

"You got a safe place tonight?" Roland asked as he followed me toward the door.

This man never seemed to want to give up.

"Always." And with that, I was out the door and headed off down the street at a brisk trot to get to my car.

I couldn't figure out what Roland's deal was with me. I understood that he was a cop, but every other cop in town held no interest in helping any of the homeless. They were all too happy to arrest us and throw away the key.

So what was Roland's deal?

Why did he always look at me like that?

Why did he care what happened to me and if I had anyone or anywhere else to be?

Even if he believed I was underage, that shouldn't be enough for him to act this way. He had to want something from me. Everyone wants something from everyone. I just couldn't figure out what that could be, but I had a feeling my life could depend on figuring that out.

Arriving at my car, I was pleased to see that it was still there and wasn't damaged. After using the key to unlock the back, I crawled in and lay down. I had the back seat down flat so I had a bit more room.

Some people had asked me how a homeless guy could have a car, even a piece of shit like mine. When I aged out of the system, I got some money to help me get on my feet. It was supposed to be enough to get me through a month or two for rent until I was able to secure a job or if I was lucky enough go to College.

I had really looked forward to that money I'd been told I'd get. On the really rough nights, I would dream of having my own place where there was no yelling or violence. A place where I had full control.

Only, on my eighteenth birthday when I got the check, I discovered that the amount was far from what I expected. I hadn't expected a lot. I knew the system sucked and there were an endless number of flaws. But I had expected something like five thousand dollars, or twenty-five hundred. Something that would allow a person to pay first and last month's rent.

Instead, what I got was eighteen hundred dollars.

The system paid out one hundred dollars

for every year I was in foster care. A hundred bucks a year to make up for all of the abuse, for the hell that I had been put through.

It was just another slap in the face.

I couldn't find a place to rent for that money. Not to mention, no one told me that I wouldn't be able to rent an apartment without a job, or that I couldn't get a decent job to pay for that apartment without a home address.

It was a catch twenty-two, so I did the only thing I could think of.

I bought a shitty car for a thousand bucks and saved the eight hundred to use for gas while I worked various delivery jobs and other odd jobs that I could. I still hadn't made enough to get my own place and now I was completely broke once again.

I angrily wiped the traitorous tear that ran down my cheek. I wasn't going to cry. Crying never solved anything and it sure as hell never made me feel better. I had been in this position before and I would get myself out of it. I didn't need anyone. I could make it through this world all on my own, and that's exactly what I was going to do.

CHAPTER FOUR

Roland

IT WAS JUST after nine by the time I walked back into my home. The deafening silence always hit me hard. Even after all of this time, I still expected to find Shane in the kitchen or curled up on the couch watching some romance movie. The loss of him was still fresh, even though it shouldn't be. After just over a decade, one would think I would be over what happened, but I wasn't. It's always there, right below the surface, threatening to break through and pull me under.

It wasn't healthy, I knew that, but knowing it and accepting it are two very different things. I was perfectly fine just where I was. I didn't need to be fixed.

I didn't *want* to be fixed.

The ringing of my cell phone split the silence. I dug it out of my pocket as I made my way to my fridge to grab a beer. I wasn't much of a drinker, but I could use a drink tonight.

"Wright."

"Evening, Roland. Do you have a minute to chat?" Isaiah's voice had my mind shifting away from my past trauma to a current problem that I could potentially solve.

"Hey, Isaiah. Of course I do." I opened the beer as I made my way over to the couch and sat down as he spoke.

"So, I've managed to track down your Tyler from St. Marks. It wasn't easy with just a first name and description, but I managed to pull it out. Now, I can't legally tell you everything in his file."

"I know you can't and I'm not asking you to. I just need to know the basics so I can try and find him a safe foster home to be placed in."

"That's the thing... He's not fifteen, he's twenty-two."

Wait, what?

No way.

There was just no way. He couldn't be twenty-two. I didn't know if he was fifteen for sure, but he looked between fourteen and sixteen. There had to be a mistake. He just couldn't be twenty-two.

"That's not possible, man. You must have gotten the wrong name. There's no way he's older than sixteen. If you saw him, you would agree."

"It's your guy. He's been blessed, or cursed, with a baby face. Full name is Tyler Foster, and, before you ask, no, that's not a coincidence. He was born in the foster system and both parents didn't want him. Protocol is to give the baby a generic last name. Sometimes it's the street name that the parents were living on or the street name of the first foster home. The last name that the nurses give the baby as an ID in the hospital. He is twenty-two and nothing in his file since he aged out. I did run a security check and he hasn't been arrested. Most likely, he has been homeless since he aged out."

This was not what I was expecting at all. I thought it was bad when I thought he was fifteen, but to know that he had spent his whole life in the system and was now homeless, that made it worse.

"I thought kids who age out get money to get their own place for a couple of months."

"Yes, every child gets paid on their eighteenth birthday when they are kicked out of the system. Good foster parents will allow the child to stay there until they get on their feet, others toss them out that morning. What people outside of CPS don't know, though, the amount that a young adult gets when they age out is based on the number of years you have spent in the system. You are awarded one hundred dollars for every year you are in the system."

"A hundred bucks? That's it? How the hell are any of them supposed to survive on their own with eighteen hundred max?"

That was bullshit.

We were all told that children who aged out got enough money to support themselves for two months, three max if they were able to find a cheap enough place. But eighteen hundred was nothing. Most places were a thousand bucks for the first month. They wouldn't have enough to cover first and last month's rent, assuming they found a place that took them without a job. I thought the foster system was built solely to help kids, to protect them from their parents, if they needed it. They shouldn't get screwed over yet again when the time came for them to face this world alone.

"It's not much, I agree. It's a problem with the system that is on a Government level. On a regional level, if there was enough support for it, you could increase the amount, but that would require a lot of political and local support. We don't have that. Most people want to believe everything is fine in our quaint town, but the foster system is still the foster system, I'm afraid. Tyler has been through quite a large number of homes, but that isn't uncommon. Unfortunately, though, I can't place him in a foster home. It's on him to try and get a steady job and secure an apartment."

"Yeah, okay. Thanks, man. I'll see what I can do for him. At least now I know there isn't a family out there looking for him."

"I wish there was more that I could do for him. He's had a hard life, Roland. Be careful with him. He won't trust easily."

"I will," I promised before I ended the call.

I could tell that Tyler had been through some hard times, that was made very clear by his demeanor toward me. I wasn't stupid. I had eyes. He was unsettled by me and my size. I hated it, but I couldn't fix his natural reaction to me. It'd been happening since I was eighteen, I was used to people finding me intimidating, but it still hurt to know that Tyler was a bit scared of me. I was going to have to work my ass off to start building any semblance of trust with him.

There was one other emotion that ran through me at hearing that Tyler was in fact twenty-two. Relief. I wish I could say it was because that would mean a child wasn't living on the streets, but it wasn't. I was relieved because I'd been feeling a slight attraction to Tyler. Yes, he was smaller than I normally went with, he looked young, not to mention the skittish behavior. Tyler is what I would call man pretty with his soft features and lack of facial hair. I tended to go with larger guys that were full of confidence and were more rugged looking.

However, every now and then when I was able to catch his gaze, I couldn't help but notice how beautiful his eyes were. He had amazing blue eyes that pulled you in. I could get lost in them easily, and that wasn't something I was used to. He was the exact opposite of what I normally found attractive, but he was haunting my thoughts and even my dreams. It was a huge relief to know that I wasn't some pervert finding a kid attractive.

Knowing he wasn't a minor didn't make things any easier, though. I still had to earn his trust. I still needed to try and help him get off the street, something that would not be easy. I could offer a hand out to him, but it was all up to him to take the offered hand. I was hoping he would.

As for my attraction to him, I didn't even know if he was gay. I wasn't going to put him in that position. He needed a friend. He needed someone on his side and that was exactly what I was going to be. If him being gay came out down the road, I could reevaluate then.

Taking a drink from the amber-colored bottle, I grabbed the remote and started to flip through the channels, looking for a hockey game to watch. I wasn't going to sleep anytime soon, so I might as well try to turn my mind off.

The last thing I needed to do right now was continue thinking about Tyler.

CHAPTER FIVE

Roland

AFTER DROPPING OFF my jacket at my desk, I made my way into the break room at work. The station wasn't very big, especially compared to what I had been used to out in New York.

The station I worked out of in New York, had been eight floors, with multiple break rooms on each floor. There were ten different units within the station and all of them were detective units.

Here, though, it was half of the size of one floor in my old station. The whole building was roughly a thousand square feet and it held four detectives, myself included, the twelve patrol officers, and my Captain. There wasn't any elbow room and often no coffee, but the cases that I worked were a hell of a lot easier on my mind than any case that came across my desk in New York.

"Can you believe they actually let a fag into the academy?" Baxter's voice traveled down the short hallway.

His words instantly had my whole body on edge. It wasn't necessarily just his words. I knew that most people in town still didn't accept or like homosexuals and the police force was no different. I'd come across problems in New York when I decided to come out. That was after Shane. My fear of not being accepted had put him in that car that night, I wasn't going to make the same mistake twice. It was who he was talking about. I knew there was only one new cadet within the police academy that was gay.

Devon.

While Devon had been healing from his attack, I'd made a point of going by to see him once a day whether he was in the hospital or not. One day we got to talking and I discovered he had wanted to be in the Rangers, but his lack of a spleen, thanks to his asshole of a father, had cost him that dream.

I had suggested he could be a cop, even without a spleen. As long as he took vitamins to help with his immune system and saw a doctor to prescribe him a coagulant to ensure he wouldn't bleed out from an attack.

I was very pleased and happy for him when he told me he had been accepted into the academy. That was a month ago, and he'd started a week ago in the academy.

I had been checking in on him and the instructors all said he was a natural, especially his marksmanship. They were already talking about training him on being a sharpshooter, should we ever need a sniper. I doubted we ever would. This town wasn't one that had hostage situations or even the need for a police raid. Still, I couldn't have been more proud of him.

"I heard he was good," Jarod commented.

"He's probably sucking their cocks to give him a decent mark. This is what we're letting to happen to our station? We're going to let fags and homeless people in? He's going to be too busy staring at our asses and daydreaming about our dicks to be doing any work," Baxter said snidely, letting out a chuckle just as I walked in the room.

See, in my option this is where a smart man would look down and shuffle out of the room. They both knew I was gay and they both knew I was the one that helped Devon get into the academy and saw him often. They knew this, and yet Baxter just smirked at me as Jarod started to shuffle slowly toward the door.

"You know what I'm talking about, Wright. You're from the big city. You know what homeless people are really like. They're all messed up with different mental illnesses, not to mention lazy drunks or junkies. We can't have someone like that wearing the uniform. Besides, we already got our residential queer with you here," Baxter said with a smirk.

My hands balled into fists as I tried to push down the anger. Normally, I would do one of two things: walk away and just ignore the ignorance, or I would put him in his place with a verbal lashing. I did out rank him and often it wasn't worth the effort to try and change his opinions about homosexuality.

Maybe it was the lack of sleep over the past few years.

Maybe it was from learning more about Tyler.

Maybe it was because I knew Devon and what he had been through with his father.

Whatever it was, I lost it. I threw a punch, catching him right in his jaw, and knocked him flat on his ass. The sound of the coffee mug in his hand shattering on the ground and him falling into the cart on his way down was enough to catch the attention of everyone in the building. Everyone including my Captain, who stormed in just as I was considering punching Baxter again as he sat there dazed on the ground, coffee from his broken mug slowly working its way over to his pants.

"What the fuck is going on in here!" Captain Perry demanded.

"I punched Baxter," I easily admitted. I was man enough to own up to my actions and decisions. Plus, it was pretty clear that it was only me, Baxter, and Jarod in the room. We all knew Jarod wasn't going to be punching anyone. He was more quiet and timid. He was the guy that went along to get along.

"Get your ass in my office now, Detective Wright!"

Captain Perry stormed out of the room and I looked down at Baxter, as Jarod, who'd finally snapped out of his daze, helped him up. I should have felt bad for punching a fellow officer, but I didn't. He deserved it and maybe now he would think twice before he started to mouth off.

Turning on my heel, I strolled out of the break room and made the short walk down to my Captain's office. I closed the door, not that it would matter if he started to yell. Giving him my full attention, I started to explain myself.

"Sir, if you knew what Baxter was saying..."

"I don't give two shits if he told you he slept with your wife," Captain Perry cut me off, but before he could continue, I cut him off.

"Husband, sir. If I had a spouse, it wouldn't be a wife, but a husband. Which you know, because I told you in my interview that I was gay and wouldn't entertain accepting your offer if that was going to be a problem for you or anyone within your force. I've been dealing with Baxter's crap for years. I've been listening to his little snide comments about gay people for years. Today was the first day that I've hit him and he had it coming."

I didn't hide that I was gay and I'd finally had enough. I wasn't going to continue to deal with hearing those nasty little homophobic comments all the time. If I ever did find a man to fall in love with one day, I wanted to be able to bring him to my work. I wanted to be able to hold his hand in public without having to deal with any comments or looks about it from the men that are supposed to be my brothers, supposed to have my back. It was time everyone knew I wasn't going to tolerate it any longer.

"I have no problem with you being gay, Wright. I told you that from the jump. But that doesn't mean you get to knock out another member of this department. You think I don't know that Baxter is an asshole? His daddy was one, too. Yep, same as his daddy. He's a tenth generation asshole, but that doesn't give you the right to hit a subordinate. What the hell is going on with you?"

Gone was the harsh tone and it was

instantly replaced with a softer one. It always amazed me how he could go from one high emotion to the next within seconds. He could get to a boiling rage and then flip a switch without any effort.

I didn't know much about Captain Perry, but I knew he was from out west, California, and had seen his fair share of trauma in his time. I suspected it was one of the reasons why he picked me for this job. He understood my need to get out of a big city.

"Nothing. I'm fine."

"Bullshit you are. You think I haven't noticed how you've been going downhill over the past three years since you got here. I thought that haunted look in your eyes would dissipate after you had some time to recover from the traumas you have gone through, but instead it has only gotten worse. You're not sleeping, you're working even when you are off duty, you're no longer social, and now you are punching people. You've left me with no choice, Wright. I'm suspending you."

"What? You can't suspend me!"

This couldn't happen.

He couldn't suspend me.

I'd never been suspended in my entire adult career. I didn't have black marks on my record. I'd always made sure to do my job to the best of my ability and I respected the Upper Brass. I needed to work. I needed to keep busy. I couldn't be stuck in my house with nothing but my own thoughts to keep me company.

"You punched a subordinate in my station. You're damn right I can suspend you. I could suspend you for a month in accordance with the regulations. But I'm not about to bench my best detective, small town or not. The length of your suspension is completely up to you. All you have to do is provide me with a signed note from a licensed therapist that says you went and spoke with them."

"You want me to do what?"

A therapist.

Ah, hell no.

I wasn't going to talk to some shrink who

would only turn around and tell me I was crazy and shouldn't be allowed to carry a gun. That wasn't going to happen.

"You need to see a shrink. It's time, Roland. I don't know what you have been through. I can make assumptions based on what I've been through, but I know that my traumas are not the same as yours. I struggled for many years before I moved here. It cost me my wife of twenty years and my two children, who still, to this day, refuse to take my calls. By the time I went and saw Dr. Alex Howard, I had lost everything. I don't want that for you. And I don't want you worried that you are going to lose your job because you are seeing a therapist. You're not, no matter what they say. I know you can do this job and you are the only person within this department that I know without a doubt can handle pretty much any damn situation that comes up. This is about your mental health and that is just as important as your physical health."

I swallowed around the lump that had formed in my throat. I had no idea he had seen a shrink. A local shrink. I just figured he was like every other cop, you push the erase button and override the memories. You bury it down deep inside of you and move on. That's how you are taught in the military and in the police academy. It's how I'd always operated and now he wanted me to open all of these boxes of horror.

My knee jerk reaction was *hell no.*

It wasn't going to happen.

He would cave eventually.

The problem was, he wouldn't. He wouldn't cave, because he believed one hundred percent that I needed to do this. Rationally, I knew he was just looking out for me, but irrationally, it felt like he was out to get me.

"See Dr. Howard, or see someone else in town, I don't care. But if you want to come back to work, you need a session completion form signed and given to me. And you need to do that every time you go, twice a week, for the next few months. After three months, it'll be up to you if you wish to continue. Mandatory, twice a week for ninety days. You've gone to war four times, Roland. You've faced gunshots, knives, bombs, terrorists, and everything in between. You can face a therapist. I believe in you and I will always be there for you, no matter the time of day or night."

I didn't want to hear this. I didn't want to hear any of this, especially in his soft and understanding tone. Life was easier if I kept people at a distance. Even Zane, Daryl, and Devon. I was friendly with them and I had no problem talking to them if they had a problem. But I kept my personal life private.

Talking about my time overseas, as an NYPD Detective, Shane, it made my chest tight. I didn't want to talk about it. I didn't want to hear the words that I had been dreading. Words that I had thought myself in the quiet of the night.

That I had PTSD.

Logically, I knew it wasn't a terminal illness. Lots of cops and soldiers have it and operate perfectly fine in the field. The home life could be a little off, but it was something they could live with. That didn't make it any less terrifying, though, and I had been doing everything within my power to convince myself that I didn't have it.

That the nightmares were nothing.

That the bouts of depression and anti-social behavior were normal.

That any insomnia was just because of work and my mind was busy working out a case.

Sitting down with a therapist could make it all real. It could cement what my mind had been trying to tell me for years and that absolutely terrified me.

"Couldn't we just compromise and I take a week off?" I tried. I had to try and at least bargain with him.

He gave me a warm smile that did nothing to remove the cold that had seeped into my bones.

"No, but you can go and see someone tomorrow and come back to work right afterward, if you want. And no one will know that you are suspended. I'll tell them you are on a special assignment for me. This stays between us. You can do this,

Roland, I know you can. And I promise, you will be happy that you did one day. I know it might not seem like it, but you will be."

That wasn't going to happen. I was being given a prison sentence of ninety days and I was going to hate every second I was stuck in that shrink's office. At least it was only two hours a week. A grand total of a hundred and eighty hours. I knew I would be keeping a mental calculator in my head and counting down until I was finally free.

This was going to be the longest three months of my life.

"Don't be holding your breath for that. I guess I'll see you tomorrow."

I didn't wait for his reply. It didn't matter right now, anyway. He knew I wasn't happy about this and he accepted that. I made my way out of the station and made sure to not make eye contact with anyone. I needed to get out of here. I needed to work these emotions off.

The gym.

Yes, I needed the gym, but first I had to head home to get changed and lock my gun up. I just needed to keep busy until I could get this over and done with.

CHAPTER SIX

Tyler

THE HEAT WAS starting to get to me today. It was always hard during the warmer spring and summer months for my asthma. The result was more asthma attacks that required me to use my inhaler more frequently. Today, I had to get a refill, which is why I was stuck out in the hot sun standing outside of a free clinic waiting for my turn.

Why was I outside?

Because the waiting room was full of other patients. All twenty of them. You wouldn't think in a town this size that there would be much of a wait for a free clinic, but it was always busy and under staffed.

The doctors didn't want to work here, because they wanted to make real money. But the doctors that were in town had to volunteer here so many hours a month to keep a discount on their malpractice insurance, so they grudgingly did what they had to for a few bucks back in their pocket.

They often didn't care too much about the non-paying patients they had to see. The whole process was basically the same. You go, sign your name on a clipboard, wait to be called, get called, wait even longer in the room. When the doctor does finally appear, they get your name wrong, they only listen for a minute before they either give you a drug you might not have needed or they tell you that you're fine when you really aren't. If you were actually paying, you wouldn't be able to get out of the room because the doctor would talk your ear off.

It was complete crap, but it was another piece of my reality.

At least today I just needed a refill, so hopefully, it wouldn't be too much of an issue. I was only allowed to have one cartridge at a time. Apparently, they were worried I could be selling it to someone. Even if I could find someone that would pay me for it, why would they buy it?

It's not like steroids could make them high and it wasn't a pill that they could crush up to snort or inject. It was annoying, because sometimes a single cartridge could last me a month or longer, but sometimes it only lasted me two weeks if we were in a heat wave and I was working outside. The past two months, I'd been using it a lot while working outside at the construction site.

Feeling a little light headed, I went and sat down on the ground with my back against the bricks. I wished there was some shade, but there was nothing around me that I could use to get some relief from this heat.

I wasn't the only one out here in this heat, there were four other guys waiting in line ahead of me. They were all waiting for their methadone. I wasn't judging, but I had seen them around quite a bit and I could see the signs of withdrawals starting to creep in on them. I also knew that before they even got in there, they would be getting worse and starting to get aggressive until they got their fix.

Letting out a small sigh I bent my knees up and placed my head in my hands to try and push through the tightness in my chest.

"Tyler?"

This isn't happening.

How is it he was always around when I felt like complete crap?

It was like he had some type of radar or something. Slowly lifting my head and squinting in the harsh sunlight as I looked his way, I spoke.

"Detective."

Roland moved so he blocked the sun with his enormous body before he bent down in front of me, still managing to block out the sun.

"Are you okay?" he asked in a caring voice as his eyes scanned over the parts of my body that he could see. "Is your eye bothering you?"

"It's fine. I need a refill," I said as I held up my inhaler slightly while also managing to look away.

That feeling was back. What was it about him?

"You have asthma. It must be pretty bad in this heat. They need to listen to your lungs, I'd imagine."

His concern for me was confusing. I wasn't really used to someone being concerned for me. I didn't understand why he would be worried or concerned for my welfare. I was just some homeless guy. I wasn't anything special.

"I'm waiting to get my refill. I have to wait for a doctor to give it to me."

They wouldn't listen to my lungs. The doctor wouldn't even be bothered to know my name. That was just fine with me. I had my share of doctors growing up.

"Can I see that for a second?" he asked with a nod at my inhaler.

I wasn't sure why he wanted to see it, but it wasn't like he could do anything to damage it. I doubted he would run away with it. I held it up for him and he easily took it and popped the cartridge out.

"Yeah, I thought so. You see this red diamond by the prescription name?" he asked, turning it back to me so I could see it. I gave a slight nod before he continued. "Any prescription with that mark lets pharmacists know that it is safe to be refilled without a prescription. You don't have to wait for a prescription from a doctor, you just go into any pharmacy and they will give you your refill." He handed it back to me as I spoke.

"Wait, are you serious?"

I didn't have to wait?

I could actually go into a pharmacy and just hand my inhaler over and they would give me my refill, just like that?

If that was true, then why didn't any

doctor ever tell me that?

Every month for the past four years I'd had to wait in line to see a doctor. I'd had to go through this dance every time I needed a refill. I had to wait hours just to be treated like a nuisance because I needed medication for my lungs. It always made me feel like I was being a burden or bothersome to them. Like it was my fault that I had asthma, like I had done something wrong and this was the end result.

It always felt like I was the problem child. I was always made to feel like I was causing problems with my health. I was born premature and that came with health problems. Problems that I had to live with for the rest of my life. Thankfully, the worst of it was my asthma, but that brought other problems with it. I had to be really careful not to get any chest infections because it would be made worse with my asthma. I'd had a hard time with my weight and getting up to an average level. All I had to do was eat a healthy diet and often, but that didn't work with life on the streets.

"Yes. I don't know how long you've had to be on an inhaler and why no doctor has ever told you. But you just need to go into a pharmacy and they'll take care of it for you."

Unbelievable.

This whole time I could have just done that. This is what people don't seem to understand. People who are homeless are treated like we're less than the dirt everyone walks on. We're an annoyance, an inconvenience, and no one holds any interest in helping or making things a bit easier on us. All it would have taken was one doctor or even a nurse to open their mouth and tell me and then they could have never seen me again.

Why have to go through this whole process as a doctor if you could have avoided it by just informing me of something this simple?

It was ridiculous and not something that I would have had to go through if I wasn't at a free clinic. They would have had no problem if I was paying, but I wasn't paying so I was going to get the least amount of effort they could provide. Like I wasn't a human being just trying to survive like everyone else.

"Thanks." Letting out a sigh, I stood up. There was a pharmacy not too far from here. Hopefully, they would fill it without giving me any problems. The last thing I wanted to do was to have to be at the back of the line.

"I'll walk with you. Make sure they don't try and give you the runaround," he offered, but I could tell it wasn't a suggestion.

I wanted to argue that it wasn't necessary, but I truly didn't know if it wouldn't be. At least if he was with me, I wouldn't have to worry about the Pharmacist giving me a hard time and denying my request.

I simply gave a nod and we headed down the street for the short walk. He didn't talk and for that I was thankful. I wasn't sure what I would even say at this point. He still believed I was underage and I wasn't in a real hurry to correct his assumption. It wasn't anyone's business how old I was, especially a cop. If he thought I was underage, then he wouldn't be trying to arrest me for some bullshit excuse. There was a safety in being perceived as young to the police.

Arriving at the pharmacy, we immediately headed back to where the prescription counter was. After a quick explanation, the Pharmacist had no problem giving me my refill. I still couldn't believe how easy it was to get it. I expected to have to argue with them and then inevitably have to go back to wait in an even longer line at the free clinic. The whole task took seven minutes and then we were back outside on the sidewalk.

"Thank you for this. I really appreciate it," I said, a small smile turning up the corners of my lips.

"It's no problem at all. There's something I wanted to talk to you about. Why don't we grab some food at the diner? My treat."

Going anywhere with him didn't seem like a good idea. That odd feeling was only getting stronger when I was around him and I still didn't know what it was.

At the same time, if he wanted to talk to me about something, could I really say no?

I didn't know what he wanted to talk about but if it had anything to do with him suspecting I did something illegal, it would be better to get it sorted out early before it grew into a monster.

Plus, I hadn't eaten since dinner at the soup kitchen, how could I turn down free food?

"Okay," I said, but I couldn't hide the uncertainty in my voice.

He simply gave me a warm smile and started to walk down the street toward the diner. I wasn't too sure about this, but my feet seemed to move all on their own and I followed.

He didn't say anything again and I couldn't help but wonder if he was a man of few words or was just terrible at small talk. Either way was fine with me. It wasn't like we were friends and I didn't hold any interest in filling the silence with pointless conversation.

As we approached the diner, I couldn't help but wonder if maybe Devon would be working. I knew he was going to be a police officer, but I wasn't sure if he was still working at the same time. A quick scan when we walked in told me he wasn't there. We sat down at a booth off to the left side of the building as one of the female servers brought our menus to us.

"Do you have a go-to diner food?" Roland asked, after we placed our drink orders.

"I've never eaten in a diner before, so I'll go with no."

Diners and restaurants were a no go growing up and especially after being homeless for four years now. Whenever I got food, I always tried to make sure it was something that could last a few days. Going out to eat was a waste of money to me, because it was money I could use to get food for a few days, as opposed to a single meal.

"The food here is really good. I'm a burger guy myself."

I liked burgers, but my body had a hard time processing that much protein in one sitting. It always left me feeling heavy and that wasn't a good feeling to have when living on the street. The omelets looked good, though. At least the photos of them did.

The words got all mixed up in my head so I just ignored them. I didn't normally get breakfast food. When the waitress came back over with our drinks we both placed our order before she walked off with a warm smile.

"The omelets are really good here. I'm a big breakfast guy, it's the most important meal of the day, but I like eggs and hash browns. Sometimes I'll make it for dinner."

"I used to cook it a lot. It's cheap to feed multiple people."

"While you were in the foster homes?" he asked, gently.

It was a logical assumption that I had been in foster homes, but the look in his eyes told me it was more than just an assumption. He was a cop, so he could easily have tried to find a file on me. I had never been arrested, but in the system was in the system. It was all the same, especially in a town like this.

"You pulled my file," I easily stated, as I sat back. I wasn't mad. I wasn't anything. I had accepted that the police in this town would do whatever they wanted. All you could do was hope you didn't get on their bad side.

"No, no. I called my friend in Social Services and he was able to find your file. I don't know much of any of it, actually. He would never betray anyone like that. He just told me that you were in the foster system since you were born and that you were twenty-two. Now, before you get upset, I only started trying to find information on you because I believed you were fifteen or so. I never would have done it had I known you were of legal age."

I believed him.

For some reason, I actually believed him. He didn't intend to invade my privacy. He had done it with good intentions and I couldn't fault him for that. I looked young and as a cop he'd decided to try and make sure I was safe and off of the streets. I could respect that.

"It's okay, and yeah, once you start becoming the oldest it's on you to take care of the kids. A dozen eggs and a bag of potatoes can feed six kids for a few days," I said with a small shrug.

"Not much food for that many kids," he said as his brows crinkled slightly.

I could understand his point. It wasn't much food. And often, I would go a few days without eating just so the younger kids would get something each day. It was hard, especially when I had to tell one of them that they couldn't have more. I made it work, though, because it wasn't their fault. They didn't ask for it any more than I did, but I could at least give them some semblance of safety and care.

"The foster system is far from sunshine and rainbows. The kids all work together to do what they can to survive."

"And you haven't been able to get on

your feet since you aged out?"

"The small amount that I got for aging out wasn't much. It wasn't enough to cover first and last month's rent for a deposit. The places that I could afford to rent, they wouldn't take me because I didn't have a job and no one was willing to give me the chance to find one while living there, either. I bought my car and now I live in it. I've been trying to work wherever I can, but most places want an address and I can't give them one."

"I agree with you on that completely." He shook his head as he spoke. "It's insane how people treat those that are homeless. I know a lot of great guys that have been struggling and trying to get on their feet, but no one will rent to them without a job, but they can't get a job without having a home. No one seems to want to help. I've been trying to help where I can, but I also know as a cop I can be off putting because of that."

"Not a lot of people trust cops, especially in this town. Plus, physically, you don't help yourself."

He was making me nervous and we were just sitting here. I knew it wasn't his fault, though. It was mine from my own traumas. But I also knew I wasn't the only one with those kind of traumas within the homeless community.

"I know. I have this unique ability to clear a room by just walking into it." He chuckled. "I never used to be this size. I was actually closer to yours when I was younger. But I joined the military and that started me on a strict training schedule. It stuck with me."

I wasn't all that surprised that he used to be in the military. His very slight accent told me he was from the New York area. Someone his size and with his accent, it made sense that he was military.

Most likely the Army in one of the divisions.

It also made a lot of sense why him and Devon hit it off right away. Devon had always wanted to be a Ranger before his abusive father ripped that away from him.

The waitress was back with our food and at the delicious smell of it my stomach growled. The food looked even better than it did in the photos and the smell was to die for.

"I don't know if you are interested, but my friend, Oswald, he's got a bar and he's looking for a bartender. He's been having a hard time trying to get someone that actually wants to work. Now, it's a dive bar so it's not fancy. Most people just do a beer and a shot, and the people that go there are blue-collar workers. But if you're okay with that, I could set up a meeting for you and him to sit and talk it over."

"Are you serious?"

Was he actually going to give me the chance to get a stable job?

I had never bartended before, but if it was just a beer or a shot, I could do that. I wouldn't be very good at fancy drinks, but I could handle basic bartending. If I could meet with someone and have the chance to convince them that I would be a good fit, that could be exactly what I needed to start getting back on my feet.

"Absolutely. He's a great guy. I met him when I first moved here. I've been going to his bar since day one. It's a small and old building, so the bar isn't anything to rave about in terms of decor. And the majority of the customers, like I said, are all construction workers and low income people. There are also only four servers, two on each shift and one bartender a shift. So it can get busy, but the tips are decent, from what the girls have said."

I didn't care what the bar looked like or how busy it would be. It was a chance to have an actual steady job. That was the only thing I cared about. I didn't care what I had to do if it meant I could have the chance to actually get a place to live and make steady money.

"If you want to set something up I would appreciate it. I've never done any bartending before, but I'm a quick learner."

I was a quick learner if it was away from books. Working with my hands and following a routine was something I excelled at. If I could meet with his friend, maybe I could convince him to give me a chance.

"I don't doubt that. I'll set it up for you. He'll be happy, I'm sure of it. He hasn't been able to find anyone and he's been working doubles for a couple of weeks now. I'll call him later and get a time for you. I'll be at the Soup Kitchen tomorrow night, so if you swing by, I can let you know the details."

I easily agreed. I wasn't planning on going to St. Mark's for a couple of days, but I would if that meant I could have a potential interview. Today had turned out a lot differently than I had expected. I thought I would be stuck in a line up for the day, only to now have the chance to have a real job. If Roland was able to get me a meeting with his friend, I would make sure I did everything I could to secure that job and keep it.

This opportunity could be the very thing I needed to have a real chance at a true life and I was not about to let that slip through my fingers.

CHAPTER SEVEN

Roland

THIS WAS STUPID and completely unnecessary. Baxter was being an asshole and deserved to be laid out for the crap he was spewing. If it had been anyone else, I doubted that Captain Perry would be forcing them to speak to a shrink over it.

Damn it.

I was fine.

I didn't need this.

So what if I had nightmares every night?

So what if I didn't sleep some nights?

So what if there have been moments where I could swear I've seen or heard him?

I was fine.

I didn't have a problem.

I didn't need to be fixed.

There was nothing wrong with me.

Ugh.

I was going to this appointment and then I would be back at work tomorrow. The fact that I had to do this for three months was complete shit, but if I wanted to keep my job, I had no choice.

Walking into the office had me feeling a mixture of emotions. The first was shame. Dr. Howard's office was the only one in this building so the receptionist would know I was here for him and anyone that saw me outside would know I was here for him as well.

People knowing my personal information made me feel uncomfortable. Like I was on display at some freak show and everyone paid ten bucks to see the show.

As a cop, I had referred many victims to

speak to a therapist in the past. Easily over three hundred victims I had introduced to a therapist, someone that could help them overcome the trauma that they had endured. Never, not once, had I ever thought less of them or told them that they should be ashamed. Yet, as I walked through the door it was all I could feel.

I couldn't help but wonder if they felt the same way as well. If they thought I was a liar because I told them it would be fine. Because I told them they had nothing to be ashamed of when that might have been all they felt.

This was ridiculous.

I wasn't a victim.

I had been through some hard shit in my life, yes, but I survived and I was one of the lucky ones that got to keep living. I didn't feel very lucky sometimes, but that is what everyone always said when you survived a tour. You were one of the lucky ones because you didn't get shot, blown up, or tortured while you were off fighting for your country. A country that was made up of thousands upon thousands of people that didn't appreciate it and assumed you were just a paid government assassin.

Pushing back some of the bad memories from my time overseas that were banging on my mental door, I turned my attention to the office. It was warm and welcoming with a rich brown paint on the walls and pieces of local artwork hung up. There were a few couches that made up the waiting room.

With the town being on the smaller side, it allowed for doctor offices to be more intimate with nicer furniture compared to plastic chairs that you typically found in larger cities. It was designed to be welcoming and to put you at ease, but it had the opposite effect on me.

I wanted to run from the building.

I wanted to lie to the receptionist about why I was here. I would have rather walked into a crime scene of a triple homicide than to be standing here right now. And wasn't that the screwed up part, because I would rather be called to a tragic crime scene to see the horror that waited me inside that house, than to be safe here in a doctor's office.

"Detective Wright, it's good to see you," Alexis said, a warm smile turning up the corners pf her mouth.

Alexis had been Dr. Howard's receptionist for close to ten years now. She was another one of the sweet older ladies that made up the heart of this town. She was always up for a fundraiser and to help organize any event, even at a moment's notice. She believed very strongly that a lady should never show her age, so her hair was always dyed brown to cover any of the grey. She never left her house without wearing makeup and dressed ready to impress. She could be a bit nosy, but if you needed someone to command and corral hundreds of volunteers, Alexis was your girl.

"It's good to see you, Alexis. You look beautiful, as always," I said, flashing her a warm smile. Regardless of how I felt about being here, she didn't deserve for me to take it out on her.

"You are still sweet as honey. You go on back, Dr. Howard is expecting you."

I offered her another small warm smile and then I headed down the hall toward Dr. Howard's office.

I felt like I was a dead man walking to my execution.

It was just an office. There was no threat on the other side of the door. There was no man with a gun or a bomb standing on the other side lying in wait. It was just a room with a man sitting in it. There was no danger, and yet, my heart rate was spiking the closer I got to the door. I knew I didn't have a choice, though. I had to go through the door. If I ever wanted to get back to work, I had to do this. I *would* do this because my job was all I had and I was not about to lose it.

Not for anything.

Walking through the door did nothing to slow my pounding heart, but I didn't let it show on me. I closed the door and gave Dr. Howard a simple nod of acknowledgement as I made my way over to the couch that sat across from his chair.

"Detective, it's good to see you," he started.

"Can't really say the same here, Doc," I responded honestly.

I didn't intend to keep it a secret that I didn't want to be here, nor did I feel like I needed to be. There was no point in lying about it. That would only cause problems later on when he quickly discovered I was faking my enthusiasm.

"I get that a lot. I know this wasn't your idea and that you are not all that happy to be here. I take no offense to any of that. Let me start by saying that anything that is said within this room, stays in this room. I'm not going to be mentioning it to anyone outside in the community."

"And I appreciate that, but anyone that sees me walking into this building knows what I'm doing here. People will already talk and whisper about what's going on."

"I don't know much about you, but I do know that you came from New York City and before that I know you did a stint in the army. Most soldiers and law enforcement officers all share the belief that talking to a therapist is a sign of weakness. That you are to hit the erase button within your brain and override all of the horrific images that are stored within your memory box. However, as I am sure you've noticed, there's only so many times the mind can be overridden before all of those horrors explode out and drag you down into the darkness. Sometimes, there are experiences in life that you can overcome without talking about them. Then, there are traumatic horrors that need to be talked about in order for you to ever have a healthy life. I'm not here to judge, Roland. I'm here to listen and to help."

His calm and understanding voice did nothing to ease my racing heart or my nerves. I knew what he said was true. Logically, there was nothing for me to feel ashamed of. That didn't make this any easier, not even the slightest. Letting out a slow and deep breath, I decided to suck this up and get it over and done with.

"I punched Baxter and now Captain Perry believes I need to talk to someone."

"Assaulting another officer is not exactly how things normally work. Have you ever assaulted a colleague before in your career?"

"A few times, yeah. Not like Baxter, it was at crime scenes when there was a young gunshot victim and the ambulance was too far away. It went against protocol to transport a victim in a squad car, but if we had waited they would have died. My partner at the time was in agreement with me in taking them in our car, other officers felt differently. I've punched six patrol officers who stood in my way and each time my Captain understood and let it go."

"Well, I can understand that. If it's a choice between saving a child's life and doing nothing, I would pick punching an officer each time. What happened with Baxter, then?"

"He deserved it."

"I'm sure there must have been others over the years that have deserved it as well, but you didn't assault them. What happened specifically with Baxter?"

He wasn't going to let this go and there was no point in trying to stall for an answer. Punching Baxter was the least of my issues and it was the safest topic to be discussing.

"There is a friend of mine who I met three years ago at St. Mark's. Devon. He was homeless, had been since he was seventeen and ran away from his very abusive father. He was able to fall in love with a great young man, got a job, and was accepted into the police academy. Baxter was talking trash about him, about him being gay and homeless. I got tired of hearing it so I knocked him out."

"It must be hard for you being the only gay officer within the police department. I'd imagine when you were in New York, you weren't a unicorn over there."

"It wasn't easy in New York, either. Bigger city holds a lot more bigots than the town square could hold. You learn to deal with it and you know who your friends are and which ones just want to watch you burn. I never kept it hidden from day one in the police academy. Moving here, I was honest and straightforward with Captain Perry about being gay and not hiding it. He was fine with it and assured me I wouldn't have to deal with any backwards, redneck comments about it."

"And then Detective Baxter started to make comments about it. But surely that couldn't have been the first time."

"No, he's made jokes and comments for three years now. He doesn't like it, but I have superiority over him and he knows I can knock him out if I wanted to. I normally ignore it."

"But not this time around. Could it be that perhaps there was something else you were dealing with at the time? Another personal issue and you lashed out at Detective Baxter?"

Well, there goes that safe topic. Of course he would try and dig deeper and find some deep root psychological reasoning behind me punching Baxter because I was sick of hearing his bullshit. The trick was going to be getting through three months, two hours a week, sitting here and not divulging any personal or previous issues in my life. It was bound to come up at some point and there was nothing I could do about it. Might as well rip the band-aid off and get it over and done with. Letting out a sigh, I spoke as I leaned forward with my elbows on my knees.

"Okay, I am only going to do this once. I did three tours overseas and killed my first person when I was eighteen. In my life, I have shot and killed a hundred and eighteen people, the majority of them men, and all of them were either firing upon me and my team or they had a suicide vest on. Their deaths don't haunt me, because they were trying to kill innocent people. I didn't tell anyone within my unit that I was gay. I kept it hidden, including my boyfriend at the time, Shane, who I loved, lived with, and wanted to marry. He wanted more. He didn't want to be a dirty secret. We got into a huge fight eleven years ago. He stormed out and was killed by a drunk driver twenty minutes later. After three months of the cops not finding the driver, I decided to join the police force and track the bastard down myself. It took two years, and he had killed a mother and her young child in another DUI. I arrested him and was promoted to detective due to my investigation skills. Sometimes, I get nightmares and don't sleep all that great. A combination of my time overseas, losing the man that I love, and working homicides. But that doesn't stop me from doing my job. I was simply sick and tired of hearing Baxter's shit talking, and now he will think twice before doing it."

I made a point of keeping my voice calm and even. I didn't want it shaking with emotions and letting him know how much it hurt for me to even say the words out loud to him. I'm not a stupid man. I know it's not normal for someone to be having nightmares every night practically. I know it's not normal for me to be staying awake as long as possible. To be refusing to date anyone, to have not even touched another man in close to eight years.

After Shane had been murdered, I was a wreck. I couldn't even stomach looking at another man, much less touch one. It took three years and a very drunk night at a local gay bar for me to have sex. I would never forget how I felt that next morning, waking up to some stranger in my bed.

The bed that I shared with Shane.

I was sick all day from it and I felt dirty. I felt like I had cheated on him. Ever since, I've been terrified of touching another man, terrified that I would feel that way again. It was just easier to use my own hand when the itch became too much. But that wasn't something that he would understand.

"You've been through a lot in your life. It's natural that you would have days, have nights, where you struggled harder with all of that trauma. Like I said, Roland, I'm not here to judge you. I'm here to help you. To make those hard days and nights fewer in between. To give you ways to cope with them. Do not mistake this as any judgment or me looking for a reason to tell Captain

Perry he needs your badge. He doesn't get any reports from me. All I do is sign the form that states you appeared for our session. I'm here to help you work through the trauma so you can be healthier. So you can go out and be an even better cop to the people of this town. That's all."

He obviously took what I said as me being defensive, and I probably was.

How could I not be when I was sitting in this position?

"I don't do shrinks," I simply said.

"Most people don't. Don't think of me that way. I've known you for four years. We've worked cases together before, shared beers. I'm not the enemy, Roland, I'm your friend. I'm the one person in this world that you can talk to without any judgments or lectures. If you want to do that in this office, okay, or we can do it in the park with coffee, at a bar after shift. I don't care where we do our sessions, as long as we are doing them. Just not the gym. Please, not the gym. It's extremely depressing how little weight I can lift."

I couldn't help the small chuckle that escaped me. He wasn't old, only thirty-five, but he looked like a wet paper bag could take him out in a fight with a strong gust of wind. He had a wonderful grandmother that was still alive and kicking that could cook comfort food better than anyone I know. Dr. Howard, though, was blessed with a fast metabolism, the only thing he claimed was saving him from obesity. He would have to bulk up quite a bit to even be able to be considered a lightweight fighter, something he made very clear he had zero interest in. He was right. We were friends. He was one of the first friends I made when I moved here. There had been plenty of nights we shared a beer. Plenty of times, when I had unexpectedly unleashed a rant about one case or person to him. I couldn't let the situation around me being here change the fact that we were friends. I wasn't sitting here talking to a therapist. I was sitting here talking to a buddy that just happened to have schooling on how the human mind works.

"Okay, I'll try."

And I would.

He was right. I didn't want to fully admit it right this very second, but he was right.

If I could have fewer horrible days, then why not fight for that?

Men died so I could come home, so I could make something of myself. If I could honor their sacrifice by being a better man, a better cop, and saving more lives, then that is what I needed to do.

Even if that meant facing the darkness within my mind.

CHAPTER EIGHT

Tyler

THIS WAS SURREAL, absolutely surreal.

When Roland had told me he could get me an interview with his buddy, Oswald, I didn't truly believe it would happen. Whether he needed a bartender or not, most business owners didn't hire homeless guys. Yet, last night, when I went to St. Mark's, Roland told me to meet Oswald at his bar, Brotherhood Tavern, for an eleven o'clock interview.

Even hearing that I had the chance at a real job wasn't enough to convince me that I truly had a shot. I figured he was just agreeing because Roland was his friend and a cop.

Turned out, I was wrong.

Oswald had already decided to hire me, before I even came through the door. We sat and talked for a good hour about the systems and he told me about his life and I shared some of mine. He didn't care that I didn't have a set address. He didn't treat me like I was worthless or less than anyone. He treated me like every other human being and it almost brought tears to my eyes.

I had been at the bar ever since. I had been working with Tammy, a server, and learning from Oswald how the computer system worked. There was food here and we had a day and night cook. Oswald had explained to me that we were all a team, so if one person needed help, someone would jump in.

For me, I would be the only bartender working at night and on weekends, but

Tammy and the other three servers could make drinks as well, if I got slammed. And apparently, I would be getting slammed, especially Thursday, Friday, and Saturday nights. I was just fine with that. I had no problem being busy and working hard. In fact, I preferred it to be busy and having something to do over it being dead and getting paid to stand around.

Tonight was Wednesday and it had been fairly slow all day. I had been training and learning what I could. Tonight, I was going to be closing with Oswald showing me how it all worked, then tomorrow night I was on my own.

I couldn't believe he trusted me this easily. Yes, there were cameras all over the bar, but still, I could easily steal all of his cash and leave town. He would never know until the morning and by then, I would be long gone. I would never do that, but he didn't know that. It was a huge show of trust. One I was not looking to break in any way.

At the sound of the door, I turned to see

who was walking in. I was making an effort to know the regulars and remember their drink orders. Tammy said that a lot of the regulars would come around the same time either everyday or every other day after their shift at work.

At the sight of the man that walked through the door, my heart fluttered and that weird feeling was back. I didn't know what it was about Roland, but every time I was around him, I felt so weird. At first, I thought maybe it was my old instinct of fear at his size, but after the diner, I knew that wasn't it. I didn't know what it was, but it had nothing to do with fear.

That feeling completely disappeared at the sight of Jasper walking in right behind him. They were partners, so it only made sense that they would go out for a drink together, but that didn't make it any easier to see him. I instantly wanted to go and hide, but I couldn't. This was my job. I had to speak with him to take his order.

I could do this.

I *had* to do this.

"Hey, you look good back there," Roland said, flashing me a warm smile.

"Thanks, what can I get for you, Detectives?" I kept my voice even and professional. I wasn't going to let Jasper know his presence affected me.

"Two bottles of Bud, please," Roland answered for them.

I gave a nod and headed over to the beer cooler. I grabbed them each an amber-brown bottle, opening them before bringing them back over.

"Keep the change. This is my partner, Detective Jasper Monroe." Roland handed me the cash for them as he spoke.

"It's nice to meet you, sir."

Jasper grunted and scowled as his only reply.

I could have told Roland that I already knew him, but I wasn't sure if that was something that Jasper wanted him to know. I was sure Roland knew that Jasper was a foster parent, but I didn't want him asking me questions about him and he would if he knew that I was one of his foster kids. It was better to pretend that I had never met him before.

"How is it going? Are you liking it here?" Roland asked next.

"It's good, yeah. Thank you for setting this up. I truly appreciate it."

"Don't worry about it. Oswald is a great guy and he's too old to be working so much. You're doing him a huge favor by taking the job."

Which was exactly what Oswald had said. He'd been working a lot without having a night bartender and as energetic as he was, he was older and it wasn't good for him to be working eighty-hour weeks.

I offered them a small smile before I moved on to help the other customers.

Once we were closed, Oswald was going to show me all of the paperwork that needed to be done each night at closing. I was worried about it, especially with how my mind worked, but hopefully it wouldn't be terrible. He was going to walk me through it, though, so with any luck, I would be able to easily follow along with him. It wasn't something I needed to worry about right now. Later, I was sure to be a ball of nerves with it all.

CHAPTER NINE

Tyler

THE PAPERWORK WASN'T so bad, but I was worried about trying to do it on my own last night. I was not about to tell my new boss that I had some type of learning disability. I would be taking that to my grave. I didn't want to give him a reason to question my abilities or his decision to give me a chance.

"That's it, Tyler. You did good today," Oswald said, flashing me a warm smile.

Hearing that, it made me feel good. I took pride in my work, no matter what it was. I always strived to do my best and to make my boss happy. It felt good hearing that he was happy with my work.

"Thank you. I truly appreciate you giving me this opportunity."

"Believe me, you are doing me a huge favor. I couldn't find a bartender no matter what I did. You're helping me out immensely with this, Kid. I'll be here tomorrow when you get in, but then I'll be heading home around six. You go on and get out of here. I got some paperwork to finish up and then I'll be right behind you."

"Have a good night, Boss," I said warmly.

"Good night, Kid."

I let myself out the heavy wooden front door and made my way into the back parking lot where my car currently was. I wasn't too sure where I was going to park it moving forward.

Today, I had driven to work because it was a bit of a walk for me in the heat. My asthma was acting up and I tried to avoid having to take my inhaler so it would last longer.

For tonight, I was going to sleep in the parking lot and then tomorrow, before work, I would find a place close by that I could keep my car and sleep in it. It was going to take me a few months to save up enough money for an apartment, even a cheap one, but I would at least be able to start saving up money.

Climbing into the backseat, I grabbed the small blanket, quickly set the alarm on my watch, and lay down. I closed my eyes and tried to calm my mind down enough for me to fall asleep.

Some time later, how long I wasn't too sure, there was a knock at my window. Snapping my eyes open, I was fully prepared to see a light from a police flashlight, but instead I was greeted by Oswald's face.

Sitting up, I moved and opened the door, climbing out so we could chat. I wasn't sure what he wanted, but I hoped it wasn't to tell me I was fired.

"Are you sleeping in your car?" he immediately asked me.

"I thought Roland told you I was homeless."

I prayed that Roland had disclosed that. I figured he would have and that Oswald had hired me knowing I was homeless. If he didn't tell him, there was no way I would be able to keep this job.

"He told me you were having a hard time finding steady work. He knows I don't care if someone is homeless. I care about them being able to and willing to work."

"I'm not fired?" I asked, holding my breath for his answer.

"God, no. You were great tonight, why would I fire you over being down on your luck? Come on, this way," he said as he waved two fingers at me and headed off to a set of metal stairs attached to the back of the building.

I closed my car door, locked it up, and trotted after him. I had no idea why we were going over there, but I was not about to not follow if my boss told me to. I was lucky enough that he wasn't going to fire me over being homeless. I wasn't about to insult him by not following after him.

We trudged up the surprisingly sturdy stairs and he pulled out a key to open the door on the second floor. We walked in, and Oswald flicked on the lights as he cleared the doorway.

I looked around in awe. The place was a small studio apartment with a little kitchenette and a bathroom off to the right. There was a bed off to the right of the kitchenette in the corner and the other half of the room held a small bistro table, loveseat, and a coffee table. It was clean with everything one would need for an apartment in it.

"Now, it's not much, I know, but it's got more room than that car of yours."

"What?" Now I was even more confused.

Why was he showing me this?

"I've been sleeping here sometimes at night since I've been having to work the night shift. I use this space as a safe place for my employees. You are not the first homeless person I have hired. Jose, he used to live here up until eight months ago when he was able to secure his own place. I will not tolerate you sleeping in your car. You can stay here, make this your home. You don't pay rent, all you have to do is save up and when you are able to get your own place, you move out and this becomes available to whoever may need it next."

"Boss, I can't stay here for free. You have to let me pay you something." This was unbelievable. This wasn't actually happening. Tears clouded my vision and my voice wavered slightly at this man's generosity. To say I was overwhelmed would be the least of my emotions at the moment. This sweet, old man couldn't actually not only be giving me a job, but a place to live as well. It was too much. I couldn't possibly accept this.

"You will do no such thing. This place here is for people who need it. I've been doing this for twenty years, now, and have never regretted it for a single second. This is your home, now. Here is a spare key," he said as he held out a key out to me.

Out of instinct, I opened my hand and took it, but I was still in a state of shock. He placed the key in my hand and then placed a comforting hand on my back.

"You'll process this soon enough, Kid. You get some sleep and I will see you tomorrow. Make sure you come down and get some breakfast. I don't want you not eating. You look like a good fart could knock you right over."

I chuckled at that. He was a very straightforward and interesting man. "Thank you for everything. I truly appreciate this."

"We all have hard times in life, it's important to help those that need it. See you tomorrow, Kid."

"Drive safe, Boss."

He waved me off and I could tell he was not a man that liked someone worrying about him. I didn't know much about him at all, really. He had a wedding ring on his left hand, so I figured he at least had a wife. He didn't talk about anything personal, though, so as far as kids went, I had no idea. He was well into his sixties and if he had only owned the bar for twenty years, I couldn't help but wonder what he did before that. He didn't seem like a small town guy, so I suspected he moved here, possibly for work. I would have to ask Roland more about him when I saw him next.

Moving further into the apartment, I took a moment to soak it all in. I had an actual roof over my head. I had a small stove and fridge. I could cook food for the first time in four years.

I had a bed.

A *real* bed.

It wasn't some thin old and dirty mattress on the floor. It was a double bed on a bed frame with pillows and a blanket and there were sheets on the bed. I couldn't even remember ever sleeping with sheets on a bed before. It might seem like a small thing to some, but to me it was huge. This was set up as a home, a real home, and I got to stay here.

I stood on the floor of my first real home.

A few tears leaked from my eyes and I didn't bother with wiping them away. I was not going to risk losing my job, losing this opportunity. I was going to show Oswald that I was worth the risk and I was worth all of his generous help.

Sitting down on the loveseat, I sucked in a deep breath to try and calm my emotions down. I would be going to bed soon, but first I wanted to take this all in. I never wanted to forget this moment and the joy that it brought to me.

I had never felt actual true joy like I did right now and I wanted to savor this moment for the rest of my life.

CHAPTER TEN

Roland

THE TRILL OF my phone echoed in the quiet of the night as I sat in my living room. It was just after midnight and old instincts told me there was a crime scene waiting for me. Only, I wasn't in New York City anymore, so the likelihood that my Captain would be on the other end was extremely low. Even though it was late, I still picked it up and saw that it was actually Mason, my kid brother.

"You know it's late right?" I said as I answered.

"You know you don't sleep right?" he countered with a light tone.

He wasn't wrong, but apparently he didn't sleep anymore than I did if he was still awake.

"Said the man calling me after midnight. What's going on, little brother, you have a bad dream?"

I was teasing him, but he also knew he could call me even if he did have a nightmare. I would always be there for him. We had no parents, no other family alive, it was just us. He was eighteen when they died, so I didn't have to raise him, but that didn't change that I felt responsible for him.

He was twenty-five, now, and worked with Homeland Security going after organizations that committed crimes against children. He traveled all over the country and even overseas when he needed to.

When he told me when he was sixteen that he wanted to be a Federal Agent, my heart went to my throat. I couldn't fault him for it and it wasn't my place to tell him no. By then, I had already been in the Army and was a New York Police Officer. I wasn't in any position to tell him not to do it.

So, I did what I could and made sure he worked out, got fit, taught him how to shoot and how to fight. I couldn't change his mind, but I could make sure he would survive anything that came his way.

"Just in the middle of a case. These cases, man, they are getting harder and harder. It seems like every time we kill one snake another five show up."

I could hear how stressed and burnt out he was getting. I couldn't do what he did. I couldn't dedicate every waking moment of my life to seeing abused children. He was solving vicious crimes against children and I couldn't be more proud of him.

"You need a break. Come down for a bit and give your mind a rest."

"I've been thinking about that, but I gotta wrap this case up first and it could be a month or more before that happens. I got a shit load of vacation time saved up, so I was thinking about coming down, seeing my big bro, and resetting my brain."

"You're welcome here anytime, you know that. You got a room with your name on it, always. You've been doing this for about seven years now, Mason. You need a break before it breaks you."

"I know. I will. What are you doing up still? Or is it one of *those* nights?"

"No, it's not one of *those* nights. Do you remember the kid I was telling you about?"

I had mentioned Tyler to Mason a couple of times over the past few months, about him being young and homeless, and how I hoped to get close enough to earn some trust with him to get him off the street. Mason had advised me to be careful and to reach out to someone within Social Services here, which is what led me to talk to Isaiah.

"Yeah. Tyler, right? You were looking to see about getting him set up in a foster home."

"Well, it turns out he's not a minor, he's twenty-two and the definition of a baby face. I introduced him to Oswald and he had his first shift as the night bartender tonight."

"No shit? Wow. Well, that's good that he's not a minor, but it's unfortunate that he's homeless and there's nothing you can do about it, really. It's good that he's working, but I don't really understand. Why is that keeping you up?"

"I went there to show my support and I brought Jasper with me. I introduced them and everything seemed fine, but after a couple of beers Jasper told me he actually knew Tyler. That he had been a foster kid with him for two years, between twelve and fourteen."

"Ouch. And Tyler didn't act as if he knew him?" Mason asked, his tone making it clear he was confused as well.

It seemed like a simple thing that could be looked over, but at the same time it didn't sit well with me.

Why would Tyler pretend to not know Jasper?

Why did Jasper never say anything?

He knew I was looking into Tyler's background when I thought he was underage. I had even shown him a photo that I had managed to sneak one night. There was no mistaking his face.

So why didn't he say something then?

"Nope. And I've talked about Tyler before to Jasper, plenty. Even showed him a picture. I'm telling you, there is no way you'd forget his face. Yet, Jasper waited until we'd had a few beers last night to tell me. I don't know, it's just not sitting right with me, that's all."

"I agree, I think something is there. It's one thing to not remember a foster kid if they are young, but at the age of twelve, most foster parents remember them. Or if nothing else, they recognize them. You're in a small town, it's not like Tyler was one of thousands that came through his door. You haven't asked Tyler about it yet?"

"No. He works again tonight. I was going to mention it then. We haven't really talked about his time in the system. He was a foster baby, so it's the only life he's known.

At the diner the other day, though, he had mentioned that he used to cook for the younger kids and that a dozen eggs and a bag of potatoes could feed six kids for a couple of days."

"That's not enough food," Mason instantly said, before the words could even come out of my mouth.

"That's what I said, but he didn't get into it. I don't know, maybe because it's a small town, I guess I expected foster parents here to be different, but maybe they're not. It's something I'm going to look into, either way."

"Some of the worst foster homes I've come across are the ones in the small danky towns. I'd look into it on my end, too. The least I can do is help you make sure the kids in that town are safe. Let me know if you need any help running any names."

"I will. I'll talk with Tyler tonight and see what I can get out of him. I'll loop in Isaiah, too. Doing a check on the current foster homes wouldn't be a bad idea. I'll have to see when the last spot check was done. This is my town. It's bad enough that I can't do anything about the homeless problem we have, I'll be damned if I'm going to turn a blind eye to any problems with children."

"Damn right, Brother. I'll be here if you need me."

"Appreciate it. Now, get your ass into bed, I'll do the same. I love you."

"Love you, too."

I ended the call and stood up to head into the bedroom. I wasn't really tired, but it would be better for me to be lying down at least. Give my body some form of rest and I just might luck out and fall asleep in the process. Tomorrow, or rather tonight, I would talk with Tyler and see what I could squeeze out of him. Hopefully, there was nothing there and it was all just in my head.

CHAPTER ELEVEN

Roland

THE BAR WAS already busy by the time I got there just after nine. Thursdays were always a good night, and it would leave Tyler with a good amount of tips.

I went and sat on a swivel stool at the bar and watched as he moved around getting drinks for customers and for Tammy. He was a natural behind the bar and I loved the confidence he had, even though it was only his second shift. He had made a point of knowing where everything was and how it all worked. He was a hard worker and I knew Oswald would be happy with him. It was a good five minutes before he made his way down toward me and I flashed him a warm smile.

"You're a natural back there."

"Thanks. You want a Bud?"

"Yes, please."

He gave a nod and grabbed an amber bottle from the beer fridge, turning back to slide it across to me.

"Hey, real quick, I know you're busy. I wanted to ask you about Jasper. He told me last night that he was one of your foster parents."

The easy smile on his face slowly disappeared at the mention of Jasper and I kicked myself for being the one who made that smile disappear. It was also concerning, though, and did nothing for my suspicions.

"Yeah, I've had a lot of them. I tend to rather just forget about them and focus on the new set of parents and their rules. I didn't know if people knew he was a foster parent, so I figured I would leave the ball in his court," he said, before he headed off to deal with the customers.

What he said was logical and made sense, yet I couldn't shake the feeling that there was more to this than what he let on. I was still going to be looking into the foster system here in town. I wanted to make sure everyone was safe and okay.

I spoke to a few people that were around me, but I kept my gaze on Tyler. He was looking good, rested. Oswald had texted me this morning letting me know that he was sleeping up in the studio. He would be getting proper sleep and he would be able to eat properly and hopefully gain some weight. It was a good thirty minutes before he came back my way with another beer.

"Sorry, I've been neglecting you," he offered with a small smile.

"No apologies needed. Everything okay with you? You getting along with the girls and Jose?"

"Yeah, they are great. I um... I actually

have a date with Tammy," he said, sounding slightly surprised.

"Really? How did that happen?"

"I honestly have no idea. We were talking and she was mentioning Noelle, her daughter, and next thing I know she asked me out and I said yes. I'm not really sure how it happened," he said with a small shrug and a fake smile.

"Either you have very good game or terrible game." I forced a chuckle out.

"Terrible, it's terrible. I don't know, guess we'll see what happens." He shrugged again before he headed off to grab some drinks for the tables.

I took a long drink from my beer as I tried not think about the fact that he would be going on a date. I had been attracted to him for a while now, I knew that. It got worse once I discovered he was actually legal. At one point, I thought maybe he was into me with the amount of times he'd looked at me or shied away from me, but now I knew for a fact that he was into women. The fact hurt more than it should have and it made me slightly sad to know it. I was happy that he was getting his life back on track and going out and meeting people, but it did hurt to know that anything that happened between us would only be in my own fantasies.

CHAPTER TWELVE

Roland

IT WAS JUST after two thirty when the last customer had finally left the bar. I knew Thursdays were busy nights due to the construction and factory workers that came down on their night off from the nearby towns, but tonight had seemed extra busy for some reason. Oswald had built one hell of a following and often the blue-collar workers from the area would make the drive down to have some cold beer and good food.

Guess the word about the bar was getting around more these days.

I went over and locked the door while Tyler was looking over some paperwork. He seemed to be lost in his own world as he looked at the checklist that Oswald had behind the bar.

Every night Oswald made sure the inventory was done and the money was counted. He recorded the sales manually, all so he could compare it with the information from the computer. It wasn't that he didn't trust people, it was more that he didn't trust the computer. There had been a few occasions where the computer stopped working and recording part way through the shift, losing valuable information. I had to stop him from smashing it with a hammer on a few occasions.

"You survived. How do you feel?" I asked, flashing him a warm smile as I went over to him.

"It was good. I like being busy," he answered, but I could tell he was a bit distracted as he looked over the paperwork.

I couldn't help but notice the frown that was growing on his face. He was also hovering over the same bullet point for the past couple of minutes. He rubbed his eyes and I couldn't help but wonder if maybe he needed glasses. Perhaps that was why he was having a hard time with the paperwork.

"Everything okay?" I asked gently. I didn't want to insult him or insinuate that he couldn't understand the paperwork.

He let out a tired and frustrated sigh as he looked up at me and I could see the pain and shame in his eyes. I hated seeing it. His eyes were beautiful and they should never be filled with shame or pain, ever.

"When I was in school, the teachers discovered that I had a learning disability, but they didn't know what it was. None of my foster parents wanted to shovel out the money for me to get tested. I have a hard time with reading. The words get all mixed up."

Nodding, I moved around the bar to join him behind it. I spoke as I grabbed two pieces of paper. "My kid brother, Mason, he used to struggle with reading. Finally, when he was twelve, my parents got him tested and it came back that he was dyslexic. The words and letters would jumble together on the page and he couldn't understand any of it. It got worse if he was tired. He still struggles at times, even now, if his mind needs a break. There's a trick we learned, though."

I covered the words on the page with the exception of the very first word. "You have to train your mind to read one word at a time without thinking about it. Once you can do that, then you go to two words, and then three, etc., etc., until eventually, you can read a whole page without any problems. I don't know if you are dyslexic, but the same rule applies."

He straightened up and I could see the determination in his face as he started to read a single word at a time. I stood by him, being there to help him if he got stuck on some of the larger words. I knew from Mason that even as a single word, if there were too many letters it could be hard for his mind to read it.

Together, we worked through it all and he was able to write without a problem, something that was a good sign. Mason would often get letters or numbers backward, so at least Tyler didn't have that issue.

He put the paperwork away where Oswald kept it before he came back over and leaned his left hip against the bar top, facing me.

"Thank you for your help and for not making fun of me over it."

"I would never make fun of you over something like this, over anything, but especially something like this. You don't have anything to feel ashamed of, either, Ty. The system failed you, not the other way around. If you want, we can work together on it. I'm not an expert, but I have experience with Mason. I'd be happy to help."

"I would love the help. It's time I started to figure out how to overcome it. It's my life, it's time I took control over it."

"You're off to a great start. I'm proud of you," I said, flashing him a warm smile.

The smile that I got in return, though... Hell, it warmed my whole body. It was the first true smile I had seen on his face, it even reached his eyes. He was the most beautiful man I had ever seen. A thought that didn't cause pain to shoot through my heart like it normally did when I looked at another man since Shane.

I don't know what it was about Tyler, but it was as if there was a string connecting us, bringing us together. My hand itched to reach out and touch him. To feel how soft his skin would be underneath my fingers. I had to force myself to remember that he was straight. He was going out on a date with Tammy. There could only be friendship between us.

"It's late, I should get going," I said as I stepped back. I had to get my head back on straight. He was into women, not men.

"Yeah, of course. I'll see you around."

He almost sounded disappointed, but I

quickly dismissed the thought. I needed to get out of here and get some space between us. I was not about to jeopardize our new friendship over anything, even if my body wanted his.

CHAPTER THIRTEEN

Tyler

STANDING OUTSIDE OF Roland's house suddenly seemed like a bad idea.

It had been almost two months since the last time I had spoken with him, truly spoken with him. He had stopped coming by the bar. He was still going to St. Mark's, but I wasn't so we didn't see each other there.

At the beginning, we'd started meeting for coffee and hanging out, talking with each other during my off hours. I was finally more comfortable around him. Well, at least his size didn't intimidate me so much, anyway. We had been building a friendship. At least, I thought we were.

Then, all of a sudden, he wasn't answering my calls or texts. He'd stopped coming by the bar, and we were no longer meeting for coffee. It was like a light switch had been flipped on our friendship and I had no idea why.

The past two months had been different for me. I had dated Tammy, but that only lasted two weeks before we discovered we were more compatible as friends. I started dating a patron at the bar. Casey. She was a sweet girl and we were the same age. We had a lot in common, outside of me being a foster child. She was a great girl and a lot of fun to be around. It was different to have people in my life all of a sudden.

Friends.

What I couldn't figure out was why Roland was ghosting me all of a sudden and I was done waiting around for him to come to me.

That determination was what brought me to his house tonight on one of my days off. Though, at the time it seemed like a great idea, now, standing here in front of his door, it seemed like the dumbest idea I'd ever had. I could turn back, but I was already here, and if I left, I might never get the courage to come back here and then I would never know what happened.

I had been going over every conversation we'd had to see if I could have said or done something to offend him or given him any indication that I didn't want a friendship with him. I was coming up blank, though. Something was off. It had to be. Roland was the only one with those answers and I deserved them.

With newfound courage, I reached out and pushed the doorbell before I could change my mind. After a moment, the door opened to reveal Roland, who seemed surprised at my being there. I didn't even wait for him to invite me in. Instead, I started to speak as I walked right through his doorway.

"What is your problem?"

"Excuse me?" he asked, confused, but there was no edge to it.

"You've been ghosting me for almost two months now. I deserve to know why you have decided that we aren't friends anymore. What, now that I'm not some pathetic homeless guy on the street you want nothing to do with me?"

That was an actual worry of mine. It might sound illogical, but it was the only logical explanation I could come to that would explain the one-eighty from him. I wasn't about to quit my job and be homeless just so we could be friends, but I deserved the truth, even if it hurt.

"I haven't been ghosting you, Tyler," he denied, but I was not about to let him get away with it. I was not going to tolerate lying.

"Bullshit, Ro. You no longer answer any of my calls or texts. You no longer go for coffee or grab something to eat. You're not even coming by the bar anymore. If you have a problem with me, then fine, but say it. And you don't get to take it out on Oswald, he doesn't deserve it after everything he has done…"

My rant was cut short by a pair of lips capturing mine. I hadn't even seen it coming. I was looking just off to the side of him, not directly in his eyes because I still had a hard time with confrontation and it was easier to not look at the person while doing it. His hands were on the side of my face, cupping my cheeks and holding me against his lips.

His lips.

Holy shit, I was being kissed by a guy.

Shock didn't seem to cover what I felt in that moment and before my brain could even register what to do, he was pulling back from me.

"That's why I haven't been coming around you. Because every time I'm alone with you, all I want to do is kiss you. I haven't wanted to kiss another man since the man that I loved died eleven years ago. And then you came into my life and it took all of my strength and restraint to not push you up against a wall and kiss the hell out of you. Hearing that you were dating a woman, it killed me inside and I couldn't do it. I thought I could, but I can't. I like you, Ty, and not in a friendly way."

Holy shit.

I needed to say something. I knew I needed to say something, but my mind wouldn't work. All I could feel were his lips still against my own. The tingle that it sent right through my body.

Oh God.

A tingle that still lingered.

I had to say something, anything, right now, but no matter how many times I opened my mouth, no words, no sound would come out.

My instinct to run when being exposed to confrontation or uncomfortable feelings went into overdrive and before I even knew what I was doing, I practically ran out of his house. By the time my mind had caught up to what I was doing, I was ten blocks away. Bending over, I tried to catch my breath.

Running was not something I did often and it was not advised with my asthma. I could already feel my chest getting tighter, so I pulled out my inhaler and took two puffs.

Slowly, I felt my lungs start to loosen up. I started back to the bar, walking this time. I hadn't brought my car because Roland actually lived only fifteen minutes away from the bar. It was better to walk than to risk my car breaking down on me. I was saving everything I could to be able to afford an apartment and have a little bit of a cushion, just in case. I had been looking at different apartment for rent ads in the newspaper, so I had a rough idea of the amount I needed to save up. I was about halfway there, as long as my car didn't crap out on me.

Roland kissed me.

Fuck, I couldn't get over that. I knew he was gay and I didn't care that he was gay. That was never an issue with me. I didn't think he would ever be interested in someone like me, though. He was built, successful, good looking, he had his life cemented.

Me? I was the exact opposite of that. I was homeless all of two months ago. I didn't have family. I was riddled with trauma that made it hard for me to trust people, especially men. I had no high school education. I didn't even have a diploma. That was all before you factored in my health and my size. I was not attractive to men like Roland. I was barely attractive to women.

How could he possibly be attracted to me?

That wasn't even the most confusing part, though.

I think I liked it.

I could still feel his lips against mine and it didn't bother me. I was a twenty-two year old virgin. It sounded farfetched, but I was.

There was no time growing up to date and have sex because I was not in school and I took care of the younger kids in my foster homes. I couldn't go out on a date. And then, I was homeless and it wasn't like I could bring a girl back to my car.

I had been kissed when I was thirteen by a girl in my foster home, but we never went past heavy make out sessions. The first time I had done anything besides kissing with a girl was Tammy. We had made out plenty of times and we felt each other up, but I never had sex with her. Then, there was Casey, who I had been with for about a month, now, and we still hadn't had sex. It wasn't that she didn't want to, I didn't. When she touched me, yes, I got hard, but I wasn't filled with this desire or need to be inside of her.

The lack of desire, I thought maybe that was just how I was wired. Maybe it was normal for me to not want to rip her clothes off. Maybe it was normal for me to not feel sparks when we kissed or touched. But now, I don't know.

Now, I couldn't help but wonder if maybe that was why I didn't feel anything. Maybe I was gay. Maybe that was what this weird feeling I got around Roland was. Maybe it wasn't fear, but attraction. I don't know. The more I thought about all of it, the more confused I got. I needed time. Time to think and figure out who I was and what gender I was attracted to.

The second I arrived back at the bar, I got into my car and headed over to Casey's place. I needed to talk to her. I had no idea what I was going to do, but I did know it wasn't fair to her to wait while I figured it all out. If I was actually attracted to men over women, I wasn't about to string her along and I was not about to hide who I was.

That was something I was confident in. Once I knew who I was and I accepted it, I was not going to be hiding in any closets. I just needed to figure out what gender I was attracted to. I needed time to process the events that happened and my own feelings.

Pulling up to Casey's apartment, which was the bottom level of a house, I parked and turned off the engine. I wasn't sure what I was going to tell her, but I wasn't about to lie. I would still see her at work and I didn't want to cause any hostility. Letting out a slow breath, I climbed out of my car and strolled to her door. She opened the door a moment after I knocked and I could see she was pleasantly surprised to see me.

"Baby, what are you doing here?"

"Sorry, I should have called or texted first. There's just something I need to talk to you about. Can I come in?" This was not a conversation I was about to have over the phone and definitely not through text messages. She deserved better than that.

"Of course, yeah," she said as she moved back.

Normally, I would kiss her and I could tell she expected one, but I couldn't bring myself to do it. I was afraid that if my lips touched hers that I would lose the feeling of Roland's lips. I wasn't ready for that yet.

"What's on your mind?" she asked as she closed the door.

I didn't even know where to start. When Tammy and I called it quits, she started the conversation off and I jumped on it. Maybe being honest was the best way to go here.

"A guy just kissed me," I blurted out.

"Wow, are you okay?" she asked

sincerely as she walked over to her couch.

"I didn't kiss him back and it came out of nowhere." I spoke as I joined her. The last thing I wanted was for her to think I was cheating on her.

"I know you well enough to tell that you aren't the cheating type. You know, I would be lying if I said I hadn't wondered if you were gay," she said carefully.

"What?"

"I don't mean it against you at all. I have a few gay friends, both guys and girls. It's the twenty-first century, love who you want. But yeah, I've wondered. A girl can tell when a guy isn't all that hot and heavy into her. I didn't want to push, figured maybe you were trying to work something out yourself."

Of course she would have noticed. I should have figured as much. It would be pretty obvious that I wasn't dying to get in her pants when every time she tried to move things along I put the brakes on it.

"Honestly, I don't know. I've never looked at a guy that way before, but if I'm honest with myself, I've never looked at a girl like that before, either. Dating wasn't a thing for me growing up. There was no time for it. I haven't really put any thought into it."

"When you kiss someone, especially the first time with that person, it leaves you feeling like electricity just shot through you. Your whole body is covered in goosebumps and you tingle. Have you ever felt that way when you kiss a girl?" she asked with complete patience and understanding in her voice. She wasn't mad that we were having this conversation. Apparently, she had been waiting for it.

"No. I'm sorry, that sounds mean considering what we've done." The last thing I wanted to do was make her feel bad.

"It doesn't sound mean at all. Lots of people can have a great time together, a great friendship, but zero chemistry. It happens all the time. The world didn't move when I kissed you either. There's no deep love between us and that's okay. There's nothing wrong with us being friends. What did you feel like when he kissed you, beyond the obvious shock and surprise."

"Shock and surprise mostly sums it up. It happened so fast and it didn't last long, I didn't even have the chance to respond or push him away. Afterward, though, there was that tingling feeling. It wasn't strong, but there was something there."

That was the confusing part, because apparently I should have felt that way kissing her, but I didn't. Maybe I was gay, maybe this was a piece of myself that had been missing, a piece I didn't know was missing. This conversation had me feeling better in the sense that I wasn't hurting her by breaking up. However, it was only leaving me even more confused by how I felt toward Roland.

"I think the best thing you can do is take some time to be single and let your mind process everything that happened. Right now, it's all new and your mind is probably overloaded with new feelings. Take your time and see how you feel about it in a few days. Then try and think about what you want."

She was right. I needed to take some time to myself, process, and then re-evaluate my feelings toward Roland. I'd give myself a week to be on my own, in my own world, and hopefully, by the end of the week, I'd have a better grasp on what I wanted.

CHAPTER FOURTEEN

Roland

HOW COULD A single week feel like an eternity?

It had only been a week since Tyler stood here in my home with my lips against his. It was a single moment in my life that was both good and horrific.

Horrific, because it caused Tyler to flee from not only my home, but from his job as well. He hadn't been to the bar in the past week and that was all my fault.

It was also good for me, though, because of how amazing it felt to feel his lips. To feel him against me. I never thought I could ever feel that way toward another man, not since Shane. I would have sworn on my life that Shane was my soulmate. That he was who I was meant to be with. Yet, one single sort of kiss with Tyler and the world moved. I had never felt that way with Shane, which brought on its own confusion.

During my session with Dr. Howard, he could tell that something was off with me. I had been a bit depressed, something that got worse as the days without seeing Tyler added up. He had explained that perhaps at the time I believed that Shane was the only guy for me in this life, that he was my soulmate, it was because he was the only male I had been with. He described it as puppy love, often what teenagers feel, versus true love. He mentioned that it is normal for young people to feel this way until they become an adult and they go through a few relationships and eventually discover that what they felt when they were younger was nothing compared to the real thing.

I didn't want to believe that Dr. Howard could be right, but as each day went on, that single kiss invaded my entire body and mind. I dreamed about Tyler and his lips all over me. My lips all over his body. Being inside of him. My thoughts of him were all consuming, all from a single kiss.

Maybe what I did have for Shane was puppy love. Maybe I clung to him and his memory so hard, because that's who I believed to be my soulmate, like most teenagers.

It hurt to think of Shane like that and I knew he would always live within my heart, but it was possible that he didn't need to live in my whole heart. He could live in a piece of it as my first love. I hoped that maybe, just maybe, over time, the hurt would decrease until I no longer felt it. One thing I did know from kissing Tyler, I could have a chance at finding love again one day.

My problem, though, I craved Tyler and his body. Not just his body in a sexual sense, but his presence. I had grown used to having him around. To grab a coffee or a meal together. To see him at the bar after a long day of work. He had become the best part of my day and now for the past week that sunshine was gone. It had been pouring rain and no matter what I did I couldn't escape it.

I hadn't even been to the gym all week because I didn't feel like doing anything. I would drag my ass to work and to my sessions, but then just come right back home and sit on the couch. Eventually, my eyes would start to burn from exhaustion and then I would crawl into bed just to be haunted by dreams of him. It was exhausting and it dragged me down more than anything ever had before.

A knock at my door brought me out of my depressing spiral. Letting out a tired sigh, I mentally debated if I should get up or not. It couldn't be anyone important, because if it was they would have called me.

The knock came again.

I forced my body to move and get up.

Whoever it was on the other side of my door, they were clearly not going away. I wasn't sure who I expected, but when I opened my door the last person I expected stood there.

Just the sight of Tyler was enough for my heart to jump right into my throat. For a week, I had been worried about him. For a week, I had been terrified that I had scared him off and he had left town. That he had thrown all of his progress away because of my reckless actions. Oswald had said he had asked for some time off, but that didn't ease my fears.

"Hey, um... can we talk?" he asked with complete uncertainty to his voice.

I hated hearing it. I used to hear it all the time when I first met him. He wouldn't make eye contact with me and he would often shy away, stutter. But we were past that, or so I thought. I hated that I was responsible for putting that timidness back into him.

"Yeah, of course. Come in," I said as I moved back and he cautiously walked into my house.

He was a ball of nerves and I knew I had to be careful with my actions and words toward him. I didn't want to scare him off again. I had no idea how we were ever going to get back to being friends with each other, but I was determined to make it happen. If there was one thing that I had discovered this past week, it was that I didn't want him out of my life. Even if that meant we would only ever be friends. He was special and I was not about to lose him again.

"Look, Ty, I'm sorry. I shouldn't have kissed you. It was wrong of me. It came out of nowhere for me, too. I knew I had been attracted to you, but I never thought I would act on it. I know you're straight," I started, but he cut me off with a very soft and confused voice.

"I don't know about that."

"Don't know about what?"

"I'm confused. I've never looked at guys like that before, but I've never looked at women like that, either. Growing up, I just thought I was too busy to notice and then I was homeless. I didn't have sex with Tammy or Casey. I've never had sex with anyone. The interest or desire to have sex has never been there. I just thought it was *me*. But then, you kissed me and now I can't stop thinking about it. When you kissed me, my whole body tingled from it and the feeling lasted for hours afterward. I've never felt that way before. So, yeah, I'm confused and I just needed some time to process what happened. To try and figure out what I felt."

Two thoughts ran through my mind. The first, *holy shit he's a virgin*. The second, *he might be gay*. I thought the possibility of me and him having some type of a romantic relationship was completely off the table, but now it was actually on the table. There was a true chance that we could build something, if that is what he wanted. It made sense why he needed time.

I could still painfully remember what it was like for me when I first discovered I was gay. Mason had handled it so much easier than me. He was fine with it, accepted who he was since he was twelve.

Me, though, I denied it. I tried everything within my power for me to fit within the straight box. I dated a lot of girls. I was a player and I kept having sex with them. I was going to be straight, because I couldn't be the gay soldier. Even at the age of sixteen, I knew I was going to be in the army and I knew I couldn't do that as a gay man.

But no matter how many women I slept with, I never felt satisfied.

On my eighteenth birthday, a week before I was to ship out for boot camp, I went to a gay club with my fake ID. It was there that I met Shane and we hooked up that night. The first time being touched by another man sent fire all down my spine. I could still feel his touch lingering long after we had parted. I knew exactly what Tyler was feeling right now.

"When you've gone your whole life believing and thinking you were straight, it's not easy to accept that you could actually be gay. Taking the time to be alone and to gather your thoughts was the best thing you could do, Ty. There's no pressure here. We can pretend that the kiss never happened and just go back to being friends. You have the control here."

The last thing I wanted was for him to feel pressured into being with me. If he wanted to be with me, I wanted it to be because he felt attracted to me and not out of some sort of obligation. I didn't want anything fake. I wanted something real between us.

"I don't think I want that. To go back to just being friends, I mean. But I've never done this before and I don't know if I'll even be any good, at the sex or the relationship part. But, I want to try. I know when you kissed me I felt electricity for the first time in my life and I know I want to feel that way again. I just need you to be patient with me while I try and figure it all out."

"We have all the time in the world. We'll take it slow and you dictate what you are ready for in terms of the sex department. We'll go as slow as you need. I'm not in any rush."

Sex was an important part in a relationship in terms of chemistry and connection, but it also wasn't the only part. I wanted to connect with Tyler on an emotional and mental level as well and not just a physical one. I had no problem waiting to have sex with him. Hell, it'd been eight years since I'd had sex. He wouldn't be the only one nervous and unsure.

"Will you..." he started, but then stopped, clearly scared and unsure.

I moved closer to him, placed my hand on the side of his face, and tilted his head so he was looking at me and not the ground. He needed to start building up some confidence. He needed to understand and learn that he was not less than in any way. Especially to me.

"Will I what? You can ask me anything, Sweetheart."

I never wanted him to hesitate with me. He needed to feel like he could be open and honest with me. I wanted him to feel like he could tell me anything or ask me anything. I didn't want secrets between us. If we were going to have any chance of a real relationship, we needed to build a strong foundation.

"Will you kiss me?" he asked softly.

"Always." I closed the small distance between us. This time, when I pressed my lips against his, I kept it soft and gentle. Last time, I had kissed him out of raw need, and this time I wanted to savor it. I wanted him to savor it.

His lips were softer than I remembered them being. He felt amazing and unlike last time where he froze at the contact, this time he pressed back. He was still unsure and slightly apprehensive. I could feel it. I understood it.

When I first kissed Shane, even though I had been kissing girls for years, I felt like I didn't know how to do anything. I knew, though, that Tyler would get more comfortable and loosen up. Soon, the pleasure would kick in and he would take more control.

He started to get a bit braver as he

pressed his lips a bit harder against mine. I moved and his lips easily followed me. I could feel his body starting to loosen up, so I pushed my tongue out to trace against his lips, asking for permission, which he easily gave. The second I felt his tongue against mine, we both moaned. He tasted better than I ever could have imagined.

He ran his hand up along my chest as I moved us back so his back was up against the wall. I wanted nothing more than to press against him fully, but this was only a kiss. I needed to go slow and let him dictate how fast we took things. It wasn't even the fact that being with a guy was a new experience for him. It was the fact that he was a *virgin*.

Your first time is supposed to be special, something I didn't believe in when I was younger, but I did believe in it now. He deserved for his first time to be romantic and sweet, especially after all of this time. I could have kissed him all night, but we needed to talk more first.

Reluctantly, I pulled back, stopping the

kiss in its tracks. He gave a small whine at the loss of contact and that was a very good sign. He liked it and wanted more. Hopefully, that would help ease some of his confusion about his new discovery.

"Wow," he said softly.

I let out a warm chuckle. I was feeling the same way.

"Come on, let's sit down and talk."

If we were ever going to have any chance at something real, I needed to be honest with him. And that meant telling him about Shane. It wasn't going to be easy at all, it was going to hurt to talk about, but I knew I had to do it. I had been talking to Dr. Howard about it in between my stories from my army days. It was hard, but I had to admit, it was helping. We went and sat down on my couch and I turned so I could face him.

"You shared something very personal with me and it's only fair that I do the same. First, I want to let you know, though, that I would like to build something real with you. It's not about sex, and like I said, we will take it as slow as you need. There's no pressure on my end."

"I'd like to build something with you, too. I'm not good at this and I don't really know how to be in a healthy relationship, but I'm willing to learn."

"To be honest, I don't really know, either. I've only dated one guy in my life. *Shane.* He was the first guy I had kissed when I turned eighteen. I didn't handle it well when I discovered I liked boys over girls. I still tried to like girls, to fit into the box I thought I had to be in. I slept with thirty girls between sixteen and eighteen, but none of them ever left me feeling satisfied. Friction was the only reason I could even get off. But a week before I was to leave for boot camp, I decided to go to a gay club. It was there I met Shane. We were together for three years, but I kept him a secret. I stayed in the closet and it was a serious issue for Shane. He was out and proud and he didn't like being a dirty secret. We got into a huge fight when I was twenty-one and he stormed out and drove off. He was hit by a drunk driver. He was dead on impact."

"I'm so sorry. I can't even imagine."

"It was hard. It was *really* hard. I was set to go into the Rangers, but his death changed everything. They didn't find the driver and that wasn't something I could live with. I joined the police force in New York City and, eventually, I was able to find the man that killed Shane. I came out when I went into the academy. I wasn't going to make the same mistake twice. It took three years, though, before I could bring myself to touch another man. The next morning, I felt horrible. I felt like I had cheated on Shane. I swore I would never feel that way again, so I haven't been with anyone in eight years. You are the first man that I have kissed in eight years."

I could see the shock flicker across his eyes. It was surprising and that was why I never told anyone. Whenever someone at work asked me about my dating life, I kept it private and said it was none of their business. To go eight years without sex seemed unheard of where a guy was concerned. Even more so when you factor in I hadn't even touched a man in eight years.

"Really?"

"Yes. So all of this is new to me again. I wanted you to know that so you can completely understand and believe me when I tell you that sex isn't important to me. We can take as long as you need. If all we do is kiss, I'm good with that. The most important aspect is you feeling comfortable with taking any of the next steps."

"Thank you for sharing that with me." He reached over and placed his hand in mine as he spoke. "As much as you want me to be comfortable, I want the same for you. I don't want you doing anything that you aren't ready for either."

"I promise."

It was an easy promise for me to make. One that I would be keeping, and I knew he would keep his promise as well. Tonight had gone so much better than I had ever expected. I never thought I would even get to see Tyler again. Now, here we were sitting on my couch and actually going to start a relationship together. It was a dream come true and I couldn't wait to see what the future held for us.

CHAPTER FIFTEEN

Tyler

LISTENING TO ROLAND tell me about Shane really cemented my certainty for him. I was a bit worried that he was looking for sex right away, or that he wasn't looking for a relationship. He was older than me by ten years. We were at two different places in our lives and it would be natural that he wasn't looking for anything serious. It felt amazing to know that he wanted to take things slow with me, too. That he wanted to build a strong foundation with trust and honesty on both of our ends so we could form a strong relationship. It matched everything that I knew about him and it only made me feel more certain that I was making the right choice.

It hurt to hear him talk about Shane. Not because I was jealous, but because I could hear the pain still in his voice. Even though it had been eleven years, that wound was still fresh and had yet to scar over. I'm sure some would feel like they were competing with a ghost, but I didn't feel that way. I had never loved someone before, but I could imagine that if I lost the man that I loved, that I thought I would marry and be with forever, it would be devastating. He needed to heal from it and I had no problem helping him heal. I had no problem listening to stories about him. I already knew he must have been a special man if Roland loved him so deeply.

We decided to put on a movie and just relax on the couch together. I had to work tomorrow night and I was looking forward to going back to the bar. When I had asked Oswald for the week off, he was very sweet and kind about it. I was worried he would deny my request, but he was good with it and he didn't push to know why. I'd tell him my reasons tomorrow so he knew I wasn't just taking time off to flake on him or because I didn't feel like working. He had been nice enough to not only give me a job, but a place to live and the last thing I wanted was for him to feel taken advantage of or that I was ungrateful.

I was trying to pay attention to the movie, I really was, but it was a lot harder than I thought it would be. Feeling the heat from Roland's body right next to me, all I could think about was how good it felt to feel his lips on mine. I wondered how his body would feel against mine.

If the weight of him would leave me feeling claustrophobic or safe.

I was still trying to get used to all of this. To being attracted to him, to a man, but also being interested in sexual activities. I was also still trying to get used to him being huge.

My whole life I had been afraid of men that were big, much less massive like he was. I kept reminding myself that he wasn't going to hurt me. That I didn't need to flinch and curl up whenever he got too close to me. That when he reached out for me, it wasn't to grab and hurt me. The fear, the reaction, was deeply ingrained in me and I knew it would take time for that instinct to be erased. But I also knew he had been good about it.

He always made a point of making sure I saw when he moved his hand toward me. Even little touches here and there to help me get used to his presence. The signs were there that he had been developing feelings for me, but to me those little touches weren't affectionate, just a man moving around. Knowing that they were actually affectionate touches, it left a warm feeling in my chest.

We were halfway through the movie, but I truly had no idea what was going on with it. I was looking at the screen, but my mind wasn't taking any of it in. I couldn't focus on anything but his body. The feel of his lips against mine. He was allowing me to have complete control over our situation, meaning he wouldn't kiss me again tonight until I initiated it.

The problem was, I didn't really know how to do that.

With a girl it was easy, and more times than not, she would be the one to initiate it with me. Normally, by sitting on my lap and kissing me. I wasn't really sure how to go about initiating it with Roland, but if I wanted to feel his lips against mine again, I would have to figure it out. The only thing I could think of would be to straddle his lap.

I mean, if it works for a girl, why wouldn't it work for me?

Right?

Oh God.

Gathering up all of my courage that I could muster, I moved and straddled his lap, snapping his attention away from the movie. He gave me a warm smile as I started to close the gap between our lips.

The second our lips touched, a fire shot right through me. I had never felt this way before and it was all consuming. The need for more, the need to feel his body against mine, it was overwhelming in a good way. This time around as we kissed, I moved my hands up and down his chest, feeling each and every single muscle that was lying underneath his shirt.

His hands ran down my back and landed on my ass. He squeezed it slightly, causing my hips to rock forward just the slightest, but it was enough for our crotches to rub together. That slight touch was enough to cause me to moan and I needed to feel it again.

I rocked my hips, causing friction between us and, apparently, I wasn't the only one with the desperate need to feel it again, because Roland used his grip on my ass to rock my hips even more. We both moaned and I could feel his dick was already hard, straining against his pants. I was already hard and to feel his dick throbbing against mine, with only material separating us, was pure and utter bliss.

I picked up my pace and Roland started to roll his hips to match mine. It added to the friction and we were both moaning and panting. I had to pull back from the kiss as it became too hard to keep going while we were moving.

"Oh fuck," I moaned.

Never in my life had I ever felt this good before. Not even with my own hand or that from a female.

"That's it, just feel it, Baby," Roland said as he started to kiss and nibble along my neck.

That's all I could do right now, was *feel*.

Everything around us disappeared. I couldn't even hear the movie anymore. All I could hear were our moans and heavy breathing echoing throughout the room. All I could feel were his hands on my ass, his lips on my neck, and his glorious thick dick against my own.

It was like everything in my life was clicking at this exact moment. Gone was the confusion of being attracted to men. Gone was the uncertainty if this was the right call to make. Our bodies fit together so perfectly, and it felt too good to be anything but real and right. I was gay and I was going to embrace every aspect of it.

I had no idea how the sex aspect would work. I had to assume that it would be my ass that he would be pounding into and not the other way around. It was slightly terrifying, but if he could make this feel good and we weren't even skin to skin, shit, I couldn't wait to see how good it would feel when I could feel every inch of his body and dick against my own.

Our panting and moans picked up and I could feel his dick hardening more against mine. We were both close to the edge and I was torn between wanting to come and wanting to hold off so we could keep doing this. I wasn't ready for the pleasure to end, but my body had other thoughts in mind. After a moment, I was coming hard in my own pants, something I had never done before.

"Ro," I moaned deeply as he continued to

move my hips up and back over his cock so he could follow behind me.

I pulsed as I listened to his delicious grunts as his own climax quickly approached. He held my hips down over his dick as he gave a deep groan and then I could feel his dick pulsing underneath me. The feeling of it caused my own dick to pulse in return, pumping me for even more cum.

I placed my forehead against his as we both fought to regulate our breathing. Everything was tingling, absolutely everything, even my lips. I knew it was from a combination of pleasure and lack of air from panting so much.

"That was the best movie I've ever seen," he joked.

I couldn't help but laugh at that. It was a great movie. One that I would be very interested in seeing over and over again.

"Well, that cleared up any confusion. I'm definitely gay."

It was his turn to laugh at that. Not having that confusion hanging over me, over us, was going to be a huge relief. At least I knew for a fact that I was gay, completely, and we could work on building a strong relationship. I would also hopefully not be scared or as nervous with the next aspect of our sexual relationship as we progressed.

"I'm glad we could clear that up for you. Now, we're both sticky and tired. I haven't come in my pants since I was a teenager."

"I've never done it. I have to agree, though, things are getting a bit sticky."

The journey to get here had been amazing, but now that the pleasure was starting to taper down, I was getting a bit uncomfortable with wet cum in my pants. It wasn't a fun and enjoyable feeling, but I knew I would be more than willing to go through it again.

"Come on, let's turn in. I have a spare room you can sleep in. As much as I would like to have you in my bed, I don't think either of us would be able to keep our hands to ourselves and I don't want to move too fast."

That might actually be the sweetest thing I had ever heard. He truly did want to take things slow and he was making sure I would be comfortable with whatever we did. It was sweet and I greatly appreciated it.

He was also right.

I don't think I would be able to keep my hands to myself if I was in bed with him. I could have walked back home, but I was exhausted and wanted to get cleaned up. Plus this way, I would get a good morning kiss and that was very appealing to me.

"Sounds good," I easily agreed.

I got up off his lap and he turned off the TV and the lights before we made our way up the stairs. He showed me where the bathroom was and the spare bedroom. He had his own bathroom in his room. He gave me a slow and passionate kiss that left my knees weak and had my dick half hard by the time he pulled back.

"Good night, Sweetheart," he said warmly.

"Good night, Babe."

He gave me a wink before he turned and

headed down the hall to his own bedroom to get cleaned up himself.

I watched as he walked away, noticing his ass and how amazing it looked in his jeans before he disappeared. Letting out a soft sigh, I headed into the bathroom to get cleaned up. Tonight had been a whirlwind of emotions, but I was glad I had decided to take the risk and come here. It had more than paid off and I couldn't wait until the morning when I could see him again.

CHAPTER SIXTEEN

Roland

JUST AS THE coffee finished percolating, my front door opened and I heard the telltale sound of clicking against my floors. The smile that rushed over my features was instant as I turned and saw Koda running straight for me as Mason closed the door. Koda was Mason's gorgeous German Shepherd that he trained for work. The sight of the dog filled my heart with happiness.

Koda was five years old now, but he was still full of energy. He was the sweetest dog. Mason got him when he was just eight weeks old and started to get him trained. After five years, he was now trained for attack, scent tracking, and to detect anxiety. Mason often used him with the children he came across in his job, and Koda had made a huge difference to thousands of children. Whether they were anxious with being away from the only life they had known, or they were too scared to sleep at night, Koda was there for them and made them feel better, made them feel safe.

I was thankful that my brother had companionship in Koda. I knew the horrors that he often saw with his job, and Koda would be there to protect and help him heal from the toll it could take on him.

"Hello, my sweet boy," I said as I started to pet him. "You know he loves me better, right?" I teased my brother, who very maturely rolled his eyes.

"He only likes you because you slip him food from the table when you think I'm not looking."

I chuckled at that, because I really thought I had gotten away with it. It never failed, though, every time I saw Koda I always told myself that I should get a dog, yet I still haven't. Maybe this time around I would.

"How was the trip?" I asked as I reluctantly moved away from Koda and gave my brother a hug.

Mason was not built like me, but he was still muscular and I knew for a fact he could take anyone in a fight. I had trained him, after all. We did look similar, though, in terms of our hair and eye color, the shape of our face. We were both cursed with being handsome and, oddly enough, were both gay.

"Not bad. Airplanes are nothing for me."

No truer words had been spoken. Mason was built for flying. It didn't matter if it was two hours or twenty-four hours, he could do it standing on his head. I was all right with flying, but those long flights were not something I had missed since being out of the army.

"So, what's been going on since I talked to you last? You seem to be in a better mood than you were a few days ago. I expected to find you on the couch in sweatpants with empty pizza boxes and beer cans all around you."

That wasn't all that inaccurate.

I really wish it was, but a few more days and I probably would have reached that level. I wasn't a health freak, but I usually did make sure I ate right. It wasn't often I would eat greasy pizza, but if I did then you could assume I was feeling sad or stressed.

"Tyler came over last night. We had a great conversation."

"Oh, just a conversation?" he teased as he grabbed some coffee and headed for the table.

"A bit more than that. It started off with a conversation. He told me that he needed time to get his feelings in order and to process everything that had just happened."

"Makes sense. He thought he was straight his whole life. Having a guy kiss you out of nowhere can be shocking.,” Mason said with complete understanding in his voice.

“And that was my fault for doing it that way. It came out of nowhere. Thankfully, though, I didn’t scare him off for very long. He told me he had feelings for me, too. That he didn’t even sleep with the two women he had been dating in the past two months. He’s actually never slept with a woman before, or anyone.”

“Damn, you bagged yourself a twenty-two year old virgin. Now I’m jealous.”

I couldn’t help the sigh. My brother, he was a sucker for smaller guys and virgins. They were his kryptonite and I swear one day he was going to sleep with the wrong guy and be on the wrong end of a gun.

“The point is, we are taking things slow. We watched a movie and made out a bit last night before we went to sleep, in separate rooms. I’m trying to make him feel comfortable and allow him to stay in control of the sexual progress.”

It wasn’t easy, because I would have

loved to have him underneath me. However, I did remember what it felt like to first discover you were gay. It was terrifying and confusing. The last thing Tyler needed was for me to be a jerk and pressure him to go faster.

"I am happy for you. It's been a very long time since you've allowed yourself to be with another man. I know what happened with Shane was devastating, but you've kinda been putting your whole life on pause, Bro. I don't know what it's like to lose the man you love, and I didn't know Shane as well as I should have, but he wouldn't want this for you. He wouldn't want you to be alone and heartbroken for the rest of your life."

His voice was calm and gentle and it reminded me of the voice he often used with child victims. What he said was true and I knew that. Shane wouldn't want me to be miserable. The whole point of the fight was he wanted me to come out of the closet. For us to have a true relationship and potentially get married. He wouldn't want me to be alone and miserable forever. It was something I was trying to deal with during my sessions with Dr. Howard.

"I'm trying. What about you? Any new men in your life?"

"Not right now, no. I've been too busy with work. I'm not really the dating type, anyway. It's easier to keep things to friends with benefits or one-night stands."

"Always such a romantic," I teased, sarcasm lacing my voice.

Before he could comment, Koda's head snapped up and looked right at the door. I caught the tension that flared through my brother's body and I couldn't help but wonder if more was going on with him then he had been telling me.

"You expecting someone?" He tried to keep his voice calm and casual, but I could hear the tightness in his voice. He was on edge. Something else was definitely going on with him. I knew he wouldn't talk about it right now, but I would be keeping an eye on him.

"It's Isaiah. He's coming by so we can talk about the foster home situation," I answered as I got up to let him in.

I had told Mason about Jasper and Tyler's reaction to him. Even after Tyler tried to blow it off, I still felt uneasy about it, so I reached out to Isaiah to see what he could discover for me. He had called last night before Tyler came over to tell me he found something and we needed to talk about it. He wanted to come over last night, but I knew Mason would be here in the morning and told him to come by now. If something was going on, it helped to have a Federal Agent around.

"Hey man, come on in," I said warmly as I opened the door.

Where I looked well rested, a strange thing for me because I didn't have a single nightmare last night, Isaiah looked like a train wreck. His hair stood in spikes around his head and there were dark rings around his eyes. If I didn't know him better, I'd assume he'd gone on a bender and this was the end result. But, I did know him better. This was no bender. I had no idea what he had discovered, but it looked like it had him up all night tossing and turning.

"Is your brother here?" he asked as he walked in.

"Yeah, in the kitchen. Come on back and grab a coffee. You look like you could use it. Rough night?"

"You wouldn't believe what I found, Roland," he said as we headed toward my kitchen.

I had no idea what he had found, but by how he was behaving, he found something huge. Something I wasn't going to like. I did the introductions as Isaiah grabbed some coffee.

"Mason, this is Isaiah. He works with Social Services and is who I mentioned that I reached out to about intel on Tyler."

"It's nice to meet you," Mason said with a nod as he held his hand out to Isaiah.

"Nice to meet you. I have a feeling we're going to need your help on this one." Isaiah clasped my brother's hand in his easily as he spoke.

"What did you find?" I asked, getting things started.

"I started by looking through Tyler's time with Jasper. As you know, he was there between the ages of twelve and fourteen. He was one of eight foster kids, sometimes a little less, over the two years. It all seems perfectly normal and there weren't any red flags in Tyler's file for Jasper. Before that, he had been through a lot of rough homes and had been abused. It all stopped for two years before he was sent to another foster home and then it picked up all over again."

"Okay, but I'm not hearing anything to imply that something is wrong with Jasper. Sounds like you need to review all of the foster homes in the system, though," Mason said.

"Tyler was diagnosed with a protein deficiency when he was eight. It makes it hard for him to gain weight. Aside from that and the asthma, he was perfectly healthy. Broken bones and bruising, but no illnesses. For the two years he was with Jasper, everything was perfect. *Too perfect.* Bruises were gone, he went to school, everything was normal and without complaint. Then all of a sudden, he's being transferred, at Jasper's request, to another home and the hell started all over again. Only, he was there for two days when he started to get very sick. His social worker saw how sick he was and took him to the hospital. They ran his blood work and discovered he was going through cocaine withdrawal." Isaiah ran a hand through his hair, mussing it even more.

"Whoa, what?"

I wasn't expecting that. I figured maybe Jasper had lost his temper with him at times and hurt him. Jasper did have a temper on him and if you pushed the right button he lost his shit. I had seen it at work before. We had been partners for three years now, but I thought I knew him. I thought I had seen the ugliness he had inside of him.

"There was no way of telling how it got into his system, just that it was there. His social worker asked where he got the drugs, but he clammed up. They brought Jasper in to be questioned, but he was a Detective, even back then, so the worker believed everything he said. He said Tyler must have gotten it from school, that he had no idea. They went with Jasper's story and never looked into his home or any of the other children." Isaiah shook his head.

"It's not uncommon for children in their young teenage years to get their hands on cocaine. I find it hard to believe that no one would have noticed. If he was going through physical withdrawal, he'd have had to have been doing it for months and in large doses. Were any of the other children checked out?" Mason asked.

"That's the thing, the social worker never spoke to any of the current children or looked through his home. So, I did." He placed a rather large brown file on my table as he continued.

"That is Jasper's and Dana's fostering file. It includes every child they have ever taken in, including the current ones. Currently, he has nine kids all between the ages of nine and fourteen. I've started to go through the process of pulling the previous foster children's files, but there are over a hundred and fifty of them."

"Shit," I said, shocked that it was that many.

I didn't really know much about Jasper's fostering situation. I knew he was forty-eight and he and Dana, his wife, had been married for twenty years or so, now. I knew they were foster parents, but I had never actually met any of the kids. I've never been over to his house. Whenever we'd met after work, it was at a bar or a restaurant for a meal. He didn't have photos of them. He didn't talk about them. I figured he was just a private person. We were partners, but that didn't mean we had to share every single detail of our lives with each other. He didn't even know about Shane.

"It's going to take some time to pull all of their files and go through them to see if any doctor reports were made after their time with Jasper. Some were also moved to another city or out of state and I don't have access to their files," Isaiah continued.

"I can get 'em. I just need their names

and I can pull the file, no matter where they were placed in the country. We need to do a sneak and peek at Jasper's house and see what is going on. I'm assuming you are operating under the impression that Jasper is cooking drugs in the house," Mason asked.

"Last night, I looked through twenty files. Twelve of the kids were admitted to the hospital with withdrawal-like symptoms. Not all of them were given blood work, most were told it was the flu and they would feel better in a few days. It's enough for me to make the hypothesis that cocaine is being either cooked at the house around the children, or the children were weighing and packaging the cocaine." Isaiah looked thoroughly disgusted as he relayed the information.

"That sounds like a reasonable hypothesis. I've never noticed any problems with Jasper being sick, though, in the three years he's been my partner," I stated.

It wasn't that I doubted his assumption, it did sound like something was definitely going on in that house, but I also figured Jasper and Dana would have to be sick as well.

"Depends. I've gone into a lot of homes where the drugs were made in the basement and the kids were sick but the foster parents weren't. The kids were the ones touching the drugs and breathing it in as they were either cooking or packaging it, while the parents were fine, because the ventilation system in the upstairs of the house was solid. It kept the fumes down in the basement and when they needed to go down there, they wore the proper protection. It's completely logical that Jasper isn't breathing it in. Just like it's logical that he is breathing it in, but he's never not been around it. His body could be addicted to it and he gets his fix by being in the house," Mason pointed out.

That could be true.

I had never seen any signs, but I hadn't known him for twenty years. His temper could be a side effect from the drugs in his system. Big city police get random drug tests, but they don't do that here. They only do drug testing if the Captain thinks you are on drugs. That's never happened yet, and apparently hasn't in the last ten years. There were stories about a previous patrol officer twelve years ago that was fired for being a pothead. That was it, though.

"Let's get the files and go through them. See which kids were hospitalized after leaving Jasper's. I'll loop in Captain Perry so he's aware of the situation. We'll need to do a sneak and peek at his house. Mase, can you get a warrant from a judge? We gotta keep that out of town." There was no way we could do that here.

"I'll get it. With the files we'll have enough for a warrant," Mason said confidently.

"Okay, I have to go to the office and start pulling them. Do you want to join me there, or do you want me to bring them back here?" Isaiah asked.

"It would be better to do it here. We don't know who might talk to who. I want to try and keep this as quiet as possible," I answered.

Small towns and their rumor mills.

All it would take is for someone to see Isaiah grabbing the wrong file and it would be all over town that he was pulling files and looking into something. The very last thing I wanted was to tip Jasper off.

"I'll be back in about an hour or so, then," Isaiah said, before he finished his coffee and headed out.

"I'll grab my bag and get my laptop out of it. I'll get A.S.A Crawford up to speed and he'll grab us a warrant."

"Not exactly the vacation you were looking for. I'm sorry."

"It's okay. The drug cases are the easiest. Have you thought about just asking Tyler again? Tell him you know that Jasper could be mixed up with drugs."

It would be very logical for me to ask Tyler. Hell, he was there, why not get a first person perspective on the matter? The thought of bringing him into this, though, had my stomach up in knots. I didn't want something to happen to him. Even if he did tell me and didn't blow it off or clam up, he could be at risk if Jasper suspected he started all of this. I had to protect him.

I wasn't about to lose him like I lost Shane.

"No, I want to keep him out of this. I don't know what is going on, but I know that when drug dealers feel threatened, they'll attack the one they feel is responsible. I don't want Tyler getting hurt. It's better to leave him in the dark."

"It's your call, I'll support you. I'll go grab my gear," Mason said with complete understanding to his voice.

Once I was alone, I let out a long breath. This was not what I had expected, but at the same time, I wasn't about to turn my head away from it. If Jasper was dirty, I was going to put him behind bars and I would save those nine children. They deserved better and I was going to make sure everyone got justice.

Especially Tyler.

CHAPTER SEVENTEEN

Tyler

THE PAST TWO weeks had been a whirlwind. Things between Roland and me had progressed wonderfully. I was a little worried that our friendship would be compromised by our new sexual relationship. It wasn't, though. It actually made us closer and I couldn't have been happier.

I wasn't living in a naive world. I knew that we would have problems. We would have arguments and we would be mad at each other. That was natural in any relationship. As for now, though, I was happy to keep living in our little bubble and I was not in any hurry to pop it.

For the past two weeks we had made out again and we had progressed to actually touching each other's dicks. I had touched myself plenty of times and I'd had women touch me, but the feel of Roland's hand on me, it was addicting. I felt like a drug addict off of his touch. I constantly craved it and when he had to work late and we couldn't see each other, withdrawal would set in. I never thought I would be like this, the type of guy that always wanted to be around someone, but I was. My body had been starving and now it was being given an all you can eat buffet and, damn, was it eating.

Tonight, we were at my place above the bar for dinner. It was really nice being able to share domestic tasks together. I enjoyed cooking and it was good to have Roland here helping me with it. He was a good cook as well, and he apparently enjoyed it, too. It was something we could do together outside of the bedroom.

"How has work been?" I asked, once we finished eating and were relaxing on the couch.

He had been working a lot these past two weeks. I suspected he had something going on that was a pretty big deal with the amount of whispered phone calls and how much time he was spending with Mason.

It wasn't just that he was spending time with his brother. That was completely normal. What made me suspect it had to do with work was how they spent their time going through files and down at the station. They weren't going out to dinner or the movies. They were working on something and I hoped he would open up to me about it, even just a little bit. I wasn't sure if he could talk about it with it being work related and him being a detective. I would never ask him to compromise a case or his ethics, but it would be nice to hear about some of his day at work. He knows about my day. Hell, he's here for the most of it. It would just be nice to know more things about him.

"I've been working on a big case recently. I'm sure you've noticed."

"I have. I didn't want to ask, because I didn't want to pry, but you seem stressed."

"I am stressed. It's a major case and Mason has been helping me. Isaiah has as well. He's a friend of mine that works with Social Services in the Child Protection Division. This case is very sensitive and we have to be extremely careful with how we proceed. My Captain, Captain Perry, is the only one other than me in the department that knows about this case. I've been trying to not bring it home with me, to not involve you, and it's not because I don't trust you or anything like that. I just didn't want to drag you into it. If people knew you were involved, it could be dangerous, and the last thing I want is for you to be hurt."

I didn't want to be hurt, either, and I could tell how terrified he was at the prospect of me being hurt. He had lost the man he loved already due to a drunk driver.

He didn't want me to suffer the same fate. He didn't love me. I knew it was too soon for that. It didn't matter that I was already falling for him, too soon or not. My heart wasn't listening to me on the matter. He might not love me, but he did care for me, and it would hurt him if I was seriously hurt or killed. I reached out and placed my hand on his thigh as I spoke.

"I know you don't want me to get hurt and I don't want that either. But, I also don't want you to feel like you can't talk to me because of that. I know we're not in New York City, but your job can still be dangerous and sometimes that danger might come home. We have to be able to talk about it so I'm aware of it and can be careful. I can't avoid the landmines if I don't even know they're there, Babe."

He gave a nod and placed his hand on mine as he turned to face me.

"You're right, and if I'm being honest, I could use your help. I wanted to keep you out of this, because I knew it was going to be hard on you and the last thing I want to do is cause you pain of any kind. The case that we're working on... it's Jasper. We're investigating Jasper."

A cold dread washed over me.

Jasper, his partner, my old foster parent, the man that still haunted my nightmares. I had worked hard to try and forget about him, forget about what he had done to me, to the other kids.

Why would he be investigating him?"

"For what?" I managed to get out.

"The way you reacted to seeing him and how he was about mentioning he was your foster father for two years, well, it just didn't sit right with me. I asked Isaiah to look into it and see if there was something there. He discovered a lot, including that you were addicted to cocaine at fourteen."

I went to open my mouth to say something, but he cut me off before I could even form any words.

"I know you weren't a drug addict. There are a hundred and seventy-five foster kids that they've had within the past eighteen years and out of them we can prove that a hundred and eight of them were addicted to drugs after they left Jasper's home. Others could have been sick, but were never taken to the hospital. Mason was going to use a judge outside of the city to get a warrant to look in Jasper's house, but due to Jasper being a detective the judge wants more proof first. What we have isn't substantial, because any lawyer could argue the statistics of foster children being addicted to drugs. What we need is a witness, one of the foster children to speak up and be willing to go on record about what was happening in that house. We've reached out to some, but none are willing to do that. Isaiah is working on trying to find new homes for the nine children that are currently in Jasper's home, but it's hard to move them without any legal reason to."

I slid my hand out of his and got up. I needed to move. I couldn't sit still right now, not with my mind racing like it was.

They knew about the drugs.

I didn't think anyone would ever find out about that. With Jasper being a detective, he knew how to cover his tracks, how to work around the system that he played in. No one ever suspected he was doing anything wrong, even the social workers that came into the house. They never suspected anything. But maybe the difference was Roland wasn't a small town detective or social worker. He was from a massive city and he knew what signs to look for. He had to trust his gut in the field and that instinct was still strong in him.

It didn't surprise me that no one would talk. They all knew better.

I knew better.

You kept your mouth shut no matter how many years it'd been. It's like fight club, you don't talk about fight club. We don't talk about what happened in that house. All we'd had was each other. It didn't even matter if you were in the house at the same time, we still were there for each other.

When I got to leave at fourteen, I had met another boy when I was seventeen who had just left Jasper's house. He was really sick and I knew what it was from. I was there with him for the whole two weeks as his body went through withdrawal. It didn't matter that we didn't go through Jasper's house at the same time, all that mattered was we had and we were both lucky enough to survive. Roland had no idea just how bad it was.

How bad it *is*.

He would never find anyone that would be willing to talk. I wasn't stupid, though, because if no one talked, then Jasper couldn't be shut down and he would be free to keep doing this. To keep hurting children until he eventually died. He was only forty-eight. He could go on doing this for another thirty-five years. That's thirty-five years of more pain, more children being hurt, killed, sick, and abused.

Nothing changes unless someone speaks up.

I let out a shaky breath as I leaned my back against the kitchen counter. I didn't want to be the one that spoke up, but I couldn't continue to be the one that stayed quiet and let another child be hurt or killed.

All of the times growing up I wished someone would storm through that door and save us. I dreamed about it. About the cops that would bust the door down and finally stop Jasper. I knew those nine kids in that house currently were feeling the same. They were waiting every minute of every day for someone to come and save them.

And here Roland was trying to just that. He was armed and ready to kick the door down. All he needed was for someone to be brave enough to speak up.

To tell their story and face the monster, once and for all.

"Pull out your phone and turn on the recorder."

"Baby, no," he said as he shot to his feet and came over to me.

"I wasn't telling you this so you would talk about it. I just wanted for you to know in case something happened and Jasper mentioned something to you. It's not safe for you to be going up against him."

"And you'll protect me by arresting him. It's more than just drugs, it's more than what you know. I was trapped there for two years and all I wanted more than anything in the world was for someone to storm in and stop him. And that is exactly what those nine kids want right now and that can't happen if no one talks. The others won't talk, because there's no one there to protect them, but I have you and I know you will get him. Let me help you get him. Let me help you free those kids."

There was fear in his eyes and I couldn't blame him for it. I was terrified, too. Within the fear, though, I could see he was proud of me. He was proud that I was going to stand up to Jasper, stand up for those kids. If it wasn't for the fact that he did have children currently in his home, I might not have said anything. I might have taken this to my grave, but he *did* have children and he would continue to have them.

I had to stop the cycle before more children were ruined.

"Okay, but if you need to take a break,

just say the word. I'll record the conversation and sometimes I'll have to ask questions if I need more details. But if you can't handle it, then tell me and we can stop."

I simply gave a nod and he took my hand and guided me over to the couch once again. We sat down and I let out a shaky breath as he pulled out his cell phone and hit the record button. He said his name, the date, time, and his detective badge number before he gave a nod to me and I started to tell my story.

A story I never thought I would ever talk about.

"I was twelve when I was placed in Jasper's home. I was there just over two years before being transferred to another one at his request. He stated that I was getting to be too problematic and he was worried about the younger children. The second the social worker left me there, Jasper made sure I knew the rules. I was used to having *the talk*. Every foster parent did it. I had gotten good at following the rules, no matter what they were. If you followed them and didn't make any trouble or too much noise, the foster parents would leave you alone."

"What were Jasper's rules?"

"You don't do anything that causes attention. So, no fights at school, no skipping school, all marks had to be kept hidden. You never talk about what happens in the house. Unless addressed, you don't talk to him or Dana. We learned that also meant no talking around them. You eat once a day before school and if you missed it, you had to wait until the next day. He always said he wasn't going to be poor because we kept eating. No complaining, and you do as you are told when you are told to do it, no matter what it was. You break the rules, you get punished and the level of punishment would depend on how bad the violation was."

"Could you give me an example of some of the punishments either you went through or saw happen?" he asked in a gentle voice.

"He would lock us in this crawl space

under the back deck. It didn't matter what the weather was like, you were in it for hours. One time, he put me in it for three days in the middle of winter. I was only in a shirt and pants and socks. There was no food or water. I used to catch the snow that fell through the slats of the deck boards and eat it for water. He hit us everyday, always where a shirt or pants would keep it hidden. Sometimes, he would use a belt or Dana would use a frying pan. The worst was when one of the kids would disappear."

"Disappear? What do you mean by that?"

"If one of us became too much of a problem, or a liability, Jasper would make them disappear. You could normally tell when something horrible was going to happen. He would get this look in his eyes and he would get really quiet. Me and the older kids would always make sure the younger ones were kept hidden away when that happened. He would grab the kid later on and that would be the last time anyone saw them." I sucked in a breath.

"I snuck out one night to see what was

going on with Sammy. He was just nine and he almost started a fire by mistake. He dropped a chemical. It was an accident but Jasper was furious. I saw a man with Jasper. He handed over a wad of cash and took Sammy. Jasper did that about twenty times in the two years I was there." I twisted my fingers together, the memories pushing my anxiety up.

"A few times, though, one of the kids would do something that Jasper saw as unforgivable. The kid would be grabbed at night and we could hear screaming and then it got really quiet. In the morning, there would be blood on the floor, a big pool of it, and we were told to clean it up. No one ever saw the kid again. Jasper used to threaten us about putting us with the Forgotten Kids, that's what he called them."

I wiped my cheeks as the tears started to come down. I had never talked about this before, not with anyone. We didn't talk about it, especially the Forgotten Kids. None of us wanted to be one of them, so we always did what we could. We always went above and beyond our duty just to avoid it. All of the older kids would protect the younger ones and make sure they didn't lag behind. We always hit our quota, no matter what, because we knew that anyone of us could be added to the Forgotten Kids list, and that would be on us.

Roland reached out and took my hand in his as he spoke. "Do you know where he might have buried the kids?"

"No, he never said. And he didn't really say anything about the kids that were taken in the middle of the night. But Dana and him were arguing one night and I heard them. She was upset that they weren't getting more per kid. Said they should start getting younger kids because they go for a higher price. Jasper said you can't guarantee a younger kid won't talk, that it was better to stick with nine and up."

"Okay, can you tell me how you got the cocaine into your system when you were fourteen?"

That was the easiest part to talk about. I wasn't happy about it, and it was horrible going through the withdrawal. I was sick for two weeks and completely on my own. I spent it on the bathroom floor curled up just waiting to die, essentially. My current foster parents didn't care. The father would just walk over me and use the bathroom as if I was a floor mat. He had actually stepped on me plenty of times because I was in his way.

"In the basement there's a lab where we were to cook the cocaine, weigh it, and package it. We didn't have gloves or anything to protect us from it. The whole basement had some type of venting system, though, because it was loud. The older kids said it was to protect the rest of the house from the fumes. We worked in the basement from the moment we got home from school until two in the morning. On weekends, we would work all day and night. When the shipment was ready, we would get into his van and drive to other towns around us and deliver the packages to different drug dealers. We had a set quota to fill each week and we made sure we always hit it. If we didn't, we would all be punished. Me and the older kids would sometimes stay awake for three days straight to give the younger kids the chance to rest. We made masks for them out of what we could salvage from around the house to try and protect them from the fumes."

"Why didn't you ever say anything? To a teacher, to your social worker, or to your next foster parents?"

I knew he wasn't asking in a rude way. He had to ask because people would logically assume I would have told someone. The thing was, they didn't grow up in the foster system. Any foster child would tell you that you never talked about anything that happened within the walls of any house.

"Jasper made sure we all knew not to say anything. As for my social worker, he didn't care. In all the foster homes I had been in, they were all abusive. Teachers looked the other way. My social worker only saw me as an annoyance. The system is broken. It's been broken for decades. No one cares about foster kids. We're a burden that no one wants to truly take on. They take on foster kids for the status of it. *Look at me, I'm helping this poor child.* But when something goes wrong in their life, we're the first person they take their frustrations and anger out on. We don't matter and no one ever listens."

"I'm listening and I'm not going to let it go unnoticed or ignored any longer. Thank you, Tyler."

He closed out the recording before he turned it off and then instantly he was pulling me into his arms. Feeling the safety that surrounded me, I couldn't hold back the tears any longer. I completely broke down against his chest as the pain from the memories became too much. He didn't say anything and I appreciated that.

There was nothing he could truly say that would make me feel any better, that would make this any better. I hoped that he would be able to stop it, that he could stop Jasper, but I truly didn't know. Jasper was a cop and there was no telling what connections he had. At least it would be known, though, and hopefully that would save some children.

"I'm so proud of you, Baby," he said, and pressed a kiss to my head as my sobs finally started to calm down.

"It was really bad."

"I know. I'm so sorry you had to go through that. He can't hurt you anymore. I'm not going to let him. I'm not going to let him get away with what he's done and he's never going to hurt another child again. This is what we needed to arrest him. Thank you for being brave and telling me this."

"Just get him, okay?"

"I will. I promise." He kissed my head once again and I could feel my body getting weaker. I was hitting a wall and I really needed to get some sleep.

"Will you stay with me tonight?" I asked as I moved back so I could see him.

"Of course. Come on, you get ready for bed and I'll clean up. Then, we can curl up in bed together."

I gave a small nod before I got up off the couch and headed into the bathroom. I needed a minute to try and get my thoughts and breathing back under control. I thought maybe I would feel better after talking about it, but I just felt heavy and exhausted. Hopefully, some sleep would do me some good and tomorrow I wouldn't wake up feeling like complete shit.

CHAPTER EIGHTEEN

Tyler

THE LOUD BANG of thunder instantly had me sitting up and breathing heavy. The apartment was filled with the sound of rain hitting the window and the stairs out back. Thunderstorms were something I was not very good with. I hated them, always had, since I was a little kid. I couldn't help the flinch at the feeling of hands on my arms.

"Hey, it's okay. It's just me, Baby."

"Sorry, I hate thunderstorms."

"Come here."

Roland pulled me down and tucked me against his chest. I instantly curled up against his heat, soothed by the sound of his heart thrumming under my ear as he held me tightly.

His arms were so big, but they made me feel safe. I never thought I would feel safe in his arms due to the size of him, but I did. He felt amazing and for the first time in my life, I felt truly safe. I never wanted that feeling to disappear. I wanted to stay in his arms forever, in this safe bubble where nothing could hurt me. I flinched at another loud crack and rumble and he ran his hand up and down my back as he spoke.

"When I was eighteen, on my birthday, I was on the bus to boot camp. Boot camp was only six weeks, so I was placed in the infantry division and sent on tour three months later. We were all told what it would be like, we all knew that we were walking into a war zone, but seeing it and hearing about it were two different things. I thought I was fine with it, but then two weeks into my six month tour, the base was attacked in the middle of the night. Suddenly, there were bombs going off around the outside perimeter and gunfire was echoing throughout the night. We were in the barracks when it started and the guys all got up, threw their boots on, and were out of there. But me, I was frozen. All I could focus on were the bangs from the explosions. A soldier that had been in for five years came over to me and told me to count the seconds in between the blasts, to focus on the seconds. It helped me to calm down and I was able to go out there and join in on the fight. I kept counting, though, and I knew that when the blasts got longer in between, that meant it was almost over. When I got back from my tour, that first thunderstorm scared the hell out of me. I snapped out of bed and grabbed my gun thinking I was still on base. It took me a minute to realize that I was at home and it was merely thunder. The only way I could relax was to count the time in between the booms."

I liked it when he shared pieces about his time either in the army or when he was in New York. He was older than me and he'd had a life before we met, before he got in town. It was nice to hear him share those pieces with me.

"The further the time in between, the further away the storm is," I said with understanding.

"Exactly. You're safe, Baby. I promise I'm not going to let anything happen to you."

"I know. I still don't like thunder," I said with a soft smile against his chest.

He rolled us over so he was on top of me as he spoke. "Let's see what we can do to change that."

"I like that idea."

I couldn't help but grin as he wiggled himself between my legs and closed the gap between our lips. Now this was a much better way to get through a thunderstorm. We had our own storm approaching and I hoped that we would make it through. We were stronger together. I believed that with everything in me, and I knew with Roland by my side we would get through any storm that tried to take us out.

CHAPTER NINETEEN

Roland

"ALL RIGHT, I got the no knock warrant," Mason said as he walked into the tactical room.

I had been there getting ready with Captain Perry. Isaiah had arrived a few minutes ago as well. This morning, I had come straight into work to speak with Mason and Captain Perry about what Tyler had told me last night. I played the recording for them and I could instantly see how furious they were. I could understand it perfectly. I wanted blood myself.

When we started this, when *I* started this, I thought maybe Jasper had let his anger get the better of him and he had hurt Tyler. I never expected to discover he could be involved in drugs, and now, we not only knew he was involved in producing and distributing drugs, but he had killed children and sold them. He was far more dangerous than any of us ever knew and we had to be ready for anything.

It was why Mason went with the recording and personally delivered it to his judge friend in Baltimore. He had called me an hour ago, letting me know he was on his way back with the warrant.

Captain Perry had rounded up everyone that we had at the station, all ten detectives, to go and make the arrest on Jasper and Dana. What they didn't know was that they were arresting one of their own. It was going to be a problem and I knew most wouldn't want to believe it or be involved. They wouldn't have a choice, though, with Captain Perry giving the orders.

I wasn't sure how this was going to go over, I really wasn't. I knew the blue line was extremely important and cherished by every cop within the country. You didn't go against the blue brotherhood, even if that meant keeping quiet about a dirty cop. For the most part, I went along with it. I was not about to go through the headache of trying to get a cop fired for taking bribes to look the other way on tickets or even drug dealers.

In New York, there was no point because once you got one drug dealer off the street, five more took their place. I had learned that it was better to deal with the devils you knew then get some hotheaded moron that just wanted to drop bodies on the streets.

But we weren't talking about a shady cop letting drug dealers off. What Jasper was doing was putting children, innocent children, at risk. He was having them making cocaine and selling it. He was abusing them, starving them, selling them, and killing them. That wasn't something I would stand for. I wasn't about to stand by and let that continue. I didn't care who I pissed off in the process. If the guys that worked here didn't like it, then, as far as I was concerned, they didn't need to work here and I knew Captain Perry felt the same.

"We brief everyone in ten," Captain Perry said before he turned on his heel and strode out the door.

"Grab whatever you need," I said to my brother, gesturing to the supply table, knowing he didn't come down here with all of his tactical gear.

He gave a nod and headed over to grab a vest and one of the tactical long guns as Isaiah spoke.

"What about Koda?"

"I'll bring him with me so he can help with the children. We have no idea what the kids are going to be like. Do you have transport for the children?" Mason responded as he started to get ready.

"I have a fellow social worker on standby

with a van to transport the children to the hospital. I haven't found new placements yet, though. I need to see what their medical conditions are like and if they have any cocaine in their systems first. Chances are they will and they'll need to stay in the hospital for at least a week. What about the other children, though? The ones that were sold. We can't just forget about them."

That was going to be the trickier part, because unless Dana or Jasper talked, we would have no idea where they were. It would take time to try and track anyone down. We would need to go through all of Jasper's finances, emails, phone calls, everything to see if something stood out and if it didn't, we would be at a dead end.

"I've already contacted my boss about the situation down here. He wants me to stay here and build a task force to track down the missing children and make sure the foster system down here is safe for every child within it. Looks like you and I are going to be around each other for a while yet," Mason said to Isaiah.

"I'm happy to have the help and I'm more than willing to help in any way that I can," Isaiah easily agreed and flashed a warm smile.

He was going to need all the help he could get. Trying to rework a system that had been functioning this way for decades was going to be one hell of an undertaking.

Each foster home, past and present, would need to be investigated to ensure no wrongdoing to any child. It wasn't going to be easy and it was going to take a lot of time.

At the same time, though, I was happy that Mason would be here longer. I was worried about him and not just what this job was doing to him. He seemed jumpy, on edge, like he was waiting for an attack. That wasn't like him. Something more was going on with him and I was going to get to the bottom of it. First, we had to take care of Jasper, and then he and I would be having that discussion.

"Who's heading the task force?" I asked as we finished grabbing the last of our gear.

"I am. My boss is putting me in charge and allowing me to pick who I want on it from Homeland, local police and a child protective worker liaison. I assumed, Isaiah, you'd wish to be that liaison."

"Yes, I would. Thank you."

"You better be placing me on that team," I said with a knowing smirk.

I knew I would be. There was no way my little brother would be running a task force and not have me as his secondhand man. I was very proud of him. He was getting to run his own task force. This was huge and it would be an amazing career opportunity for him. He had worked his ass off from the ground up and his boss clearly noticed his skills and potential.

"Wouldn't think otherwise. Let's go get this bastard," Mason said as he put the clip into his gun.

We all headed out and crowded into the small briefing room that also worked as the roll call room. This place was very small and I couldn't imagine being able to house a task force. Mason would need to figure out where to put up his new team while they were setting up shop in town. This station would not be able to hold them. Not to mention, we didn't have anywhere near the computer power they would need to run their investigation.

Captain Perry was already in the room. He stood at the front, ready and waiting for us. We moved over to the side of the room to give Captain Perry our full attention.

We were operating on everyone not knowing that I had started the investigation into Jasper. It would be better, for now, if people believed the Captain had been looking into it. When he had told me he was going to play down my role in all of this, I wasn't happy about it. Not because of glory or recognition, I could care less about that. It was about him feeling like I should have to hide what I was doing.

I didn't want to hide behind someone.

I didn't need to.

I had gone up against a lot worse than anyone in this building. I didn't shy away from terrorist cells. I was not about to give

Jasper that privilege. Still, he was my Captain and I firmly believed in following the chain of command, so I kept quiet and focused on being a silent support.

"Before we begin, I want to make one thing very clear. This is *not* a training exercise. You are the more experienced detectives that I have. Some of you have never done a raid before outside of a training exercise. The majority of you have only ever done one or two raids when a nearby town needs more bodies. Due to the type of raid that we are about to go on, I am going to rely on experience to lead us. Detective Wright and his brother, Special Agent Mason Wright, will be taking point on this raid. I expect everyone to follow their orders and do as they tell you, myself included. What matters most is that we all come home alive and no one gets killed tonight. Do I make myself clear?" He paused to allow the reality of this situation to sink in.

Captain Perry was right. None of them had any real experience doing a raid. They were used to training exercises or helping out in the back on a raid. There wasn't anyone we could call in for this, it had to be the men in this room, and the only reason I wasn't more concerned was because Mason was standing next to me. He would be able to handle anything that we come across in that house.

I quickly scanned the room to see everyone's reactions. Some were concerned and worried about just what we were about to do. Others seemed excited at finally being able to do something active on the job. My gaze traveled over to Baxter. I wasn't really happy that he was here. It wasn't that he was a dirty cop or anything, just a lazy and bigoted one. He was also close with Jasper and I wasn't too sure he would believe what we were saying about him. He could be problematic, but we didn't have much choice right now.

Next to Baxter stood his partner. Jarod. He stood behind him slightly and looked very uncomfortable. He was a younger guy, but he had a lot of potential. When I got into town, he was a rookie patrol officer, but he wasn't content to just sit around a desk all day. He was out there on the streets talking to people, watching them and getting involved. He was always reading a book. Sometimes it was on forensic science, profiling, criminal law, federal law, and even negotiation tactics. This kid was always learning and I suspected he had a higher IQ then he allowed others to see. He wasn't timid, but he was shy and didn't tend to speak up. He seemed a bit apprehensive with people. Even after the past few years, I still didn't know anything about him personally. He had managed to impress Captain Perry a year ago with his work ethic so much so that the Captain had promoted him to detective and partnered him up with Baxter.

The two of them didn't click at all and I had been considering asking the Captain to switch our partners. Jarod seemed to want to learn, but Baxter had zero interest in teaching him. It was something I might have to actually do once the dust settled on this raid.

"Keep an eye on Baxter tonight. I don't know if he'll be a team player," I whispered to Mason.

He simply gave a nod and I knew I didn't need to tell him who exactly Baxter was. He had already heard about him from me after I punched the asshat. Mason would keep an eye on him tonight so I could focus on Jasper.

"We have secured a no knock warrant for the home of one of our own. Jasper Monroe. He has been under investigation for the past few weeks for suspected drug trafficking. We secured the warrant based on an eyewitness account of drugs being produced in the basement. We also have evidence of him killing foster children and selling them to pedophiles for close to two decades. We have an arrest warrant for Jasper and his wife Dana," Captain Perry continued.

"You expect us to believe that one of our own, that a cop who has almost thirty years on the job, is not only a drug dealer, but a child killer? Who is this eyewitness, Santa Claus?" Baxter asked, clearly not believing anything Captain Perry had to say.

I knew he wasn't going to believe it. I could see the doubt in almost everyone's eyes. Interestingly enough, I didn't see doubt in Jarod's eyes.

"Why doesn't the kid seem surprised?" Mason whispered to me. Apparently, I wasn't the only one who had noticed.

"That's Jarod Lopez. He's Baxter's partner. He's only been a detective for a year, but he joined the police force at eighteen. He's only twenty-one and has a shit load of potential. But I don't know anything about him. He keeps everything personal under wraps. He's smart, though. Smarter than he wants people to know. He could have easily seen something," I whispered back.

"The witness' identity is being kept a secret, for obvious reasons. We have more than enough evidence to back up the claims. Once we get into the house, we'll find the lab in his basement. He currently has nine foster children that we will need to ensure are safe before they are transported to the hospital for evaluations. Due to the nature of this investigation, all cell phones will be left here in the station. I don't want anyone reaching out to either Jasper or Dana. Agent Wright, you wished to say something," Captain Perry said with a pointed look at Mason.

Mason moved to stand at the front of the room and I was hit with a strong sense of pride once more. He was so confident in himself and it warmed my heart. I was a proud big brother and I couldn't wait for him to be around more. It was going to be really good for the both of us.

"Due to the connection Jasper has to this police department, his charges will be placed by Homeland Security, making them federal charges. He will be eligible for the death penalty, which means anyone that tries to contact him or help him in any way will be charged with aiding and abetting a wanted criminal, as well as an accessory after the fact. You will be facing hard time in a federal prison, and I will personally ensure you are placed within general population and not solitary." He paused to allow the seriousness of the situation to sink in before he continued.

"We are going to hit his home in two teams. Roland's team will hit the front door and my team will hit the back and hold down the perimeter. Once the arrests have been made, Isaiah will then handle the children. If you cannot do your job, then speak up now, because once we leave you will have no choice but to do your job and ensure that Jasper does not evade arrest."

You heard him, does anyone want to be kept here?" Captain Perry asked.

I waited to see someone raise their hand, but surprisingly no one did. They weren't happy, but they were riding with us. Nothing more needed to be said, so we all got divided up into the two teams and once we dropped our phones off into the basket, we headed out.

The drive up to Jasper's house was done in silence. There was nothing anyone could say and we were all on edge. The guys weren't happy about arresting one of their own, especially a veteran with almost thirty years on the job. It wasn't a good situation to be in and I understood that. I wouldn't want to be here, either, and I might not believe the evidence if I was in their position. They would believe it, though, once they saw the lab. Once they saw the kids in that house. I just hoped everything went smoothly tonight.

The convoy of police vehicles pulled up to the house as one. We all got out of our vehicles and instantly made our way into position with our respective teams. Mason ran around the back of the house and when he was ready, he gave me a nod to go ahead. A quick look over at my Captain, who gave me a simple nod, and I kicked down the door.

We ran in with our guns up and ready for anything. I wasn't even in for two seconds when the backdoor was kicked in and Mason came into the house. He had three guys in the back and I had three in the front holding the perimeter. As we all made our way through the main level of the house and then up the stairs, we quickly discovered that the house was quieter then we expected. It wasn't until we reached the bedroom when we found Dana in bed on her laptop with headphones in that we understood. Now it made sense why she didn't hear us. I easily went over and once I was close enough, she looked up and promptly screamed.

"Put your hands up," I ordered, not even bothering with lowering my gun.

"What are you doing here?" she demanded as she removed her headphones.

"Dana Monroe you're under arrest for crimes against children and drug trafficking. Get your hands up," I ordered, keeping my voice sharp so she knew I wasn't playing around.

"Are you out of your mind, Roland? You know me. You know *us*. We're not criminals."

She wasn't going to make this easy on me and that was just fine by me. I looked over and saw that Jarod was in the room with me and he had his gun trained on her. I lowered mine and grabbed her, pulling her out of the bed and slamming her face first into the floor before cuffing her. After reading her her rights, which she yelled and screamed at me throughout, I dragged her to her feet as Mason's voice came over the comms.

"House is cleared. Jasper isn't here."

"Fuck," I said under my breath as I headed out of the bedroom with Dana.

As we made our way toward the front door, I noticed that Isaiah was already being escorted into the house and they were starting to round up the children. I brought Dana out to one of the cars and tossed her into the backseat.

"Where is he?" I demanded.

"He went away for a boy's weekend. It was a surprise for him. He's going to be pissed when he comes back home to find out you arrested me. Your career is over, Roland."

"The only career that is ruined is his.

But don't worry, we have a very nice ten by ten cell with your name on it."

I slammed the door and ordered one of my guys to drive her back to the station and process her. I made a direct order for no one to talk to her or let her call or talk to anyone.

"Apparently, he's away on a surprise boys' weekend," I told Mason and Captain Perry once I reached the house.

"Bullshit," Mason instantly said.

"He's up to something. You think he caught wind of the investigation?" Captain Perry asked.

"Someone who has almost thirty years of experience on the job holds a lot of connections. There's no telling who he could have heard something from. Could have been someone within social services. It would make sense that he had a mole on the inside. Someone that could feed him the children that no one would think twice about when they went missing. Someone to help cover it all up. He could have been made aware of the investigation once files started to be pulled," Mason stated.

"Shit. And now he's in the wind," I said as I shook my head.

We should have seen this coming. *I* should have seen this coming. Of course Jasper had connections within our department and social services. He grew up here. He would have known everyone in that damn building. He had been planning his escape for weeks now and he left Dana here to take the fall for it all.

"Detective Wright, sir," Jarod said with uncertainty in his voice. He was clearly nervous about walking in on our conversation, but he seemed determined to do it. He clutched a folded up piece of paper in his hand and he spoke as he held it out to me.

"One of the children said he was told to give this to you."

"What is it?" Captain Perry asked as I grabbed the paper.

As I opened it, the words on the page brought a cold dread to flood my entire body.

It's your fault for him breaking the rules. Dead men tell no tales, Wright.

"Roland, what is it?" Mason asked, now on edge.

"Tyler," I said, before I turned and bolted for my car.

Mason climbed into my passenger seat, slamming the door closed as I gunned the motor and slammed the car into gear simultaneously. The tires spun for a moment before catching the pavement and, in seconds, we were rocketing down the street.

Jasper was going after Tyler, after the man that I was falling in love with. I wasn't going to allow that to happen. I wasn't going to lose another man that I loved.

Not tonight. Not again.

CHAPTER TWENTY

Tyler

DRAINED.

Completely and utterly drained seemed like the best way, the only way, to describe how I felt tonight. Between the thunderstorm and telling Roland my story, I did not sleep well. Having to get up this morning was a Herculean effort, one I wasn't certain I would be able to pull off.

Roland had been very sweet this morning, though. He had made me breakfast in bed before he had to head out for work. I knew he had to get the recording in so he could get a warrant, but I appreciated him taking the time to make breakfast and spend the time with me.

I spent the rest of the day hanging around the apartment before going down to the bar for my shift. Tonight had been busy, which was nice to make the time go by faster, but it left me feeling even more exhausted. It had died down for the past hour with it being a weeknight. It was so dead, I had sent Tammy home and Jose had closed the kitchen so he could head home, too. It was just me in an empty bar, something that was odd but also nice. It allowed me to start doing the cleaning and getting things ready for when I could close.

I checked my phone to see if Roland had sent me any texts. I knew he was stressed and busy working tonight, but I wasn't sure if he would have the time to send me a text and check in with me. I wouldn't hold it against him if he didn't. He was busy trying to get Jasper in jail and I knew that was not going to be easy at all. I hoped to be able to see him tonight so I knew that he was okay.

"What the hell is that?"

There was a clicking sound coming from somewhere. I thought I had heard it a few minutes ago, but with the traffic on the street that often sounded through the walls, I blew it off. Now, though, I was certain something was clicking. Moving around the back of the bar, I looked to see if there was something back there that would be clicking.

It sounded like an old school clock where the second hand ticked as it moved around the clock. The thing was, there was no analog clock behind the bar and I couldn't find anything that would be clicking. It was just liquor bottles and glasses along the back of the bar. There weren't any electronics and the cash register wouldn't click. I couldn't find a reason for something to be making a random noise.

All of a sudden the clicking stopped.

The eerie silence rang out in the bar for a split second, and then pain exploded across my chest.

The world faded in and out all around me. I fought to keep my eyes open, but all I could see was fog. I couldn't seem to clear the fog away, everything was blurry.

Something was wrong.

I knew I needed to do something, but I couldn't seem to get my mind to function enough to tell me what I needed to do. I could hear a loud alarm going off. At least, I hoped it was an alarm and not my ears. I closed my eyes again and this time I couldn't seem to bring myself to open them.

I took the time to attempt to figure out what was going on, but for the life of me I couldn't. I took inventory of my body and focused on my other senses. My body ached and it felt like something pressed on my back. I could feel the cold floor underneath me, my shirt wet with what smelled like gin.

A coughing fit suddenly overwhelmed me and, to my horror, I couldn't seem to get a decent breath in. My chest felt tight, constricted. I couldn't get my lungs to expand and a fire raged within my chest. It felt like an asthma attack but worse. It hurt like hell each time I gasped in my desperate need for air and my throat burned.

I forced my eyes open, only to have to shut them as they started to burn and water. In that split second I noticed there was smoke. Black smoke, billowing throughout the bar, filling it up and sucking out the remaining oxygen at a rapid pace. I could hear more than just the alarm going off, I could hear the roar of a fire.

The bar is on fire.

The clicking, it must have been from a bomb or something.

I had to move. I couldn't stay here. Forcing myself to get up turned out to be a lot harder than I expected it to be. I couldn't get up, there was something heavy across my back. I was stuck until someone came to help me lift whatever was on me.

Another coughing fit shook my body and it left me fighting even harder for a breath. It became harder and harder to breathe, to not choke on the smoke. My vision kept going in and out. I could feel myself getting weaker. I could feel the heat of the flames becoming hotter, creeping closer to me.

I suddenly realized what it meant that I was lying in liquor. If the flames got too close, I would be on fire along with the bar. I had to get up, but I couldn't lift the weight off of me. The back of the bar must have fallen on top of me and it was a good three hundred pounds so it could hold up the liquor bottles.

The world was starting to get darker, but before I could sink into the blackness, I heard the rapid barks of a dog. It was random and for a second I thought I imagined it, until a very wet tongue ran up my cheek. I forced my eyes to open and sure enough there was a large dog in front of me.

"Roland, over here!" A male voice called out from my left.

I wasn't sure who it was or who he was calling, but someone was here. They could get help. They could get me out of here before I barbecued. I was losing the fight with the darkness once again, but then the sweetest sounding voice I had ever heard in my life dragged me back to consciousness.

"Ty! Baby, can you hear me?"

"Help me lift this," the first man said.

I could hear Roland and whoever was with him shuffling and suddenly the weight disappeared. I felt teeth around my wrist before I was being pulled away from whatever had pinned me to the ground.

The dog.

The dog was pulling me free and once I was far enough away he let me go. The world spun and by the time it cleared, I was up in Roland's arms and we were running out of the building. Even the fresh air wasn't enough for me to be able to breathe properly. For some reason, it made my breathing worse as another coughing fit overcame me, one that had me feeling weak and on the verge of passing out.

"Medics!" Roland yelled, and again the world passed me by in a blur as I fought to catch my breath.

Something was wrong.

I couldn't catch my breath. I couldn't get

a proper breath even though we were outside in the crisp night air. My chest was still on fire. It was tight and burned. I needed it to stop. I needed to breathe.

Roland's arms were suddenly gone and I was on something soft with blurry strangers standing over me. Everything was blurry and spinning. I couldn't make it stop. They were talking to me, I could see their mouths moving, but I couldn't hear them.

I couldn't hear anything.

Everything was fading, the blackness at the corner of my eyes was moving in, threatening to swallow me whole. They were panicking, I could see it in their eyes, by the looks they were giving to each other.

Roland was scared.

I wanted to tell him it would be okay, but I couldn't get the words to form before everything went black.

CHAPTER TWENTY-ONE

Roland

SITTING IN A hard plastic hospital chair next to a hospital bed that contained the man that I loved was the hardest thing I had ever done in my life.

When we arrived at the bar and saw that it was up in flames, my heart tried to escape my body through my mouth. I thought I would actually throw up and my heart would be on the ground.

Thank God Mason was with me and had

reacted so quickly. I was right behind him, but him flying into the burning building without thought or care for his own safety was what snapped me out of my complete terror. When we found Tyler in the middle of all of those flames, I thought he was dead. It wasn't until I reached him and saw that he was alive and breathing did I feel like I could catch my breath again. Only to feel like I was dying once more when it was clear he was having extreme trouble breathing. Having to stand there and watch as the paramedic shoved a tube down his throat...

Fuck, I was going to have nightmares about it for years to come.

It had been a day since Tyler had been admitted into the hospital. He was still intubated, but his oxygen levels were going up. The doctor was just being cautious because of Tyler's asthma. The smoke he'd inhaled aggravated his asthma and that made it harder for his lungs to function on their own. They had also been keeping him sedated so his body didn't fight the tube.

I was thankful that he was asleep right now. I couldn't imagine trying to be awake with a tube down my throat. I would be pulling it out the first chance I got. Even though the doctor said he would be okay, I wasn't going to relax until I saw for myself that Tyler would recover.

Until I could see him awake and talking again.

The door opened and I turned my attention to see who had walked in.

"Any update?" Mason asked as he headed over to me and handed me a coffee.

"The doc isn't going to give him any more sedation. He thinks it'll be okay for him to wake up today and then he'll pull the tube out."

"Good, that's good, Bro."

"Is Koda okay?"

Koda had run into the bar before either Mason or I could even start running. He'd jumped right through the window and immediately started to search for victims. He was trained for it, but I knew Mason hated it when Koda was put in danger.

Koda had been the one to find Tyler first, though, and his barking alerted Mason. The fire was all around us by then and I knew Koda's paws had been injured from the heat on the floor.

"He's good. A doctor checked him over for me and put some cream on the bottom of his paws. First degree burns, but in a few days he'll be okay. I've got his paws wrapped to keep from any dirt aggravating his burns. He's hanging out in the kid's playroom right now on the floor."

"You left him there?"

That surprised me. Koda always went where Mason did. Always. It didn't matter who was there, Koda always followed Mason when he left a room, even at the house.

"Jarod was there with the kids as Isaiah worked with one of the doctors. I called him, but he didn't want to follow. Apparently, he's happy to lay next to Jarod."

I couldn't help but chuckle at that. "Maybe Koda finally sniffed out your soul mate."

He rolled his eyes in a dramatic fashion. He didn't believe in soul mates and even if he did, I doubted he would see Jarod as his. He liked smaller guys, but Jarod wasn't small. He wasn't my size, but he was equal to Mason. That right there was a no go to him. Still, they would be cute together, assuming Jarod was even gay.

"What do we know?" I asked, moving my attention back to what mattered the most.

"Well, the tests have started to come back and, so far, it's looking like all the kids are addicted to cocaine. The doc is going to keep them for at least a week, possibly two depending on how bad the withdrawals are. Dana has lawyered up. Apparently, she expected Jasper to come back and rescue her. Once she figured out he'd left her holding the bag, she clammed right up and yelled lawyer. I'm trying to get her denied bail, but I don't know if it'll stick. We have all of the electronics from the house and more than enough evidence of the drugs. But we still can't find him. None of the kids are talking about it. The few that have talked, all said it was Dana. That Jasper didn't even know about the drugs."

Fuck.

"Bullshit. It was in his basement. Of course he knew about the drugs. He's trained them to put all of the blame on his wife, like fucking a coward."

Just when I thought the man couldn't go any lower, he took off and left his wife to face the full punishment for his crimes. It wasn't going to be an easy open and shut case. The case couldn't even *be* closed until they found Jasper.

"I got a BOLO out on his ID and his photo is being sent to every federal agency all across the country. I'll find him, but it might take some time. I'm going to bring Jarod onto the task force. He seems smart and like a good person. He's good with kids, which will help as we come across victims."

I doubted that was his only reasoning. I think my little brother had a crush on the young detective, but he wasn't willing to accept it yet.

"He's got potential, I think he'll do great.

Once Ty is set back home, I can help you with finding Jasper."

"You're not on the task force, Roland."

"What the fuck are you talking about?" I snapped. There was no way I wasn't going to be hunting down that son of a bitch.

"You can't be out there looking for Jasper. I know you want to, I get it, but if you are out there with me, who the hell is going to be here protecting Tyler? The only way to make a case against Jasper for multiple counts of murder and child trafficking is Tyler's testimony. Jasper knows that and he won't stop until Tyler is dead. You need to be here with him, protecting him."

He was right.

I didn't want to admit it, but he was right. Jasper was not going to stop at anything to silence Tyler. If I was out there with Mason trying to track him down, that left Tyler vulnerable to an attack. I needed to be close so I could keep an eye on him and ensure he was safe. I let out a sigh and gave a small nod in defeat. He placed a comforting hand on my shoulder as I spoke.

"I'll get him, I promise you."

I knew he would. If there was one thing my brother did better than anyone, it was hunt down monsters. He would find him and he would make sure he paid for every sin he committed.

CHAPTER TWENTY-TWO

Roland

IT WAS NEARING nine at night when finally Tyler started showing signs of waking up. It had almost been a full two days since he had been admitted and even though the doc said he would be okay, I had a hard time believing it with how long it was taking for him to wake up. The second his hand twitch in mine, I was on my feet and sitting down on the edge of the bed, making sure that Tyler would see me when he opened his eyes.

"That's it, Baby, let me see those mesmerizing eyes of yours," I said as I reached out and rubbed my thumb against his cheek.

Slowly, Tyler blinked his eyes open and I could finally see him awake. It only took a second before they were filled with confusion and panic set in. I reached over and hit the call button for the nurse as I spoke.

"It's okay. You're okay. I know it's hard, but you have to stay still. You had to be intubated from the smoke, but the doc will remove it for you. Just relax your throat and don't fight it. Let it breathe for you, Baby."

I wiped the tear that escaped from his eyes. He was scared, but he was listening to me and not fighting against the tube. I knew fighting it would make it worse. I didn't want him choking, because I wasn't certain I wouldn't pull the damn thing out myself if that happened. The door opened and I was thankful it was actually the doctor and not a nurse. He spoke as he made his way over to the other side of the bed.

"Good evening, Mr. Foster, it is good to see you awake. I'm Dr. Richards. I've been treating you for smoke inhalation from the fire you were in. You had to be intubated to help your lungs recover from the smoke. I'd like to remove the tube and see how your lungs handle breathing on their own. Do you understand?"

Tyler gave a very small nod and I squeezed his hand to make sure he knew I wasn't going anywhere. I watched as Dr. Richards moved around and grabbed what he needed to get the tube out. I could see the tension in Tyler's body and I couldn't blame him. It wasn't going to be comfortable getting that tube out. Once he was ready, Dr. Richards spoke.

"I'm going to start pulling the tube out now. I need you to give deep coughs as I do, it will help relax your throat and make it easier for me to get the tube out, okay?"

Once again Tyler gave a small nod, and

the doc started to pull on the tube. Tyler did as he was supposed to and coughed until the horrible tube was finally out of him. The coughing instantly got worse and I reached over to grab him some water.

"Small sips," Dr. Richards warned.

"Try some water, Baby." I brought the cup over to his mouth as I spoke.

I helped him take a few sips before I pulled the cup back and I was pleased that it did help to stop the coughing. Dr. Richards went on to check Tyler's breathing and listen to his chest. Neither of us spoke while the doctor worked and I was relieved when he didn't appear disappointed.

"They sound good. I want you to keep this nasal canal in for the rest of the night and, if your oxygen levels stay stable, you should be able to go home sometime tomorrow."

"Are there signs we should be looking out for?" I asked, as the doctor got Tyler set up with the oxygen line under his nose.

"The smoke will aggravate his asthma, still, so if there are any signs that it's getting worse, page a nurse. We might need to do some breathing treatments with a nebulizer to help clear his lungs out. The best thing for him right now is to sleep."

"Thanks, Doc," I said on our behalf.

"I'll be back to check in on you later on tonight," he said to Tyler before he turned on his heel and strode out the door.

Once we were alone, I instantly bent down and placed my lips against his. He weakly kissed me back and I could feel how exhausted he was. I pulled back, but stayed close so if he did talk I would be able to hear him. I ran my hand through his hair as I spoke, my voice thick with emotion.

"I thought I had lost you."

"I'm okay." Tyler gave me a weak smile and placed his hand on my thigh.

His voice was very raspy and raw from the tube and smoke. I hated it and wished I could have made it better for him. If there was one thing this whole experience had taught me, it was that I was madly in love with him. I wasn't falling in love, I had already fallen, hard, and it wasn't puppy love like with Shane. This was all consuming, it might kill me love and I wouldn't change it for anything.

"I love you. And I know it's too soon and I don't expect you to say it back," I started, but he cut me off with his own raspy voice.

"I love you, too."

He gave me a warm smile and instantly I smiled back. All of my worries and fears for the past couple of days melted away with those four simple words from him. I leaned down and kissed him once again. I made sure it was gentle still because he was exhausted and his body wasn't in any condition to be doing anything physical. But my need to feel him connected to me was too strong. After a moment, I pulled back and kissed his forehead before I sat back.

"Move in with me. I know you are trying to get your own place and if that is what you want, then I will support you and respect your decision. But I don't want to waste any time that I'll get to spend with you. I want to go to sleep at night with you curled up in my arms. I want to wake up to you. I want everything in between, the good and the bad. Move in with me."

I was hoping he would say yes, but if he didn't, then I would respect that. I could understand him wanting to get his own place, to have a true home for the first time in his life. At the same time, though, I didn't want to live without him. I wanted to build a home with him.

"On one condition," he started weakly.

"Anything," I easily agreed. I didn't care what that condition was, I would be happy to agree to it.

"The curled up in your arms part, it starts now."

Now that was a condition I could live with and agree to all day. I instantly moved and crawled into the bed with him. Carefully, we got him turned so he was lying on his side against my chest. I wrapped my arms around him and placed a kiss to the top of his head as I spoke.

"Get some sleep, Baby. I'll be right here if you need me."

"I love you," he said, already sounding half-asleep.

"I love you, too."

If you had told me that I would eventually find a guy that I would be madly in love with, I would have denied it until I was blue in the face. I never thought I would ever be able to love another man. That I would ever be able to touch another man without feeling guilty and dirty.

Now here I was, about to start a new life with the man that I loved. It all felt like a dream, one I never wanted to wake up from. There was still work that needed to be done. Tyler would never truly be safe until Jasper was dead or in jail. But for tonight, I wasn't going to think about any of that. I was just going to enjoy the feeling of having the man that I love in my arms and think about the wonderful future that awaited us.

EPILOGUE

Tyler

WE STUMBLED INTO our bedroom as Roland's lips devoured mine. We were finally going to get to do this. We were finally going to get to have sex.

The past month had been a huge challenge for the both of us. My lungs had healed up, but we were under strict orders by the doctor for me to not exert myself for at least a month. I had to do breathing treatments just to get my lungs back to one hundred percent, or at least one hundred percent for me.

We hadn't been able to do much of any sexual activity outside of kissing. Tonight, though... Tonight was going to be different, because I was now officially cleared to resume normal activities.

We had both been counting down for this night. I knew Roland wanted to make it special, but I didn't care about that. All I wanted was his body and to finally feel him in me, against me. I didn't need anything special.

I just needed him.

Roland kicked the door closed. Mason and Koda were still living here until they found their own place in town. The task force was up and running and Mason was currently trying to find Jasper and the missing children. We rarely saw him, but he made a point of checking in on us and keeping us informed.

Roland pulled back, breaking the kiss, and I couldn't help but whine at the loss of contact. He smirked as he turned me around and I finally saw the room. He couldn't help the small chuckle at the sight of it. He had put candles all over the room, candles that were battery operated and not by flame. I'd had enough of fire for a lifetime and I knew he felt the same. There were also rose petals all over the bed and the floor. It was very sweet and only showed me how much he truly did love me.

"Look at you, being all romantic," I lightly teased as I pressed my ass back into his groin, causing him to moan.

"I told you, your first time should be special."

"It is special, because it's with you." I turned around and started to pull at his shirt as I continued. "But if you don't get naked, I'm going to play all by myself."

He spoke as he moved his hands over to the bottom hem of my shirt. "Now that is something I'd be happy to watch, but not tonight. Tonight, you are mine and I have every intention of keeping you very pleased all night long."

"That a promise?"

God, I hope it was.

"It's a guarantee," he said against my lips, but he didn't kiss me. Instead, he pulled back and my shirt quickly hit the floor. That was all we both needed before we swiftly rid the other of their pesky clothes and then, I was on my back on the bed with him on top of me.

I loved the feel of his weight against my body. It wasn't suffocating at all, but comforting and still, to this day, made me feel safe and wanted. I was his and I had no problem with that. Tonight, I was finally going to be his and only his, officially. He would be my first and I was hoping he would be my last.

Roland kissed his way down my neck as he ground his crotch against me, causing us both to moan. He continued to kiss his way down my chest and made sure to lick and suck on each of my nipples as he went further down until he reached my hard dick. He gave it a long lick along my shaft, causing me to instantly moan, before he took me down to my base in one go.

"Ro," I moaned as I moved my right hand and tangled it in his hair.

This was only the second time he had given me oral sex and it was still just as amazing as the first time. I can't believe I had gone for so long without ever feeling this way. He continued to work his mouth along my dick, bringing me closer and closer to the edge.

"Oh fuck, I'm close." I couldn't help but thrust my hips up slightly to get even deeper inside of his mouth.

Roland didn't seem to mind, though, if the moan was anything to go by. His moan sent vibrations straight down my shaft and it pushed me over the edge. I came deep into his mouth and pulsed as he easily swallowed what I had for him. Once I had finished, he pulled his mouth off my dick with a pop. Kissing his way back up my body, he reached over and pulled out some lube from the bedside table.

"I need to stretch you so it doesn't hurt when I'm inside of you. It's going to feel a little weird, at first, but it will feel good.

Trust me."

"I always trust you." The honesty in that sentence hit him and he flashed me a warm smile.

There was nothing that Roland could do that would take any trust away from him. He had more than earned my complete trust and faith in him, in and out of the bedroom. I wasn't sure what I expected, but it was not for him to grab me by my hips and flip us around.

He was lying down on his back with me on top of him, only I was facing the opposite direction of him. He seemed to have felt my confusion, because he explained instantly.

"It'll be easier in this position for you. Plus, this way your mouth will be busy and it will distract you from the slight pain you might feel."

I wasn't sure what this was going to feel like, but I was happy for the distraction. I easily bent forward and sucked on his tip, tasting the precum that had been collecting. I felt one of his slicked up fingers circling my hole before he gently and slowly pushed it inside. It was a weird feeling, for sure, but I trusted that it would feel good soon enough.

I focused on making Roland feel good with my mouth as I took him down to his base. I did my best to focus on what I was doing and not the weird feeling of having Roland's finger moving in and out of me.

After a moment, he added a second finger and that one hurt slightly, but it wasn't too bad. I had only done a bit of research on gay sex and, apparently, I should have done more, but it seemed so straight forward at the time. Everything changed the second his fingers hit something inside of me and caused me to see stars. A deep moan escaped my lips.

"You like that, Baby? That's your sweet spot. Just think how good it is going to feel with my dick hitting it," Roland said as he made sure to hit that spot all over again.

I couldn't stop moaning at the pleasure that shot through me. My hips moved on their own accord as they pushed back, trying to take more of his finger inside of me.

All too soon, he was adding a third finger and instead of pain, it only added to my pleasure. Once he felt that I was stretched enough, he removed his fingers from my hole and I moved my mouth off his dick.

Once again, his hands were on my hips and he flipped us around so he was sitting up with his back against the headboard, but I was straddling his lap facing him this time.

"Nice and slow, Baby. You control the pace, go as slow as you need."

He was letting me control how fast he was pushed inside of me and I loved him even more in this moment. He didn't need to be in control in the bedroom. He knew how much this moment mattered to me and he was allowing me go at my own pace.

It only made it more special.

Slowly, I lowered myself down onto him. The feel of his tip against my hole should have scared me, but it only turned me on. We were finally going to be connected. We were finally going to share something special and I knew it was going to be amazing and something we would both cherish for the rest of our lives.

Going slow and carefully, I lowered myself until his tip breached my hole and I took him inch by inch down to his base. Once he was fully inside of me, we both moaned and I kept myself still for a moment to adjust to his size. Roland began to slowly kiss me with a great deal of care and passion. We didn't need words, because the kisses said it all.

After a few minutes had passed and I was no longer feeling the sting, I slowly began to move up and down as Roland kissed his way along my neck. I wrapped my arms around his shoulders so I could better hold myself up as he placed his hands on my hips and angled them into a better position. I wasn't sure why, but the second I felt his tip hit my sweet spot, I couldn't stop the loud moan that erupted from me.

"I told you it would feel amazing," he said and flashed me a big smile.

Amazing didn't even come close to how that felt.

I continued to move slowly, but I did aim for that spot each time. With each second that passed, we were both moaning and riding on that edge. I wanted to feel him come inside of me.

I needed to feel it.

Roland wrapped his arms around my hips and once again he flipped us, this time putting me on my back with him on top of me.

"You're loosened up enough, you ready to go to the moon?" he asked with a smirk.

"Hell yeah." I had no idea what he was going to do or how this could feel any better, but I was more than happy to find out.

He moved my legs so they were up on his shoulders. He slowly pulled out almost all of the way before he pushed back in, hitting my sweet spot in the process. That was the only slow thrust that he had, though, because after that his pace picked up rapidly. He repeatedly hit my sweet spot dead on, causing me to let out a scream as pleasure shot through me.

"That's it, Baby, let it out. Don't hold back."

"Oh fuck, don't stop. Harder." I moaned as I reached up and gripped the headboard behind me.

He was going to take me to the moon all right. My whole body was tingling from the pleasure he was giving me. He pushed as deep and as hard as he could each time and I had never felt so amazing before in my life. I never wanted this to end, but I could feel myself getting close and I could feel him getting close, too.

We had been waiting for this for a long time now and all that waiting was making us have short control. I knew Roland was close when he snaked a hand between us and started to touch my leaking dick.

"Shit, I'm close, Babe." I moaned.

"Come for me, Baby, I'm right behind you."

I couldn't hold off any longer and I gave a long and deep moan as I came, shooting it all over my stomach and chest. If I thought I was sensitive before, it was nothing compared to the feeling of pulsing while he continued to hit my sweet spot at a rapid pace.

I couldn't contain the soft screams as the pleasure shook through me. After another ten thrusts, Roland gave a final thrust and I felt him coming deep inside of me. He held still as he pulsed over and over again.

Both of us were breathing heavily and our bodies were covered in sweat and shaking. Roland leaned in and kissed me gently a few times as he lowered my legs. My whole body was shaking and I had no interest in moving at all. I didn't think I would be able to move, even if my life depended on it.

"Damn," Roland said softly as he broke the kiss and placed his forehead against mine.

"Damn, Damn," I agreed, flashing a big goofy smile.

There was nothing that could go wrong

in this moment. It was perfect. Absolutely perfect. I had been dreaming about this moment since Roland first kissed me and my dreams didn't even come close to reality.

Reality was so much better.

Slowly, Roland pulled out of me and he managed to climb off the bed and head into the bathroom. By the time he came back, I hadn't managed to move.

"Did I break you?" he asked with a chuckle as he wiped away my stomach with a warm cloth.

"In all the right ways."

Once we were cleaned up, Roland turned the lights off and helped me to get under the covers before he joined me. I instantly rolled onto my side and curled up against his chest as he wrapped his arms around me.

"This was perfect. Thank you," I said as the drowsiness started to take over.

"You're perfect. I didn't hurt you right? You're okay?" he asked and I could hear the worry within his voice.

"You didn't hurt me, I'm good, Babe."

"You might be sore in the morning. We can always take a bath together."

"I'd like that."

I'd like to do anything that involved us both naked at this point. He was perfect.

The perfect man for me.

It's crazy when I think about how far we have come. I used to be terrified of him, I couldn't even look him in the eye, and now here we are. He was the man that I was madly in love with and wanted to spend the rest of my life with. The world operated in crazy ways, but I did believe that the world put people in your path that needed to be there and I was forever grateful that the world put Roland in my path.

I had no idea what the future was going to hold for us. Between our new relationship and Jasper still out there, any given moment could change anything.

What I did know, though, was I planned to embrace and cherish every moment that I could have with him and I knew he was going to do the same with me. I had always wanted a home. I just had no idea that my home was a person and not a building. Laying here in Roland's arms, I was finally home and it was more than I could have ever wished for.

Thank you for reading Jaded, book three in From the Edge.

If you enjoyed Jaded, please return to your retailer and leave a review. Even a few words can mean the world to an author. Plus it helps other readers like you find our work, too.
Share the love! ;)

Turn the page to read a preview from Rescue, the next book in the series.

PREVIEW

Thad

GOD DAMN IT.

This was not a good start to the evening. I was running late, close to thirty minutes now, and I already knew my parents were going to be pissed at me over it. It was bad enough they were already going to be annoyed by my presence. I wasn't looking to make it worse, but apparently the stars were not aligned with me tonight.

At the age of nineteen you would think I wouldn't be so worried about what my parents thought, but I wasn't worried about me. It was my kid brother, Danny, that held all of my concern. Growing up with very religious and strict parents was never easy, but it got increasingly dangerous when you were gay. Luckily for me, I didn't figure out my attraction to guys until recently. Danny, though, he hadn't been so lucky. He knew when he was twelve that he was gay. He kept it hidden, even from me, until he was fourteen.

I could still remember the night he told me as clear as day. I was seventeen and had been working a lot to save up for my own place. I wanted out of that house the moment I legally could. It was late and I heard him crying in his room. I wasn't about to walk away when I could tell he was in pain. That was never something we did with each other. Whenever we needed each other, the other was there.

No questions asked.

Growing up in a very strict home made

us rely on each other for basic needs like comfort and love. Whenever one of us had a nightmare, we would go to the other. Whenever we were sick, the other one took care of them.

I was the one that walked him to and from school. I was the one that gave him baths. I was the one that would sneak him food when he didn't like whatever fancy crap our mother cooked. It was him and me against the world and I wouldn't change that.

Yes, it would have made my life easier if I hadn't had to practically raise my kid brother since I was eight, but he was my kid brother and I loved him. I wanted the best for him. It was just that simple.

So, when he was crying in his room, I instantly went in to see what had happened, what had upset him. He was a complete mess and hysterical from emotional pain.

It was that night that I discovered he was gay.

He was upset because our father had

gone on a long rant about a gay guy he'd seen at church. He called the guy horrible names and those words cut deep in Danny.

I knew our parents would never accept him, they would do anything they could to force Danny to keep it hidden and to be straight. To me, though, I just wanted him happy. I didn't care who he loved as long as he got to experience it.

That night, I knew I wouldn't be able to leave him behind when I left. I started working even more to save up more so I could afford a two bedroom apartment. Once I turned eighteen, I moved out and Danny followed behind me six weeks later when he came out to our parents. They didn't handle it well and they kicked him out. That was eight months ago, and they had never reached out to him since.

I hadn't been so lucky.

They called every week to see if I had managed to convince my brother that he wasn't gay. They believed it was a phase or a hormone imbalance that was causing him to feel the way that he did.

They had no idea.

To them, being attracted to the same sex was a mistake and God couldn't possibly make a mistake like that.

They would never accept him.

They would never accept me.

They didn't know I was gay.

I hadn't told anyone, not even Danny. It wasn't that I thought he wouldn't be okay with it, obviously he would be. It was more about me. I wasn't really ready to admit it out loud just yet. I was still adjusting to it all. Adjusting to my new reality and the new piece of myself.

Growing up, I had never looked at another guy like that before. Changing and showering in the locker room was nothing to me. I still didn't understand why all of a sudden I started checking out guys and watching gay porn.

I had started watching porn when I was seventeen, like most teenagers do, but it was always straight or girl on girl. The *typical guy* porn. The thing was, it never got me aroused. It was as if I watched a documentary on frogs or something. I chalked it up to not finding anything that interested me.

It wasn't until six weeks ago when I was feeling horny did I decide to try porn again. I just so happened to pick one that had a threesome with two guys. They were interacting with each other and, for the first time, I was able to orgasm while watching porn. The problem, though, I was busy watching the two guys and not the girl. That started to open up some questions, questions I was still dealing with. I could accept that I was gay. That wasn't too much of a big deal to me.

The problem was, I had no idea what to do about it. It was bad enough when I thought I was straight. I had been confused and self-conscious enough about sex when it was with a woman. I was nineteen and not only still a virgin, but I had never even been kissed.

My parents never allowed me to be alone with a girl. I had dated a couple in the past before I moved out, but I was always supervised. They believed that your first kiss should be at the altar. Now, I was a nineteen year old gold star virgin who was gay. It was a whole other world and I had no idea how to do any of it or how it would make me feel.

Was I a top or was I a bottom?

How would I know?

What would I do if I didn't like giving oral sex or if I didn't want to be a bottom and the guy I was with was a top?

It was so much more complicated and I still wasn't ready to be active on it.

I let out a sigh as I parked in my parents' driveway. I wished I could have just turned around and gone home. I was exhausted from working so many hours this week.

I worked eighty hours every week, on average, just to be able to afford the apartment and have some money saved up for Danny's college education. He would have to get student loans as well, but at least he would have something that he could put toward it.

He wasn't sure what he wanted to do yet,

but he was certain he didn't want to be a mechanic, like me. He wasn't interested in working with his hands and he wasn't very good at it, either. He was more book smart than street smart, but that was okay. He deserved to go off to college and I wanted that for him. Even if that meant I worked more hours than I slept in the week.

My parents hated that I was a mechanic. They always had. Ever since I was little, I'd loved cars and being around them. I loved taking mechanical things apart and putting them back together. I used to do it all the time with the lawn mower. It drove them crazy, but I was always able to put it back together.

When I turned sixteen I used some of my money that I had saved up and bought this clunker of a car. My parents hated the thing and made me hide it in the garage so none of the neighbors would see it. I loved it, though, because I could spend all of my free time fixing it up and cleaning it. I had rebuilt the whole engine from parts I was able to pick up. To this day, I still drove it and you would never believe it was the same car.

When a position came up at one of two mechanic shops in town, I quickly grabbed it up and I'd never regretted it since. To my parents, though, I was a disgusting working class citizen. I was less of a man and person because I worked with my hands serving others. To them, I belittled myself because I choose to not work in an office like they did. It didn't matter to me, though. I loved it and I never wanted to do anything else. I hoped one day I could open my own shop and run my own business.

Climbing out of my beloved car, I headed toward the door. I just needed to get this over and done with and then I could go home and relax with Danny. I knocked and waited for one of them to answer the door.

You would think with this being my parents' house that I could just walk right in, but I couldn't. I wasn't allowed to do that, because they found it disrespectful. As a guest, son or not, you waited until you were granted permission to enter the home.

It was ridiculous, because I shouldn't be classified as a guest.

I was their son.

I should be able to walk right in.

With that being said, though, they were not allowed to just walk right into my apartment. But that wasn't because I wanted to be rude and make them feel like they had no control of the situation. It was because I worried they would try to grab Danny if they could come in whenever they wanted. I had gone out of my way to ensure that Danny felt safe at home and I was not about to jeopardize that.

The front door opened and my mother stood on the other side. She wore her perfectly ironed sundress with the matching kitten heels. Her hair and makeup were done as if she was going out to church instead of just having dinner at the house. She looked me up and down and I could tell she was disgusted by what she saw. I wore my work clothes so there was black grease on my pants. I had wanted to go home to change before coming over, but I had lost track of time working on a car and didn't have the chance to. At least, I had managed to get the grease off my hands.

"Hello, mother." Always *mother*, never mom. Just like it was always *father* and never dad. To them, anything less would be disrespectful.

"You couldn't have at least bothered to change?"

"I was working late and I didn't want to be any later than I already was. It's dry, it's not going to rub off on anything, mother."

That was another thing we were never allowed to do growing up, get anything dirty. Everything was always pristine. It had to be perfect in case anyone were to surprise us by coming by. It wasn't easy when you had two boys running around. We always had to be hyper vigilant with what we were doing outside. We couldn't play football after it rained, because if we dragged even a speck of mud into the house, we were stuck scrubbing the floors for hours until our mother was satisfied.

Always having to have the house

immaculate growing up was why my apartment looked lived in. It wasn't dirty or messy, but when you walked in you knew people lived there. There was always a coat hanging over the back of a chair and there were dishes in the sink from breakfast. It was lived in and that was exactly how I liked it.

She let out a huff before she moved back and granted me permission to enter. I walked in and instantly removed my boots as she closed the door. There were no hugs or a kiss on the cheek. She would never allow it with me having dirt on my clothes. Even though it was dry and wouldn't transfer, she would never take that risk.

"Dinner is ready," she simply said as she turned on her kitten heels and headed off for the formal dining room.

I couldn't stifle the eye roll as I followed behind her. The formal dining room was always a sight to see. It was a long table, big enough for twenty people to sit at. It was often full for holiday parties that my parents would throw in extravagant fashion when we were growing up. It was always a big deal and the food was disgustingly fancy.

The type of food that a normal person would never eat.

I used to have to force it down, but Danny was never able to. It got to the point that my parents would have Danny up in his room for the parties and just make up some lie about why he couldn't be there. I used to sneak him up real food, normally a cheeseburger from some fast food joint.

One of the antichrists according to my parents.

Fast food and junk food was never supposed to be in the house. We were to have healthy food and only healthy food. Some kids would hide porno magazines under their bed.

We hid chocolate bars.

Of course, my father sat at the head of the table with my mother sitting next to him. I had no choice but to sit on the other side. The food was, thankfully, not that bad. It was chicken and vegetables, at least.

"Good evening, father," I said as I sat down.

"You're late. A man of faith is never late."

"I'm sorry, father, Work ran late."

There was no point in telling him that a man of faith didn't kick his son out or disown him, either. Just like there was no point in telling him I hadn't stepped foot inside of a church since I left home on my eighteenth birthday last year.

He led saying grace before we were able to grab some of the food. I took a small portion because I knew my mother could barely cook. It might look good, but taste was a whole other beast.

"We need to talk about Daniel," my father started.

Apparently, we couldn't have a meal together as a family without some ulterior motive. I had suspected something was going on when my father had called and ordered me to come for dinner tonight. Normally, when they reached out to me it was over the phone and it was to tell me about some event that I was apparently obligated to attend. I never did, but they still felt the need to reach out to me and tell me. They felt like they could control me, still, and I was not about to let them feel that way. Whenever I could avoid it, I always did. Tonight, I knew something was going on because they had never invited me over for a family meal.

We didn't do family meals.

We did fake shows for the society they were connected to. If my parents wanted to sit down and share a meal with just me, they wanted something and I'd suspected it had to do with Danny.

"He's doing great. He's getting all A's in school," I said. I knew that wasn't what they wanted to talk about, but I was not about to just yield to what they wanted.

"Lord knows what he's doing for those A's," my mother said under her breath, and I was instantly pissed off.

Of course she would think that Danny was trading in deviant sexual favors in exchange for a better grade. It wasn't even the fact that she thought Danny would have to stoop that low, but that she thought he couldn't be smart enough to get straight A's without the help.

Not to mention, what kind of teachers did she think were at that school?

"We have tolerated this silly phase of his long enough. It's time to get serious. He needs to understand and see the light. He is not a queer. He is not a deviant living in sin. He needs to be cleansed of the demon inside of him and shown the light," my father lectured.

I was really getting sick of these beliefs of his. Homosexuality was only proof that demonic possession was real to him. It didn't matter how much scientific fact you provided him that sexual orientation was decided long before you were born. That it was within your genetic makeup and not some curse from God or the Devil trying to overtake your body.

"It's genetic, father. He can't control being gay anymore than you can control being straight."

"Deviant behaviors can be controlled and

corrected. I have reached out to a man that runs a facility that is equipped to handle this very situation. He runs a highly successful conversion camp and he has a place for Daniel."

A cold dread flooded my body.

He wanted to have my kid brother sent to a conversion camp?

Hell no.

I had heard of those places. It wasn't like a bible study group. They used any means necessary to try and rewire a person's brain to believe they were straight. They were taught how to suppress a major part of who they were just so they could fit in with what society dictated for a man to be. Danny couldn't go to a place like that. I wasn't going to let that happen.

"You can't send him to a place like that. Father, do you know what things they do to the kids there?"

He couldn't actually be educated properly on this. There was no way he would be willing to risk sending his own son there. They used any type of methods to "save" the boys there. Including sleep deprivation, starvation, abuse, borderline torture, and more. There was a reason the camps had been getting shut down whenever one was discovered.

"I am well aware of what goes on in the facility. I've already toured it. Daniel will learn how to be a real man and to finally be rid of this ridiculous phase. He will return to be a man of God and live how our Father wanted him to. It is on you to ensure he is here Saturday morning and ready to go. He doesn't need a bag, they will provide the proper clothing."

He actually thought I would not only agree to this, but to gift wrap my baby brother for them. That I could somehow convince him it was a good idea. He was more insane than I thought. There was no way I was going to allow this to happen. I would to do whatever I had to to ensure Danny was safe.

I'd stupidly thought they would just leave us alone. Allow Danny to stay with me until he was eighteen and then he would be an adult so it wouldn't matter. Now, though, I could see our father was not about to let that happen. He was not going to risk someone finding out that he had a gay son.

It looked like I was going to have to do something I had hoped to avoid, but now it seemed like the only way to save Danny from that level of pain. I would have to file for custody of him and fight my parents in court for him.

This dinner looked like it would be the last supper for our family. Because coming morning, it was going to be a bloody fight. One I was hoping Danny and me would survive.

Watch for Rescue at your favorite online retailer.

OTHER BOOKS BY EVIE

Federal Protection Agency

Mason

Rafe

Ryzen

Cooper

Noah

Damien

Sebastian

Gabe

Logan

Ruthless Empire

Courting Danger

Chasing Danger

Kissing Danger

Smokejumpers

Hawke

Cyrus

Jase

Gage

Jackson

Xavier

Jasper Springs
Cade
Dawson
Drew
Grayson
Riley
Mitch

From The Edge
Shattered
Runaway
Jaded
Rescue
Hidden
Tormented

Gray Vale Pack
His Fated Mate
His Wounded Warrior
His Healing Heart

ABOUT THE AUTHOR

Evie Riley is a prolific, neurodivergent author known for her captivating MM romance novels. She has gained a significant following and topped the LGBT+ action and adventure bestseller charts with her series.

Evie's writing style often explores dark and gritty themes where her men must overcome difficult obstacles in their search for love, but she has also ventured into sweeter small-town romances, incorporating tropes like enemies-to-lovers, friends-to-lovers, age-gap, and forced proximity. She is known for crafting engaging romantic suspense novels and has a knack for creating interconnected series worlds that keep readers invested.

EVIE RILEY

Interestingly, Ms. Riley has hinted at exploring new genres, such as Alien Omegaverse Romance, in the future.

Outside of writing, she enjoys spending time at the beach and has a quirky personality, described by her partner as ranging from cute to deadly, depending on her blood-chocolate levels.

Evie spends her nights writing bad boys in love, and her days wrangling the sweet boys she loves.